A Breath of Time

Short Stories

This is a FLAME TREE Book

FLAME TREE PUBLISHING
6 Melbray Mews, Fulham,
London SW6 3NS, United Kingdom
www.flametreepublishing.com

First published 2026

26 28 30 29 27
1 3 5 7 9 10 8 6 4 2

ISBN: 978-1-83562-782-2
Special ISBN: 978-1-83562-932-1
Ebook ISBN: 978-1-83562-784-6

A copy of the CIP data for this book is available from the British Library.

Printed and bound in China

Represented in the EU for product safety and compliance by Authorised Rep Compliance Ltd, Ground Floor, 71 Lower Baggot Street, Dublin, D02 P593, Ireland. Contact at www.arccompliance.com

MIX
Paper | Supporting responsible forestry
FSC™ C005748
FSC
www.fsc.org

A Breath of Time

Short Stories

Romantic Fantasy

FLAME TREE
PUBLISHING

Contents

Foreword

Georgia Summers

Romantic fantasy, fantasy romance, romantasy – at this point in time, these are all terms for a subgenre that you may be very familiar with. Since its introduction in the early 2020s, romantasy and its iterations have come to dominate the landscape of science fiction and fantasy publishing as an unstoppable trend, carving out premium space on bookshelves and on tables in bookshops everywhere. In its most technical form, it's defined as a story where the plot is driven by its romance, within a fantasy framework. But genre definitions are inherently blurry at their edges, and colloquially, it's often used to describe any fantasy story with a strong romantic subplot. Maybe romantic fantasy is a zeitgeist desire, a fleeting dream that we will awaken from in one collective gasp, before hurtling towards the next exciting trend.

But I don't think so.

Romance in fantasy is as old as its fairytale bones, and almost certainly older. It's there in every princess who has awakened from a prince's kiss, every knight who has pledged his sword for true love. Think of great, genre-defining fantasy, and often you'll find an equally defining romance shining within: Arthur and Guinevere, Aragorn and Arwen, Buttercup and Westley. Even when love is ruinous or ill-fated, such as in *A Game of Thrones* by George R.R. Martin or *The Song of Achilles* by Madeline Miller, we find ourselves drawn to it.

These terms are simply a new way to categorize and highlight stories that have existed for much longer, slipped between well-worn genres. Even if you haven't noticed, we're almost always reading about love.

Anywhere, any time

When exploring romantic fantasy through the lens of time, we might instinctively consider the love that endures across centuries. In stories of time travel, these are loves that were never supposed to happen at all, and perhaps it's this improbable element that continues to capture our collective imagination. For example, it's impossible not to acknowledge the cultural impact of *Outlander* by Diana Gabaldon or *The Time Traveller's Wife* by Audrey Niffenegger. And even though the time travel element is arguably science fiction, it's the romance itself that becomes the fantasy that shines through on every page.

These romances defy the logic with which we live our lives, and yet entirely reaffirm our deepest held beliefs:

that love knows no bounds. Of course these two people have found each other despite the centuries that separate them. Of course their connection proves stronger than the circumstances that threaten to part them.

Love (and time) is a battlefield

Sometimes time is not the enemy or the limiting factor, but rather the playground in which the romance blossoms and holds fast. For example, in *This is How You Lose the Time War* by Amal El-Mohtar and Max Gladstone, time itself is their shared weapon and means of communication. Red and Blue leap through centuries, untethered to anything except themselves – and perhaps that's why their connection proves so profound.

Likewise, for Owen and Una in *The Everlasting* by Alix E. Harrow, it's both their prison and refuge, as they work to escape a grim future. In their rewinding of time, they may forget one another, but the body keeps the score and remembers. And there is a reassurance in this physical remembrance, even as it also includes the trauma they've endured. Some things are not as mutable as we first believe.

Time, posed as a setting and a magic system, is something to be made pliable for a greater force; if we tweak the past, we can redefine the future. But even if the very nature of how we understand history proves unreliable, our own memories untrustworthy, then these characters are each other's constant anchor. They give us the opportunity not just to see what might have been, but what might yet be – and how love can craft that ever-hopeful future.

Destiny calling

Time can also be a stand-in for fate's immutable hand – and in this, it's not always our friend. For Simran and Vina in *The Isle in the Silver Sea* by Tasha Suri, it's the cyclical nature of their doomed love that carries the narrative forward, with each iteration of the curse reinforcing both their love for one another and their hand in each other's deaths. Likewise, in *The Raven Cycle* by Maggie Stiefvater, we know by the very first sentence where the characters' tragic ending lies. And what seems improbable in those early pages is unquestionable by the story's climax.

Their narratives ask us to consider their romances in the past and future at the same time, and to hold this paradoxical balance in our heads. Their love is certain, but so, too, is its end. The dilemma posed to the reader, therefore, becomes not whether they will fall in love, but how – and what happens when love proves to be their undoing.

Even in other storytelling mediums, such as Anaïs Mitchell's musical retelling of Orpheus and Eurydice, *Hadestown*, the characters themselves comment on their entrapment in a tale that ends in tragedy, as they send us back to the beginning in their final song. They ask: *is this love still worth it, if we know all that's to come*?

Love, defiantly

It's this last question that is so personally fascinating to me because it speaks to a joyful human defiance. Because against all the odds, against a story whose ending has been written so definitively across endless iterations that to rewrite it risks unravelling the very story which we retell, we hope that Orpheus and Eurydice walk out of the underworld together. We hope that this time, fate will show us a little grace.

In other words, we hope for love to endure.

It's with this hope that I invite you to consider the stories in this anthology of romantic fantasy through the lens of time. There are fated lovers and chance meetings with the fae, centuries-old curses and midnight encounters held in a stretched-out second, women fighting to carve a future of their choosing or reflecting on the unchangeable roads of their pasts. They reflect the breadth of romance – stories of regrets and what-ifs, of joy and discovery – and the thrill of its reimagining through the possibilities of fantasy.

The Negative Serpentine

Chase Anderson

0.

I spend my hours waiting for your return by wielding a blade of my own, freeing your face from the unshaped void like I've done countless times before. The smell of maple yielding to the chisel is grounding. These actions are meditative, to chip away at the negative space until the image so clearly set in my mind takes form in reality.

Like you, I have work to do, in the name of keeping our city safe, but the Ministry will survive without the blocks for their newest poster. Instead I carve our tomorrow.

"The war shall be over soon," you said last night, in the dark of our room before sleep took us. "The enemy draws closer, but their numbers only dwindle."

I could only believe you. Civilians aren't allowed upon the wall, and the siege is still so young that supplies won't be an issue for many moons. Our kingdom is at war, but with you at my side, nothing felt any different.

I couldn't help but smile. "What will we do if you're robbed of your glorious battle against evil, O Hero?"

You huffed indignantly. "If no one smites their foul leader, then he'll only rise once more." Yet your fingers interlaced with mine. A quiet end to the war meant you'd surely come home. Another warrior would take your place, someone just as devoted, just as willing to die to protect the innocent.

Someone who isn't you. I know the image I carve is a fantastical one, a mix of mountains and rivers and crops that surely can't cohabitate. But you're there, working the land, with me, and the children we've yet to have. Your muscles would shift as your body took to swinging a hoe instead of a blade, perhaps even soften through age and peace.

I had fallen for the hero you so wished to be, grew to love the woman you are, and wanted to spend the rest of our days with her, with you.

The day stretches on, and you still do not return. I rise from my work desk, legs protesting after unfolding for the first time in hours. I need more movement, more than just my hands and mind, so I throw on my shawl and step outside of our apartments.

The hall is dim, quiet; the local mage hadn't come through to recharge the lights today. Perhaps he was a soldier, too, and been summoned, or he was sick, or the landlord forgot to pay him.

There are countless reasons why, and I put it out of my mind as I descend the stairs and step out into the fog. I can't see the great wall through it, but I know it's there, protecting us from the sea on three sides and the rolling hills – and the invaders lurking between them – to the south.

My feet take me towards the market; we still have plenty of spices and preserves, so I'll turn our rations into something celebratory for today's victory, no matter how minor it may be.

A dark figure fades into view. It's not one of the local guards, but someone from the Ministry. His uniform is suitable only for ink and scrolls, the tallying and replicating of numbers in perfect hand. Reducing our warriors and their efforts into faceless values.

"I'll have to ask you to return to your home, ma'am," he says.

"Is something the matter?" I ask. The city is unusually quiet; it could easily have been from the thick fog chasing people inside as it has a penchant for obscuring dangers in the distance.

"It's of no concern to you."

"As a matter of fact, it *is*. My wife is out there, and—"

The Ministry man steps forward, his boots striking sharp upon the cobblestones. I stand my ground, glaring.

"You're Miss Ai, aren't you? The poster maker."

"Designer," I correct. "I'm not the one who—"

"Then you should know how *important* it is for every citizen to perform their duty during military operations."

Something flutters within me. The early-morning summons hadn't said it was anything of the sort, just that they were short-handed at the barracks and needed you quickly. You were so sure that it was nothing that you didn't even request the time for your morning prayers.

"I understand," I say. "I'll leave at once."

I tend to the altar as best I can. I always knew I should have taken the time to learn the rites, the words worthy of offering, but my family was never particularly devout. It feels strange to pray to Ootara when I'm not a hero myself. I don't know anyone else from this century who has her as their patron. I can only hope that my attentions are enough to forgive your singular lapse.

Yet you still do not come home. For the first time in countless years, I find myself in bed, alone. My arms wrap around the bolster. It fills the negative space, but nothing more.

I do not awaken to you joining me in bed. I do not awaken to a messenger, dragging me to a hospital to see your lopsided smile. I do not awaken to a nosy neighbor telling me of any late-night misdeeds, as so many warriors do, but not you. Never you.

I am awakened by a stern, solemn knock at the door. And, in my sleepy state, I am sure that it's you.

It is the Ministry man, his uniform just as pristine. "Miss Ai?" he asks, as if we hadn't spoken just yesterday.

"Yes?" I am still too bleary from sleep to recognize the severity of the situation.

"I have been entrusted by his highness and his royal army to inform you that your wife, Kiitoa Ai, was killed defending our great city."

I understand each word in isolation, in couplets and more, but not in their totality. Not what it means for me, meant for you.

"We were unable to hold proper ceremony for the deceased, as the city—"

"No, that can't be true."

"Ma'am?"

"Kiitoa wouldn't just. . .*die*." You're too skilled, too practiced. Ootara wouldn't steal one of her most faithful in such silence.

The Ministry man is still speaking, but the words do not register.

And then he presents your sword. It's the only one like it in the world, bright red cords winding on the grip, an antler pommel shaped into a twisted swan. The blue gems of its eyes hold their familiar cracks, scars from your ancestors' battles, the ones you so revered.

I take the blade, wrapped in some random cloth, and the Ministry man leaves. I can see the stains from the blood that was only wiped off, not properly cleaned. What happened to you, my love? What beast or blackguard slew you, robbed you of the grand battle you've always wanted?

I try to clean it like you would. I'd watched you do it countless times, but never learned how. You were the warrior, were always so proud of that fact, and I didn't want to intrude. I had thought that our kingdom would always be at peace, that the day would never come when this life would take you from me. I had thought I was doing you a kindness, letting you strive for a dream that made you so happy, even if it should never be.

I don't know what else to do with it, with what remains of you, so I place it on the altar and pray. I pray to make up for every missed day of my entire life, to ensure you died with honor, that your soul would be at peace.

But I can't. I'm angry at Ootara, the invaders, everything that must have happened to take you from me and that peaceful life I'd envisioned for us, that I'd been too afraid to share.

But I should have told you, stopped you. I should have known that this was to be our last day, then I would have… done something differently. Kissed you differently. Found a way to keep you with me, forever, instead of letting fate trample over us both and this inglorious end.

I don't know when the thought entered my mind, if it was even my own. Perhaps Ootara was listening, or some darker being had slithered by and chose to intervene on her behalf. I lift what's left of you, so thin, so heavy, and do what I so desperately wanted to one last time.

I took you into myself, even if it meant my own life would come pouring out.

1.

I awake to you in my arms, heart frantic and fresh like a clear sky after a storm. I must have moved, as you nuzzle into my neck.

"What's wrong, love?"

I weep and pull you even closer. I can feel the press of your heat against my skin, your hard angles and soft curves.

I can smell the coyote mint of your hair rinse, the sweat from my fear.

"A nightmare?" you ask. Your arms find their way around me, shifting the covers and letting the cold night air snake across my skin. It takes me several moments to draw up the courage to speak.

"You died," is all I can bear to say. I wanted all of those memories to disappear forever, to be nothing more than a dream. I wanted that to be true more than anything.

"Worry not, my love, for no man can best Kiitoa in battle."

It's the same sugary line you've said to me countless times before. Sometimes boastful, always earnest. It's everything you ever stood for, and I cannot help but crack a smile.

"Then it's fortunate that I'm no man, huh?" I had felt so very clever when I first thought of that retort, and had never felt so elated when it earned me that first kiss. And, like every time since, it earns me another, where we can take things slow, where you can chase off the nightmare that had scared me so.

The frantic knocking at the door makes me jump, you tense.

"Lady Ai?" comes a male voice from the other side.

You wordlessly move off me, quickly put up your hair and put on your robe. It's only once the door opens and you speak to the sudden visitor that I recognize it.

This is the same messenger from before, from the day you—

"I'm sorry to leave you like this, my love, but I'm needed." You're at my side and I latch onto your form.

"You can't go. If you go, you'll *die*." My voice breaks upon the words.

"The barracks are simply short-staffed, and they need me to—"

"No! No, it's…" Isn't this what you said before, in the dream? But this is irrational, my memory fallible. This isn't the first time you've been called for such a task. I am conflating different events.

"There's no need to fear," you assure me. "The invaders can't get past our walls, they simply do not have the technology. I'll be inside, away from any stray arrows. Nothing shall harm me."

I so want to believe you. "Can we pray before you go?" My voice is so frail; my attachment to everything feels so tenuous, a single, wobbly line balanced upon the edge of your blade.

But you don't question it, only smiling and explaining the steps to me. You do not tell me the words that pass through your head as you offer them to Ootara, but I try to offer ones just as worthy. Thanks for keeping you safe all this time, a request to bring you home once more, an offer of eternal devotion if you do come home.

I help you dress, assure the messenger that you will be ready momentarily. Your loss, no matter how temporary it was, has flushed me with new-found appreciation. Of how every movement you make is with such purpose, touching every object with such care. I want to savor every moment I have with you, even though I'll have so many more when you return.

Before you step through that door, you take my hands into yours and look me straight in the eyes. I shiver.

"Ukuri, I promise you, I'm coming home." Your vow is singular, solemn. "It's always my plan, but…I can tell how rattled you are. I'd do anything to save you from unnecessary grief."

"I'll be okay." I say it for my sake as much as yours. "It was just a bad dream." I stretch up to kiss you on the lips. "Now go do your boring tasks, O Hero, and I'll see you later."

And so you leave.

* * *

I spend my hours waiting for your return by wielding a blade of my own, carving out your face like I've done countless times before. The Ministry never wants specific individuals on their posters, only the theoretical ideal citizen, warrior, hero. It's embarrassing to admit, but even when they order for a man, I give them your eyes, your hands, your determination.

They've never said a word; I doubt they pay much attention to my work, as long as the words are correct. Doubtless, the printers have noticed by now, but they must be wise enough to keep this observation to themselves.

The day stretches on, and you still do not return. The last dregs of the nightmare rise, illogical, unignorable. The air of the apartment is suffocating, allowing my dream to drape heavily across my shoulders.

I'm on my feet in an instant, joints screaming after the sudden action. I need to move, feel the sun on my face, burn away these accursed thoughts before they can further envenom me. The building's hall is dark, still; the local mage hadn't recharged the lights. I keep a hand on the wall as I descend the stairs and burst outside.

But the sun I so crave is obscured through the fog. Like every summer, it hangs thick, spilling over the walls and shrinking our world ever smaller. There's more out there, I know, you're out there, but the sight of every space filled with cloud makes it feel impossible.

"I'll have to ask you to return to your home, ma'am."

I freeze. The only noise is boots striking stone, the swish of cloth-on-cloth born of bodily movement. The form of a man from the Ministry takes shape.

"Wh–what are you doing here?"

"It's of no concern to you."

The nightmare is only being reinforced. Wasn't this exactly what he said before? This is the man who told me you died, delivered your sword.

"What's really happening? Was there fighting? Why did my wife—"

"You're Miss Ai, aren't you? The poster maker."

"Answer me."

He glares at me. I recognize how irrational I must sound and deflate. This is not the person to give trouble. If not for your sake, then for mine. You would be just as heartbroken if anything happened to me.

I duck my head. "I apologize, I've not slept well. I'll be going now."

I scuttle back home and lock the door behind me, terrified that I've been followed. It's many long, painful minutes until I decide that I'm safe.

Once again, I return to the altar, praying even more. There's no possible way that I am living through the dream, that this isn't a case of a day-long delusion. Things are already different: we prayed together, I worked on a different block, you took several minutes more to leave. Things would not take the same path.

And yet you do not return for dinner, and I refuse to go to bed alone. I pray, mine my brain for every detail about Ootara I can find, searching for some additional aspect of her I could beseech to ensure your safe return.

Her battle against the world serpent.

Her labors of the rivers.

Her children fated to war against the end of time itself.

And then I'm pulled to the present by a stern, solemn knock at the door. I'm jolted into awareness and wrench open the door.

It's the Ministry man. Already I see the familiar bundle he carries.

"Miss Ai?" he asks, as if he hadn't done this before.

"What happened to her?" My voice cracks. It had been no dream, but a vision of the future. One that I had been helpless to prevent.

"I have been entrusted by his highness and—"

"Who killed her?" I've never felt such anger as this, but who is it even for?

The man takes a moment to respond. "It was…several invaders. Miss Ai had been run through, so there was nothing that could be done to save her."

I couldn't imagine it. This isn't the battlefield, but our city. You were supposed to be in the barracks, so how…?

"We were unable to hold proper ceremony for the deceased, as the city is now under conservatorship by enemy forces."

"A…what?" I understand the word in isolation, but not what it means for me, meant for all of us who remained. "What do you mean?"

The Ministry man shrugs, as if this is merely as inconvenient as a spilled bowl of maize. "It means that we are no longer a free state. Our king is currently discussing the details of the surrender as we speak."

I want to ask more, but he shoves your sword into my grasp and leaves. Surely, there are more widows he'll have to inform tonight.

I'm so numb, so unsure of what the future would even look like for our kingdom, for me, without you. Perhaps you have protected some civilians with your life, your comrades, but it's all for naught if the city falls to the evil you sought to destroy.

I return one last time to the altar, direct a hateful thought at Ootara, and once more take your remains into myself, cursing all who have betrayed you.

2.

I awake to you in my arms, pulse throbbing like a shuddering earth. I must have moved, as you nuzzle into my neck.

"What's wrong, love?"

I can only freeze, breath catching in my throat.

Again.

"A nightmare?" you ask. You lift your head, eyes meeting mine, even in the dark of the room. It takes me several moments to weave together what to say.

"You will die today." I'm unsure if I've even uttered the words, as you do not respond at first.

But then you say, "Worry not, my love, for no man can—"

"No! I, I…" My fingers claw into your arms, I can feel your muscles tense, in shock? Fear? For me? Of me?

"Ootara, what is she the goddess of?" The words leave me, breathlessly.

"Ukuri, this isn't—"

"I have to know, it's…I think it's the answer."

You are thoughtful; I'm unsure if you believe me. I've never shown interest in her before, so why—

"She is the patron of warriors, heroes…"

If this were a normal day, you would have added, "like myself" or, "like my ancestors," but you know this isn't time to boast. I need reassurance, even if the truth would make things infinitely worse.

"…and of time," you end.

"Time…?"

"Yes. It's been foretold that, one day, her power will be stolen, she will be made mortal, and that time itself shall end. Her children must fight countless monsters to prevent it."

"Of course." I swear as tears of frustration cut my face. "Of course I anger Ootara and she sends me back to—"

The frantic knocking at the door makes us freeze.

"Lady Ai?" comes the male voice from the other side.

"Don't," I whisper, as if he can hear us, as if Ootara could hear us.

"It's Gin, a messenger from the barracks," you say, as if it would calm me.

"I *know* that, which is why—"

"Lady Ai, are you there?" he calls again.

You rise, make yourself presentable to outsiders, just like last time, me begging you not to all the while. You speak to the visitor while I desperately think of something that could convince you to stay.

"It's of no concern, the barracks—"

"It's not!" I cry. "Something, I don't know what, something *happens* and the city's invaded and falls! And you're killed!"

You wrap me in your arms, as if your steady form can convince my body to stop trembling. "It was only a nightmare. The city cannot fall."

You do not deny that Ootara would curse me.

You do not deny you could die.

Only that the city itself will stand regardless.

"They have no siege weapons, a guard is stationed every ten paces upon the wall. Every drain and passage is blocked or under watch. There is *no* way the city can be breached."

The only explanations I can imagine are catastrophic in nature, the ground tearing, a massive wave. Things that could not have happened without my notice, even through the numbing fog.

Maybe the Ministry has it wrong. Maybe you're in a hospital, maybe you dropped your sword. Maybe there's so many explanations besides your death.

Maybe I have been the fool, leaving my body for you to find. Surely, you would have followed me, and Ootara was enraged for losing her most faithful. And so I was forced to make it right by living this again, the only power she held over a civilian like me.

I swear again. "No, I…I must be wrong. Go, just…be careful. Come home to me."

You nod solemnly. "When I arrive, I'll don a shirt of maille. It will be a burden, but it will keep me safe and remind me of you."

You tip my face to meet yours and kiss me. I want it to last forever, but I know there's no such thing, and soon you depart.

* * *

I keep my mind occupied as I wait for your return by wielding a blade of my own, carving out channels to erase the would-be darkness of the print block. My tools only know the shape of you, so even though it's meant to be an image of Ootara, she has your blade, your poise, your resolve. She's slicing a serpent in twain, one with a single head that branches into many tails.

I don't know if depicting her is a sin, if the beast is meant to be invulnerable. I don't know the names of her children that are supposed to end the end of time. I don't know why she's doing this to me when you are the one she's so concerned about.

I have the urge to step outside again, to encounter the Ministry man once more, but I force myself to remain, working on the print. The base layer shall be red – the sky, the serpent's blood, the pleats of Ootara's pants. Next would be blue: the gleaming eyes of her sword, the waters above and below. A final layer of black would give her your inky hair and stormy eyes, the texture of the serpent's scales and the folds of clothes. The negative space would use the paper's white and allow the stars and moon to shine between the clouds.

There are so many questions I want to ask you, about her, her children, what parts of her you saw in yourself. I never thought of her as a mother, but neither have I of you, or of myself. We might have discussed it, years ago; I recall you saying you'd adopt the orphans made from the wars you'd ended, protecting them even once your sword had been forever lodged in the heart of evil.

Do you still feel this way? I've always assumed that you wanted the same things as I, that part of you understood that becoming a hero was a dream you could never experience. Perhaps this was the reason: Ootara had always meant for you to be the hero, to receive the happy ending you have earned, one that I had robbed you of out of sheer panic. I was to be hounded until I complied.

And so I work, determined to be the dutiful wife that the divine ordained me to be.

* * *

I am awoken by the stern, solemn knock. I had fallen asleep hunched over my work desk, and my limbs beg for mercy as I rise.

And, once again, the Ministry man is at the door. The cloth around your sword is stiff with blood, his uniform just as stained.

"How did she die…?"

He takes a moment to inhale; a tremble passes through his limbs. "It was…several invaders. The other soldiers had been run through, but Miss Ai…she was wearing maille, it seems. They…well, perhaps it is a mercy we were unable to hold a proper ceremony for the deceased."

He transfers your sword to my arms, says more useless words, and then disappears. I let the cloth fall away to see what remains of you. Dents along the cutting edge, dried blood flaking off the cords. One of the swan's eyes is gone.

You had fought back, fiercely, against their cruel weapons, amongst your slain comrades, and yet you still fell. I had felt your blood countless times before and I just knew it to be yours.

My intervention had done this to you. I had let you go, given you the knowledge of what would happen, and it happened again, even crueler than before.

I no longer care what Ootara thought of my actions. I have to fight just as fiercely to save you, and it would start by spilling my own blood once again.

13.

I stop warning you, stop asking you to pray. I let you go as you had the first time. My plan was to follow you at a distance, discover what would happen, and tell you exactly the right movement to make at the precise moment that would save you.

But I'm no hero. My body is not made for sneaking. I am caught, again and again, either chased home and losing your trail or detained.

When the invaders raid the jails, I can easily imagine what happened to you that second time, having felt the cleaving of limb from torso myself.

It's how I discover I needn't end my own life for time to be uncarved, and it needn't be upon the altar, or with your blade. A small mercy, that.

I'm unsure of what compels me, but, on this turn of time, I tail the Ministry man instead of attempting to evade him. He is the one who acquires your sword, after all, so he must have discovered where you fall, or was told by someone who did. I have learned much about the movements of the guards in these repeatings, but nothing of yours.

He walks far, until the guards fade away and we move through crowds of people, civilians unaware of what is to come. Even in the fog, their sunny faces stand out, unknowingly enjoying their last day of peace.

Soon even the sounds of people fade back into the fog. The imposing shapes of warehouses hover out of sight. He stops before one such building, the figures of workers sculpted in relief under graceful arches.

It's some part of the waterworks systems, I recall. There's a labyrinth of aqueducts under the city – nearly every building and street had been raised a century ago to accommodate them – and they've been heavily guarded to prevent their use in breaching the city.

The man disappears inside, and I wait. There are countless benign reasons he could have done so, yet I still wait.

And then I hear you, clear voice suddenly cutting through the fog like your glimmering blade.

It could only be you. You speak so kindly to your fellow warriors, despite what is to come. This is a minor errand, I glean, alerting the workers that the water pumps have ceased functioning. There are no messengers to be found, strangely, so here you are, in numbers for safety through the fog.

"What's got you so rattled, anyways?" your compatriot asks. "It's not like you."

You take a moment before you respond. I can imagine the tilt of your head, the ripple of your hair. "I know it sounds strange, but…I left so quickly this morning that I couldn't pray to Ootara."

At this, someone groans.

"You may think it superstition, but, thanks to her, I return home to Ukuri every night. It's the only thing that…"

The shuffle of feet has grown steadily louder despite the fog, and now in number. I've heard these sounds of strangely cured leather scuffing upon cobblestones so many times that I know what it means, and I'm reaching towards your voice.

"Kiitoa!"

The yellow light of the streetlamps are but pinpricks, floating just above our heads, useless for seeing the ground.

"Ukuri?" Oh, how I want to sob at hearing you call for me again. That you're alive, for now, a new version of you I've yet to meet, even if I doubt she would last.

Your keener sight finds me first, and your pounding footsteps approach.

"Kiitoa, finally, I—"

But you dodge my reaching arms with a face carved from stone. I feel the breeze of your passage, hear the whine of your sword being drawn, smell the copper now suffusing the air. The shrieks of men ring out behind me and weights strike the ground.

The other soldiers stop next to me, out of breath. I turn to see your back, shoulders trembling and blood dripping from your sword. The bright weave of your cloak is a familiar island of chaos amongst the grey-on-grey void framing you.

"My love, you need to leave."

"But—"

"Now!" you bark. "I–I don't know how, but…" Your head dips to the slain invaders, their blood seeping into their thinly padded armor. "It's not safe. If anything happens to you, I…"

I step forward. "I know, that's why…" What can I even say in this moment? Could you ever believe me if I spoke the truth?

But that possibility is stolen from me. You hear something none of us can and take off, leaving the other soldiers chasing after you and me bringing up the rear. Your comrades falter when they hear it, but I've already grown used to the sounds of the invaders killing civilians. Most use pikes, but some have swords, plain steel and twisting wires above the hilt.

They're like children playing war, swinging as hard as they can with glee, unafraid their opponent would ever harm them. You flow like a river, your banks carving out a safe space between your people and your enemy.

I'd never seen you fight before. I've seen you practice, of course, duel with dulled blades, where all parties knew they'd live regardless of their performance. I'd imagined you gallantly protecting me from a shapeless monster, a faceless enemy, countless times before.

But I'm finally seeing you live the version of you you've always wanted to be.

"We need to leave," I say once the last invader falls. The red feathers from their caps grow redder as they drink up their owners' blood. The grooves between the cobblestones become an ever-growing crimson web. The other soldiers poke the bodies with their own weapons, ensuring you've succeeded in your dance.

"Leave?" you ask.

"The city."

"What? No, my duty is here."

"The city *will* fall." It all tumbles out of me, breathlessly. How you always die, or me, the surrender, that this is the first time I've found you and could, perhaps, save you.

The tip of your sword quivers, your face unreadable. "And…what brought you here? To this part of the city?"

"I followed—"

A crack of thunder echoes, casting the fog with a red-hot glow. I hear screams, but my eyes are fixed on only you. You pitch forward and crash into the ground.

A strange smell burns my nose and my hands grow slick as I grab you, pull you to me. Your breaths are wet and ragged and horrible, you cannot speak, as if I even could myself.

"You'll surrender if you wish to live."

My head snaps up to meet the eyes of the Ministry man. Others like him, with their suits never marred by battle, flank him. They each carry one of the strange weapons of the invaders, metal tubes with long wooden grips. The man who's heralded your death so many times holds one that weeps smoke.

Your hand grasps mine fiercely. You understand: you've found the villain of this tale, but you will not be able to stop him.

"Were you the one who always killed her?" I ask.

He glares at me. "What are you saying?"

Your strength is already fading. This turn of time will end soon, but I know what I must do.

This time, at least, we shall go together.

28.

I master the art of slipping out of bed without your notice. It will cause your behavior to change, having to leave without knowing where I am, but I need those precious extra minutes to evade guards and make my way to the palace. It's on the opposite side of the city from the warehouses, upon a green hill with a view of the western seas.

There are fewer guards than there were in peaceful times, and they never notice another woman entering alongside all the other servants. Still, they will find reasons to imprison me if I act suspiciously enough. The halls are difficult to navigate, walls and doors with endless carvings of herons and tides and the horned serpent's many heads and rattling tail. I make one wrong turn too many, and then I'm spotted as the outsider I am.

It's difficult to gauge the passage of time in the lightless dungeon, but someone will always come and quickly execute the prisoners late in the day, or else sometime into the new.

Perhaps they need the room, perhaps they fear what we might say. But it always happens. Another small mercy, that.

My success is entirely by mistake. A guard grabs me by the arm as I search a new hall and I assume this to be another failure. She orders me to the kitchens to deliver the king's breakfast instead.

My arms tremble, causing the tiny porcelain dishes to clatter together as I walk down the hall. Some of the foods I recognize – preserved lemon and quail eggs, acorn jelly, blue flatbread with strawberry compote – and plenty I don't. Slices of huge fruits with bright red flesh. Roasted orange tubers and a soup whose sediment swirls with my every step.

The two guards stationed at the dining chamber's doors open them for me without further question.

"*Finally*, I was beginning to wonder if you'd forgotten."

I knew the king was young, was forced to take the throne after illness took all his parents last summer. I hadn't realized how young he was until he was before me. His hair is tousled and his purple robe is almost indecently askew.

The apprentices at the press shop hold themselves with more dignity and grace than he.

There are no others in the chamber, so I can speak freely. "Your Highness," I say, laying the tray on the table before him, "I have a matter of grave importance to discuss."

"And?" He picks up a spoon and begins gouging chunks of sugar from the miniature sugarloaf. "The matters of servants are beneath me."

"It's about the war, your Highness." He continues to ignore me, too focused on the sugar for his coffee; both had become scarce since the traders had become the invaders, at least for the common people. "A traitor is planning on allowing our enemies into the city."

The spoon falls, clattering to the floor.

"What?" The king's voice drops to a hush.

"Through the aqueducts, your Highness. He plans on doing so this evening."

"How do you *know*?" His knuckles grow pale as his hands clamp around the chair's arms.

"I...overheard." I wouldn't have expected him to believe the truth, so I leaned into the role as a nameless servant instead. "I was helping at the Ministry of Information, when—"

The king swears loudly, making me jump. "I *knew* he couldn't be trusted to keep his mouth shut."

"Y–your Highness?"

I haven't the chance to ask him anything more, as the guards quickly come and haul me away.

* * *

Ootara grants me one final kindness, it seems. You are placed in the cell next to mine and we can talk, for however long we have until all the threats are exorcised. You came willingly, too, thinking the palace needed your protection. You couldn't even conceive that we'd been betrayed so thoroughly, and why would you? This is the first you've heard of any of this.

You are quiet when I finish my explanation.

"I imagine he believes he'll be allowed to keep ruling if he rolls over for the enemy," I wonder aloud. "Even if only as a puppet. Why else would he drive us off such a cliff as this for the scavengers below?"

You still do not speak.

"Kiitoa?"

"I…I don't know what to think."

"I understand if you don't believe me, it's—"

"It's not that, my love. There's…no other explanation for how things turned out this way." You pause. "I cannot understand how such evil was allowed to lead us for so long, and to such a degree as this."

We are both silent. I know there are others here, in other cells, but they don't speak. They don't agree, or call me insane. I can hear their bodies shifting on the bare rock, but they might as well not exist. The world has been reduced to the dark space in front of me and the singular sound of your voice in this far-reaching void.

I wonder if the king is evil, or had been compelled into evil deeds by others. I wonder if he sees 'surrender' as the lesser of two evils, that he is doing us a kindness. I wonder if he even cares.

"If you knew what would happen," I say, "that we were to be betrayed, that you would die…would you do anything differently?"

You take a long moment to think it through. I know what I want to hear you say, and what Ootara wants you to believe.

I wonder if I'm strong enough to do this again, if only to change your answer.

Finally, you sigh. "No…no, I don't think so. If my death could save just one civilian, one other soldier, then it would be worth something."

"Even if the villain still wins…?"

"A hero cannot vanquish every evil." There's resolve in your voice, but it's tired. Small. "Even a small evil stopped is one less in this world, and that is enough."

* * *

Time flows at a pace we cannot know, in the only direction it ever should. The end is only heralded by the first prisoner begging for his life, and then his strangled scream.

"Kiitoa, I—"

"I know," you say. "And if—"

Another prisoner begins screaming.

"If this happens again, remember what I said."

"But—"

"Ukuri, promise me."

"I won't forget," I whisper. "I promise."

You die as nobly as you can, denying them the pleasure of hearing your despair.

I wish I could have done the same.

29.

"The war shall be over soon," you say, in the warm dark of our room. "The enemy draws closer, but their numbers only dwindle."

The moments grow long as I recognize when I am.

The night before. I've been gifted more time.

"Is something wrong, my love?"

The memories of what felt but a moment before sink their red-hot fangs into my mind. I can imagine the outlines of that final pain, even through the heavy press of all the others I've experienced so many times, and yet you not once.

Not yet.

"What would you do," I ask, "if you were robbed of your glorious battle against evil, O Hero?"

Shift

Kim Claussen

The *Starfish* isn't a fear-inducing name for a pirate ship, but that's why Baz likes it. It's a small brigantine vessel that glides through the Celestial Sea, over misty pink nebulas, weaving among the stars like any ol' ship. Others don't recognize the threat to their treasures 'til it's too late.

Sail the Celestial Sea, expect danger from the Celestial Sea, as Grandad used to say. Baz knows that well. Really, you had to be out of your head to live like he did, and Grandad before him. The Sea is brimming with the weird, wonderful, and downright deadly. *The Sea isn't just the dreams of plane-bound mortals*, Grandad would say. *It's their feckin' nightmares, too.*

It's the only life Baz has ever known, but he's loved it since he was wee, old enough to lash around the decks, trailing his blue-skinned palms along the ship's rails.

Something's off kilter today, though he can't cop on what.

"Alright, Baz?" Captain Daltyn tilts her red, dragon-scaled head. "You look worried."

Baz hesitates, glancing at the looming black-hulled ship off the starboard side of the *Starfish*. The dark behemoth is in a right state – tipped arseways, big ol' hole punched in the scorched hull. It has the illusion of a beached whale, hovering in space. Bits of ash linger in the Pocket surrounding it – 'course, he can't see the Pocket, but that envelope of air and magic wrapped around Sea ships keep gravity normal, air breathable, and the like – ships don't exist without it.

"Just a feeling, I guess." Baz fiddles with his ivory-handled guns, hanging at either hip.

He's done this before, hasn't he? He can't have – he's never been to this region of space before, never seen this ship – he'd remember if he had. But he can't shake the feeling, even as he boards the charred, abandoned vessel with a couple of crewmates, Grymes and Volaxia.

The three of them pick their way through the dark interior. Volaxia curls her cat-paw hands, conjuring small orbs of golden light that float like fireflies, lighting their path. Baz darts his arm out, stopping Grymes from putting his foot into a hole, charcoaled and weak – he would've crashed through, down and out the hull, plummeting out the Pocket into endless space.

"Whew, that was close, man!" Grymes swipes his webbed fingers over his sweaty forehead. The Amphibianoid is always glistening, but even more on this difficult trek. "How'd you see that?"

"Just lucky." Baz flashes him a grin, but his gut twists – he'd known it'd be there, like he'd seen it before. *Can't have*. He shakes his head, moving on.

With the ship sideways, they walk on the walls – now floor – and jump over or climb through doorways. It's disorienting, slow progress as they maneuver through the maze of hallways, stepping over debris. Most rooms don't contain anything of real value, but the best goods are usually locked up towards the stern anyways.

Baz leaps over a doorway. He stumbles, tripping across an old painting bolted to the wall-now-floor. The heel of his boot slides, tearing a slash across the stern-faced man depicted in the brushstrokes.

"Apologies, sir." Baz tips his black tricorn at the man. He's relieved he doesn't remember this painting, at least, but déjà vu still clings to him like a burr in his buttocks.

At the end of the next hall, there's a whopper of a door, heavily reinforced with thick strips of iron.

"Huzzah!" Volaxia claps her paws.

Baz grins – with a mighty door like that, it certainly looks like a room for goodies – but when an ominous rumble shakes the wood under his feet, he stops smiling, as do his crewmates.

"What in the blue blazes...?" Goosebumps race over his arms.

"Just the ship settling," says Grymes, but his bulbous eyes dart around. Another rumble shudders through the ship. Louder. Closer.

Animalistic.

"Maybe we should turn back," Volaxia suggests.

A figure melts out of the shadows, its growl like thunder. Baz has the impression of something huge and terrible looming towards them, spindly claws of smoke reaching out

– that's all the convincing he needs. He's legging it full tilt back the way they came – no treasure is worth getting sliced to ribbons by some shadow beast.

"It's haunted!" Grymes bellows, bounding after Baz.

Baz loses track of Volaxia in the frantic scramble. He risks glancing over his shoulder and glimpses what might be needles or teeth wreathed in black smoke, bearing down on him. The half-second look costs him. His boot catches the edge of a doorframe, and though the doorway isn't too wide to jump, he can't stop his over-balanced momentum. Baz falls.

A nasty crack.

Darkness.

* * *

"Alright, Baz?" Captain Daltyn surveys him with concern.

Her concern is fair, given Baz just hollered and spasmed like he'd been electrocuted. A few crewmates raise eyebrows at him. His heart thrashes in his chest, like he's been yanked awake from a terrible nightmare.

While standing up. On the deck of the *Starfish*.

Baz swallows, giving Cap a nod. "Boris's brew last night has me still scuttered," he lies. He has no idea what happened, but his attention is snagged by a massive black wreck off the *Starfish*'s starboard. He's seized by a strange wave of fear and déjà vu, but Grymes laughs it off, saying Baz is being paranoid and the likes.

"There's sure to be grand loot in there." Grymes rubs his webbed hands together.

Baz opts to go with, if for no other reason than to prove he's not catching a dose of the heebies. He's not normally afraid, so the prickling fear makes him extra uneasy the deeper they explore.

He stops Grymes from crashing through a hole in the wall-that-is-the-floor, unsure how he knew about it, but he's distracted when he hops over a doorway, skidding on a ripped painting of a man. He's seen this before – with this *exact*...rip? How?

When they arrive at the big ol' iron door, Baz hisses for the others to be quiet. His skin crawls and he jumps at every creak.

Grymes chuckles. "What, you think it's haunted or something?"

"Or something," says Baz and makes a shushing motion. "Just *whisht*."

Together, they wrench open the huge door. It slams to the floor, kicking up dust and ash, making them cough. Volaxia sends her magic orbs into the room, lighting it up. There's a couple of busted, dusty barrels in the middle of the room and off to the left is an old mattress piled with rags and moth-eaten blankets. At the back is a massive chest, bent open on its side. Pieces of gold have spilled across the floor, glinting in the light.

Grymes whoops and goes for the chest. Baz and Volaxia grin and step inside.

The rags on the left stir and Baz freezes, anxiety notching up. There's a distant rumble and he hushes the other two with a slicing hiss.

We waltzed into a feckin' trap, didn't we?

The blankets shiver. A white hand and emaciated white face emerge. Baz gapes, wondering what fresh spectre is about to eat them – but no, it's a proper person, not a ghost. A woman.

"Help me," she chokes out in a dry rasp.

Baz drops to his knees beside her. "Hey, petal, you alright? What happened?"

The floorboards tremble. Sweat breaks out on the back of Baz's neck – he's sure something horrific is coming but he doesn't know what.

"We need to get you out of here. Can you stand?"

The woman's long dark hair is a tangled mess as she extricates herself from the rags. Baz snatches up the canteen of water on his belt and holds it to the woman's chapped lips. She sips gratefully, then gulps greedily, watching him.

"Name's Baz. What's yours?"

Her eyes are a vivid, unnatural sea-green and he could tip right into them and stay there. He feels like he knows her, though he'd swear on his guns he's never met her. She doesn't answer and has a strange expression he can't parse out, but it shifts to fear when thunder shakes the room.

He tries to help her up, but she folds like wet paper on her skeletal limbs.

"I'm going to carry you – is that okay? Do you understand?" At her nod, he tucks his arm under her knees and scoops her against him. She's horrifyingly light – his guns might weigh more than her.

"What's that noise?" Volaxia's furry ears twitch.

"Probably that feckin' shadow thing, but we're not waiting to find out," Baz snaps. The woman looks at him sharply, but he's quick to reassure her. "We'll get out."

"What shadow thing?" says Grymes. He's trying to haul several bulging sacks of gold by himself. Volaxia rolls her eyes and heaves two of them onto her back.

"From…" Baz trails off. From *before*? "Never mind, man, just *hurry*."

Baz is barely out the door when shadows seep and roar down the hallway towards them. He curses and legs it, best he can, while carrying the woman. Hopping over doorways is much trickier – his balance is all over the place and they're not going to make it—

Behind him, Grymes screams.

* * *

It's surreal to board the scorched black ship again, to traverse the maze of halls and discover that iron door… again. Baz insists that they *must* lower the door quietly this time.

"This time?" Grymes raises his eyebrow.

Baz just shrugs.

When the door's open, Grymes is too buzzed about the treasure to notice much else. He leaps over the busted barrels and starts filling sacks. Baz dashes to the pile of rags – the woman is there, and she sits up a little easier.

"What happened to you?" he asks.

"Who cares?" Grymes says from the back corner.

"Shut it," Baz snaps over his shoulder. Volaxia watches him, her paw resting on the pommel of her rapier.

"Calliope," the woman says.

Baz stares. He'd been about to ask that, too. "Sorry, do I… know you?"

She laughs like it's a delightful inside joke, then surprises him with a soft kiss on his jaw. "Maybe next time."

"What in the seven heavens is going on," says Baz. Is he light-headed?

They're both startled by a crash. Grymes heaves another bulging bag of gold towards the door, and shrugs at the glares from Baz and Volaxia.

"*Don't—*" Baz hisses.

The floorboards shake.

Too late.

"That's not good," says Volaxia, throwing a couple of loot sacks over her shoulders.

Baz scoops Calliope into his arms and takes off, hollering at the others to follow. Grymes struggles under the weight of the gold. The thunderous noise gets louder but Grymes slows, panting, sweating, and determined not to drop a single coin. Volaxia drops her bags in favor of speed.

"*No*, whatcha do that for?" Grymes stops to retrieve the fallen sacks, but he can't carry them all. Gold spills out, clinking over the wall-now-floor, dripping through open doorways. The hallway trembles, the roaring reverberating.

"*Leave* it, man!" Baz shouts, shaking off a lil' wave of dizziness. Calliope whimpers, clutching his neck. "Almost there, petal, promise."

He makes it to the ragged hole in the hull serving as their exit. He sets Calliope down in the floating dinghy outside the hull, a bit rougher than intended, and spins, rushing to get his crewmates, guns drawn.

Baz is furious that Grymes is going to die for stupid gold – worse, Baz is going to die saving his shitehawk friend. He hasn't gone far towards the horrifying monster sounds when he's met with a screech and a wall of black smoke.

Tendrils like claws shred into his chest.

* * *

"*Feckin – NO – getthef—*"

Baz falls onto his rump on the deck of the *Starfish*, arms flailing.

"Uh…alright, Baz?" Captain Daltyn raises a scaly eyebrow.

Baz claps his blue hands to his chest. Shirt – skin – both undamaged. Off the starboard side, a massive banjaxed ship looms.

"Well, *feck* me."

* * *

Grymes says Baz is being grumpy and weird, but Baz doesn't care. He hops onto the painting of the man. It's marred by multiple ragged rips, coated with dusty bootprints – he'd bet his beloved guns those prints belong to the boots on his feet. He's breathing harder than he should be – it feels like a marathon this time, but Baz is also really hurrying.

"How do you know where to go?" Even with her cat-like limbs, Volaxia is straining to keep up with Baz. He doesn't have an answer for that, nor for the way he darts straight to the woman in the storeroom the moment they've oh-so-gently lowered the mighty iron door. "How'd you know she was here?"

"Instinct?" He has no reasonable explanation.

Calliope has color in her cheeks and she's not as thin as he remembers.

"Tell me what happened," he says, pausing to catch his breath.

"They ripped me away from home." Calliope's lips tremble. "They bound me to this place – left me to die when that thing attacked. But..." She wipes away the tears threatening to fall. "Baz, you already know all this."

"I *don't*, petal, I don't understand. I wish I did, believe me." Baz sighs. Thunder rolls in the distance. He stands and says to the others, "We need to go, right now. Forget the gold."

"Forget the—?" Grymes snorts.

"C'mere to me," Baz says, low and stern. "You wanna die by shadow monster? On your head be it. I'm not going back for you again." He rushes from the room with Calliope.

"Again?" comes the confused chorus behind him.

In no time at all, the ship's hull shudders. Baz launches himself over doorways, drops down others with the ease of familiarity. At least with repetition, it's making him quite adept at the simplest path through, even with Calliope in his arms, even as his limbs are burning.

He sets her down in the dinghy. "Be right back – don't go without me."

Back in the hull, his crewmates argue, no doubt drawing the monster closer with their noise. Baz finds them as Volaxia is vaulting over doorways, the treasure and her crewmate abandoned. The smoke is closing in, but *buck eejit* Grymes won't leave the gold.

Baz curses and draws his guns. "Leave it, you *gowl*!"

Whatever Grymes hollers back is lost in the din as he is enveloped by monstrous smoke. Baz surges forward. He doesn't get a shot off before the teeth and claws are on him.

* * *

"Alright—"

"Yeah, yeah, fresh as daisy." Baz marches to the dinghy where Grymes is letting out the line, preparing to board the black ship. Before the Amphibianoid can get a syllable out, Baz tells him, "You're not coming."

Grymes blinks his speckled eyes. "What?"

"I *told* you I'm not dyin' for you and your gold again, you gobshite."

Grymes sputters, but Baz shuts him down. Despite Grymes appealing to Cap, she ultimately sides with Baz.

"Baz's instincts are strong," she says. "If he thinks something's off and doesn't want you on this one, I trust his judgement."

Grymes pleads and curses, but neither Baz nor Cap change their minds. Sure, they're here to find loot, but not at the cost of their lives.

* * *

Baz's boots tramp across the painted man. The canvas is torn up and muddled with bootprints, like it's endured a stampede. Baz sweats in his coat, feeling knackered, but he pushes on.

"You want to explain what's going on?" Volaxia lands deftly beside him, her tail twitching.

"Couldn't if I wanted to."

Getting the iron door open is tough without Grymes' muscle, but they manage. The thud is louder than Baz would've liked and his pulse trips with worry. *Did we wake the beastie already*?

He's surprised to find Calliope sitting on the rags, smiling.

"Whoa, what—" Volaxia draws her rapier, but Baz puts his arm out.

"Steady on, it's alright. Just keep your ears open."

Volaxia backs off, but he can feel her checking on him as she pushes gold into sacks.

Baz meets Calliope's stunning gaze and he doesn't want to ask, but—

"Are you doing this?"

"No," she insists. The intensity of the fear and upset in her expression breaks his heart. "I swear, Baz – I'm trapped by the monster, too."

She's so earnest, but he can't deny the strangeness of her continued transformation every time he loops back. That has to mean *something.*

Feck. He prays he isn't the purest eejit in the Celestial Sea as he helps her stand, this time on her own two feet. Her smile makes his pulse race and he curses himself for being so weak.

The door must've been enough noise after all, because the hull's shivering already. The monster is closing in. There's no more time to chat, so he scoops up Calliope – she's like a person instead of a paperweight this time.

When Volaxia falls behind, she at least has the good sense to ditch the gold and her pack so it doesn't weigh her down, but not soon enough. Baz goes back for her and fires three times, realizing too late that even enchanted bullets are useless against smoke.

* * *

Baz still takes Volaxia with him the next time, but he warns her about the monster.

"I think it's attracted to noise, so be *quiet*, and if you hear anythin', you *leg it*."

She eyes him. "This something your grandad told you about?"

"Sure."

They nearly injure themselves bringing the door down as softly as possible. Baz's arms tingle and he mops his sweaty face with his sleeve before he steps into the room. He's shaky like he hasn't slept, has missed a few meals, he's sore and achy, but he fights off the gammy feelings best he can – doesn't have time for it.

He thought they'd been quiet enough, but he barely talks to Calliope before the monster is roused, storming in their direction. Volaxia bolts like she's supposed to, but again carries her load farther than she should've. Because Calliope can stand, Baz gets her most of the way before he turns back.

He knows his guns won't help but he can't think of a better option, so he fires at the bellowing toothy maw bearing down on him. He should've been able to shoot five times total, but his guns click empty after only two.

* * *

It's hard to convince Cap to let him go alone, especially when he can't give a good reason why. So he pulls her aside to her cabin and tries to explain the time loop. Daltyn claps his shoulder and asks him to wait a moment. He realizes his mistake too late when she locks him in.

The door doesn't open until Doc comes in, arms full of medical equipment and healing scraps from the chest in her quarters. She tilts her head of seaweed hair, offering him a placating smile, like he's completely off his rocker.

Baz hears the distant screams of Volaxia and Grymes coming from the black ship while Doc is taking his temperature.

* * *

One moment he's promising Doc he's fine, and in the next blink, he's out on the deck. Cap asks Baz for the tenth or fiftieth or hundred-and-thirteenth time if he's alright.

So it's just like that, I guess.

His next tactic to convince Cap goes better – he doesn't mention the time loop. She's skeptical but agrees to let him do recon alone. He thanks her, then runs below deck to stuff supplies in his bag: rope, a couple of crowbars, a large hook, and some bullets. A hunk of hardtack to ward off the weak, dizzy feeling that keeps sliding over him.

On the black ship, when he's made it to the storeroom, Baz rigs up a makeshift pulley system so he can lower the door with as little noise as possible – excluding his grunting as he strains to keep his grip on the rope. This was way easier with Volaxia and Grymes.

Calliope is waiting for him. She's the healthiest he's ever seen her: complexion rosy, cheeks and body filled out. He drops to his knees beside her, exhausted.

She greets him, and then says, "Baz, I…I love you."

"Love me?" Baz chuckles. "Flattered, petal, but you hardly know me."

"Don't I, Bastien Cummerband?" Her smile is soft, radiant, warm. "Been sailing the Celestial Sea since you were a babe. Bit of a chancer, loves a good tale, pineapples, and Grandad's guns. Hates tight spaces."

He's flustered. He doesn't *tell* people about his claustrophobia—

"*Don't* I? How long has it been?"

Baz flounders. "I don't know – it's hard to keep track…I guess…a week or two?"

"Oh, Baz, no, I'm so sorry." She lets out a heartbroken sob. "No, darling, it's been *ten months*."

He stares, his heartbeat muffling his eardrums. It's not possible – he hasn't eaten, he hasn't changed his clothes, he – he'd remember, he'd know, he'd—

Explains a lot. Explains her. Why he's so drawn to her, feels connected to her, but still can't understand why. Why—

No, he can't process this. His brain grinds to a halt.

"Sometimes…it doesn't come for a while," Calliope continues. "So, we talk. You don't always remember. Well, you…mostly don't. That's been harder than anything."

He's at a loss. It's like his heart remembers, yearns and reacts to her, but his mind doesn't have the time spent or the memories to go with it. It's confusing and cosmically unfair – the way she looks at him, the way his heart flutters, and he doesn't know why.

The ship rumbles – he was quiet this time, so what summoned the monster? *Maybe this is it. Forever.* Inevitable. There's no escaping it.

But Grandad didn't raise a boy who gave up the fight.

"You gotta help me, Cal. How do I break us out of this? How do I save you?"

The roar lumbers closer. They need to run, but Calliope steps back, her face drawn, sad and resigned.

"You can't fight a shadow, Baz."

* * *

"Alri—"

Baz ignores Cap and bolts below decks. He'll be sorry about breaking into the locked chest in Doc's quarters later. For now, he digs through the organized scrolls of magic until he finds the right one. Downs a hearty potion to give him some strength back. *Doc, if I live, I owe ya one.*

When he reaches Calliope, she's standing, and as always, her smile sends warmth radiating through his chest. He takes her hand. Together they navigate the ship's maze-like hull. He stops when they're almost to the exit and draws his freshly loaded guns, fires them down the empty hall. It's explosively loud.

Calliope gasps, clutching at his arm. "What are you *doing* – you'll call it right to us!"

"Bang on." He flashes his trademark grin. Sure enough, the hull shakes as the monster batters towards them. Calliope begs him to run but he waits 'til it's rounding the corner.

"How do you fight a shadow, love?" His grin widens. Baz leans in close. "With *light*."

He unravels the scroll.

It glows bright as the sun. The monster screeches like a banshee in a shredder, piercing Baz's skull, cascading off the walls. He grips the scroll's edges, his eyes shut tight against the incredible light. Cold and hot wind blasts around them, fierce and acrid, deadly strong.

Calliope clings to him like an anchor in a maelstrom as Baz plants his boots and grits his teeth. The scroll is scorching hot under his fingertips – his knuckles are burning, scalded, scraped, bleeding, but he doesn't let go – he can feel the monster right in front of him – *this is it*—

His heart beats. Stops.

Silence.

After a breath, he cracks open his eyes. Debris and chunks of shadow monster are suspended in the air around him, lanced through with brilliant rays of sunlight. It's like gravity has disappeared...

Or time is frozen.

Calliope releases him. He's about to warn her, but her expression is anything but surprised.

"I'm so sorry, Baz." Those sea-green eyes sparkle with tears. "I lied…I do know what's happening. I was captured and stolen from home, bound here. This ship was attacked by this thing – that's true. But…"

The tears make shining tracks down her flushed cheeks.

"I'm a Time Siren. I lived by feeding on the essence of the sailors who were here before. And who…came after."

Baz tries to swallow, but his mouth is tinder dry. His exhaustion…

"Looping time… I trap them, take their time for my own, until there's nothing left. They cease to exist. But you…" Her voice catches. "You were kind – from the beginning and in every variation, you were always kind. I liked you and I…I kept you…"

He doesn't know what to say – think, feel. He's in bits. It's all a jumbled, half-remembered mess. His eyes sting, turning her into a blurry smear.

"I don't want you to be trapped anymore. I don't want *you* to cease to exist." She steps close, tears trailing down her lovely face. "So I give it all back – I let you go. Because there's one more thing I didn't lie about: I love you, Baz."

Her lips press to his.

His heart hits the next beat.

The sound of a rushing waterfall blasts over him. Calliope is brighter than the scroll still clutched between his fingers and Baz squeezes his eyes shut again. A sudden rush of energy courses through him – not painful, but something like adrenaline. No – *vitality*. His strength—

A noise like a lightning strike rattles his teeth, makes the entire shipwreck shudder, and sends him sprawling to the floor, banging his head and elbows. Stars burst across his vision.

Silence.

* * *

"Alright, Baz?"

He's in the dinghy jetting over to the black ship before anyone registers him lashing across the deck. The halls and doors are so easy to navigate, he does it easy as breathing. No more dizziness. The only sound is his pattering footsteps and the settling groans of the hull.

His heart stutters when he reaches the iron door, because it's already open, flat on the wall-now-floor.

"Calliope?" he calls. There's no reply.

In the storeroom, the treasure is untouched. So is the pile of rags. He overturns them, keeps calling for her, running through the ship, heedless of the monster. There is no monster, there is no answer.

Nothing but an empty, creaking ship.

* * *

Back aboard the *Starfish*, he informs Cap that the black shipwreck is empty: he searched every nook and cranny.

He might throw up, though. It's completely, utterly, terribly empty.

Calliope is gone.

His heart aches, and he'll never even fully understand why.

Cap peers at him with her wise, dragon eyes. "Baz? Really though – you alright?"

Not even a little. And then, despite everything, he can't help himself. His lips quirk up. He says:

"Probably will be…in time."

Shift • /SHift/
(1) small movement
(2) a change in direction/position
(3) informal Irish: a kiss

Stitching Time

AnaMaria Curtis

Irialen Eldentry was seventeen the first time she was invited to the Second Duke of Correct Behavior's manor house in the off season, when the petals and the ash from the bonfires mingled in the air of the city. There was no blood in the air that summer, for which she was grateful, but the open air of the country was a relief all the same.

Even better was the library in the late afternoons, when most people had retreated to their rooms or to intimate little clusters in various sitting rooms to which Irialen, too young and too willing to venture an opinion on things she knew little about, was not invited. The library had soft leather seats and big bay windows that looked out onto the lawn of the manor. On the third day after arriving, Irialen finally found the interesting books – a small shelf of new mysteries tucked behind a larger and much more imposing shelf of astronomical observations. She happily plucked the latest installment in her favorite series off this shelf and settled into the curve of the nearest window without noticing that she was not alone in the room.

In fact, it wasn't until she was halfway through the novel and regretfully aware that she ought to begin thinking of going upstairs to change for dinner that she saw him, a long, lean scholarly type hunched over one of the books that had undoubtedly come from a prominent shelf and probably held scientific observations of plant anatomy or something equally puzzling. He had a pen and a small notebook, where he was clearly jotting down observations.

Now that she was looking at him, Irialen realized that they somehow hadn't been introduced. It wasn't a large gathering at the Duke's manor, just four or five families, all of whom had been known to her for years, though she was only just officially out. This man had the dark coloring and the long, sharp nose of the Duke, and the thick, even eyebrows of the late Duchess, but Irialen felt certain she'd never seen him before. She would have remembered that face.

A cousin, surely, a near cousin, for the resemblance was strong. He must have been newly arrived.

Irialen was conscious of her manners. She would wait to be introduced at dinner.

But she hit her elbow against the window standing up to leave, and the young man looked up, caught her gaze, and immediately fell to his knees, bowing his head.

"I beg of you," he said, his voice low, "do not speak." Irialen shivered; the timbre of his voice was clear and strong.

She did as he asked; she did not speak.

Finally he looked up, and the look on his face was wretched, abject. He was a picture of misery. "It was not right, what happened to you," he said. "I mourned you, as did the city, though none of us could show it."

Irialen stared at him, frozen. What in the world was he talking about? As far as she knew, nothing worse than two dances with her second cousin Dromley had befallen her in the last few months.

In the face of such strangeness, she did what she often castigated her mystery novel heroines for not doing – she fled.

* * *

Irialen recovered her bravery after dinner – glazed venison and carrots, with a pavlova with lemon curd for dessert to really bolster her spirits – and crept back down to the library before she could be ushered to bed.

There was laughter down the hall, and as she rounded the corner to the library doors, her elder sister, Sariel, emerged from the other end.

Sariel had always been the beautiful one, with piles of warm brown hair, clear, rosy skin, and bright green eyes. Irialen knew that they were only entertaining the visit with the Duke's family because her father thought Sariel might catch the eye of his heir, or, if they were lucky, the Duke himself. That, at least, was not a fate she envied.

"What are you doing?" Sariel whispered, seeing her. "You ought to be in bed."

"I wanted to finish my book."

"You're not meeting someone in the library, I hope." Sariel sighed. "You have to be careful, you know. The Duke's family is in the House of Correct Behavior."

"I didn't agree to meet anyone," Irialen said, which was true.

"Come on, then," Sariel said, and followed her to the door.

The young man was in the library again, or perhaps still, for he hadn't been at dinner after all. He looked up when Irialen entered, but she avoided his gaze, heading to the spot where she'd left her book.

"You didn't think I would move it, did you?" he said. She couldn't see him, focused on the book in her hands, but there was a smile in his voice, something warm. She blushed, waiting for her sister to comment on her lie, on the beautiful young man addressing her with such familiarity, but when she turned, her sister was standing in the doorway, gazing at her own reflection in the window, completely in her head.

"Well," Sariel said finally, seeming to snap out of her own reverie, "you have your book? Make sure your light's out by the time I come up, please. There's talk of a phoenix hunt tomorrow, so the household will be up early."

"Of course," Irialen said, drifting toward the door. She kissed her sister on both cheeks. "Goodnight."

She leaned against the outside of the library doors, pretending to be absorbed in her book, until her sister had rounded the corner.

Then, of course, she went back inside.

"Why didn't my sister notice you?"

The young man looked up from his book. "Who?"

"The woman who was with me just now."

He frowned. "I didn't know you had a sister."

"Of course I do. She's usually a lot more observant."

"Lucky us."

Irialen narrowed her eyes. "You don't mind me speaking now. What changed?"

He smiled, a slow unfurling of amusement across his face, masking something dark. "I've decided I don't believe in ghosts."

Irialen sat in the chair across from him, close enough that she could reach out and nudge him with the toe of her slipper, if she wanted to. She didn't do it, of course. But she did want to.

"I'm not a ghost."

"Sure you are."

"I'm not! I've never died. Ask anyone."

He closed his book. "What's your name?"

"Irialen Eldentry, of the House of Memory." She wrinkled her nose. "A distant branch, through my mother's line."

"Yes," he said. "That's what I thought. And are you the same Irialen Eldentry who walked in the king's gardens four months ago? Who killed one of his birds, however accidentally, only days after your debut?" He gestured to the windows, where of course nothing but their reflection was visible. "Is it not your blood in the ash that flows from the capital this season?"

Irialen sat back, head swimming. She opened her mouth, swallowed, tried again. "I'm not," she said. "I'm *not*. I never walked in the king's gardens. I meant to, a few months ago, but Sariel asked me to stay in and help her with something, and I never got another chance."

Now the man across from her was speechless. He stared at her, and there was something raw and powerful behind his eyes, something so strong that Irialen could not look away. Grief. Hope. Longing.

He stared at her for so long, in fact, that Irialen began to recover her own courage.

"If I am not that Irialen," she said, "then who are you?"

His jaw shut with a click. He took a deep breath through his nose. "You don't know who I am." It was the first time that beautiful voice had sounded flat to Irialen. She shook her head.

"I am Royden Marsenius," he said finally, his voice rough. "The second son of the lord of this house."

Irialen blinked at him. "But you're dead. You've been dead for almost ten years."

He blinked back at her. The absurdity of the situation wrote itself across his strong features just as it rolled through Irialen's mind; they broke into laughter at the same time. On impulse, Irialen reached across the table to take his hand. He drew back, but not quickly enough – her palm met the air above the back of his hand like a bolt of lightning to a yearly sacrifice. It was like nothing she'd experienced before, the jolt and the pain and the not-quite feel of his skin.

Her palm itched into the night.

* * *

The next day, most of the party did go hunting, heading out in a clamor of spears and flame-warded shields and high, bright bells. Irialen's riding skills were poor enough that she was excused as a matter of course; she ventured back to the library, and Royden, and they curled up in cozy leather chairs in a secluded reading nook and built each other explanations.

Royden was twenty-two, and he'd never learned to ride. He was near to finishing his studies at the University of the Full Court, which required a great deal of travel between the various Seasons. He expected to do well on his examinations and hoped to earn a place in the Summer Court working for the House of Glass, so that his father could not obligate him to come back and work for the House of Correct Behavior. The House of Glass had lost many of their officers during the plague – "A plague?" she'd asked, horrified. "We didn't have a plague" – so he thought he had a good chance. At this, he looked up at her, smiling a sideways smile Irialen had begun to get used to. "I have good prospects," he told her, and she looked back down at her hands, unable to speak.

He told her very little about her own family. It clearly pained him to speak of her. "We were friends," was all he would say, tracing the woodgrain of the table with his left hand. "I thought – but everything happened very quickly.

It was an accident; even the king knew it was an accident, I think. But the rules had been written."

For a second, Irialen wanted to reach for his hand again. This time she stopped herself.

* * *

The night before they were due to depart, Irialen turned in her narrow bed toward the side of the room where Sariel lay and asked if she could borrow the needle.

It was still dark, moonlight glancing over everything like the gilding at the temple, and she could only see Sariel's temple, the bridge of her nose, and the soft jut of her cheekbone.

"You're sure?" Sariel asked quietly.

"I've been thinking about it."

"Do you need my help?"

"Have you ever used it?"

Silence. Irialen thought about the way the Duke's cousin had smiled at Sariel at dinner, the way the Duke's eyes had passed over her. She wouldn't know if Sariel had used it. And her sister was twenty-one; she would have had plenty of opportunities.

"Yes," Sariel said finally. "Yes, I've used it, and yes, you can borrow it. Be careful. And don't tell anyone."

* * *

Anyone meant anyone.

As Irialen had told Royden, she was from a very distant part of the House of Memory, on her mother's side. The House was an illustrious House, with many Favored Objects. There was one that had gone missing so long ago as to become more legend than object, the needle that stitched time together. The Great Queen had used it to rescue her most beloved courtier, three thousand years ago. Her granddaughter, Regent of the Autumn Court at the time, had used it to bring the islands back from the oceans. Not even a millennium ago, the Great Sorcerer of the missing continents had used it to cast the Faithless Few from the land, unwriting their very existence so that the songs only spoke of them in absence and riddles without an answer.

And then it had disappeared.

Disappeared, as it happened, into the hands of Irialen's great-great-great-great-great-great-great-grandmother, passed down daughter to daughter, aunt to niece, and never spoken of except over piles of embroidery, which they were all uncommonly good at.

They mostly used it to guarantee good marriages, as Irialen understood it. Stitched together good outcomes for favored suitors or manipulated timelines so that any suitors they sought to avoid would pass them over as well. Anything bigger than that could draw attention. Anything bigger than that was dangerous.

* * *

At first, Irialen used the needle to stitch little pockets between time where they could exchange letters.

This was a great comfort when the drought hit.

She wrote to Royden of failing crops, of a land so dry that the air sparkled with the potential of violence well before the season for bonfires and sacrifices.

There is water for the greenhouses, she wrote to him, *but little for the grain. The rivers are dry. The lakes are low. The wells are empty. The House of Abundance proclaims every day that they are arranging trade with the other Seasons, but so far nothing comes. The King has even shut up the gardens. There is no water for the flowers even in the center of the Summer Court.*

I know you won't remember the plague, he replied. *You won't remember the days after the plague then, either, and for that I almost pity you. When the infections ceased and the dead were buried, and the flowers bloomed and were not needed for the medicines. We braided garlands of them, for the temples, for the throne of the King, for every loved one we still had. I threw a wreath of marigolds around my brother's neck. I swear to you: the flowers will bloom again.*

* * *

The promised supplies from the other Seasons did come. And one day, finally, so did the rains – thick, heavy sheets of rain, like the sky was giving everything it had withheld all at once. Irialen dragged Sariel out into the streets of the city, where everyone was standing, shouting, reveling in it.

The sisters joined them, holding each other around the upper arm, jumping and screaming up into the sky. They stayed out long after the streetlights turned on, long after the first wave of people had gone back inside. Their dresses were plastered around them, drenched and heavy and mildly itchy, and it didn't matter.

Sariel wrapped her arms around Irialen. "I'm so glad," she muttered into Irialen's shoulder. "I'm so glad, I'm so glad."

* * *

It was three years after they'd met before Irialen and Royden could see each other again. It was hard to match their lives to each other, like fitting pieces from two different puzzles together. But through their letters they managed to find a few places of overlap that were relatively sparsely populated.

There was a public fountain across from the public offices of the House of Glass surrounded by benches. Various family members and friends often waited there while people shopped in the stores circling out from around the fountain, so it was easy enough for Irialen to find a reason to be sitting on the bench facing due east in the hour before sunset. She watched the passersby, took note of a bag going missing and clutched her own to her, and then looked up – into his face.

It had been three years. They had had letters. The letters were not enough.

His eyes were steady on hers, dark and glossy with tears the longer she looked at him. Something was twisting and knotting in Irialen's chest, a complicated, shaking thing. It had been there the whole time, she was realizing. She took in the line of his nose, the sharp angle of his jaw, the even, thick brows, the slight sideways curve of his smile. It was all very dear to her.

"It's really you," he said. "I thought perhaps I'd made it up."

She smiled helplessly. "Me too." He pressed a handkerchief into her hands, and the fabric shivered slightly under her fingers. The time transference, she thought, pressing it to her wet cheeks. She wondered if he would try to touch her, if it would still feel like a shock.

"Sit," she told him, and he did.

"Your letters," he said, after a long moment. His voice was rough, but still that pleasant, low timbre. She had tried to remember it, reading his words, but it was better than she had thought. "They've been like a breeze through a still, hot day. Even when you wrote to me of the drought…it was beautiful, to know you were alive somewhere, writing to me."

The words pressed against a thought Irialen had often had but never found a way to ask in the letters. "Royden," she said, "what were we to each other, where you are? Before I died?"

"Friends," he said. "You were young. I was young. But I always thought…if I did well on the examinations, if I got that post in the House of Glass…"

She nodded. "I'll never have those memories, you know. I'll never be the friend you had and lost."

His voice was thick when he replied. "I know. But the same things I loved about her, I love about you. The jokes you make, the tiny mole under your left eye you always complain about, the way you turn to me as though I have the solution when one of your books ends badly. But there are things I only know about you that I never knew about her. I love the way you write your g's with an extra loop, you know, and you always draw a different flower at the corner of your letters depending on what's in bloom outside your window. You tell me what you think more, too. Of course I wish you hadn't died, but—"

"I wish *you* hadn't died," Irialen said. "I wish I had been your friend when we were younger. I'm sure you were delightful."

She looked down at his gloved hand, on the bench between them. "Can I?"

"It'll hurt."

"It'll hurt either way."

The shock lit her up from the inside out this time. She closed her eyes against the wave of pain, the edge of *wrongness*, and kept her hand where it was, until the sensation simmered down to a constant sort of buzz, disconcerting and, yes, unpleasant, but not unbearable.

As she looked down at their two hands, he flipped his palm over slowly, maintaining contact the whole time, and wrapped his fingers around hers.

* * *

I've been thinking, Irialen wrote to him a few days later, *what if there was a way to bring you over to my world? Would you want that?*

The reply was a single word: *Yes*.

* * *

It wasn't that simple; of course it wasn't that simple. To bring him into her timeline, she would have to bring enough of his universe that he would also have a family that recognized him, his position at the House of Glass...

It all got that much harder when he sent another letter. *Dearest*, it began. *I don't know how to tell you this, but in my timeline, your sister died in the plague. I never met her. I didn't even know she existed, until I asked around after meeting you – this you. Anything you do – and I don't know what you're contemplating, or what's in your power – don't let that be something I bring with me. I would hate for you to lose something to gain me. You will always have me, even if it's only ever from here.*

Irialen stared at this letter for so long she feared she might set fire to it with her eyes, as her aunt had once done with a letter from an ex-lover. But the paper only grew creased and slightly damp in her grasp.

Royden had lived, and her sister had died, and she, eventually, had died as well. Royden had died and her sister had lived and so had she. They stood across an impossible gap.

Irialen reread the letter. She didn't know what was in her power either.

* * *

Sariel announced her engagement to the head of the House of State to Irialen by tackling her into her bed as they were getting ready for dinner one evening. It had been almost two years since Irialen had seen Royden and started her preparations. Sariel had never asked for the needle back.

"I'm so happy," Sariel said into Irialen's shoulder, repeatedly poking Irialen's spleen with her elbow in her excited wriggling. "I really am. It's what I wanted. It's what I waited for. I didn't have to change anything at all."

* * *

The next three months passed like a slow nightmare. Irialen helped Sariel with wedding preparations – the dress, the trousseau, the firedancers, an endless checklist – and wrote to Royden and tried to understand how she could hold the happiness of two people in her palms and not let it drop.

The thing was, time wasn't like a linen or a cotton that Irialen could embroider beautiful, complicated dreams on, so long as her hand moved true and sure. The warp and the weft never lined up the same way twice. There were gaps where there ought not to be. Instead of fabric, perhaps time was better visualized as a river of threads, clumping and bunching and tying themselves together in chunks, drifting apart in others.

Irialen was on one strand of thread, reaching out to snag the thread Royden was on every now and then, hoping it didn't get lost the longer they spent apart.

She had the needle; she could bind the two threads. But at what cost?

* * *

I miss you, Royden wrote. *A lightning dancer came to court yesterday, and I reached my hand out and nearly touched his shoulder, before one of my companions knocked my hand away. It wouldn't have been the same as touching you, I know, but I find myself yearning for lightning nonetheless.*

"I want you to be happy," Sariel told Irialen, one night when she'd snuck in and asked to brush Irialen's hair in the place of her maid while she still could. "That's all that matters to me. You know that, don't you?" She stroked the back of Irialen's head almost absentmindedly. "I hope you don't resent me."

Irialen didn't quite know where this was coming from. Marriage must be making her emotional. Or perhaps it was the fractiousness of the Court. The King was in a temper. The House of Fire was feasting.

* * *

On days that ash and blood wafted by the window, Irialen stayed inside and worked on the problem. She wrote to Royden and asked him questions, asked him for details she'd never considered before, trying to understand what separated the worlds in which each of them had been allowed to live.

In his: Royden had never learned to ride, having taken a dislike to horses at an early age. There had been a plague when he was young, in which Sariel had died. At the age of seventeen Irialen had gone walking in the King's garden and most unfortunately tripped over an ailing bird, snapping its neck with her heel in the presence of four witnesses. For this, she had been condemned to the fires.

In hers: Royden had died in a riding accident as a child. There had been no plague, so Sariel had not died, but there had been a drought. Irialen had lived a mostly happy life. She had never visited the King's gardens.

Irialen thought about this last difference while waiting for her sister to return from the dressmaker so they could have lunch. She was curled in a nook in the informal sitting room, nearly finished with the embroidery – pink roses, meant as a gift for Sariel – but the needle went loose in her fingers when the thought struck her.

Why had she not gone to the King's gardens after all?

She had been quite set on it, she remembered. But Sariel had insisted that she stay in, that she help with some piece of embroidery Sariel meant to take to a friend. When Irialen had insisted, indignant, Sariel had actually raised her voice at her.

Irialen had been too annoyed to notice it at the time, but now...

What had Sariel said, the other night? I hope you don't resent me?

Irialen looked down at the needle in her hand. Sariel had used the needle once, before she'd given it to Irialen, but she hadn't gotten engaged until years later. She hadn't used the needle on a suitor at all.

* * *

This didn't fix Irialen's problem, of course, only made her feel more guilty about it.

Sariel had saved her. And here she was contemplating something that might risk Sariel, so that she might have Royden. It felt like a betrayal of the highest order. Incorrect Behavior. She could almost feel the flames.

* * *

It didn't occur to her until the night before Sariel's wedding. She crept into Sariel's room, the light of her candle wavering in the breeze from the window, the needle tucked into her sash. Sariel sat up immediately, not even pretending to have been asleep.

"What is it?" she whispered.

"Were you ever going to tell me?"

The candle illuminated the edges of Sariel's face. Her round cheeks, the red gleam in her brown hair, the way her lips opened on an *oh* as she understood what Irialen meant. Sariel opened her arms, and Irialen set the candle on the nightstand and crawled into them.

"I didn't want you to feel as though you owed me something," she said finally.

"Okay," Irialen said into the quiet of the room. "Thank you."

She let Sariel wrap her arms around her.

Then she broke the silence again. "I had an idea, but I need your help."

"Go on," Sariel murmured into her hair.

Irialen told her about the timelines, the way the three of them never all survived. How she'd finally worked out that she lived because Sariel lived, but that that didn't bring back Royden, who she missed, who she longed for. Sariel's arms tightened around her in silent sympathy.

"I was thinking," Irialen finally said, "that if you do the stitching, if you wield the needle, maybe it won't be able to unmake you."

She could hear Sariel's smile in her voice. "If I make it, it can't unmake me."

"Exactly. Because in the unmaking, it too would be undone."

Sariel straightened, and Irialen sighed in relief. She hadn't really been worried Sariel would refuse her, but it was no small thing she was asking.

"Light the lamp," Sariel said. "Let's do it now."

"You're sure?"

"I've always had a steady hand. Plus, I want to be here when it happens." Sariel grinned. "This way I can chaperone."

Irialen lit the lamp, pulled out the needle, held it in the air, unwilling to snag it on anything until she was sure she needed to.

"Together," Sariel said. She wrapped her hand around Irialen's and pulled the thread.

* * *

It took him another three hours to find them once the threads were bound together, but he was rapping on the front door by the time dawn was creeping over the rooftops.

"Go on," said Sariel, her nose pressed against the window. "I'll be right behind you."

Irialen met him at the base of the stairs. He was still tall, still beautiful, but she thought to herself that she'd never seen him smile like that before. His happiness carved his face wide open, bright and disbelieving, and this time he held his hands out to her.

It didn't feel like lightning when she touched him this time, but her heart skipped a beat all the same. His fingers were warm under hers, a little calloused from all that writing. They were real, real, real.

It was a sensation she would get used to.

Stupid Cupid

Sarina Dorie

Being a cupid is a lot of hard work, more than one might expect.

Hidden behind a tall stack of files on my desk, in my disturbingly glittery, pink office, I signed off on cases to give the go ahead to shoot. Bill Eros edged around the mounds of reports in my office. It was always like this in mid-January, being pre-V Day.

I smiled at Bill as he set another file on top of the mountain on my desk. If anyone in our firm is close to looking like a cherub, it would be Bill, with his short, paunchy build and receding hairline. I'm fortunate to have the fashion sense to sport the Greek god look with my dark, Mediterranean features and bronze biceps. It would drive mortal women insane if I didn't use glamour to tone down the real me. Then again, I didn't have to resort to using glamour, as I rarely made it out of the office these days.

I opened the folder as Bill attempted to slink away. "Wait a minute, this one hasn't been filled yet," I said.

He coughed. "There isn't anything I can do for her."

I gestured for him to take a seat. Sighing, Bill lifted the stack of papers from the chair and set them in his lap while I skimmed case PAAC897692. She was a twenty-nine-year-old who lived in Florida. Occupation: rocket scientist. Employer: NASA. Okay, maybe she was a hardworking nerd. Was that why she couldn't get a date? Too busy for love? Name: Pandora Athena Artemisia Chronis, preferred name, Dora. I chuckled. An obvious Greek, but that shouldn't have been a drawback in itself.

I shoved aside the papers covering my keyboard and pulled up her profile on my computer. In her photo, she was stunning for a human; long, black hair with the kind of natural wave most women would be jealous of, an adorable, dimpled smile, full lips, and dark, sultry eyes.

Smart and attractive. How could Bill say he couldn't do anything for her?

I turned the screen for him to see. "Look at this goldmine. You just aren't trying hard enough. I'm worried about you. What's going on?"

He ran a hand through the little brown hair he had and shrugged noncommittally. "Nothing. It's not about me. Read the report, and then *you* try to make her fall in love."

"This is why you're still doing field work and you're not a supervisor." He'd been here longer than I had and was still in the same position he'd always been in, whereas I was now regional manager. My early days of partying with Bill were now replaced with overtime and administrative work – and a prestigious position I'd earned.

"I like playing matchmaker," he grumbled.

"Did you try troubleshooting? Is her preference women? Does she have a self-esteem issue? A brain tumor?"

"No, no, and no! She can't love a man."

Can't. There's no worse four-letter word in our firm. I stood up, looking him square in the eyes. "I'm sure *I* could find someone for her."

Bill didn't take the bait like he would have two thousand years ago. He crossed his arms, looking amused and self-assured. "Fine, go ahead and try. But you aren't going to be able to find a man for her."

"Let's widen the scope and say *human*. How much do you want to bet?"

Bill smirked. "Five hundred big ones. And I want you to get off my case for being lazy."

"Deal."

* * *

It isn't like we help all humans find love. At *Aphrodite's Helpers* we just focus on individuals who have a deficit. Unfortunately, there's a lot of love deficit, and with the human population growing at an exponential rate, our piles of eligible candidates are pretty high.

I stayed at work late reviewing Dora's profile. No major abnormalities. She had what seemed like a normal family life and, as expected, a high IQ. Her hobbies included watching romantic comedies, volunteering to read to the blind, and belly dancing. She seemed too perfect. In high school, she'd had boyfriends and crushes. Oddly, the only time she'd ever slept with a man was when she'd been twenty-one and in college. That was eight years ago. The note in her profile simply said, 'Latin club dorm party'.

I scratched my chin. Probably some creep had taken advantage of her and left a lasting, negative impression. Though there was no evidence in her medical history of assault, serious depression, or negative feelings toward men.

Because I wanted to get to the bottom of this trauma, I decided fieldwork was in order. I dropped in on Dora's belly dance class at the health club. No one could see me in the well-lit, mirrored room, as I kept to the realm between worlds.

Dora was even cuter in person than in her picture. She was clumsy and unco-ordinated in an endearing way and kept to the back of the room. She had the curves of a Greek goddess, and the kind of smile that was contagious to everyone around her, myself included.

I carefully selected an architect from the group of body builders in the weight room next door, used a suggestion dart to plant a seed in his head to be thirsty, but not be able to find the vending machine, and guided him to the dance class. When he opened the door, Dora turned to look at the hunky human. Some of the other ladies giggled and became distracted from their dance choreography.

"Do you know where the vending machine is?" he asked in a deep, manly voice.

Dora's smile was shy and polite. "I think it's on the second floor next to the bathrooms."

Before he turned away, I drew two infatuation arrows, shot him in the chest and then her.

Immediately, his eyes twinkled, his grin grew broader, and he seemed to melt a little. Her expression didn't change. She went back to dancing.

Well, not all humans are expressive in their faces. I stuck around to see how things played out after her class was over and – Score! – he asked her out on a date. But she declined.

I was perplexed. Hadn't my arrow affected her at all? Was she just too shy? Was she afraid of men?

I decided to give the arrow a few days. But every time I checked on her, she seemed unaltered. I observed how confident and friendly she was at work. With her coworkers she wasn't at all shy or intimidated, though she was completely oblivious to the admiring stares of male coworkers.

The next time she went to her belly dance class, I unleashed a true love arrow when he walked by her. He even struck up a conversation, but she didn't seem particularly impressed. It took another two weeks before she agreed to go out on a date with him. Unfortunately, she stared out the window the entire time and didn't call him back. Maybe he wasn't her type. I had to pull his arrow so he wouldn't go on pining for her.

I tried a lean, blond man from her work. Nope, had no effect. I shot an arrow at a woman Dora smiled at in a coffee shop to see if that was her type. Nothing. I tried men again; a slightly older man, a younger man, a Greek man, but nothing. I tried true love, love at first sight, infatuation and slow-and-burning love arrows, but none of them worked. She seemed to be completely immune to cupid love charms.

I was just about to give up, drowning my sorrows with mug after mug of cocoa at the chocolate fountain in the break room (one of the luxuries of working as a cupid), when Bill Eros sauntered in.

He smirked. "Why the long face, Tony?"

I wasn't about to admit my failure. "I'm just tired. Have a lot on my plate."

"Opened that Pandora's box yet?"

"I'm very busy. I can only work on it a few minutes here or there." I quickly walked away.

Okay, no more Mr. Nice Cupid. I pulled out the big arrows, the ones for soul mates. I also took out passionate, crazy sex arrows. After reading profiles, I carefully selected an attractive man from a different department at her work who had a successful history with relationships, and shot him and Dora. As usual, she didn't seem in the least bit in love. But the other rocket scientist was head over heels for her. She dated him for a couple weeks, and I was ready to throw a victory party when she finally went to bed with him.

In my younger days, I might have stuck around to observe, but there's nothing more pathetic than a horny cupid, so I decided to just check on them in the morning. To my surprise, they weren't at his place, lounging in bed and cuddling. She was back at her apartment, curled up in bed, crying. She watched TV all day and ate ice cream.

What had that idiot done to her? Not just the most recent bonehead I'd set up for her, but the one that had ruined her for all men.

I hovered in the layers between worlds, more than anything wishing I could make myself visible, to hold her and tell her everything would be all right. But besides the fact that it would scare the bejezus out of her – and wasn't allowed – I didn't know if I could make everything better.

* * *

Extreme times call for extreme cupidry. Which is why I allowed myself to be visible as I strolled into the bustling coffee shop while Dora was in line for her latte. The aroma of mocha greeted me as I flashed her my most charming smile. Naturally, I'd toned down the real me with a bit of glamour.

"Do I know you?" Dora asked.

"You do now." I held out one of my business cards.

Antonio Cherubim
Matchmaker extraordinaire
Aphrodite's Helpers

She cracked a smile when she read it. "Do I look like a desperate, single girl who can't get a date?"

She looked as radiant as always, oblivious to the stares of the men around her. I leaned against the counter, trying to act casual and not too eager. "Not at all. The problem isn't about getting a date, it's about finding true love."

She rolled her eyes. "Whatever."

Mortals usually lapped up the f–word, so I dropped one in. "It's *free* for ladies."

She looked at me again. I could tell she was considering it now.

"No commitment from you. I can set you up with some profiles to look at in my office. If you like what you see, you can pick one to meet. If you don't, that's fine, too."

I'll admit, it's slightly unorthodox to bring humans into our office, and I did get a little smirk from Bill, but I didn't care. This wasn't about my pride or some rivalry between us anymore. It was about the client.

She sat in the chair on the other side of my desk. I'd taken the liberty of removing half the files from my office, making it appear slightly less messy than before. Her lips twitched as she hid a smile, her eyes dancing over the excessive pink décor. I hoped she didn't think I had chosen the color scheme.

"Tell me about your relationship history. Have you dated anyone recently?" I coaxed.

She fiddled with the vinyl purse in her lap. "Yeah, I've dated a few different men. None of them were right for me, though."

I leaned forward with interest. "What do you mean? What was wrong with them?"

"Nothing. That's the thing. I think…something's wrong with me." She burst into tears.

My heart broke seeing her like that. I handed her the tissue box and sat on the edge of my desk across from her. "Nothing's wrong with you. Men are morons. It isn't your fault if none of them were good enough for you."

She took a few deep breaths and went on. "You don't understand. I don't feel anything for anyone. I mean, I like men platonically, but I don't feel anything. I've tried, but I can't. I thought it was a phase or something with my hormones because I liked boys in high school. But my doctor said my hormones are fine. I just don't understand why I feel numb inside."

I thought back to her only two sexual experiences. I took her hand in mine. "Did someone hurt you? Someone you were intimate with? Someone…in college, perhaps?" Human traumas usually won't overpower cupid magic but perhaps I'd underestimated this one.

Shock crossed her face. "No, nothing like that."

I tried to word my next question carefully, not wanting to give away that I had been spying on her. "Tell me about the man you dated most recently."

"He was nice. There was nothing wrong with him. But when we were together…"

I suddenly felt protective of her. Invested as I was in her happiness, I wished I'd stayed that night to make sure he hadn't messed up.

She sighed, listlessly. "It didn't feel special to me. There was no chemistry. Maybe I'm too picky. Or I've romanticized love to the point that I think it has to be love at first sight or something impossible—"

"It isn't impossible." Ignoring protocol, I moved closer and hugged her to my chest, noticing how she smelled of roses and vanilla. "And if love at first sight is what you want, that's what I'll give you."

She gazed up at me, the earthy chestnut of her eyes so bewitching it made my breath catch in my throat. The familiar beauty of her classical features stirred something deep inside my chest. I loosened my hold on her, aware that she might think I was crossing the bounds of professionalism.

It was a relief when she laughed, tears still clinging to her spidery lashes. "You probably think I'm silly, telling a perfect stranger all this. I'm not usually such a blabbermouth. I guess you just seem pretty trustworthy."

Guilt clawed at my insides. She trusted me; I couldn't let her down again. I tried to concentrate on her problem, but it was hard with the warm mocha of her breath rushing so close, the softness of her hand in mine. "Tell me your idea of the perfect man and I will find him for you."

She smiled a little sheepishly. "Well, someone who's caring, thoughtful, respectful. I want a gentleman. Maybe someone with the same interests as me, but most importantly...I want someone who will love me." I saw the pain in her eyes on that last note.

Now, I hadn't matched her up with losers. I'd used plenty of arrows to give her men who loved her, and all the men I'd found fit those qualities. There had to be something more. "That's a good start, but those things are kind of generic. Tell me *exactly* what you want. Your fantasy."

She blushed, but her gaze still held mine. "My fantasy... he'd be tall, with black or brown hair, have the body of...a hero from a romance novel—" I hurried behind my desk and typed this into her profile. "He'd know all the names of the constellations, have an interest in philosophy, science and ancient history. He'd be intelligent enough to have a conversation with, but not condescending. And he'd be more incredible than Eros in bed."

I laughed at that. But her expression was serious. I cleared my throat. "When you say Eros, do you mean figuratively, or do you mean..."

"I'm sorry." She sighed. "I'm describing a man I – well, that I met at Yale. It was at a toga party for the Latin club. I think he said he was visiting from Harvard. He had beautiful costume wings, and he was supposed to be the god of love."

I tried to swallow the lump in my throat. There was no way this could be Bill Eros. Not without a whole lot of glamour.

"I thought it was love at first sight, but I guess I was a little tipsy. I remember staring at his face and thinking I would never fall in love with another man again. He was too beautiful to be real. But then in the morning when I woke up, it was all fuzzy. I couldn't see his face anymore or even recall his name. He disappeared like a dream."

A chill washed over me.

The pieces were starting to fit together now.

The reason Dora couldn't fall in love with a human man was because she was in love with a cupid. And not just any cupid; it appeared she was in love with my good friend, Bill Eros.

* * *

That's how these things happened millennia ago before such strict rules were in place to help mortals. A few cupids or other immortals would slip into a party while everyone was dancing and drunk, seduce a mortal and then afterwards, pass out in a drunken haze. It was safe enough if the mortal stayed asleep, or the stupid cupid didn't get so smashed they lost their ability to cloak their true selves with glamour when they passed out.

But the cupid Dora had slept with obviously hadn't. Still, I couldn't believe Bill Eros would be so irresponsible. He'd been an experienced veteran of cupidry.

After Dora went to the waiting room, I checked the date of the college party at Yale, then did a cross check of any cases that might have been active and near campus within three days of the dorm party. Not that this would take into account any rogue or freelance cupids with their stray arrows – or stray seducing.

I lucked out. There had been three cases active at Yale that night. And the cupid assigned to them had been…Bill. I cringed.

Was that why he'd given me this case? He hadn't known what to do about it? Yeah, well, I had a pretty good idea of how to fix things now. I got out a bolt of true love for the crossbow.

I shouted out the door. "Sharlene, please tell Bill I would like to see him in my office. Now."

Lowering his glamour like that wasn't just dangerous to our operation, but he had hurt a mortal in the process. I was shaking with rage as Bill strolled in. To his credit, he didn't flinch when he saw my crossbow aimed directly at him.

"You ruined this flawless woman for all other men and made her a slave to infatuation for eight years." I said through clenched teeth. "How could you be such a stupid cupid? Were you drunk?"

He leaned against the doorway. "I save the drinking for after the parties. I like to remember my pretty little mortals."

"So you're saying you did this to her *knowingly*?"

He crossed his arms. "Mediterranean virgins are not my type. Use your brain. What's my preference?"

The truth was, I'd never seen him with a woman. He was a man's man; always the center of attention in groups of fair-haired, blue-eyed *men* with rock solid muscles… Oh, that was his preference.

"If it wasn't you, who was it?" I lowered the crossbow and set it on my desk.

He shrugged. "Must have been someone I took with me."

Toga parties. They used to be all the rage. Bill used to take all of us to them. That meant I had a hundred suspects.

Bill studied his watch. "Did she mention any details about him?"

"She said his name was Eros and that he'd been a student at…Harvard."

Bill smirked. "Well, Sherlock, we already know I wasn't the cupid who seduced her. Look in your computer to see who was working at Harvard during that time."

A sinking cold cramped in my belly. I didn't need to check who had been working at Harvard.

I swallowed, meeting his eyes. I tried to remember any details from the toga parties Bill had taken me to while I'd been working at Harvard. I rarely drank, but on one occasion, when I'd been celebrating my promotion, I'd definitely drunk too much. Bill had introduced me to someone that night; a beautiful, dark-haired girl…a girl I'd carelessly used and then forgotten?

Silently, Bill closed the door to my office, leaving me alone to wallow in self-disgust. Here I was, accusing Bill of being irresponsible and unprofessional when I'd been the big jerk.

I thought of Dora's adorable smile, her endearing humanness, and her eight years of pining…for me, the stupidest cupid of all time. I knew what the right thing to do was. Maybe it wasn't necessary, considering how much she'd grown on me since I'd taken on her case, but I snatched up my crossbow and held it to my chest. It probably would have been easier to ask Bill to do it, but I felt too humiliated.

* * *

I called Pandora back into my office. She deserved better than me, but I was the one she wanted – if she didn't change her mind once she knew I was the one who had caused her so much pain. I cleared my throat, leaning against my desk and knocking down a pile of papers in my nervousness. Being the kind-hearted soul she was, she immediately left her seat to help me pick them up.

My heart was thundering, my hands uncharacteristically clammy. Is this what my clients went through? I shuffled the papers together haphazardly, unable to take my eyes off her. "I realize this is highly usual, but…would you consider going on a date with me?"

Her eyebrow jerked up in surprise as she handed me another paper. "Mr. Perfect Matchmaker is single?"

My insides twisting, I took her hands in mine. "I'm hardly perfect."

I let a fraction of glamour slide, knowing the moment she recognized me she might slap me. Her gaze was intense, but I wasn't sure she remembered my face yet. I let a little bit more glamour dissipate; I didn't want to overload her. A gasp escaped from her perfect lips.

This was the moment she might scream she never wanted to see me again and run out of my office and my life, leaving me the one with the wounded heart. Instead, she threw her arms around me, knocking me flat on my butt, slightly undignified for a cupid, but she didn't even seem to notice.

"I knew you somehow looked familiar," she said.

I kissed her tear-streaked cheeks, unable to hold her close enough, unable to kiss her enough. If this is what humans felt when they were in love, this extraordinary euphoria, I was ready to give up immortality to be with her.

I was sure Bill would say I lost the bet, but I was too in love to care.

When the Moon Cradled the Sun

Kate Duarte

It was a house – a perfectly good one at that – and Robin had been a nestless bird for far too long. She was in no position to refuse.

She chose not to look the gift horse in the mouth. Even if its teeth were chipped and decayed, tongue rotten, she could wash down the odor with a bit of whiskey.

She could pull a rug over the broken planks, a bucket if there were holes in the ceiling when it rained. She could ignore the house's flaws and call it her own.

Finally, something that was *hers*.

Sitting in the middle of nowhere, woodland surrounded the house, birds chirping loudly on the lower branches – a welcoming song, a good omen. Robin took a deep breath before trying the key, rust flaking at her feet, paint chipping off the entrance's walls. She blew off the dust covering the door handle and stepped inside.

Oh, she loved it already. With its scratched wooden floors, frayed carpets, and low chandeliers, it was lived-in; it had character. Robin took the stairs two steps at a time, each one creaking under the soles of her combat boots, and found herself in a paneled corridor, an arched doorway to her left, rooms to her right.

Here was a living room, a small hearth to one side, tucked like an alcove, two wooden benches flanking it. Over the hearth there were panels with *fleur-de-lis*, lions, and towers carved in white. Robin loved it here.

Once more, she stepped into the corridor, its ceiling all stained-glass, tinting her skin green like the forest outside.

Robin settled for one of the bedrooms, beautiful like everything else inside the house and equally hearty. With dusk thundering toward her, she only had time to unpack a few books, three bottles – whiskey, vodka, a sweet liquor – her cigarettes tossed onto the bedside table. As soon as the moon peeked from behind a cloud, Robin collapsed on the bed, clothes and all. She tried clinging to the light one moment more, not long – enough to hear the scratches, like claws against wood.

* * *

Robin woke up gasping for air.

Throwing the windows open, she started looking for signs of woodworms. But the wooden beams holding the ceilings were pristine, the floors only showing marks of use.

She could call someone over. With how remote the house was, and how extensive, perhaps they'd have to work until night came knocking. She couldn't risk staying alone with a stranger at night.

Propping a blank canvas on its easel, Robin decided to ignore the scratching. It could've been in her head – God knew she had had her share of lulling alcohol already. She sketched the house. A loud caw cut through her favorite room, and she dropped her brush.

"Shit," she said, eyeing the stain on the ancient carpet.

The day was almost over. Robin had not gone into the basement yet, and she had made up her mind that she'd explore it first. Surely, she could do it quickly and return upstairs before moonrise. If not, she could sleep on the stairs. It'd be hard on her back, but she could deal with back pain if it meant reaching *the itch* spreading rapidly inside her, telling her to go.

She wasn't known for her sensible decisions.

Despite its extensive wings, the house had only two floors, an attic, and the basement below. Robin tiptoed downstairs, then pulled open the hatch leading to the basement. A spider scurried out, stealing a tiny whimper from Robin.

Robin descended, brushing the cobwebs aside and coughing dust. She turned on the flash on her phone, illuminating the boxes scattered across a stony, cracked floor, filled with broken bikes, children's dolls missing an eye, old clothing.

And the monster chained to the wall.

As she stumbled back, her calves hit the edge of a broken piece of furniture, and Robin went tumbling. Her phone flew out of her hand, drowning her in darkness. Crawling, she groped around blindly, until her fingers closed around her phone. She pointed the flash at the monster. He was still there, chained and silent, long grey hair covering his face. Two pairs of horns protruded from his head, one short, at the forehead, and the second pair longer, curving inwards, dark brown and ridged. His shirt flapped open, exhibiting a chest peppered with scars from wounds long healed. He wore a pair of trousers that looked taken out of the historical romances Robin enjoyed watching, the heels of his boots not touching the floor, as if whoever strung him there wanted him to struggle.

No, she couldn't think of him as a man. *It.* It was a creature with long black talons, who did not stir even as Robin rose slowly to her feet. She was afraid she might wake it. But would it not have woken when she screamed and fell? How would it even be alive, if the house had been vacant for decades? And how had no one noticed the monster in chains, when they came to fix the house to receive her?

"Are you alive?" Robin asked, feeling stupid and exposed. Would it even answer, or would it wait for her to come closer and bite a chunk off her neck?

When it didn't respond, she took a step toward it, and another, until she was a breath away. It didn't so much as twitch a muscle. Robin snapped her fingers in front of its face. Nothing. Holding her breath, she brushed back the long strands of grey hair, and dirt came off on her fingertips like ashes. Its hair wasn't grey at all, only covered in cinders. She could now get a full view of its face – white eyebrows over white lashes fluttering lightly. It was *asleep*. There was a dimple beneath its bottom lip, so human it brought tears to her eyes.

It was monstrous, too. Half of its face was covered in thick skin like…bark? Yes, black bark, stiff, moving with its breath.

"Please, don't bite. I taste horrible," she murmured, grimacing at the beast.

She pulled its upper lip, inspecting. A row of sharp, fang-like teeth, all pointy and made to tear apart. She dropped her hand with a start, stepping back. Still, the creature did not wake.

Robin might as well continue her inspection. She tested its chains, and they rattled but didn't snap. She poked its scarred chest, blew on its face, pinched its bicep. Nothing could wake it up, almost like—

Night was coming.

Robin fumbled to turn her phone around, to check the hour. Time had passed faster than she expected, as if the basement had swallowed the minutes, trapping her inside with the strange creature. Through the only window in the room, a horizontal slit which barely illuminated the space, the sun coughed its dying breaths, burnt orange turning purple, bleeding into blue.

She had a few minutes, then.

"Wake up!" She shook the monster.

She was giving up when its eyes cracked open the slightest bit, one dark grey, the other black, sclera and all.

Robin tripped backwards, gaze widening, never leaving the beast's. And then she ran for the ladder, scratching her palms as she fell a step. Almost reaching the hatch, she heard it croak out, "Release me!"

Freezing with a hand on the latch, Robin's breath fogged in front of her face.

"Release me," it said again, its voice a raw, wounded thing. "Please…" The last word broke in half like a twig, and when she turned to look at it, the creature's chin was touching its collarbones, as if it couldn't lift his head anymore.

"What are you?" Robin asked, but it didn't answer. "If you don't tell me, I can't help you."

"Why should it matter?" it snarled, head snapping up. Rage flashed in its eye, the black shimmering like onyx, no need for the flash of her phone anymore. "Have you come here to keep me, like the ones before you?"

"To *keep* you? No, I inherited this house. I didn't even know the man who lived here before. I knew none of them. I was adopted."

He – she could no longer pretend it wasn't a man – cocked his head to the side. "Are you not an Ashford?"

"Not by blood."

His eyebrows shot up, and a new life colored his features, like he was using all the strength he had. "Please. Please, *let me go*." His voice had such desperation, such emotion, she couldn't help but move back down.

"I don't have the keys. And night is coming."

He furrowed his brow. "If you fear I might maim you, I could do it at dawn or at the eve all the same."

She gnashed her teeth together, determined not to let him know. "I can't stay. I'll be back tomorrow and…break your chains. I'll find a hammer."

"No!" Again, his tone was jagged edged with anguish. "Let me go now."

Instead of checking the hour again, Robin stole a glance at the window, so quick he shouldn't have noticed.

"You said you *can't* stay," he said, going quiet.

The breath caught in her throat. How could this stranger know of her condition, how she could not rise from sleep before the daylight. A captive of the sun, Robin could never get a good look at the moon, nor party until dawn came, like other people her age.

"There's still time," he said, licking cracked lips. "Give me a glass of water, and I'll be strong enough to break them myself."

"I won't make it to and from the kitchens in time." There was no more reason to lie; she knew, in her heart of hearts, he was *aware*.

"I am cursed the same as you. If you do not let me escape now, I won't be able to when you wake up. And if they come for me then, I'll be done."

"No one will come for you. I'm the last Ashford," Robin said. "And if they did, I wouldn't let them in." She shouldn't make promises to beasts, yet this beast looked, and talked, and felt, like a man. It'd be cruel, inhuman, not to help.

"I—" She didn't get to finish the sentence.

* * *

When Robin opened her eyes, she first touched the bump at the back of her head, then sat straight and stared at the stranger.

He slept.

"Hey," she walked toward him, shook him. He towered over her, shoulders wide, legs thick, but Robin wouldn't fear a muzzled dog. "I'm here now. I can release you."

The creature didn't acknowledge her presence, eyes flitting behind his lids. What did monsters dream of? Liberty? The vast woods outside?

Already, Robin knew they'd only be able to meet for a brief moment, at dusk, when time held its breath. Perhaps at dawn, too, just before the mountains cradled the moon. She sprinted upstairs, pulled a notebook out of her still-packed baggage, and started scribbling. She told him how she came about the house – a man unceremoniously informed her there was no one else to inherit it – asked him about his life, how he ended up chained to a wall, why he had horns.

All day, Robin paced back and forth, searched the cabinets for hammers, stared at her watch. No one came to the door, which was well and good, because she didn't want to have to fight them off. She had decided not to let anyone hurt the man. It might be idiocy, but she felt a kinship with him.

And as the small hairs on the nape of her neck started to rise, sensing night coming, Robin went to the basement.

He was awake!

"I'm Robin," she said. "I don't have much time, but I wrote you a letter. You can read it when I go to sleep. Now, I think I might have the key." She said all this in a single breath, words tripping over one another. "See? It must be in this set of keys."

"That one." He strained against his chains, leaning forward. "The red."

A rusty key, ornamented in a vintage way, dangled from the set. Robin lifted it to the lock, standing on her tiptoes, her body pressing against the stranger's. She could feel his breath on her hair. "How do I know you won't kill me?" Robin murmured, suspended mid-action.

"I vow it on my honor," he said, with such vehemence it made it seem as if no one would ever swear falsely on their honor. "I won't harm you."

Robin gazed at him, his mismatched eyes, the dimple under his lower lip. "What is your name?"

He considered it first, like his name was the only possession he still had and he couldn't very well hand it over to the first stranger who showed him kindness. "Garth," he rasped.

Garth. Robin rolled it around in her mouth.

Swiftly, she reached for the lock. As soon as the chains clattered down, Garth fell into her arms, too weak to stand. She propped his back against the wall to relieve herself of some of his considerable weight.

"Forgive me," Garth said.

"It's okay." Robin adjusted her arms around his waist, helping him slide down to the floor, and sit with his back to the wall. "I brought water." She reached for the bottle she'd left at his feet, pulled the stopper, and brought it to his lips.

Garth drank in sloppy, full gulps that escaped the corners of his lips and rained down the scars on his chest. He squeezed the plastic between his fingers, until there was no drop left, and then cast the bottle aside. Already, a healthy flush was returning to his cheeks, his posture straightening.

Robin knelt before him, between his legs stretched either side of her.

"Why did you unchain me?" Garth asked, his voice thunderous, free of the hoarse quality it previously had held.

"You asked me to."

"Do you do everything you're asked to?" A menacing current ran under his question, his eyes glinting liquid, like petrol, like a viscous, dangerous thing.

Robin licked her lips. "It'd be cruel to leave you here."

"Do you never do cruel things?"

"Sometimes. Never like this."

Her lids weighed down her eyes, numbness spreading through her limbs. *Shit.* She had meant to be out of the basement before night, preferably locked in her bedroom, the dresser blocking the door, and the windows shut. But here she was, at the mercy of a stranger. A stranger, which her family had apparently captured, maybe tortured.

"I must go—"

"Shh." Garth lifted his thumb to her eyelids, closing one at a time. "Rest now."

* * *

Tangled in her sheets, Robin almost fell off the bed. She stretched her arms over her head, lay with her eyes closed for a while longer – until she remembered the rough touch of Garth's thumb. *Rest now.*

He had carried her upstairs, strong as he promised he'd be after drinking water.

Robin tossed back her sheets, paper crinkling under the soles of her feet when she hopped out of bed. *An envelope.* She ripped it open, feasted on the words like a starved woman. While she slept, Garth had apparently cleaned the kitchens, lit a fire in her favorite room that she could rekindle when she woke, and he'd read the books she brought to the house. He hoped she didn't mind. The Ashfords had always kept him; he scarcely remembered the world outside. His kin were long gone, but horns ran in the family. He was fae. He was chained so they could better bleed him, hence the scars, and his blood kept the family wealthy and lucky. Once upon a time, the Ashfords had asked for a source of power – here was Garth.

Immediately, Robin reached for her notebook and wrote another letter. Garth had beautiful cursive handwriting, but her words looked like crickets, jumping up and down the page, escaping the lines. Today, she planned on working on her painting and exploring the rest of the house. She'd see if she could find him clothes, but she'd order them online if she couldn't find any. He wouldn't know what *online* meant, but she could explain it later. Then she'd visit him. Robin finished the letter telling him that was what she was most excited for.

* * *

It was, perhaps, madness.

She'd blame the alcohol, but Robin hadn't touched her bottles since arriving at the house. For the last few days, it'd been hers during the day, his at night. She explained the light fixtures to him, and how to use the shower.

Garth spoke of curses. He didn't understand modern medicine – he thought she was cursed to the sun, as he was to the moon. And, in truth, Robin had started to believe him. Doctors had never found an explanation for her peculiar sleep pattern.

Picking up a new canvas, Robin started to sketch Garth's horns, the curve of his mouth as he slept. She touched his lashes with a hint of silver. He was a beautiful monster asleep, knee folded, his cheek resting against his knuckles.

At dusk and dawn, they communicated. Sometimes, she waited on purpose, until it was too late to return to her bedroom by herself. He now slept in one of the rooms. She knew, at the back of her mind, she should fear him. What couldn't he do to her while she was deep in the clutches of *the curse*? But every morning she woke up clothed, and she felt whole, and she knew nothing had happened. He'd barely look at her, let alone touch her.

Robin never asked him why he didn't enact revenge on her, for the blood the Ashfords made him spill, and because he behaved a bit like a feral dog.

They had started to talk more about the curse, to theorize. His had come from a witch – yes, there were such things! And fae who came to snatch babies out of their cribs, and men who shifted into foxes. He thought Robin might have had a drop of magic in her family tree, a curse's seed well buried in her blood, sprouting when she was born.

* * *

Dusk was approaching, and Robin didn't want to miss the precious minutes when they both were awake. But she needed to explore the attic today. It was her little game, one room a day.

The attic was similar to the basement, in that it was scattered with boxes full of trinkets and memories from the past. Downstairs, the boxes had yielded no information about Garth, their shared curse, or anything that mattered. It was as if the Ashfords had been hiding a festering wound, perfuming the air not to let the odor of rot spread. Garth, their little secret – their *terrible* secret.

Digging into the cobwebs, she fished out a small trunk under a table with crooked legs. She blew off the dirt. Fingers stained with grit, she opened the trunk, a small click as it surrendered its contents. A leather-bound book lay at the bottom, straps keeping it closed, spine cracked, pages yellow.

"...For the curse to be broken, a condition must first be satisfied: for the pair to fall in love, truthfully, without the aid of potions or spells. Only when they share a kiss of true love may both be free."

Robin turned the page, ripping a corner, paper turned ash between her fingers. She read and read. The gist of it was this: they must share a kiss – of true love – but only when the moon communed with the sun.

That dusk, she didn't visit Garth. Instead, Robin stayed awake until she no longer could, and dreamed of knights, and fae, and curses that couldn't be broken.

* * *

Garth was beautiful in a way she didn't like to think about. Black bled down the side of his mouth, as if he was always stained with dyes, his eyes lit every time she entered the room, and his claws seemed more suited to hold wood to the fire than slash through flesh. He spoke low, sparsely but meaningfully.

Sitting behind him on the ground, in front of the hearth, Robin held a pair of scissors to his hair. "I can't promise it will look good."

His shoulders were so tense a tendon might snap. "You're the only one who sees me. Why should it matter?"

Did he mean he wasn't concerned about what she thought of him? Robin cared about what he thought of her. She always brushed her hair now, and wore her best nightgowns to meet him.

"You'll look handsome regardless." It escaped her mouth before she could stop it, and Garth grew even stiffer.

She set to work.

Snipping the ends, Robin preserved the length to his shoulders, lightly waved and soft to the touch. It smelled of her shampoo. But there, underneath it, she caught a whiff of his own scent, like smoke and berries.

"Do you really think so?" Garth asked, pitched so low she almost didn't hear it.

"Yes," Robin said, equally quiet.

He shifted his head, and she almost gashed his cheek. The scissors tumbled to the rug. "I'm sorry," was all she could manage.

But Garth was silent. Hunger shone in his eyes, the light of the fire backlighting him as he turned and sat facing her. His gaze slipped from her eyes to her lips.

Robin swallowed, unsure what to do. She was rooted in place, waiting for sleep to claim her. She should have made quick work of his hair instead of getting distracted.

"It's almost time," Garth said.

So she sprang forward, arms encircling his strong shoulders, as his hands caught her to his chest. Seated astride him, lips parted and eyes wide, she waited for him to do it. For him to be the first to fall.

Garth's lips fell against hers.

It was the sweetest second – darkness enveloped her before she could lick into his mouth.

* * *

When Robin rose from the bench, her heart pounded in her chest. She had slept next to the hearth, and Garth had covered her with a blanket. He rested on the bench in front of hers. Robin knelt beside it, touched the tip of his nose, slid two fingers back and forth over his lips. She wished she could wake him with a kiss, like the stories told. However, their curse was particular. Peculiar. How would she move sun and moon at her will, to allow her the pleasure of kissing him, truthfully, for more than a moment? Clearly, it wouldn't work just with *any* kiss.

No letters today. Robin left his portrait outside his bedroom and hoped he'd like it.

Slowly, the hours passed, and she wasted near a window, staring at the surrounding woods.

She hadn't thought to check the news the whole time she'd been at the house. Pulling her phone out of her pocket, she scrolled through posts until her heart stopped in her chest. Robin gasped, tears welling in her eyes, a smile blooming behind her hand.

"An eclipse," she read. "An eclipse!"

Suddenly, Robin was sure her coming here, now, wasn't an accident. Fate must have wanted this. Perhaps the witch who cursed them both was still alive, but had grown tired of her deed, pulled the strings to get them to meet. Could it be a lost Ashford, regretful for what they'd done? Perhaps it was something far more sinister, and they shouldn't break the curse at all – Robin didn't care.

Checking the time, she darted out of the room, pulse thundering, her breath a mess. She barged into her favorite room, where he still lay, asleep.

"Garth?" she called.

It was time. Why wasn't he moving?

"Garth? Please."

Oh. The book had been wrong, of course, or *she* had. Garth's face was tender while he slept, long white lashes casting dancing shadows as his eyes moved behind—

Garth opened his eyes.

He rose with a gasp, disoriented for a second.

"We can't wait. Tell me, do you think—" How could she ask it? She should have written about it first, given him the chance not to witness her reaction when he refused her. Robin had had her share of pity, and she *hated* it. "I was wondering—"

"We kissed last night."

"Ah," she breathed.

"Would you like to – that is—"

"If you want to kiss me, do it now," Robin said, words driving over one another.

Garth's hands closed in her hair, fistfuls of it, and he pulled her mouth to his.

Finally, she tasted him, savored him, inhaled the scent of smoke and berries directly off the crook of his neck. He bit and teased, gripped and caressed – and they both had such *hunger*, so long held off for different reasons.

Somewhere in the house, a grandfather clock struck the hour.

Gasping for air, they pulled apart and gazed deep into each other's eyes.

"What time is it?" Garth asked.

Robin's chest trembled with laughter, shoulders shaking, and she said, "It doesn't matter, Garth. It won't ever matter again."

Once again, her mouth sought his, lost in the taste of *forever*.

A Different Dance

Corey D. Evans

The girls in the ballroom gathered to one side of the dance floor. Their many-colored gowns mixed and swirled like the oils on a painter's palette. Silent beauties waiting for selection.

A cacophony rose from the middle of the room. Late-arriving musicians – an embarrassing faux pas on the host's reputation – tuned cat-gut strings with horsehair bows, and the animals' ghosts brayed in protest. The girls in chiffon gowns appreciated the levity afforded them by the situation. The lack of dancing music kept the other animals, the suitors dressed in black and white dinner jackets, corralled on the far side of the room. Bachelor lords prowling for their future ladies.

A pace away from the maelstrom of tulle, silk, and anxieties stood Dailey Lune-Cressey. A woman of twenty-nine years and the court's reigning possessor of the title *unwed*. While the other girls snuck glances at the men across the dance floor, Dailey admired the carvings in the crown molding. Spirals and curves as graceful as leaves dancing in the wind.

Carvings like the woodwork in her family's manor. It had been a long time since any parties, or anything more social than afternoon tea, had been hosted at the house since her parents died.

The music in the ballroom swelled in harmony before she could think long on the dead. The attention of the other girls swung round to the suitors who filed across the room like penguins with pebbles to offer a mate. None of the men came to Dailey for a dance. They went for the other girls as a predator seeks the sick from a herd. They wanted the young – sixteen or seventeen years old, with dopey eyes and narrow lips – girls with their eyes half-closed to the world, and who had few words to contain. Dailey possessed nary a feature admired by nobility. Wild hair, wide eyes, full lips, a fuller vocabulary, and a blossoming figure no corset yet devised could contain. The black-clad bachelors passed by her without acknowledgment. One by one, the penguins bowed and offered their pebbles to the girls around her. One by one, sick gazelles leaped into the throats of lions. Dailey could hardly watch the slaughter.

* * *

Her dancing shoes returned home unscuffed that night. Dailey slipped them off by the door to her room and exited her skirts and bodice like a bird leaving its cage. She found a nightgown and curled into bed with a book that weighed a few pounds less than a ship's anchor.

It was a dull book – one from the library that was short on plot and high in figures. Reading such a book was the only way to calm her mind after a dancing party. Two chapters might do the trick tonight.

A breeze fluttered the pages as she read. A cool breeze like one from an open window. It annoyed Dailey to have the pages shuffle while she read. She looked up and around the room for the open pane only to find each window shut and latched.

The book pages rustled as if touched by the hands of a specter. A whisper of wind tickled the back of her neck. Dailey turned around. The high headboard behind her – a wall of three wooden panels to prop pillows against – looked different. One panel was cracked open like a door. Dailey gasped. A false panel. How long had she slept in her bed, unaware of a trap door right behind her head?

Dailey touched the panel. It swung silently on hidden hinges. Amber light like that from an oil lamp fell through the opening. By it, she could see the most incredible sight. The panel did not open to a secret passage or hidden room but to another world. One of twilight and canvas.

A town – no – a city made of many colored tents spread out as far as she could see. Emerald tents with peaked canopies and rose tents with golden tassels. All lit from inside by lanterns or candles. She could see the black silhouettes of men and women, as well as other creatures she knew only from fairy tales: satyrs, centaurs, gnomes, and giants. Laughter tumbled through the air, along with the smells of wood fires and exotic spices. Dailey blinked twice, but the sight remained. She closed her book and crawled through the opening.

She stepped barefoot onto a street of sand still warm from the sun. Her nightgown skirted over the dust as she walked toward a green tent. A rich, burnt smell wafted over her as she neared the tent flap. She was unsure if she would be welcome inside, but green was her favorite color.

"Come in," cried a voice as deep as a well. "Come in, come in."

Another step and Dailey reached for the flap. The canvas was thick yet supple, like a well-worn boot. More of the intoxicating smell leaked into the air. She took a deep breath of the stuff and pulled the flap back.

Inside sat a man with skin darker than shoeblack. He wore green robes and a friendly smile; his ivory white eyes – blind since birth – rested somewhere between the top of Dailey's head and the sky outside.

"Hello?"

"Welcome. Please come inside. We have much to discuss."

"We do?"

"Of course, but not before you have a cup of coffee." The man lifted a black earthenware jug from which the powerful smell emanated. On the ground were two mugs, and he poured a liquid the color of ink into each without spilling a single drop. As he did, Dailey noticed his ears: pointed like a storybook elf's.

"What is coffee?" Dailey asked.

"The last elixir the gods gave to mortals." The dark elf lifted a mug in Dailey's direction.

"Is it like wine?" Dailey took the mug and sat.

"Not at all," the blind cafegee answered. "Wine muddles the mind. Coffee sharpens it."

Tentatively, Dailey brought the coffee to her mouth. The bitter drink bit the tip of her lips but went smooth over the back of her tongue unlike anything she had ever tasted. She had the simultaneous urge to spit out the coffee and swallow more.

"An acquired taste, but necessary for what's expected of you tonight."

"What is expected of me?"

"An important meeting," the elf said. "Do not fear entering any tent. In one you will meet a very important person. But no matter what, you must leave the way you came before dawn, or else you will never return home."

"I'm not sure home is where I came from," Dailey said, suddenly somber. The family manor was a house and a fine place to dwell, but it was not Dailey's home. Not if a home is a place that gives one safe feelings and love.

"Regardless," replied the elf, "do not stay past the dawn."

* * *

Stars danced like spinning tops when Dailey left the green tent. She had many hours left to explore, and she walked past several tents until she came to one of gold, her second favorite color. She did not hesitate to enter this one.

The blind elf had told her not to fear any tent, but what she found inside the gold one gave her doubts: a witch with a large warty head, a crooked nose, and a pointy hat stirred a sweet-smelling potion in a brazen cauldron. The old crone looked up at Dailey.

"You're just in time, my dear," said the woman, whose smiling eyes helped her look less like a witch.

"In time—"

Presently, a man about Dailey's age entered the tent through the opposite flap. He was handsome in a common way but clothed in purple like a royal Mohammedan. The man had a strong jaw without a sharp chin. All of his hair was present but not styled in any manner. He was tall and broad, not in the way years of toil fortify a physique but built in a way someone might kindly call big-boned.

Unremarkable as the man was, Dailey became aware of her attire – a nightgown of silk and lace – upon his arrival. A short gasp escaped her throat, and she pulled the tent flap around herself like a cloak on a blustery night. The man, shocked by the visitor and her outburst, dropped what he carried on the sand. The woman stirring at the cauldron cackled.

"I'm sorry, miss. I didn't expect you there," the man murmured while picking up what he had dropped: a platter of scones and sweets now ruined with dust.

"Don't be begging her pardon, dear boy," said the witchy woman, "she's the intruder around here, not you."

"I am not intruding," Dailey objected, "I found this place in my bedroom."

The woman shook her ladle at Dailey. "Even so, you walked through a door without asking. Oh, come now.

You're not in trouble." The woman poured her potion into a glass produced from thin air and gestured to the man. "Here. Give our guest some kompot."

The man walked over with the glass in hand. Dailey watched him carefully, but she didn't see anything like a predator in him. He was careful not to touch her when she took the glass.

"Is this poison?" Dailey asked. The man took back the drink and put it to his lips. The contents were down his throat before either woman could protest.

"Not poison," he said, grinning. The witch behind him conjured another cup.

"Must I do everything?" she grumbled. As she came from around the cauldron, Dailey could see that the woman was not a woman nor a witch at all but a gnomess who had been standing on a stool. She trundled to Dailey and handed the second cup of kompot over.

"I don't make poisons," the gnome proclaimed, "I make beverages."

"Why so much?" Dailey asked. She sipped the kompot, and her taste buds were washed by the thick sweetness of reduced raspberries and lemon, with a hint of mint.

"For the party, of course," answered the gnome. Dailey would have asked a follow-up question, but she found that she couldn't stop drinking the delicious kompot.

"Yes, and we're running late," said the man.

"Pish-posh," snapped the gnome. "I am never late." She clapped twice for punctuation, and the tent unfurled around them. Dailey gasped as her flap of modesty rolled from her hand. Everything canvas disappeared.

All around her was different, too. Gone were most of the tents. Towering giants cast long shadows over the ground, and smaller shapes of satyrs pranced in a circle. Musicians plucked at lyres and sang bawdy melodies with foreign tongues. A pair of creatures Dailey had never read of came to retrieve the cauldron. They lifted the vat of fruit syrup easily despite their dainty size and put it near a table full of other foods and drinks. Dailey leaned close to the man beside her; his shape was the only familiar thing in the whole jubilee.

"May I dance with the lady?" asked a satyr with dark horns and a lascivious grin.

"Her dance is not mine to give," said the man. He took a half step between her and the satyr. Not enough to deny Dailey the choice, but the step made his preference clear.

"I've never danced with – uhm – someone like you before," Dailey said with the politest expression she could summon. "I'm afraid I would not make a very good partner."

"Follow my lead," the satyr insisted. He reached for the hem of Dailey's nightgown instead of her hand. The man took a full step between them.

"The lady says no," said the man. Immediately, the satyr's expression darkened. He lowered his horns and snorted less like a human and more like the goat that gave him his legs. The man held his ground.

"Perhaps I'll try my luck later," the satyr bleated before backing away.

"Thank you," Dailey said once the satyr was gone. "My name is Dailey, by the way. Like Bailey but with a D."

Starlight reflected in the man's dark eyes; his purple clothes shimmered. Before he could tell her his name, a pair of nymphs – beautiful in every way except for their ears, which flared out like fungi on a stump – took hold of him.

"Give us a dance," they giggled as they spirited him away. The musicians' song sped up, and the dance swept Dailey away, too. A maelstrom of bodies whirled her around for a time that felt like hours. It was a dance like none Dailey had ever attended. A dance she actually enjoyed.

Then she caught sight of the faintest of lights peeking over the horizon. Sunrise already? She looked above and saw only the dawn star in the yellowing sky. Her time in the tent city had come to an end, but where was she to go? Dailey looked around to find any bearing at all; she found only mirth and merrymaking in all directions.

Deciding any action was better than no action at all, Dailey pushed through the revelry. The press against her was like fighting through a swollen river. Not a few hooves stubbed her toes, but once outside of the crowd, she saw the green tent of the blind elf, and beyond that was – unbelievably – the back of her bed. One panel ever so slightly agape. Forgetting all sense of modesty, Dailey grabbed her hems and ran to the bed as sunlight crept over the tent city. Voices cried out to her; she couldn't discern if they were telling her to stay or leave.

For a single moment, as Dailey reached the panel, she wondered if she should go. This world she found was exciting and no more threatening than her own of vicious lords and gossiping ladies. Perhaps she should stay with the elves and gnomes instead.

Dailey turned back to face the dance and glimpsed the man in purple being tugged along by a nymph. He looked at her as though her glance were a tap on the shoulder. His dancing stopped. The man mouthed a single syllable.

"Go."

Just as the dawn light cracked overhead like a bolt of lightning, Dailey Lune-Cressey returned to her room.

* * *

She did not wake in bed as though everything that occurred had been a dream. The panel door snapped shut behind her, catching a bit of her gown. Sand fell from her feet onto the sheets. She stumbled on the book she had planned to read and fell in a heap of tousled hair and sweaty silk.

Somewhere in the house, a clock chimed twice. Dailey looked to a window. The sky outside was as dark as a storm cloud. The whole night had passed in the other world, but less than an hour had passed in hers. She gathered herself and returned to the panel she had just stepped through. It looked as set as the day it left the joiner's shop, and when she pressed it, the wood did not budge.

Dailey got out of bed and inspected the headboard. It was not firm against the wall. An empty space existed between the bed and the plaster; she found no trap door.

The coffee Dailey had drunk kept her awake for the rest of the night. She puzzled over the tents and the satyr's dance, but most of all, she thought about the man in purple until the maids knocked on her door in the morning.

The following night, she expected the panel to open again, but it remained firmly set. A week passed, a month. Dailey attended another ball but gained no favor from the noble bachelors. As time passed, she almost forgot her journey. Almost. The man in purple always found a way to dance in her imagination. If only she knew his name.

* * *

When she turned thirty, invitations to the banquets and galas ceased to arrive at Dailey Lune-Cressey's door. The peerage no longer sought her company. A quiet pronouncement of her new title *spinster*.

She was sitting on her settee with another book when a faint tapping, like a bird rooting for seeds, disturbed an otherwise boring evening. She looked up from the pages of history to find the panel not just cracked but swung wide, with the man in purple – the man of her wistful thoughts – smiling on the other side.

"It's you," he said, just before Dailey's book hit him in the face.

"Oh dear," she cried, "you startled me."

The man rubbed the red spot left by the binding. The book was not as large as it could have been, but still hurt.

"I'm okay," he groaned. "Was that a book?" The man picked up the book that had bounced off his chin – a large volume with leather bindings – as if it were a rare flower in need of transplanting. "I've never been hit by a book."

"It would be a nasty habit for one to start," Dailey said.

"May I come in?" the man asked. Dailey saw that he still stood within the headboard panel.

"I suppose you'll have to come in to give the book back," Dailey said, smiling.

"Is that a yes?"

A terrible feeling, like that of realizing a candle was left burning too close to a curtain, fell into the pit of Dailey's stomach. Did she just invite something dangerous, like a vampire or demon, into her room? Did the man mean to harm her?

"Wait," she all but shouted. The man had yet to move an inch. "Are you going to hurt me?"

The man raised a brow. "I think I'm the one who should be afraid of being hurt. Got any more books over there?"

Dailey's head shook with a grin on her lips.

"No. No more books."

"Good."

"You never told me your name," Dailey said hurriedly.

"I'm sorry?"

"That's a terrible name."

The man's brow furrowed where Dailey's joke failed to land.

"That's not my name. It's Faraj."

"Oh, that's even worse," Dailey snickered. Faraj remained confused. "I'm only teasing. Do come in."

Faraj shrugged and raised his right, then his left leg over the panel door's threshold. He stepped onto Dailey's bed with pointed purple slippers. Once on the mattress, Faraj made a comical attempt at bowing that almost landed his face into a pillow.

"This floor is quite unstable."

"That's because it's my bed," Dailey said with another laugh. Faraj looked horrified.

"A thousand apologies." He jumped off the bed. His slippered feet made no noise on the hardwood below. Surprising nimbleness from a man of his size. He looked around the room as unconcerned for his safety as a shark in shallow waters.

"I knew you were a princess," Faraj said.

Dailey stood up from the settee, half ready to welcome Faraj, the other half prepared to flee or fight. "I'm no princess. I'm a lady."

"Yes, princesses are ladies. If not, they'd be called prince."

Dailey laughed, "No. Lady is my title. My father is – was – a Duke. Lady Dailey Lune-Cressey." She gave a small curtsey.

Faraj returned another low bow. "Pleased to meet you again," he said.

"Why are you here?"

Faraj stood. "I wanted to see you, Your Highness."

"Oh, do stop," Dailey rolled her eyes. "I am no higher than anyone else who breathes air."

Faraj took in a sharp, exaggerated breath and smiled. "Your book, milady." He extended the book out. An arm's breadth separated Dailey from Faraj, and Dailey was shocked by how close he stood.

"Can I show you the library?" she asked instead of taking the book. Faraj faltered.

"Is it close?" He looked over to the open panel above the bed. "I have to be back before sunrise."

"It's just down the hall."

"The hall?"

"Come with me," Dailey said, turning without taking the proffered book and heading for the door. Faraj followed.

Portraits of long-dead men and women lined the hallway. The ghosts of Cressey Manor. Cold, lifeless, and ever-present. Her father and mother hung somewhere in that gallery, but Dailey had no interest in seeing them tonight.

"It's this way," she said, turning left. Faraj's slippered feet fell silently on the hardwood floors behind Dailey. Halfway down the hall, she turned to make sure he was still there. He held the book tight to his chest and walked close enough to step into her shadow.

"It's that door there." Dailey pointed to a dark wooden door ahead. A clock chimed the half-hour, and Faraj gasped, startled.

"Two-thirty," Dailey said. "We have a few hours left till dawn."

"It's already so early?" Faraj asked

"I suppose time works differently on this side."

"It was just after midnight when I opened the door."

"I think it still will be when you go back. It was the same for me when I returned."

"Do you like it here?" Faraj asked as they came to the library. "Do you like living on this side of the door?"

"I suppose," Dailey lied, "but I didn't know there was another option until a few months ago. Do you like your side of the door?"

"I did until recently." Faraj looked at Dailey, eyes long with pining. Dailey blushed, then opened the library and stepped in.

In the dark, the library consisted of tall shadows and musty smells. The light from the hallway bisected the room like a wedge. Few of the many bookcases were illuminated, but an empty space on a shelf could be seen.

"So many books in one place," Faraj said. "Have you read them all?"

"I could live many lives and not even read half," Dailey said. "That one goes there." She pointed to the empty space. Faraj looked at the book in his hand with the same yearning with which he'd looked at Dailey in the hall.

"I'd like to read a book," he said.

"You've not read a book?"

"Not since I was very young. Before, when I lived on the other side."

"You didn't always live in the tent city?"

"Is that what you call it? No. I found that place when I was a boy. I went through a trapdoor in my closet and danced with pixies past sunrise. When I tried to go home, the door I came through was gone."

"You were trapped?"

"Not really. Doors appear every night. I can go through them, too, if I wish, but they told me no door would ever take me home again."

"Did you ever try?"

"Yes. For a long time. But I stopped after a while. I stopped until—"

"Until you saw me?"

"That's right." Faraj walked across the room to put the book on the shelf. When he turned around, he extended a hand to Dailey. "Can I ask you for one dance?" he all but whispered.

"A dance?" Dailey's voice cracked an octave.

"I've never danced with someone like you before." Faraj bowed once more.

"Someone like me?" Dailey asked. She cautiously slid her fingers into his invitation.

"A princess." Then Faraj took hold. He hummed a strange tune with an odd beat; a song gnomes and nymphs, satyrs and sprites danced to until dawn. Dailey let him sweep her across the room in wide loops punctuated by dips or a twirl between measures. Faraj increased the tempo, and his loops became tighter; he changed key and held Dailey closer.

At one point, Faraj lifted her into the air as effortlessly as a maid fluffs a pillow and returned her to the ground as gently as feather down. His song ended, and he and Dailey stood in the hall light holding hands.

"Thank you," he said, standing taller than before. "Thank you."

"I'd like to dance with you again," Dailey said after she caught her breath. She pursed her lips and hummed her own tune.

* * *

The maids could not find Dailey when they came to wake her in the morning. Her empty bed appeared unused except for a few places where someone might have stood on the sheets. Every window in the manor was found latched, every gate locked. No signs of kidnapping were found, nor was a letter of ransom. Even her shoes remained in their place by the door. Only a plain purple frock was missing from Dailey's closet. That, and an armful of books taken from the library.

The Hour-Glass Trap

Rebecca Ferrier

I'd always known there was darkness in her. I'd put it there myself, hadn't I? Opened her up to the temporal anomalies that lay in the gaps between each fixed event in history, then warned her never to touch them. In class, she'd always been hungrier than I was, desperate to prove herself. Although we'd studied together at the Fawkes Institute, with me assigned her mentor in the early days, she'd surpassed me in everything we'd ever been taught.

It was never enough for her.

"Muriel," I cautioned.

I could see her eyeing the fissures between moments, the time between times, the starless realm we cannot go to. It revealed itself on these journeys, stepping from one age to another. When passing through months or decades or centuries – lasting only moments for us – faint lines were revealed. Beautiful, crackling gaps that glowed with a hue I cannot describe, humming and layered with the scent preceding thunder.

"I want to know," she confessed.

"It'll kill you," I warned.

A half-laugh. "You don't *know* that."

I had no reply, for she was right. We could only speculate about where the fissures led to, and these days that's all Muriel speculated about. Our teachers said we'd be trapped forever, in unending darkness, though none had ever returned from the starless realm to confirm that hypothesis. Without time, did they simply dissolve? Or were they kept in stasis to live forever without decay, floating through eternity? I'd hate that for Muriel. Since her first day, I'd protected her from everything I could, even her own rash decisions on our assignments.

However, I couldn't protect her from herself.

She clicked her tongue and tightened her grip on my hand. "Stop worrying, Hen." As per usual, she casually shrugged off problems as though I'd invented them myself. A high wind buffeted us in that strange non-space, ruffling my tweed coat and shaking a dozen pins from her dark hair, which spiralled off to nowhere and everywhere and through the fissure itself. "I promise you'll never see me delve into the starless realm," she assured me, squeezing my fingers in hers.

"Good," I breathed.

And I did not say: *I don't know what I'd do without you.*

We never spoke that way. We were colleagues, after all. Professionals hired by the Fawkes Institute to ensure the world stayed on its predetermined course. Ever since the Houses of Parliament had been wrenched apart by gunpowder in the 1600s and London near-sunk below the Thames, the powers-that-be were touchy about unplanned disturbances in the allowed timeline.

Who could blame them?

I stepped onto a puddle-strewn Bedford Square, its cobblestones as loose as a pauper's teeth. I would know, having been one in my youth. Years ago, this street might have been impressive. Now it was damp and congealing, as was everywhere in the failing city (in this era, at least). Eventually, the broken pumping systems would be repaired and the flood barriers would be replaced, though not for another fifty years: I'd been to 1871 and seen them myself through a fine drizzle. Agents of the Fawkes Institute only traversed time when it rained. Though it's a natural weather occurrence, heavy precipitation bends light enough for other shifts in our world's make-up. Plus, it means any onlooker who might see two individuals step into their reality would think it nothing more than water clouding their vision. Yes, only a young couple in their early thirties on a walk. What else could we be?

I released Muriel's hand immediately, drawing the muggy evening air into my lungs and sweeping back my limp, ashy hair. "Remember, curiosity killed the cat."

"I know," she huffed, "and then we stepped back in time and brought it back."

That was not *technically* what we did. Our work was to nudge events into order and ensure what should happen, did happen. Or, in this case, to save a child from falling beneath a passing carriage, thus securing his important medicinal breakthroughs in the future. All we had to do was detain the child – who'd just slipped from his nanny's grasp – for long enough to have the carriage roll by uneventfully.

Well, if we were lucky.

"There," whispered Muriel.

"I see him."

Despite our noble intentions, time did not enjoy our disturbances. No sooner had I grasped the boy's coat as he sought to dash across the road after his spinning top, than the carriage bypassed him and collided with two women hurrying inside from the downpour. See, when we rescued one individual, another had to take their place. Usually, I could prevent myself from looking. I thought I'd eventually become numb to it, those instances where well-meaning passers-by tried to help or doctors were called to an emergency. It didn't matter what era it was or how the death came, it was always terrible.

"Henry," said Muriel, gently.

She was better at this than I was. Collected, able to keep her distance from the world. At times, even from me. Her gloved hand reached for mine, the white material across her fingers saturated with rain. I liked when she wore this outfit: a nondescript dress, hair finely arranged (despite the lost pins), face bare and rouged only by the chill. We always dressed the part. It helped us blend in. Although we'd been recruited from the same time period (Edwardians, I believe the term is). I doubted our paths would have crossed otherwise. I wonder, had we not been employed by the Fawkes Institute, if we'd ever have found each other.

As colleagues, I mean. At a push I'd call us friends. It would be unwise to consider my association with Muriel anything else.

"Yes, I know," I said to her, solemnly. "We shouldn't tarry."

I put my right hand into hers and – with the left – tilted the hour-glass affixed to my person in tandem with her actions. Her device was hidden in plain sight as a silver ornament dangling from a choker at her throat, whereas mine was disguised as a pocket watch.

Again, we leapt through the time between time. It's rarely pleasant and always overwhelming; imagine standing inside a giant ink pot being swirled around by an unseen hand, while you struggle to remain at its centre. That was why the Fawkes Institute had us travel in pairs. Together, we could remain upright and not fall into an unplanned age (with unplanned consequences) or mistakenly venture through a fissure. Simply hold on tight to the other agent and you'll return to the correct timeline, usually. Everyone is drawn to their own eras and ours was already eager to drag us back.

"Do you care for me?"

I turned to Muriel. "Pardon?" She did not repeat herself. Nor did she need to. "You're a wonderful colleague," I told her, lamely. "I enjoy your insights."

Even within the whirling maelstrom I heard her sigh.

"Close your eyes," she insisted.

"Why?"

"Because, my dearest Hen," she gave me a terrible smile and I pretended not to notice the sadness in it, "if you don't see what I'm about to do, I won't have broken my earlier promise."

Muriel raised her free hand, glove wet enough to make her bony knuckles stick out oddly, and placed a finger on a fissure. I hadn't the time – hah, the time! – to stop her. Only stared in horror, waiting for death. Instead, a dozen lights popped around us, beyond us, within us, inside my very eyes. I was nothing and everything and dying and living and I didn't care as much as I should.

I only knew that Muriel was here with me.

If I was destined to tumble forever through an unending cosmos, I'd have chosen to do it with her. As though knowing my thoughts, her thumb grazed my inner wrist. I wondered – for a dizzying second – if they *were* my thoughts at all. Or if Muriel owned them and had somehow shared them with me, as easily as handing me a flower.

Gone were the flashes. There was solid ground beneath my feet. It was a grey, highly polished material. A word garnered from my experiences through time – *concrete* – rose into my mind. Yet that seemed too industrial for what was meant to be, well, nowhere.

"I knew it," breathed Muriel.

We stood dripping from the rain in a grand entrance with the Fawkes Institute insignia – a curling *F.I.* – above a large archway. It led to a reception with an empty desk, elevators whose floor numbers rose and fell on electronic displays, as well as rooms with men and women sitting at typewriters and producing yellow slips of paper. A few individuals glanced up from their tasks to observe us, though not a single one spoke, too intent on their work.

"This way," said Muriel, fiercely, pulling me along. In the confusion, I hadn't once thought to drop her hand.

I was breathless. "What is this?"

"Hell," she hissed.

Along the concrete hallway was a final room, which bloomed out into a massive chamber. It held what I can only describe as a hot air balloon as large as a five-storey building, constructed from glass and shimmering oddly. An uncanny light passed through it and I'd recognize it anywhere: trapped within the glass were a hundred or a thousand or a million futures. Here, time had been collected. Ready, I assumed, to be assessed and the right outcome found. Strangely, I'd never assumed it would be so mechanical. I'd seen our employer – Ivan – with a yellow slip from a typewriter. There was even a desk nearby with a paperweight on it, similar to those Ivan himself used. Did he know our missives came from here?

I knew the answer immediately, for who should appear other than Ivan himself?

"Henry!" I was greeted first as an old friend, before he added, "Muriel," with a beleaguered tone. "I thought I'd find you here eventually," said Ivan, sadly, folding his hands over his pale waistcoat. He was a greying man in every sense, with pale skin and colourless eyes.

Immediately, I thought this cold, reflective space suited him.

As a child, I'd feared him and loved him in turns. Before I'd met Ivan, I'd been a starving urchin. Until one day I'd chosen to sleep in the wrong porch: the one belonging to the Fawkes Institute. Only his generosity – or Ivan had framed it that way – had spared me from death. I should be grateful. I *was* grateful. Or I would have been, were it not for the way he scowled at Muriel.

"Did you have to bring sweet Henry with you? It does complicate the situation," he said, as though ours was a casual meeting and not one brimming with threat.

I tightened my grip on Muriel's hand.

She was fearless. "Come on, out with it!

Previously, I'd assumed the pair's tense exchanges were nothing beyond a bureaucratic rivalry. Now, I suspected otherwise. Of course, the giant time-manipulating glass balloon was a sign I'd definitely overlooked one – seemingly corrupt – aspect of the Fawkes Institute's running. Foolishly, I still believed we might be wrong in our assumptions. Naturally, the right time and its events had to be discovered somehow, didn't it? Yet why did this set-up seem so offensive to every instinct I possessed?

Ivan released a laboured sound from his throat. "You'd wish me to explain that which you've already guessed?"

I spoke, then, half-fearing they'd forgotten about me in their dislike of each other. "I don't understand."

Maddeningly, the typists continued their work. I wondered how frequent it was, agents tripping off their assigned path and into these halls, if no one acted surprised.

"We usually recruit from your era," began Ivan. "Historically," and he laughed at his wit, "it's proven better to employ those from post-industrial and pre-postmodernist eras. You understand enough not to panic when witnessing future technological advances, yet not enough to challenge what we're doing here."

Muriel scoffed. "You mean we're easier to lie to."

It wasn't a question. Ivan only smiled.

"I don't understand," I repeated.

"There's no greater good," said Muriel. "There's only greater greed."

Ivan shook his head minutely. "Our work – your work, Henry – ensures the world runs on the correct course."

Muriel was not convinced. "You mean the one that provides you – and whoever hired you – with money, power and influence? This entire machine is built to further an agenda that's for nothing other than profit!"

"Understandably there are costs in our operations and we steer our work towards financial gain on occasion, though it's only to ensure we can fund our higher purpose." Ivan seemed distinctly rational and, I had to admit, he made sense. As though guessing my indecision, Ivan turned to me. "Recall, it was expensive to save you from the streets, Henry," he reminded me. "We had to feed, clothe and raise you, not knowing how useful you'd be to us."

I agreed. "It sounds reasonable, when phrased that way."

Muriel – for the first time in my recollection – dropped my hand first. I had forgotten our contact, too used to it, until her fingers unclasped from mine. At her palm's absence, the cooler air stung my skin.

"I see," she said, quietly.

Ivan's lips were tight. "Why don't we get you back to the Fawkes Institute in your era and discuss this tomorrow?" Already he was sweeping his arms wide, stepping towards us, wafting us away from the monumental glass structure.

"Tomorrow," muttered Muriel to herself, as if not believing it would come.

With faux civility, Ivan accompanied us back to the original entryway. "Simply activate your devices here and time shall right itself, drawing you to the era in which you belong."

I held my hand out to Muriel.

She…hesitated, lips curling in a mutinous sneer, and asked, "What if I don't?"

"Muriel," I said, harshly. "We'll do as we're told."

I understood Ivan well enough to know there'd be trouble if we didn't leave now. Why, at least a disciplinary hearing. Muriel's lips had gone slack with shock. I'd never spoken to her harshly before. Didn't she understand I was trying to save her?

"Listen to your superior," said Ivan. "In ten years he may well be in my position and forced to discipline errant agents such as yourself, isn't that right, Henry?"

I was a child again, desperate to obey a man who'd promised me a better life if only I'd do everything he asked.

If I was quiet and good and worked hard at whatever task he gave me, I'd never be hungry or cold or fearful again.

"Yes, sir," I answered.

I was afraid now, though not for myself – for Muriel.

"I'll talk to her," I promised Ivan.

Quickly, I grasped Muriel's wrist. She didn't pull away. Only tensed, exhaled a shaky breath, then put her fingers to her choker and span the hour-glass. Our shapes returned to the inky maelstrom, until it settled into a palette I recognized and deposited us on the Fawkes Institute's rain-slicked steps, not a second after we'd left them on our earlier assignment.

Now on solid ground, Muriel snatched her fingers away and clutched them to her chest as though burned. She wouldn't look at me.

"It's not that I—"

"Don't," she sniffed.

Impossibly, I suspected she was crying. That wasn't her. She'd never let me see her sad, keeping me at arm's length. *I'm fine*, was her mantra. She wasn't now. Fleeing, her boots scraping against the wet stone, vanishing through the grand oak doors I'd once sheltered beneath when I'd had nowhere else to go.

I'd make her understand.

Somehow.

I assumed I'd find Muriel in the women's dormitories once I was dry, only to discover her shucking off her dirty socks and wet gloves in *my* room. She was rooting through my belongings for a clean shirt. It was – usually – a tidy and compact space. I was tall and occasionally struggled with the tiny rooms given to agents at the Fawkes Institute. When I rose up the ranks, I might be awarded an entire apartment to myself on the floor above. Perhaps, if we could fix our disagreement, Muriel could share it with me…

"What're you doing?" I asked. "You can borrow anything I have, though it'll be far too large for you."

"Oh, is this you '*talking*' to me? I'm packing, then we're leaving," she snapped.

"No, we're not," I said, aghast.

In her flurried activity, she hadn't noticed what drew my eye immediately. Someone – another agent, no doubt – had snuck through time and placed a yellow slip on my nightstand. It was an assignment: *Termination: Ennis Coldstream, 19th May 2026, Via Zara, Florence.*

I hadn't realised I was shaking until Muriel took it from my grasp.

"It's a test, isn't it?" I heard the bitten-off scream in her throat. "Ivan wants to see how far we'll go for him, to prove our loyalty now we know his secret."

This couldn't be happening. "I don't want to kill anyone." I slumped down, not caring if I mussed the clean sheets on my usually immaculate bed.

"You do that every day," said Muriel. "Whenever we shift time to save one person, another must die instead." Despite the rage I could see boiling under her skin, her tone was gentle with me, almost pitying as she sat beside me to drip in solidarity. Her smaller frame was soft and warm against my lanky one. "Consider today's events and the carriage! Or even last week, for we ensured a man took a spot in a bomb shelter originally intended for another."

"I – I've never thought about it."

"I know and I didn't want to make you unhappy by…" She trailed off.

"Explaining how ignorant I've been?" It was a horrible feeling to know one's world completely and then not know it at all. Had I really been lied to? If not, I couldn't summon even the slightest rebuff to her truth. I was angry and – unfairly – I was angry at her, because she could have told me sooner. "Do you respect me at all?"

Muriel surged to her feet. "It's not about that."

I snorted. "You must think me a complete fool."

Muriel's hesitation was admittance enough. Finally, she said, "You taught me to ask questions, while ignoring the most important one. We're meant to work for good, but what does the Fawkes Institute consider good? Or does it only aspire to do good for those who run it?" On she went, pounding her knowledge and theories into my skull. Muriel returned to the small dresser and began heaving out my belongings. I didn't have a suitcase, because I'd never travelled anywhere outside work.

"I need to go," I said, suddenly.

Improvising, Muriel buttoned two shirts together and fashioned a small bag. "Yes, don't worry, I'll ensure it."

"No, that's not what I mean."

I had to think away from this place and her and the crushed yellow slip and its terrible orders. Surely there was another explanation I wasn't seeing? If Muriel was right, then everything I'd done and been and knew was wrong.

I hesitated at the door. "Will you be here when I get back?"

"Yes," she lied, and I knew she was lying because the clothes she'd been packing for me were already sliding from her hands and onto the floor.

I didn't intend to be gone long as I strode around the vast grounds which surrounded the Fawkes Institute. It was still raining. I was already soaked through, what did I care if I got wetter? Yet as I paced around ornately trimmed hedges and sifted through every memory I had from my training, I could see nothing to dispute Muriel's reasoning.

How long had she known about this?

Once, she'd been a bright-eyed woman keen to shuck off the puffed sleeves and grand expectations from her upper-class family. The Fawkes Institute had given her freedom and adventure and a lie she'd quickly unravelled. Why had she stayed? I thought I knew the answer. *Me*. Could it be? If so, I had to hear it from her.

First, I'd hand in my resignation.

Ivan was at his desk. He seemed paler than usual. I couldn't know what day this was for him. Had he been expecting me? Was the conversation we'd had less than hour ago for me, a day – or more – for him?

"It's too late," he said, as I knocked and entered his office. "She's already gone."

I almost sank into the ornate carpet. "Pardon?"

"It needn't be your fate too, son," he assured me, almost fatherly, or so I imagined.

"Where is she?" I barely recognized my own voice. I sounded murderous. I *felt* murderous. Because in my absence they'd taken her, hadn't they? "Is she dead?"

"Look," began Ivan, in a tone that suggested I was being difficult.

For a dull bureaucrat, Ivan had one extravagance: he collected decorative paperweights. There were usually at least three on his desk, routinely swapped with others from an overstuffed shelf, to give each their turn at usefulness.

"If you go after her, they'll kill you too," he warned me, levelly, as though he was a reasonable man having a reasonable conversation with someone who possessed any semblance of reason left. I wanted to scream. I *did* scream. Worse, I took a paperweight in my hand. Although my mind didn't know what I planned to do with it, my body did.

When I was done – it didn't take long – I put my bloodied hands to my pocket watch. It was inadvisable to travel between times without another person to anchor you. However, if the Fawkes Institute had killed my anchor, I had no choice but to get her back.

It was forbidden to use one's device for one's own ends.

I no longer cared. Suddenly, I was in the hall to the men's dormitory as it had been an hour ago. I didn't have long. Soon, they'd come for her. I stepped inside my room only a moment or two after my previous self had left it. I expected to find Muriel as angry as I felt. Instead, she was in tears.

Lying across my bed, face buried in my pillow, she croaked, "If you've come back to shout at me then don't bother." After too long a silence, as I tried to calm my breathing, she raised her head, frowning. Muriel saw my blood-stained hands. "You're not the Hen who left a second ago, are you?"

I kissed her. No, to call it that was lying. I locked the door behind me and knelt at the bedside, then pressed my cold mouth to her warm, tear-stained cheek, nose, lips.

Her fingers came to my chest, pushing me back. "What is it?" I crushed her questions from her and she let me. I only broke away when she laughed. "This doesn't end well for me, does it?"

"We're going to leave," I told her. "Go where they can't find us."

"No, mine was a silly plan." Muriel rolled onto her back. "You know what we have to do, Hen."

I should have shut her down, enjoyed our last moments together, and waited for our betters to pull us apart. I didn't – I couldn't – because I realized what I'd been forcefully ignoring ever since I'd learned how smart and brilliant and fierce she was. I knew everything about Muriel. I always noticed how the rain curled her dark hair and brought a rosy pink to her complexion. I adored her penchant for hats (even though they lasted three seconds in the downpours we trudged through), and how she lent her strength to me through the smallest actions, in ways I could never easily identify or thank her for.

"Tell me what you want me to do," I said. Because it was easier than saying "*I love you*" and knowing it was too late for it to matter.

In the end, her plan was simple. Ever a resourceful woman, she'd acquired (meaning: stolen) a terrifyingly powerful firearm during a recent trip we'd made to the 2030s. "There's a reason I wear voluminous skirts even when not accurate for the time period," she answered, sweetly, as though our mission was anything other than suicide.

"Right," I said, prior to holding out my hand.

Muriel slipped her fingers into mine the way we'd done a hundred times, as though it wouldn't be the last.

Remember, time seeks to right itself. It's why, after visiting an era we didn't belong to on a work errand, we could easily return back to our own year without getting lost. It's akin to a pull on a thread tied by God. I could sense it now – a plucking on an internal chord – that informed me time *wanted* this. Us, here in this moment. We dived through a fissure. No one was startled at our arrival, as Muriel and I strode along the grey corridor. Ivan should have been here to stop us, only I'd already bludgeoned that loose end. By the time – hah, time – anyone realized what I intended to do, I'd already managed to prime and load my weapon.

I hated abandoning Muriel's grasp. I had no choice. It was heavy, the weapon slotting into my shoulder oddly.

Naturally, every agent at the Fawkes Institute is trained to use firearms. Ignorant until now, I'd never questioned why.

A command rose from behind us: "Stop!"

I could hear marching boots, while a red alarm began to flash and wail.

"Do it," screamed Muriel.

I did – *BANG* – hearing the explosion and glass shatter a mere breath after I'd pulled the trigger. Endless time washed over us. All time. Forever. I saw all the different ways I might have lived or never existed. In dying – for I assumed I was – I reached for the only realities I wished to see in those final seconds: the ones with Muriel. I saw how our story might have been. A hundred alternative star-crossed meetings and blazing arguments and passionate nights and the ways I could have loved her better had our fates been different…

…and I chose one.

It burned against my skin, as though I was clutching a star – or Muriel's outstretched hand – and this time I knew I'd never let go.

The Wolf of Darkwater Loch

Janet Forbes

Mournful bagpipes wailed over the dark, churning water of the loch, echoing off the towering basalt pillars that formed the sea cave's maw. Beneath them, our rowboat looked nothing more than a toy. What was I thinking? I swallowed, fear twisting my gut to nausea. Could I really kill the Unseelie Queene's servant?

The oarsman, Hamish, was a burley fisherman who enjoyed many a woman's discomfort of a Saturday evening. Today, he relished mine. "Well Iona, you volunteered, didn't you?"

It was true. In almost a hundred years, I was the first tribute not to wake to the thorned triskele – the fairy mark – glowing beside my bed. I was the first to *choose* damnation.

A sneer painted Hamish's face, but his laughter was cut away by a sudden sharp wind, slicing through our bones as we neared the cliff. Let him laugh. My reasons were my own.

The Mayor of Dunloch grimaced. "Almost there now." Twelve years ago, when he refused his own daughter's summons, faedemons flooded from the sea – monstrous trows and horseheaded Nuckelavees. Fifty people died that night, and then the Mayor's daughter had begged to be taken. Anything to keep the Unseelie Queene's demons away. The old days of heroes – the Green Knight, the Bonnie Prince of Darkwater, the Silent Sire – were gone, and the only protection Dunloch could claim was one fragile, unarmed girl. And so each year, they paid the blood price.

As the skiff pulled into the huge cavern, the piper set down his pipes, their wail dying with a sigh. Hamish backrowed to a stop and secured us to a carved promontory. The boat bobbed uneasily, knocking against the rocks as a fist knocks on a door.

"We bring tribute, as the Queene demands," called the Mayor.

He did this to his own daughter.

"Pray, see our early arrival as a wish to appease your mistress."

From deep in the shadows, a hand beckoned. The figure stood seven feet tall, broad as an oak beneath an all-covering cloak. This, then, was the Unseelie Queene's servant.

Even Hamish was awed to silence, as the Mayor handed me up to the slippery rocks.

The stranger's deep, husky voice echoed in the cavern. "Ye'll be leaving now," he ordered the Mayor. This was no servant as I knew the word.

And so they left, oars splashing hastily as the little boat slipped out into open water. The Mayor didn't even look back. I had served his house since I was eight. Still, he would not meet my eyes.

"Come wi' me," the Unseelie Queene's servant growled, striding off down a narrow walkway bordering the deep water. I followed, picking my way across the rocks, my bile rising as I thought of all the girls before me who had taken this path to death.

At the end of the path, he drew back a curtain of sea kelp. A tunnel of hewn rock waited beyond, and he gestured for me to pass.

But I was done with obedience. I gripped the dirk hidden in my skirts, stolen from one of those ridiculous displays in the manor and, passing him, I slashed out at his belly. Gut wounds took days, but they were sure killers. I would have my revenge, even if I died to claim it.

The man let out a surprised howl, grabbing at my arm. Strong fingers clamped around my wrist, shaking the barely blooded weapon from my hand. *Iron wounded fae.* But he seemed no more concerned by the shallow cut than by a midge bite.

I flinched, thinking he would strike me, but he merely held me by the arm. Examining me from beneath the deep hood.

"Where is my sister?" I demanded. "What do you do with them?"

"Your sister?" He released my wrist at once. "A past tribute?" His voice was lilting and calm, as if I had not just tried to murder him.

"Her name was Eilidh, you brute, and if you've hurt—" I swung my fist at him, and he stepped back to avoid my punch. With a scream, I lost my balance, slipped, and fell into the sea.

* * *

I gasped at the freezing shock, water flooding my lungs. Panicking, I flailed and splashed as icy waves closed over my head, burning my eyes and nose, dress dragging me down, down into the dark water's cruel maw.

And then strong hands gripped my waist, pulling me to the surface. In the darkness, the man held me to his chest, patting my back, and all my bile and vengeance was forgotten as, half-drowned, I clung to him with shaking limbs.

"Are ye well, lass?" he asked, his voice rumbling close to my ear. I nodded, unable to speak. Paddling to the rocks, he hoisted me out of the water, clambering up behind me.

My throat and eyes stung, and I could barely breathe, barely stand for shivering. His cloak was dry – he must have dropped it before he dived in – and I caught the scent of woodsmoke and rosemary as he pulled it round my shaking shoulders.

"We need tae get ye warm, lass," he muttered. Standing behind me in the dark cave, he wrapped me in his arms. I leaned back, still spluttering and gasping for breath, as if he were the only warmth and anchor in the world. I don't know how long we stood there, until at last I could breathe again, think again.

This man – this servant of the Unseelie Queene – was responsible for my sister's death. The thought hit me like a slap, all warm feelings for my rescuer disappearing at once and I pulled away, rounding on him to give him a piece of my mind.

Instead, I screamed. In the scant light from the corridor beyond, I saw his face for the first time. From his auburn tipped ears, to his grey-speckled muzzle, to his amber eyes, the man before me bore the head of a wolf.

He winced at my scream, and again when I gasped out, "Monster." The dirk still lay at his feet and I grabbed it, darting back and almost losing my balance again. "What did you do with my sister?"

The wolfheaded man held out his hands in caution. "Ye said Eilidh's your sister? She's alive, I'll take ye to her. Just dinnae fall in the water again. I cannae take another plunge."

I glared at him. *Surely fae can't lie?* "If you're deceiving me—"

He kneeled before me, baring his neck. With the dirk in my hand, I might have cut the wolfhead from his human body right there. "May heaven strike me down if it isnae true. Or may *you*, if it please ye," he added, like a knight from the old stories.

I gaped at him. Was this a trick? "Alright," I said at last, still gripping the dirk. "Take me to her."

Standing, he led me onward down the corridor, the grey basalt alive with eerie shadows from hanging oil lamps.

"Might I ask your name, lady?"

"No." Some said fae could use your name against you. I wouldn't give this wolfman more arrows for his quiver.

He nodded, taking my reply in his stride. "Well, Eilidh'll be glad tae see ye. She's been worried sick about ye being all alone." At the far end of the corridor, the wolfman pulled aside another curtain, releasing the scent of porridge and grilled venison. This cave was huge, four times the size of the manor ballroom. And it was full of women.

"The tributes?" Old ladies chatted aimiably beside a fire, younger ones sang in time to their wool-waulking. Here was a forgotten history – a century of stolen women, paying for Dunloch's safety, year after year after year. Had they been beneath the mountain all along?

"Eilidh?" the wolfman called. The women stopped their chatter. "Eilidh, your sister is here."

Hurried footsteps slapped against rock, and suddenly there she was, pink cheeks just the same, hair longer, her figure filling out. "You're here! How – how are you here?"

I grabbed her, crushed her to me, until she squeaked in protest, then held her face hard, searching her eyes to be sure she was no changeling. "Eilidh, I thought you were—" I couldn't finish the sentence, couldn't speak of my darkest fears.

My sister was alive. That was all that mattered.

* * *

"I missed you so!" Eilidh squealed. "I was so worried about you, all alone. Come on, let me introduce you to everyone, and—"

"But you're well?" I pressed, hardly believing my eyes.

"I know it seems strange. At first, I thought Cainlean was going to eat me, or sacrifice me, or—" She broke off, blushing. "Well, he didn't do that. We all live here very happily, see?"

Eilidh led me, still dripping, to the fire. Someone brought me a dry dress, another pressed hot barley broth into my hands. Once I was dry, the next hours were spent walking the huge cavern, admiring the standing looms and the cooking pits. There was no time for questions or explanations as Eilidh proudly introduced me again and again as "Iona, her sister, the new tribute".

At length, Eilidh led me to a corner, brightly painted. At the mural's centre stood the wolfheaded man, skillfully rendered as an imposing form. "This is my work," she said. "I decorate whatever can be made beautiful."

My heart leapt. We had both dreamed of more than service, but practicality – not art and poetry – put food on the table. To see Eilidh living her dream made me, for a shocking moment, glad she had been chosen. "They're so beautiful. You're the artist I always knew you could be."

A seashell horn sounded. "That's dinner. After, you can meet Iseabail. She was tribute the year before me," Eilidh added with a shy smile, as if I needed reminding of the girl always hanging around my sister. She'd been devastated when Iseabail was taken.

I grinned at her as she led me by the hand. I could still barely believe, after all those months of grief, she was alive and well.

Eilidh stopped abruptly. "Need something, Cainlean?"

The wolfheaded man had changed into a tattered white shirt, his dark coat trimmed with blue-green tartan. He bowed with an old-fashioned flourish. "Your sister'll join me for supper. It's tradition." He waited for no response.

"Better follow him," Eilidh whispered, as the man strode up stone steps, and through a doorway hewn into rock. "Don't worry, he's kind, if not very jolly," she assured me. "And we'll have plenty of time later. All the time in the world."

* * *

The wolfman's cave was simply furnished: wooden table, a bed piled with blankets and furs, and a few stone shelves, all scaled for a seven-foot monster. I was dwarfed by the huge chair he waved me into. Falling back on my maid's training, I reached for the ladle, but he whisked it away and dished out the stew himself. Then, spoon in hand, he took a mouthful in silence. I suppose I had expected him to eat from the bowl like a dog.

I looked down at my own supper, hesitating. *Never take food from fae*, they said.

"Nae hungry?" His face was hard to read, but his amber eyes narrowed in what I guessed was concern.

"No, it's—"

His chuckle was low and sardonic. "Hand me your blade. I cannae believe ye didnae bring it wi' ye."

I scowled, but handed it over. With great ceremony, he nicked his forearm. "Were I fae, I'd be keening in pain. Iron deals them a mortal wound." Deftly, he flipped the dirk, handing it back.

I took it, laying it on the table beside me. "You could be lying."

"Fae cannae lie. And they can smell lies, besides. So that puts ye in a fix." He cocked his eyebrow. "Either I'm fae and lying. Or I am nae fae, and truthing."

I glowered. He had me there. Hesitantly, I sank my spoon into the creamy stew, thick with oats, and tangy with beer and smoked fish. "So you keep the tributes as your servants?"

"They're nae my servants," he growled, sharp teeth flashing. "And what would ye have me do?"

"Send them back to Dunloch."

His mouth twisted into a scowl. "Plenty dinnae want to go. Dunloch isnae a haven."

"But if they did?"

"Aye, there was one. Adored her husband, so I sent her back." His tone was suddenly soft, dangerous. His orange eyes glistened. "An' that husband burned her at the stake as a changeling."

I bit my lip. Every child learned about changelings, fae folk disguised as human. And everyone knew the tributes were sacrificed to the Unseelie Queene. No wonder he never sent them back.

"'Twas decades ago, now. Better safe here than that."

"Still, all this for the Unseelie Queene? Why gather these women, just to sit under a mountain waulking wool—"

"It's not for *her*, it's—" and then his voice broke into a string of angry barks.

Terrified, I grabbed the dirk.

The wolfman covered his face with his human hands. "Sorry," he muttered, his voice low. "I cannae talk about – it."

"About what?"

He gestured to himself.

"About being a monster?"

He flinched at the word, but nodded. The room was tense with his discomfort.

I took a shaking breath and lowered the dirk. As a maid, I was used to managing finer folk's feelings. "So you've been here for a hundred years?" I said, resuming my meal as if nothing had happened.

The man nodded, not looking up.

It was a risk. But anything was better than this painful silence. "And yet you don't look a day over thirty, " I said with a raised brow, "in dog years."

He snorted a laugh. Now, what Eilidh had called him? "So tell me, Cainlean, if it's been so long, why are none of the damn walls finished?"

His belly laugh made me smile. "Well, maybe your laird could send a mason instead of an assassin?" he quipped.

"If he comes calling, I'll let him know."

Cainlean shot me a grateful smile, his humour restored. "So, Eilidh has her art. What about you? Can we find a place for ye here?"

I shrugged. I'd spent most of my years in service. Hard work was my life and, after Eilidh was taken, revenge. Without that burning fire, I felt empty inside, adrift. "I'm only a servant."

"No one is only a servant," he pressed, fixing me intently with his amber eyes.

Perhaps he was right. And after all, what did it matter how foolish my dreams were? I was sitting in a fae cave, talking to a wolfheaded man. "Once, a long time ago, I wanted to be a Makkar, a poet."

"Ye ken how tae read?"

"As a lady's maid, I read to my mistress." And because Cainlean was easy to talk to, I found myself adding: "I got quite good, if only because she threw shoes when she didn't like my performance."

He leaned forward, his voice breathy. "And ye like poetry?" When I nodded, he leapt up, bounding to the bookshelf like a boy. I covered a smile.

He handed me a leather-bound book. I opened it to find poems, one after the other, written in an elegant hand. I read one aloud:

"Around me scowls a wintry sky,
Blasting each bud of hope and joy;
And shelter, shade, nor home have I;"

Cainlean smiled, teeth sharp but voice soft, as he completed the stanza: "—*save in these arms of thine, my Love*. One of my favourites." Our eyes met and for a moment, my treacherous body reminded me of when, shivering and wet, he had wrapped his arms around me.

But this man had a wolf's head. And he was in the service of the Unseelie Queene, I reminded myself.

"Take it," Cainlean said, gesturing to the book. "I'd love tae discuss with a fellow poet."

"I've never written poetry, though. I only wanted to."

"Wi' poetry, it's the soul that matters," he replied, his voice a gentle lilt. "It's a way of seeing the world, finding great truth in wee things. So if ye will it, ye already are." For a moment, his eyes caught mine, and I felt seen, pinned, like a deer in his gaze.

Then, tray a clatter, Iseabail bustled in. I stared into my lap as she stacked the stewpot and dishes. Once she had left, Cainlean stood, bowing formally. "Our dinner is done, my lady. Won't ye tell me your name?"

He would have it from the others before long. And I believed he was no fae, though what he was, I couldn't guess. "Iona, my lord."

"Iona?" He let the name roll over his tongue, as if tasting it. "It means island, a lonely name. And it's Cainlean. I am nobody's lord." He took my hand in his, and for a moment I thought – like a knight of old – he might kiss it. But then he scowled, releasing it abruptly. "I have kept ye too long from your sister," he said, turning away. "I bid ye goodnight."

Book in hand, I scurried down the stone steps, confused by his abrupt dismissal. Cainlean was at turns cold and passionate, tender and brusque, but he was neither the faedemon – nor the murderer – I had feared.

Still, I didn't trust him. He had secrets, that much was certain.

* * *

The next weeks passed peacefully. What had seemed just one huge cavern was a true homestead: footpaths led out to a scrappy flock of sheep on the hill, to a vegetable garden, and down to the shore where we collected clams and seaweed. In the evenings, good food, music and dancing made our nights cosy.

And, astonishingly, happy. A few mourned husbands, but they knew their fate if they returned. And most had found love amongst their sisters. Hushed giggles and nocturnal gasps punctuated our nights in the huge cave and, alone in my sleeping furs, those soft sounds wound me into a fever. At least *someone* was enjoying themselves.

Dunloch was not unaware of women loving women, but the priest preached it as unnatural fornication, earning you a lashing. Here, though, my sister and so many like her were free to be as they were.

Cainlean kept to himself, and when I asked after him, Eilidh just shrugged. "He prefers to be alone, I think. But if you need something, tell him. He won't bite." I smirked, but she wasn't making a joke. To them, his wolfhead had grown as normal as our human ones.

"But what do you think he is? What kind of servant of the Queene?"

"Does it matter? He cares for us, and he never orders us around or interferes."

And that, it seemed, was that. No one knew anything more about the mysterious Cainlean, but they were content.

I, however, was no such thing.

* * *

I chose a day when Cainlean stepped out early, watching him walk the path to the hill. He'd be gone a few days, according to Eilidh.

A large group had gone foraging along the shore, others searching for herbs. Laundry basket in arm, I climbed the stairs to Cainlean's room.

"Need something, Iona?" asked one of the grannies around the fire.

"Doing laundry while the sun is out. Thought I might wash Cainlean's blankets."

The woman smiled mildly. I had prepared my excuse well enough. But now there was a witness, I really would have to do the laundry, which irked me. Even on a fine day, the wind whipped across the hillside.

Once inside his room, I dumped the basket, and began to search. There must be something in here, some sign of his office for the Unseelie Queene. I scanned the stone shelves, lined with tomes of romances and histories, but although I longed to read them, I didn't expect them to be much help.

Finally, beneath the bed, I found a chest. Glancing at the door, I tugged it out and, with a pin from my dress, tried to pick the lock. The initial clicks gave me hope but then, trying to get a better position, I jabbed myself hard.

Why is it that handwounds bleed so much? I wondered, as I hurriedly mopped up the mess.

My heart pounded. Gathering blankets was not supposed to take this long. I tried the lock again and, mercifully, at last it clicked.

Wasting no time, I flung open the lid and found a pile of loose papers, a list of sorts.

Iona: passionate, fierce, curious, loves her sister Eilidh. Loves poetry. Perhaps a writing book or inks? Maybe a gift for Eilidh instead?

Eilidh: shy, creative, loves painting. Misses her sister. Would make a fine artist if given the chance.

Iseabail…

A list of every tribute, with hobbies, traits, occasional ideas for gifts. *A century of names.* The priest, the mayor, had never kept record, but Cainlean had. Every single one.

My stomach fluttered. *He thought me passionate and fierce?* At home, I was called stubborn and irascible. Mind you, he was a poet. Surely he was being lyrical, or else kind.

I dug further into the chest, through neatly folded clothes kept fresh with sprigs of rosemary, and my eye was drawn to a green-blue tartan. A clan pin glinted in one corner, the head of a howling wolf. An ancient emblem, but I recognized it from one of the manor house tapestries. I gasped aloud.

"Everything alright, dearie?" The voice was distant, but approaching.

I slammed the wooden chest and pushed it into place, yanked the blankets from the bed and threw them into the basket as, from behind the curtain, a concerned face appeared.

"I stubbed my toe," I lied, mournfully rubbing my foot. The older lady helped me gather the rest of Cainlean's laundry, though she let me carry it to the stream and wash it myself.

My running thoughts distracted me from the icy water. That wolfhead pin. The blue-green tartan. If his claim to it was proper, then I knew exactly who Cainlean was, why his manner was so old-fashioned. Our captor was a man from legend, from history. Cainlean MacMaddath, the lost Prince of Darkwater.

* * *

The next day, Eilidh bounded up to me as I returned from gathering cockles. "Cainlean asked me to give you this," she said, handing me a note.

"Dear Iona,
With hearth a-warm and oil lamp bright
Will ye grace my table tonight?
I hope your verse and rhyme tae hear,
But if ye will't not, th'ast none to fear."

An invitation, not a summons. He was giving me a choice. And I couldn't help but chuckle at his postscript:

P.S. I swear on my heart, on blood an' bone,
Sae good or sae bad, nae shoes wi' be thrown!

Cainlean MacMaddeth – a man from legend – had invited me to dinner. Wanted to hear my poetry. The Bonny Prince of Darkwater, who lived as a monster beneath a mountain at the will of the Unseelie Queene. I had to know more, to understand. I fixed my hair and changed into a clean dress before hurrying to his room.

He sat on his bed in only his breeches, awkwardly washing a wound on his back. The wolfhead balanced incongruously on his bare human shoulders.

"What happened?" I asked from the doorway.

"Iona! I hadnae thought—" He broke off, grabbing his bloodstained shirt and holding it over his chest. "I brought down a stag, but he fought back."

"Let me help."

He hesitated for a moment, before handing me the damp cloth.

As I sat on his bed to examine the wound, his scent – woodsmoke and rosemary – washed over me. *Focus.* "You don't need stitches. Just a good clean." He grunted as I swabbed the cut, a throaty sound that raised a flutter in my belly.

Small talk. That would keep my mind out of the gutter. "You've been out hunting all this time?"

"And bringing in supplies. Oats, beer. And these." From his pocket, he pulled five small vials of pigment. "I thought Eilidh would like them?"

"She'll love them. Thank you. *I've naught in thanks but heart and song*," I began, hardly realizing I was quoting from his book of poetry.

"*And both ha' wandered 'lone too long*." He turned to face me, his pulse beating hard above his collarbone. Mesmerized, I reached out, running a finger through the fur beneath his jaw that turned to the skin of his throat, down the light hair speckling his chest, converging to a darker line along his belly. It had been months since my last furtive tumble with the Seneschal's apprentice, and the nightly moaning of my fellow captives had me worked into a frenzy.

Cainlean leaned in, eyes hungry with need, closing the distance between our bodies. He laid a gentle hand on my arm and, at the heat from his skin, my breath caught in my throat. At once, he backed away.

"I'm sorry," he said, pulling on his shirt with a wince. "I dinnae ken what came over me. Thank ye for helping wi' my shoulder."

"No, I—" I began.

"I've a fine venison stew tonight—" Iseabail paused in the door. *Cainlean half-naked. Me, on his bed, blushing like a fool.* What on earth must she think? "I'll just leave this on the table then," she said archly, and bustled away.

"Sup wi' me?" He gestured to the table, and I sat as he served the stew.

"Ha' ye been well, since last we spoke?" Cainlean asked casually, as if we had not been moments from… something, before.

"I've worked my share. And read too," I added, when he seemed about to object.

"I hear ye've been asking questions?" His voice was deadpan, but his amber eyes were alive, fixing me.

I shrugged. No sense in denying it.

"So ye reckon I've done my best by ye all?"

I nodded, and we ate in awkward silence for a while. The venison stew was spiced with juniper and tart-sweet with apple and onion – Iseabail had a real talent. "Ye were in my room, I ken," he said at last, softly. "In my chest."

My stomach dropped. Was this why he asked me to dinner? Was I to be disciplined? "Sir, I—"

"Dinnae deny it. I smelled ye. One of the few benefits of—" He gestured to his face, as if he could not bear to say the words.

I squirmed, waiting for his wrath. Instead, he asked: "Is there something ye need? That ye miss?"

"No, sir," I said at once.

"Cainlean," he corrected. He didn't seem angry. "Then why?"

"Because I want to understand what it is you cannot talk about!" I said, slamming my spoon down on the table.

"My curse isnae your burden to bear." His shoulders slumped as he sighed. "Dinnae get between the Unseelie Queene an' me, or—" Again his voice descended into a growl, ending in a sharp bark of pain. Cainlean gripped his spoon with a deep breath, mastering his temper. "Tell me about your poetry, then. Have ye been writing?"

"I have nothing to write poetry about."

He chuckled. "Start wi' the classics. Nae better than a love ballad. Maybe ye've already taken a liking tae one of the lasses here?"

I blushed to hear him assume of me what in Dunloch would be considered unnatural. "My…tastes do not run that way."

"Ah," he said, wolfish brows flexed in compassion. "Then nae doubt ye left a true love behind?"

I thought of the Seneschal's apprentice, and shook my head. Our hurried trysts were hardly *true love.*

He blinked slowly. "Yet the Unseelie Queene chose ye?"

I took a deep breath. I hadn't told Eilidh yet, hadn't told anyone. "No, sir. I volunteered."

There was a clatter as he dropped his spoon to the table. "Ye – ye weren't summoned?" His eyes were wide. Afraid.

"I had to find my sister, know what happened—"

"—and ye wanted revenge 'gainst the Queene's monster." Cainlean covered his wolf face with his human hands.

"Why does it matter? Chosen or volunteered – isn't it the same?" A horrible thought crossed my mind. "Am I not worthy?"

"When ye were a month early," he muttered, more to himself than to me. "I thought *she'd* had enough waitin', but I should hae kent..." He gestured at me. "She wouldnae send me—" And then his sentence broke off into barks again. He slammed his fist on the table, and the wooden stew bowls leapt. "Just go," he growled. "Leave me. I've need tae think."

He dismissed me with a wave, like a maid. I grabbed Eilidh's pigments and ran.

* * *

Nae trust a noble, nae trust a fae. My mother's words echoed through me as I fled down the stairs.

I liked him. Despite his moods, even despite his wolfhead. But Cainlean MacMaddath was a spoiled noble, and when push came to shove, he viewed me as a servant. *He found me* – I baulked at the word, even inside my own head – *unworthy.*

I found Eilidh beside the fire. "Here," I said, pressing the pigments into her hand. "Cainlean got you these."

Her eyes lit up, then filled with concern as she saw my face. "Did something happen?"

"He – he yelled at me. He sent me away." Foolish tears streamed down my cheeks.

Eilidh pulled me into a hug. "There now," she said, as if she were the older sister, and I the younger. "A hard word won't break your bones."

I sniffed. She was right. *But*, I thought, *it might break my heart.*

"What got him so angry?"

I swallowed. "I told him that – that I volunteered," I whispered. "That I wasn't chosen."

Eilidh gasped. "You came of your own will?"

I shushed her. "To rescue you, if I could. Or for—" I swallowed the lump that still rose every time I thought those words, "—for revenge, if that was all I could take."

We hugged for a long time. "You always took care of me, Iona. I'm so sorry you came here."

"I'm not." I squeezed her fiercely. "And none of this was your fault." I took a deep, shuddering breath. "And we're alright, aren't we? You're happy here. An artist. And you have Iseabail."

Eilidh nodded. "I – I really love her. So much it scares me, sometimes. When I arrived I worried she'd have found someone else. Most of the women here are – are like me."

"Maybe the Unseelie Queene is *rescuing* you all from Dunloch?" I laughed darkly at the ridiculous thought.

Eilidh shrugged. "I've never heard of a single, unselfish thing she did. Why start now?"

"And why Cainlean?" *What had the Bonny Prince of Darkwater to do with any of this?*

* * *

Sleep eluded me. That night marked a month since my arrival, which meant tomorrow, I would learn if the Unseelie Queene had called another yearly tribute anyway, despite my volunteering. I had hoped at least to spare one girl.

I might as well pour my anxiety into something useful. Giving up on rest, I took the small path down to the shore where, in the predawn gloom, the black rocks met the dark water and granite sky. As I reached the sand, I heard a voice above the wailing wind. Eilidh had followed me.

I waved my basket at her, the iron dirk I used to scrape goose barnacles in my other hand.

"Did you sleep at all?" she asked, when she had joined me on the shore. "I thought maybe—"

A sudden, huge wave, taller than Cainlean, washed over us both. We gasped for breath at the cold water and, when I could see again, I screamed.

Lidless eyes. Bare sinew. The faedemon was skinless, like a flayed rider and horse bonded into one monstrous beast that stank of death. A Nuckelavee. The horsehead gnashed lipless teeth, the rider snarling at me. "You don't belong here, girl."

Elongated arms lunged, but I rolled away and instead the creature grabbed Eilidh in its monstrous claws. She screamed as it dangled her from the waist like a doll.

"No! She has nothing to do with this."

"Iona! Is everything—" Cainlean's voice. "Let her go!" he yelled, running down the hill. "A hundred years and a hundred lasses, your mistress promised me. We are not yet at a century. Leave this place."

"That one does not belong here. My Queene is displeased." The Nuckelavee rider sniffed Eilidh. "And this one smells delicious."

With a growl, Cainlean lunged at the demon. I was almost used to his wolfhead, but I had never seen those fangs bared, seen them rip into living flesh. He tore at the bare muscle of the horseneck and the Nuckelavee howled, dropping Eilidh. And then, the two monsters entwined in a blur of blood and fur and howling.

Eilidh lay in the wet sand, cradling her arm. I helped her up, half carrying her behind a rock. "Go get help."

Eilidh nodded with teary eyes, and ran.

Fear kicked my gut as a wolfish howl ended in a pained yelp. Cainlean staggered across the sand, his shirt torn and bloody, his leg oozing so, so much blood. The Nuckelavee stalked towards him, those cruel claws reaching out for a deathblow. Cainlean shuffled back, his face set grimly against the pain. And then he caught sight of me, and his eyes widened. "Iona, run," he yelled. "I'll lose my ain life, but I cannae lose ye."

"Enough," I shouted. The Nuckelavee ripped its raw eyes – horse and human – from the wolfheaded man. "Leave him alone. I will go with you."

The demon rider glared, and took a step towards me, then another, until it towered over me. Blood coated its flayed flanks like meat on a butcher's slab, and fear turned my bowels to water. But I stood my ground.

"Why?" it demanded, dripping suspicion. The horse snorted foul breath and I shut my eyes as its mucus speckled my cheeks. *Sniffing for a lie*, I realized.

"I won't let him die because I chose to come here."

The Nuckelavee's chuckle was like a death rattle. "Noble fool. Come, then, climb on my back." The flayed horsehead bent low, inviting me to mount. "The Unseelie Queene wants words with you."

I turned to Cainlean, still bleeding in the sand. "You've sacrificed long enough. Just take care of my sister. Take care of all of them."

I took two hesitant steps towards the Nuckelavee, then yanked the iron dirk from my skirts and swung it at the horse's head. It caught behind the jaw and I rammed it home with all my weight.

The faedemon screamed as hot blood spurted over the sand, over me, gushing in rivers. The dirk's point scraped against bone and the Nuckelavee howled again, collapsing to its knees. I backed away and, leaving cold iron buried in its fae flesh, I ran to Cainlean.

Kneeling in the bloody sand, I slipped my hand in his. "Hold on. The others are coming," I whispered, my stomach jolting as I felt how weak and cold his fingers were in mine. He had lost so much blood. Too much.

The Nuckelavee still chuckled, taunting us even as it died. "How can he survive this?" I demanded.

"Simply break the curse."

"How?"

"He must sacrifice the womenfolk, and spend a year and a day with the Unseelie Queene. She will restore him."

Fae cannot lie. It would save him. But at what cost?

"No," Cainlean's hoarse voice ripped from his throat. "I willnae pay their lives for mine."

The Nuckelavee laughed shrill and high, blood bubbling in the corner of its mouths. "Then we will both die on these lonely sands."

Cainlean squeezed my hand. "Nae lonely tae me," he said, amber eyes fixed on my face. "I would hae liked to read your poems." His voice was shaking, fading. "Your soul is beautiful."

I leaned in, my sobbing breaths stirring the fur on his face. Never again would he bound boyishly to grab a book, or wrap his arms around me, heady with woodsmoke and rosemary. I'd never see his amber eyes bright as we shared poetry. "I don't care what you look like. You're still a Bonny Prince to me." Tears falling, I held his cheeks, kissing the short fur of his forehead, between his eyes, his nose.

And, in a blinding flash the world…changed.

Urgently I looked around, but the Nuckelavee was nowhere to be seen. On the hill above us, the great basalt pillars had transformed into the golden stone of a magnificent castle, and I knew at once where we were. This was Castle Dunloch. Darkwater Castle.

I looked down at Cainlean, and gasped. His muzzle had become a straight, freckled nose. His wolfish fur was gone, replaced by a shock of long, auburn hair, and the wounds on his arms and shoulders were nothing but fine white scars. This was the true face of Cainlean MacMaddoth.

His lips curved into a warm and very human smile as he sat, pulling me into his lap. I breathed in woodsmoke and rosemary, holding him close, like he was the only warmth and anchor in the world. With a finger, he crooked my chin up, and I looked into his unfamiliar face. His eyes – those intense, amber eyes – were the same heady hue. Softly, he laid a kiss on my forehead, then on my nose, and I smiled like a fool.

"Those lips, *mo chridhe*," he muttered, and leaned in, catching them in a deep kiss, breathing me in, holding me close. I melted, feeling for the first time at peace.

Finally, he broke the kiss, whispering into my hair: "I hae waited a lifetime for ye."

"But why? Can you tell me what happened now?"

"I was cursed, *mo cuishle*. A forfeit for spurnin' the Unseelie Queene's advances," he said ruefully. "She swore me a hundred chances to break the curse, and sent me near a hundred lasses who couldnae fall in love with me – or with any man – if they tried."

"Until I came," I realized. That was why the Nuckelavee had been so furious, so desperate to take me away. "Did killing the faedemon break the curse?"

His soft chuckle was the same too, still made my belly flutter as I pressed my ear to his chest. "Don't ye ken the stories?" I shook my head, and he stroked my hair. "Och, Iona. Ye can slay a fae with iron. But it's only love – true love – that breaks a curse."

A Fate Written in Fire and Blood

Amie Glazier

Sabine was running out of time as death chased her like a marathoner hurtling toward the finish line. Despite the concoction of incurable poisons thrumming through her blood, the oracle's vision saw Sabine bleeding out under the knife of the man with purple eyes. That didn't make the poison any less deadly or incapacitating, though.

Her only chance at survival meant finding the last quill forged with the blood of a Fire Eagle's magic to write a different story for herself. With this quill she could rewrite her past – and future.

But not all fates can be changed.

* * *

"Fifty thousand!" Sabine weakly thrust her numbered paddle in the air for the crowded room to see. She was confident hers would be the winning bid. It had to be. She spent her life fighting for those who couldn't fight for themselves. And with the poison turning her limbs to lead, she barely had the strength left to fight for herself. But there was no one left to stand in her stead. The irony of that thought fueled her desperation. If she could rewrite her past, the quill would also give her a future worth living. And perhaps someone to live it with.

The auctioneer echoed loudly through the speakers above the quiet chatter. "Going once. Going twice. Sol—"

"One hundred thousand dollars."

Sabine's head whipped painfully to the back of the room following the booming voice. The man was large. His muscular build resembled a giant refrigerator box – if boxes wore silver aviator sunglasses and commanded the room with a single damning sentence.

"Sold!"

The room continued to move as the stage was reset with the next item. But Sabine's jaw slackened and her body sagged. How could this happen? She didn't even get the chance to outbid him. She didn't have the money, but still; the Fire Eagle quill had been almost hers. Now it was gone. Forever.

The Refrigerator Man walked up the aisle flanked by two bodyguards in black suits. Sabine rushed out of her seat and followed him, gasping for breath as she walked.

"I need that quill. Name your price."

A bodyguard stepped in front of him as the three men turned, but the Refrigerator Man waved him away.

"I will not leave here without that quill," she demanded.

He stepped forward to tower over her frame. He scanned the length of her, his nostrils flared and the tight set of his jaw looked as if he found her lacking. But Sabine held her chin high, despite catching her brittle and diminutive reflection in his sunglasses.

"I hope that chair is comfortable then," he said as he turned to leave.

"Please, sir." Desperation clawed up her throat as Sabine reached out and grabbed his wrist.

The muscles of his forearm tightened at her touch, and the tension rippled up his arm in an electric wave that reverberated into her core. The energy in the air hung thickly between them as he turned to face her again. His bodyguard whispered something in his ear, and he nodded.

"If you'll excuse me, Little Mouse." He pulled down his sunglasses to the bridge of his nose to wink at her, but all Sabine saw was his glowing, purple eyes. The same ominous eyes with lavender spider veins that sneered over her bleeding body in the oracle's memory of her death.

"I do hope we will meet again," he said with a smirk. "But perhaps in different circumstances." His voice was dark and smooth like worn leather, but it grated against her, leaving splinters in its wake.

Sabine's heart lurched into her throat as the Refrigerator Man walked away. She saw him holding the quill in his hands before the door to the back room slammed shut.

Rage and disappointment and exhaustion twisted in her chest like a haunted tilt-a-whirl at an abandoned fair. Within minutes she lost the quill and met the man who was destined to kill her. But she couldn't walk away. Deadly and irreversible compounds churned in her blood, but giving up wasn't one of them.

She reached into her pocket and fished out a large, black capsule, the last of what the oracle had given her. It would make her strong and lithe for a few hours, but, unlike the last two times when it wore off and accelerated her rate of deterioration, the oracle warned the last pill would be her last chance. Once it wore off, Sabine would die. She held the capsule in her palm, her stiff wrists juxtaposing her racing thoughts as mortality weighed heavy upon her.

The purple-eyed Refrigerator Man, she reminded herself, would also lead to her death. But the only path to the quill was through him. Without it, death was a certainty. But with the quill, well, at least she had a chance at survival, small as that chance may be.

So Sabine swallowed the capsule and covertly followed the Refrigerator Man to his luxury sedan.

* * *

The dark hallway smelled like sweet cake and tea, making Sabine's stomach grumble. But perhaps it was from the two hours spent in the Refrigerator Man's trunk and then climbing the trellis into an unassuming window on his estate. Sabine felt thankful for the capsule but knew it would wear off soon.

The walls loomed with shadows, and Sabine couldn't quite make out her surroundings as she snuck down the dim corridor, but everything she touched felt like velvet and luxury. It wasn't entirely surprising after spending the long drive in the back of a car that smelled like roasted vanilla and didn't have a speck of dirt. No one would keep a trunk that clean unless they were trying to hide something.

Flickering candlelight and orchestral music echoed faintly out of the open door at the end of the hallway. Sabine palmed the knife in her belt as she listened and approached silently.

"Aren't you going to come in?" The smooth leather voice immobilized her as she anticipated a servant to enter. But no one came. "I know you're out there, Little Mouse. Join me."

Shit. She weighed her options. Sabine could run and find a quiet place to let the capsule wear off and let the poison claim her. But she still wasn't ready to give up. Not yet. Instead, she took a steadying breath and entered the room with her head high, as if she had every right to be there.

The opulence of the room was staggering. The walls were lined with shimmering black velvet and the domed ceiling was a stained-glass fresco of a bird that would put the Sistine Chapel to shame. The Refrigerator Man sat at the center table in a tall, wing-backed chair that accentuated his bulky frame. The dainty teacup in his hand looked minuscule against his oversized fingers. Sabine had never seen a bull in person, but the image of the Refrigerator

Man at the center of his own tea party felt as contradictory – and ironic – as a bull in a china shop.

"Sit." He gestured to the matching chair across from him, but Sabine didn't flinch. "Sit," he commanded again with predatory grace.

Sabine willed her heart to slow as she kept her focus on his eyes. They had an otherworldly glow like the gossamer of a spider web. She was the butterfly caught in his purple spider veins with no other choice but to be consumed. She crossed the room to join him, and her joints felt tight as she sat upon the soft seat.

"Eat," he urged. "You must be famished after cramming yourself into my trunk." He sipped his tea gingerly with his hulking pinky pointed skyward and spoke with a cordial tone that made the hairs prickle on her arm.

"How did you know I was there?"

"Oh, Little Mouse," he chuckled. "You may be small and quiet, but your presence is impossible to miss."

Sabine looked down at the steaming tea and small cake. The vibrant colors on the ornate china resembled the flickering flames on the candelabra between them.

"Are you poisoning me?"

His warm laugh resonated in his chest before spilling out between his lips. "I do believe you already have enough poison in your body. I sincerely doubt adding more would really do any good, don't you?"

The Refrigerator Man had a magnetism that lured Sabine in. In a different circumstance perhaps, she would have thrown herself – and likely her clothes – at his charming smile. But this was the man with the purple eyes. The man who would kill her. The man who held her only chance at survival. She needed the quill above all else.

"Eat up, Little Mouse."

Her growling stomach felt the logic that her mind did not see. Hunger won as she consumed the small cake. It tasted like roasted vanilla and a spice she couldn't place. It reminded Sabine of the tiny cakes her mother made for her birthdays as a child. She moaned with pleasure as she devoured three more from the plate between them.

As she became sated, she noticed that the bright colors on her teacup and saucer weren't just matching the fire in hue; they were pieces of fire feathers forged into the porcelain.

"Is this from a Fire Eagle?" she asked as her voice cracked.

"You are quite astute."

Sabine then noticed all the brightly colored objects scattered across shelves and tables. There were easily over one hundred items that ranged in size from small trinkets to large tapestries. The stark contrast of the orange, red, and yellows looked like flames licking up the black velvet walls. The whole room was a reliquary for Fire Eagle artifacts. Sabine suddenly felt hot, like the flames were consuming her too. She clawed at the neck of her shirt and her arm moved slowly as she felt her joints start to harden like stone. Her lungs felt like they were imploding, and she fought to keep her eyes open and focused on the only thing that mattered: getting the quill.

"How do you have so many Fire Eagle items? They have been extinct for hundreds of years and their imbued artifacts are very rare."

"You ask questions to which I really don't think you want the answers, Little Mouse." His sultry tone dripped with honey, but Sabine felt the punch of his condescension. Suddenly her whole body felt like it had also been punched. Repeatedly.

"Why do you want…the quill…so badly?" Deep breaths splintered her question.

"I knew it would lead me to what I'm looking for," he replied, setting his teacup down with a gentle clink.

"And what is that?" she asked dryly, her tongue hot and thick.

He paused, smirking, letting the weight of his silence punctuate his answer as the candlelight flickered against the purple veins rippling across his eyes. "You."

Sweat beaded on her suddenly sallow skin and her pulse hammered in her ears. Had this been a trap? A sharp pain sliced through her core, and she squealed.

This was the end. But she knew something far more sinister than a poisoned death awaited.

Sabine mourned the life she had given in service to others and the life she wanted to have lived for herself. There were no more chances now. The poison reached a fever-pitch within Sabine's cells, and she blinked rapidly as the world fell out of focus.

She swore she saw a hint of alarm on the Refrigerator Man's face before he raised his knife – the incandescent glow of his purple eyes reflected on the blade – and her world went black.

* * *

Levi's broad shoulders heaved with exertion and fear as he knelt beside the bleeding woman. As a seer, all his visions came to fruition exactly as they should have. But he had never been able to see past the moment when he cut the poisoned woman, siphoned her blood into the quill, and rewrote her future.

He knew to collect as many Fire Eagle artifacts as possible. He knew to outbid her at the auction. He knew she would stow away in his trunk, so he cleaned it. He knew that she would devour his favorite vanilla cakes, so he made more. He knew where to cut her arm and how to siphon her blood into the inkwell, and he knew – more or less – what words to write on the parchment that removed the poison from her past but still left her there in his arms.

But he didn't know what to do once she woke up. Or *if* she would wake up. He had been dreaming of this woman for five years, and had been living his life as a controlled formula to get to this moment, and now that it was here, fear gripped his heart.

Levi pressed his large, bloodied hands into his eyes, desperate to see what came next, but nothing told him what this new future would look like. He had grown to care for this frail woman that haunted his visions, and he desperately pleaded with the fates to wake her.

Sunlight began to stream through the stained-glass ceiling, casting colorful shadows across the woman's face as she lay on his floor by the table. Her skin was no longer sallow, her face seemed fuller, and her breaths were steady. All good signs, but not enough to tamp his nerves.

Levi cupped her fingertips and brought them to his chest. It was an intimate gesture for strangers, but to Levi, this woman was his world. His *Little Mouse*. He knew he had done all he could to save her, but somehow, it still didn't feel like enough.

Her warm, brown eyes fluttered open and lingered on him like sticky molasses. Levi's mouth broke into a smile but froze. Waiting. Watching.

"It's you," she said, her voice rich and silky, and Levi's heart clenched with affection. "You saved me…" Her brows furrowed as if dainty caterpillars were chewing on her memories. "But, why?"

Levi paused, unsure what to say or how to begin. His eyes pleaded, not wanting to break the precious moment with too many words.

"Was this your plan all along?" she asked.

"Yes, Little Mouse. I have been searching for you for a long time."

"Your eyes." She reached up to cup his face, letting her thumb trace his eyebrow. She studied him with an intensity that made Levi feel itchy. Her face was so close as she examined his lavender eyes that he could taste the vanilla lingering on her breath.

"You're a seer, aren't you?" Her head tilted like a dog who just learned of her master's betrayal.

The declaration made Levi feel exposed and raw, and words caught in his throat. So, Levi nodded.

"You saw all of this. You knew what would happen."

Levi's heart pounded, and he nodded again.

"I saw you too, you know," she said quietly. "I thought it was a vision of my death, that you would kill me. But you didn't. You orchestrated all of this. To save me—" Her words broke as something unreadable passed her face.

Levi hadn't orchestrated anything. He had simply been following orders from the fates. But he didn't dare say that. Instead, he held his breath.

"I guess it's good that some fates can't be changed, then." She chuckled softly. "Who knew?"

Levi certainly didn't. He still waited for a new vision of what would come next, and his fingers tingled in desperation. For the entirety of his life, Levi had an active vision propelling him forward. Without it now, his mind nervously raced through all possible outcomes, but with no notion of which to follow.

She sat up to meet his eyes. Her body was still small compared to his, but her strong movements made it clear the poison was gone. Levi leaned back against the leg of the chair to give her space, but he refused to let go of her hand. Silence stretched between them as the morning sun illuminated where his hand curled around hers. The colorful shapes from the stained-glass ceiling projected a mosaic around them.

He had no words and no direction. Perhaps he was being given a choice, to have agency in his vision of the future. All Levi wanted was his Little Mouse. He would always choose her – if given the opportunity. But she had agency too, and the unknown direction of her choices scared him the most.

"So, Seer. What comes next?"

"I don't actually know," he admitted quietly. He lowered his head, studying the illuminated projection of a stained-glass Fire Eagle spreading its wings around them, and he hoped it would protect them from whatever came next.

She lifted his chin to meet her gaze as a slow smile spread across her face. She leaned forward into his lap and pressed her lips gently against his.

Their kiss exploded into a series of visions behind his eyelids: a wedding dress, drinking tea by the fire, children playing tag in the garden of his estate, arguing with a teenager behind the wheel of a car. But his favorite was the last one where they held wrinkled hands side-by-side on a wicker bench. A lifetime of happiness awaited them.

Levi wrapped his arms tightly around his Little Mouse and deepened the kiss.

Paths, Littlings, and Holy Things

Somto Ihezue

Beads of sweat trailed down Olaedo's body, drenching the goat fodder where she lay sprawled. She had bitten hard into the pad of leather clenched between her teeth; her incisors now grazed against each other. Her goats just stared at her. Silent. Olaedo pushed, harder, her body quivering under the screams she was stifling. This was her third pregnancy. With the previous ones, she'd had the midwives dabbing her with a cold towel. This time, hidden away in a barn, a candle dying out beside her, all she had was her strength. With a deep inhale, she pushed again, and when she felt a head tearing through, she looked over, making sure the child slipped gently onto the fodder. And as she had feared, the other came pushing, too. Olaedo had felt it for months, writhing and kicking inside her. Every night, she had prayed to Ala, to her mothers, to take it away. They did not. The second child slipped out, wet and bloodied, next to its sibling. Sedated by the pinch of snakeweed she'd taken every day for the past week, the twins slept still as a lake. The little ones looked like Olaedo's mother, and all her brothers, and all her sisters. If their eyes had been open, this is how Olaedo would describe them: owl eyes, bronze eyes, sailing eyes.

Olaedo cut the children's cords. With a cloth, she strapped them to her chest. At first, she staggered again and again. Then she ran.

Outside the barn, the moon stole behind clouds, and the stars had forgotten what it meant to shine. For the darkness, Olaedo was thankful. She made for the main hut, the one she shared with Nnadi, and found him bent over a fire, breaking palm kernels. In the firelight, the man's skin was the sheen of tarnished trinkets. He did not see her, not until the light from the flames caught her shadow.

"I woke, and you were gone." Nnadi stood, his eyes going to the bundle on her chest.

Olaedo pulled at the cloth, revealing the faces of the little ones. "It is time." Her voice was a thing unbowed. A river unparched in drought. "We must hurry."

"You should have woken me." Nnadi's eyes did not stray from the children.

"There was no time." Olaedo let her impatience bleed into the words. "You would have slowed me down."

Nnadi was one to cuddle, to linger. There was no room for it. There was no time.

Olaedo unbundled one of the twins. She undid her woolen scarf and swaddled the infant in it. Then she placed the child in Nnadi's hands. The man just stared down at it. A tremble came finding his hands. This was the first of his children he had held. He did not touch the others. They did not let him. The infant nuzzled into him, and warmth found the corners of Nnadi's body. It was like holding light.

"We have to go."

Olaedo turned to leave, and in the darkness, she found Azuka. The woman was still – a shadow on an ill-lit street.

"Azu – Azuka—" Nnadi stepped forward, shielding Olaedo with his towering frame. It was too late. Azuka had already seen.

"I heard – I heard noises." Azuka was a liar. Everyone knew this. She once spread word she'd seen Kalu, the pot maker, holding back rain. At the time, the village had been besieged by famine. The riverbeds broke and crackled under the sun. The leaves wilted down the trees. People were erratic with hunger, and Azuka's lies had taken root with ease. Kalu was strung up that day.

Olaedo and Nnadi lived on the outskirts of the village. No one could have heard a thing unless they wanted to. After Olaedo's second pregnancy, they had moved there and steered clear of everyone. But Azuka was a mango fly, ever prying, ever hovering.

Azuka's eyes darted from the child in Nnadi's arms before straining to catch the bundle strapped to Olaedo's chest.

"Gods. Not again!" She cupped the words as tears fled down her face.

"Azuka!" Nnadi tried to hush the woman.

It was pointless. The woman's voice found the night wind and kited, higher, higher.

Olaedo hated it. The crying, the mourning. She hated being treated like tragedy made an eternal abode of her home. For all her misfortunes, Olaedo had wept for herself. She had wept for days on end. It was enough. There would be no more weeping in her house.

"I have to tell the elders." Azuka wiped her running nose, nodding and agreeing with herself.

"Azuka, please, listen to me." Nnadi tried to reach for her. The woman drew back. "We – we are leaving the village. No one needs to know."

"Where are you going?" Azuka seemed to mellow.

Nnadi trailed on as he explained the details of their departure. Once they completed the crossing ritual, they would all be safe, and the rest of the village would never know. Azuka became rather calm, listening with a sincerity. A keenness. Olaedo hated that too.

When Nnadi was done, Azuka reached for him, gently squeezing his arm. She had initially gone for his hands, but the baby slept in them.

"I can help—"

This is how it happened: Azuka was standing. Azuka was falling. Azuka was breathing. Azuka was wrestling air. Nnadi did not see it happen. There was no seeing of it. Olaedo became night and befell her cousin like a curse. In her hand, a blade. And the blade came cutting. Blood splashed across Nnadi's face. The man inhaled once. Blood splashed across Olaedo's face. There was nothing to inhale. Olaedo slew her cousin with the blade that cut her children's cords.

Azuka did not die screaming. For that, Olaedo was thankful. The woman had collapsed to her knees, her hands reaching for the gash, her hands gathering her blood like harvest. Olaedo watched her – a child watching a grasshopper struggle in a puddle. In her dying, Azuka made to speak and failed, the words flooding back into her lungs. Whatever those words were, Olaedo knew they would be lies.

"Olaedo." Nnadi's voice was afraid. "What – what have you done?"

"I have lost…" Olaedo stopped, exhaling for the first time that night. "…I will not do it again."

"She had children too."

Olaedo said nothing.

"She was your blood."

"And now she is dead."

She turned to face Nnadi. In her eyes, Nnadi found her. This was her, the woman she had always been, the woman he married. Ardent, true, raging.

Nnadi made to kneel to the body. He was unsure where to begin, not with the child in his hands.

"Leave it," Olaedo called from behind him. "It will not be the first body I have buried."

And so they ran through the cornfields, past the giant Udala tree. When Olaedo was born, her mother buried her placenta at the foot of the Udala tree. Just as her grandmother had done. Just like all the mothers before her had done. Olaedo was never allowed to bury any of hers lest they curse the land.

"Wait." Olaedo went back to the tree, her breath coming in short gasps. She knelt to its roots, resting her head against its trunk. It was the first time in a long while she knew rest. Olaedo started to dig. She tore at the soil, debris stabbing her fingers. She clawed and clawed, stones bruising her knuckles. Nnadi knelt to help, balancing the child in one arm. Olaedo did not let him. This was her digging.

"They never let me bury the others."

Olaedo stopped. From her clothes, she retrieved a bundle wrapped in pawpaw leaves. She had collected it right before she left the barn.

"They called me sacrilege."

Gently, she placed the bundle in the hole and pushed the sand back over it.

"Where are they to stop me now?"

This time, when Nnadi helped her, she let him. His hands followed the motion of her hands like water finding water. Nnadi had always followed Olaedo everywhere. When they were children, he followed her to watch the spirits dance in the warm streams. He followed her to the neighboring village to steal a goat. He followed her to the heights of the Iroko trees to catch stars. And when she yelled and tried to wrestle him away, he would knock her to the ground, rather gently, again and again. So Olaedo let him wander after her. She soon found herself following him too. They got older, and she found she wanted to wrestle him in other ways. There was something about the curve of his buttocks. When Nnadi caught her watching him, Olaedo would not look away. Nnadi would kick sand in her direction, and she would lunge at him, mostly at his buttocks.

When she came of age, they readied Olaedo to join the other girls in the maiden dance. The dance was a ceremony. Young men would gather in the village square. To watch the girls sway and twirl. To find brides.

Olaedo's mother had danced as her grandmother had done. As had all the mothers who came before her. Olaedo refused to dance.

"Why don't they dance for me, like the birds do?"

This she had said. Then she went to her father's farm and plucked the largest coconut. The next day, when the sun painted the waters, Olaedo found Nnadi and shoved the coconut into his hands. She betrothed him. The elders rebuked her. The elders scorned her. A woman does not betroth a man, they said. Olaedo did not care.

But the fight in Olaedo waned with the birth of the first twins. From the moment she took in, Olaedo was certain the pregnancy would kill her. She was convinced of it when two of her molars came loose. She had been swallowing pounded yam, and they just came tumbling out. Her hair was next. It left in painful tufts until she was bald. One morning, Olaedo woke up, and it was pitch black. But she'd heard the cock crow and welcome morning. Not many things frightened Olaedo. This did.

When the medicine man tried to line her eyes with rabbit feces, she slapped his hand away.

"You will never see again!" he had cursed.

"I will!" she spat back.

When her sight returned, in gratitude, Olaedo poured daily libations to the ancestors for a month.

Olaedo also spent the pregnancy hating Nnadi. She hated that he was happy and beautiful while she suffered. Her nose was the size of an avocado. The sight of him filled her with bile. She would stare daggers at the poor man until he fled from her sight. His scent physically made her nauseous too. Above all, she hated that she still wanted him to hold her each night.

When she went into labor and the children came, Olaedo was relieved to be alive. Then the midwives gasped and scattered back. Some ran out of the room screaming. Her relief faded away. Worry took its place. In between battling pangs of labor pain and fearing for her life, Olaedo had forgotten what it meant to birth twins. When one of the midwives spat the word mmụọ ọjọọ, demon, only then did it dawn on her.

Olaedo thought the children were ugly. Like the hairless sparrow hatchlings that nested in her mother's mango tree. Their faces were red and puffy, like baby rodents hued together. They were ugly, but they were hers, and she would not part with a hair on their head. Not one strand. When they came for the children, they came with dirges and salt. Olaedo met them with bared teeth. The first priest who reached for the babies found a dagger in his shoulder. The second one found teeth where teeth should not be. But in the end, Olaedo was one woman. They took the children, and she screamed for ten days. It echoed through the village. Grief calling. The village folk thought the screaming would kill her. It did not.

When the second birth came, Olaedo met it silent. She did not touch the children. She did not look at them. When they took the little ones, she did not fight. Olaedo was tired.

People began to call her an adulterous witch. Like being just a witch was not enough. They said she had spawned demons. The village had not seen the birth of twins in decades, so Olaedo was utterly alone in her misery. She did not speak for months. Her hair tangled and fallowed. She ate nothing, willing death to take her. And death came and found there was nothing to take.

Olaedo's family abandoned her. Her father, her brothers, and all her sisters.

"You stray from us, and we stray from you."

This is what they said. If her mother had been alive, Olaedo knew she'd never stray from her. Her husband's kin were not ones for words. A line of powerful dibias, they were not ones to be crossed. They found Nnadi another woman to marry. Nnadi refused. They paid her dowry without him present. Nnadi refused. They moved her into the marital home he shared with Olaedo. Nnadi rained fire. And his kinsmen rained fire too. So Olaedo packed her things and left for the outskirts. And Nnadi followed her.

* * *

Nnadi and Olaedo stopped running when they came upon gravestones. It was the resting place of Nnadi's ancestors. The children were starting to wake. The first child, the one strapped to Olaedo, yawned, stretching up against her. Even in the dimness of near dawn, Olaedo thought it was the most beautiful, most hallowed thing she would ever see.

She turned to find Nnadi gaping into the distance.

"What are you waiting for?" she asked in a hushed scream. "Begin the ritual."

"What – what if we went south, up Iteajali hill? What if—"

"Isi gini?" It wasn't confusion etched into the creases on Olaedo's forehead. It was apprehension. "There is no running from this. No village will welcome us. Our children will be slain on sight."

"We do not know where this path leads." Nnadi took two small steps back. "My father was the last of my kinfolk to make the crossing. We never saw him again."

"We know it leads away from here. That is all that matters."

In every generation, the path opened up to a traveler from the Ihedioha clan, wielders of fire. Nnadi belonged to that clan. A few travelers in times past had returned, spinning tales about a world of distant colors. Of fireflies trapped in glass. Of steel horses. Of blackened roads of tar. In this world, the houses were not of mud and raffia. In this world, they touched the sky. In this world, spirits did not roam amongst men. In this world, twins lived.

That was enough for Olaedo. When she took in the third time, the fight in her returned. And she hatched a plan to hijack the crossing ritual. Nnadi was not next in line; neither was he the most spiritually attuned member of his clan. So Olaedo helped him prepare. It took years of dedicated edification for one to make the crossing. Olaedo and Nnadi had months.

In the passing weeks, they performed the rites of rebirth, the rituals of the sojourner.

For to walk this path is to wade through fire.

Every first market day, Olaedo washed Nnadi in the hot streams of the Afor. His body burning through the waters reminded her of their childhood, how he'd follow her to splash in those very waters. Back then, the water did not scald.

The nights when the path spoke, Olaedo would balance a calabash of bat wings on Nnadi's head and have him wander naked into the wilds. She silently prayed he did not get torn to shreds by night leopards.

Before the ones who died before you, be bare, take flight.

Between bathing in steaming waters and getting slashed by leopards, Nnadi's nights became long, damp, and frightening. But Olaedo was there. She held onto him.

For the final rites, beneath the glow of a broken moon, Olaedo slew a goat, its body thrashing beneath her knee.

She doused Nnadi in its blood and pushed him into the Orie depths. The fall could have killed him. It did not. Ancestors past had come walking through him, filling him with might. When Nnadi emerged from the stones, it was spirit fire that coursed through his bones.

Their plan hinged on Nnadi, and now he was wavering. Olaedo would make the crossing herself, but the crossing only ferried Nnadi's kin.

Olaedo looked out into the distance. Pinpricks of light told her morning was coming. In no time, the sun would set the sky on fire.

It all fell to her now.

"If you have forgotten what awaits us come dawn, let me remind you." She drew close to Nnadi, breathing in his air. "As they did the others, they will tear these ones from us and banish their lifeless bodies to the wastelands of Akacha. If we run to the ends of the earth, they will follow; they will not stop until our children are no more. Do you understand?" She peered into his eyes, their golden brown hue softened in the dark.

"Then we kill them!" Nnadi shot back. "We kill all of them!"

In the mountain wars, Nnadi had rained terror on the Ogidi raiders, ripping their bodies to bone and dust. An Ihedioha warrior, he was formidable. Olaedo knew this, the same way she knew it would not be enough.

"Nnadi." Her hand went to his face, her fingers lost in his beard. "The village will rally against us. We would be outnumbered."

"I – I cannot leave you here with these people."

"I will be all right. I promise. I will be just one woman with one child."

Olaedo caressed his arms with a tenderness. There was no time for it. There was no room for it. But if tenderness was what Nnadi needed to forge on, she would give it to him.

"And when they ask of me—"

"You went into the wilds and never came out," Olaedo smiled. "Just like we agreed."

Still, Nnadi lingered.

"What – what is it?" The words broke out of her. Olaedo did not have the luxury of breaking. "Tell me!"

"I cannot – I cannot live in a world where you do not exist." Nnadi shook his head, his voice crumbling – the way it always did when his heart grew too heavy in his chest. His body wracked with tears.

"You can, you can. I promise."

Olaedo wiped at his tears, but they came anyway. She brought her forehead to his, the babies, a space between them. A space too little, for his tears still found her cheeks.

"You must." She squeezed out of his tight grip.

And Nnadi fell to his knees, the child steady in his hands. He began the crossing ritual, binding it to the bones of his ancestors.

"Ala, mother of my mothers," Nnadi called to the winds. "Consume me with your spirit. Amadioha, the echo that is thunder, come, see the bones that bind us. Ikenga, forge me into steel, let me fell mountains. Anyanwu, light our path with fire and day. Ekwensu, be my shadow. Take us to a place far, a time, near."

And they were gone, Nnadi and the child. Olaedo, alone on the gravestones, with nothing but the memory of them, cooed to the baby in her hands, who started to cry.

And Olaedo cried.

A Possession of Magpies

E.E. King

Catherine Linton has lived above the cemetery on Drakes Bay Lane for as long as anyone, even she, can remember. She was there when Drakes Bay Lane ended right at the graveyard gates. It had been full of bird song and the cooing of mourning doves then. The only harsh notes, struck by murders of crows and parliaments of magpies.

The road has been extended, widened and now connects directly to the state highway. It has become so crowded it is almost a highway itself, a teeming throughway between the living and the dead. But Catherine's hearing is so dim, and her eyesight is so cloudy, she can barely make out the train of cars, or hear the cacophony of horns and brakes. Instead, she imagines Drake's Bay as it used to be, a small ribbon of pavement, an asphalt garden snake edging past silent tombs and mausoleums.

Catherine spends her days in a rocker, watching the magpies swoop down and gather up the ascending souls that rise from the graves of the newly dead. She does not know if anyone else can see them, emerging out of the earth like the smoke of extinguished candles. Nor does she know why the magpies are so eager for spirits. What do the birds do with the souls they collect so zealously? Are they carrying them to another world? Do they fly them halfway to heaven, then set them free, a sort of taxi service to part way to paradise? Or are they souls made visible? Maybe, she thinks, they line their nests with them? She imagines that souls would be even softer than feather down. Or perhaps, she thinks with a delicious shiver, they feed them to their young? If she were a bird, she'd prefer fat juicy worms, or the remains of an abandoned picnic.

She thinks it odd, but many people do come to picnic on the graves, young lovers sharing bottles of cheap red wine, old widows, or widowers, eating sandwiches on the graves of their departed. She wonders if the dead appreciate these visits, if the smell of old grapes and fresh bread salted with tears and memories, is food to their hungry souls.

Drake's Bay is a beautiful old cemetery, edged by slender, pale poplars that turn golden or sprout green, depending on the season. The grass is clipped by small herds of whitetail deer that wander between graves, pruning the willows that weep over grey stone angels and licking the salty tops of white marble tombs.

Catherine imagines she will be buried there someday. She wonders if a magpie will claim her. She wonders if a magpie grabbed her betrothed, Tommy, when he died many years ago, on a battlefield in France. Once, she had been bitter about the loss, but now she can barely remember his face. When she tries, she can only see a man so young, so distant from where she is now, that he might as well be a stranger.

Her eyes are milky with cataracts. It makes this world difficult to see. Sometimes it seems that the souls and the magpies are the only thing she can focus on. The magpies because they are so black and white, and the souls because she knows she's close to joining them.

It's been a cold winter. She thinks it might have been her last. Now that spring is here, she spends her time on the deck, swaying back and forth in the rocker as stiff and creaky as her bones.

As she sits there, swaying in afternoon sun, her eyes drift closed. Her breathing grows sonorous, and for the first time in forever, Catherine dreams of Tommy. It has been so long since she has seen him it is almost a visitation.

He stands before her, young and elegant in a black and white tuxedo. As he passes beneath a chandelier. The black tails of his jacket catch the light and glitter with a hundred iridescent rainbows. Tommy opens his mouth, but instead of his melting baritone, out comes a harsh caw and a thud. She awakens with a start.

A young magpie has smashed into her window and is lying at her feet. A breeze ruffles its feathers, revealing a glittering kaleidoscope of iridescent rainbows in each black shaft.

Though she's too old to fuss over anything and should just leave it to die, she cradles the fallen bird in her withered hand. It is breathing shallowly.

Once, in a past so distant it seems like fiction, she had rescued all manner of injured creatures; birds with broken wings, squirrels fallen from nests, and litters of kittens so naked and small they were not even recognizable as cats.

Tommy had called her Florence Nightingale of the Animals. She smiles at the memory, cracking her face into a million wrinkled folds.

She wraps the bird in a blanket, sets him near a heater and searches for a place to house him in. Beneath her bed she discovers an old shoe box. The dust rises from it like fog off distant mountains, like souls out of tombs. It is the perfect size for the bird, but it's filled with old photos. She empties them onto her bed, not noticing that the only photo that falls image up is one of Tommy, staring up at her from the past.

She puts the bird in the now-empty boy and searches for some ancient dry cat food, a relic from a forgotten feline. She soaks the food in water, placing it and some water in China saucers near the box.

When the bird wakes, he gobbles it eagerly, cocking his head and looking at her with one bright eye, much too knowingly for such a young bird. He is missing some tail feathers, and his right wind is bent.

Catherine straightens the wing and binds it to his chest with an old ace bandage. It's a miracle she can do such delicate work with her knobby arthritic fingers, almost like claws themselves, but it doesn't move at all.

"Smart bird," she says. "You know I'm trying to help you."

She cares for the bird for a whole month, binding and rebinding the wing once a week to make certain it stays clean. It heals whole and strong, though still bent. She wonders if it will tilt to the left because of it, able to only fly in circles. She sighs, but she has done the best she can.

The bird hops off the table and soars to the old upright piano. He seems alright. It is time to let him go. She knows it is selfish, but she flinches at the thought. It seems like forever since she has felt anything. Now love and loss come crashing down on her like a sleeper wave.

Catherine looks at the piano, instead of the magpie's dark feather's glistening in the sunlight she sees Tommy in a shining black tailcoat. He is playing 'Jeanie with the Light Brown Hair.' just like he used to, but instead of Jeanie he sings 'Cathy.'

He was a real musician. He would play and sing, and she would join in, harmonizing with his smooth baritone. She can hardly imagine it now. Her throat aches at the memory. She remembers everything she has forgotten; the way Tommy held her in his arms, the way it felt like flying when they danced, the feeling in her soul when he told her he would never leave her.

"But you did," she whispers hoarsely. "You left me alone forever."

And somehow, though she does not see how it can be possible, Tommy is both sitting at the piano and there beside her holding out open arms, it as it is as if having left her alone for most of her life, he has returned to surround her.

Catherine feels young and weightless. She does not care that it is impossible, she falls into his arms, and they waltz round the room in sweeping circles. The magpie watches as Catherine wheels around, arms wide.

Then, she collapses. She lies on the floor gasping. The magpie hops over to investigate. When his feathers brush her face, Catherine thinks she feels Tommy's black tailcoat grazing her cheek. The magpie pecks her wrist. He jabs her chin. When she doesn't respond, he flies out the open window. Despite the bent right wing, he catches an updraft and is gone.

Catherine isn't found for a week.

The house has to be fumigated before it can be put up for sale.

There is a notice in the paper. Neighbors whisper. It's a tragic reminder of what can happen when the old are allowed to live alone. Overnight the number of medical alert buttons in Drake's Bay quadruples.

Catherine is buried in the cemetery below her house. Nobody can see her soul rising like a small, transparent child from her grave, only to be snatched up by a waiting magpie.

The magpie swallows her soul. For a moment all is darkness, a dark as long and silent as eternity.

So, this is what happens, she thinks. *A black emptiness, an endless void, a never-ending nothingness.*

And then she is seeing through the eyes of the bird, flying above the earth, soaring above the world, circling the boneyard on rising currents of warm air. She is weightless. She is free. For the first time in forever everything is clear.

The magpies have been drawn to the cemetery by fresh grass, worms, berries, rodents, and the remains of an occasional picnic. And the souls? Souls have always been drawn to wings and feathers. That's why there are birds. That's why there are angels.

From out of the slender poplars another bird flies to meet her. Its right wing is slightly bent. Despite the injury, it sweeps through the air as smoothly as a melody, black feathers catching the sunlight and shimmering with a hundred iridescent rainbows as they fly away together into the rising sun.

A Ballad for a Lady Love

C.J. Larsen

An old woman lies in her bed, her gray hair fanning out around her head. "Tell me a story," she says to the old man sitting on a stool beside her. "One more time." He smiles down at her, fighting back tears. She pretends not to see them.

"Alright," the man says. "Then you rest." He brushes a wisp of hair off the old woman's face. "Once upon a time, there was a young witch who lived in the forest and spent her days brewing potions and crafting charms for the people of her village."

He looks around the cottage, neat and tidy though crowded with things. The shelf-lined wall holds a multitude of glass bottles containing liquids in every color of the rainbow. They glisten in the warm afternoon light. Each bottle is stoppered with a cork and bears a carefully lettered label. The oak workbench that sits below the shelves has been sanded and refinished many times, but is still stained from years of use. A teapot sits on the table beside the woodstove, waiting to be poured. His eyes fall on two straw hats perched on a coat rack by the door, one plain, the other decorated with a teal ribbon. Two wool cloaks hang below them, their hems just touching the tops of two pairs of old worn leather boots.

"Was she pretty?" the old woman asks, recalling the man's attention.

"Oh, very pretty. Most young maidens are pretty after all."

"Still, some are prettier than others," she says.

"If it matters so much to you," he says, "then rest assured she was the prettiest witch who ever served the village and remained so all of her days. But it wasn't her beauty that made her special. It was her talent." The man nods to himself. "Such talent. She could cast spells that would calm a chicken so it would lay twice the eggs. She could imbue an amulet with luck that could keep a child safe from injury. She could brew a potion that would break any fever."

"Psh. Simple things," the old woman says dismissively.

"Simple things done well," the old man answers. "But our story is not about eggs or fevers."

"What is it about?" she asks, though her smile says she already knows the answer.

"Love, of course," the old man replies. "One day, the witch heard a troubadour would be performing in the local inn. She wanted to see this entertainment so she made the trek into town." The man pulls a lute down from the wall beside him and strums a chord. “She was not disappointed. The lute warbled under the troubadour’s skillful fingers while he sang of longing for his true love.”

“Was he handsome?” the old woman asks.

“Oh, very handsome,” the old man replies with a wink. “The witch stayed for the entire evening listening to him play. After his last song, she approached and thanked him for the beautiful music.”

The old man softly plucks a simple melody while he continues his story. “The troubadour could not sleep that night, thinking of the witch’s smile. He wondered if she had bewitched him. The next morning, he asked the innkeeper where the witch lived. The troubadour arrived at her cottage just after lunchtime, saying he wished to purchase an elixir to soothe his vocal cords. The witch prepared it for him and also offered him a cup of tea. He stayed all afternoon, regaling her with stories of his travels.

“The troubadour remained a fortnight in the village. Every day he visited the witch’s cottage. By the fourth day he dropped any pretense of purchasing potions and would simply accept a cup of tea and help the witch with her housework and chores.”

The old woman purses her lips. “It’s a good thing he helped with the chores. I’m sure the witch had better things to do than entertain a troubadour.”

The old man laughs and sets down his lute. “She must not have minded too much. The witch came down to the village to see him perform every night while he sang of looking for his lady love. And after the last song of his last performance, she placed an amulet over his neck, saying 'I hope you find your lady love someday.'

"The troubadour had performed all over the kingdom. He'd sung before counts and dukes in their castles. He had been given gifts of all sorts. The witch's amulet was not covered in jewels or cast of gold – just a simple luck charm hung on a leather strap. But the troubadour knew the difference between opulence and true worth. He also knew he had found his lady love. He promised the witch he would return."

The woman opens her mouth, but whatever witty comment she intends to make is interrupted by a cough. A flash of worry crosses the man's face. He holds her upright until the coughing finally subsides. "You need rest," he says.

"The story's not done yet," she whispers, her head tucked against his shoulder. The old man looks like he might argue, but instead he helps her lie down and ensures she rests comfortably before he continues.

"The troubadour was not the only one who saw the witch's worth. A Lord of the Fae had heard of the pretty witch and her simple magic. And so a new suitor arrived while the troubadour traveled across the land. He came by night and stood in her garden, calling to her in a voice of silver bells."

"Was *he* handsome?" the old lady asks.

The old man smiles wryly. "Yes, even more so than the troubadour. He was beautiful in the way a bird of prey is beautiful. Poised, aloof, and slightly dangerous.

"The Fae Lord knew the witch did not want money or treasure. He knew she did not need jewels or servants. He offered her a different sort of wealth. If she married him and became his lady, he would teach her the deep magic. He would show her how to spin moonlight into silver. He would show her how to make a charm that could stave off death itself. He would show her how to sculpt a scrying bowl that could reveal the past, the present and all the futures that might yet be."

"A fine offer for a witch," the old woman says.

The old man rubs his chin thoughtfully. "It was a fine offer. But he did not promise to help her tend her chickens or weed her garden. He did not promise to sing to her or tell her stories. He valued her talents more than her company.

"The witch told the Fae Lord to come back on the day her troubadour returned. Only then could she make such an important decision. The Fae Lord acquiesced and disappeared into the night.

"At first, the witch's heart was torn between her suitors. When she sat at her workbench mixing a potion, she thought of the Fae Lord's offer as her fingers worked her simple magic. She imagined what she could do with more knowledge. In those moments, the troubadour seemed far away.

"But when she weeded her garden, she remembered the troubadour's sweet voice singing as he had toiled beside her. She felt the warm glow of his companionship. In those moments, the Fae Lord was a half-forgotten dream." A breeze flutters the curtains in the open window. The old man glances outside at the garden, vibrant and teeming with vegetables in straight rows, tidy but for a few weeds.

"As the days wore on, it seemed likely she was right on both accounts. The troubadour probably made promises to maidens at every village he visited and had already forgotten her. The Fae Lord may never have existed at all, a midnight fantasy born of weariness and longing.

"But true to his word, the troubadour did return, exactly two months after he left. He found the witch feeding her chickens in the early dawn's light. The witch's breath caught in her throat when she saw him standing at her gate. She ushered him in and offered him tea.

"They sat in the shade of the old oak tree that stood by the witch's cottage while he told her of his plan. He would buy a tinker's cart so they could travel the kingdom together. He would perform and she could sell her magical wares. She thought this sounded a pretty life and laid her head against his shoulder.

"When the sun hit its zenith for the day, a shadow fell across the garden, as if a great bird flew above them. The air rippled like sunlight on water. The Fae Lord emerged, passing through the veil that separates the Fae lands from our own. He too had returned, true to his word.

"The witch's heart hurt at the look on the troubadour's face as she told him of the Fae Lord's offer. She thought he might yell at her and call her faithless. Instead, the troubadour shook his head sadly and said, 'I cannot offer you deep magic. I can only offer you stories and songs and my undying devotion.'"

"That's not such a small offer," the old woman says, her eyes half closed. "Undying devotion is a powerful magic in its own way." She grips the old man's hand in hers.

The old man turns his head away at her touch, hiding his glistening eyes. He takes a moment to compose himself before he begins his story again. "You're right about that, of course. Undying devotion is a powerful magic, as deep as any offered by the Fae Lord. The witch understood this and it made her decision easy in the end. The Fae Lord accepted her answer and faded away forever.

"Just as he'd said he would, the troubadour bought a tinker's cart and they traveled the kingdom together. Villagers rejoiced at their arrival. Dukes and duchesses vied for their visits. The King himself invited them to court.

"After three years of adventures, the witch found herself with child. They sold their cart and moved back to the cottage. Their daughter had the voice of a nightingale and would one day surpass her father's fame. They raised a son who sat by his mother's side and learned to make remedies and cures. When he was grown, he set up an apothecary's shop in the capital."

"And after the children grew up and left to live their own lives, the troubadour helped her tend the chickens," the old woman says. "And he always sang her to sleep at night."

"He did," the old man agrees.

"She never regretted her choice." The old woman takes a deep raspy breath, shuddering from the effort.

"That is how it goes," the old man says, "in the best love stories." He squeezes her hand. "Now you rest."

He hums a soft lullaby while her breathing slows, her hand still clasped in his. Her eyes close for the last time. The old man grips the luck charm hanging around his neck. He finally lets loose his tears, now that she no longer pretends not to see. His racking sobs fill the cottage with a sound more heartbreaking than any song he ever wrote.

* * *

The water in the bowl ripples. The image disperses as tears strike the water's surface. The woman picks the bowl up from her lap and throws it across the room. It lands with a clatter, spilling its contents on the stone floor. A lady-in-waiting peeks her head through the door at the noise.

The room bristles with deep magic. Its color changes instantly to suit the woman's mood. When she's angry, the light is the red of a furnace. When she is depressed, it is the bleak gray fog of a winter morning. Right now, it is the indigo of the ocean's crushing depths.

"Go away," the woman says. She does not know the maid's name. It's not worth remembering them, they grow old and die so quickly.

The woman paces the room, her elegant silk heels tapping on the stone floor. The sound echoes off the cold walls. She likes to pretend her room is a prison. But this is only a lie she tells herself. She is free to move about as she pleases. She is free to split the veil and return to the human realm at any time. She could go there, throw off her magic and age to dust in an instant. The only prison is her own cowardice.

With a gesture, the bowl rights itself. The puddle on the floor coalesces and rises to pour itself back over the lip of the bowl, filling it once more. She picks the bowl up and carefully sets it in her lap as she sits on the edge of her bed.

The woman runs her finger around the bowl's rim. "Show me what would have been," she says as she peers into its silvery depths. The water stills.

An old woman lies in her bed, her gray hair fanning out around her. "Tell me a story," she says to the old man sitting on a stool beside her. "One more time." He smiles down at her, fighting back tears. She pretends not to see them.

The Crypt of Lost Things

J.A. Legg

I almost didn't see the door at first. It would've been impossible to miss the day it was first installed; a high, massive oak, expertly carved, bevelled, and varnished. But that had been over a century ago, I guessed, and now it hid, nearly invisible beneath the branching mask of creeping ivy that had conquered the front of the building.

It was the knocker on the door that gave it away – an ornate brass gryphon, wings spread, biting down on a heavy tarnished ring. I knocked, once, twice, breaking the dusky silence of the street. A heavy *clunk* came from behind the door, followed by the rusty slide of a drawing deadbolt. *Sshshsk.*

The door opened. An old man peered at me over the stopper on the other side; short, bespectacled, dressed in a patchy winter jacket and bunny slippers.

"Can I help you?" he asked.

"Erm, hi," I said, clearing my throat and glancing behind at the empty road. The bus had already moved on to the next stop, and I didn't think there'd be another one before morning. "I had some trouble getting here, and I'm still not sure if I've got the right address, but is this the—"

"Yeah, yeah," he muttered, and coughed. "This is it. You're in the right place."

That's good news, I thought, glancing over the front of the building. It was old, older than most other buildings in London, but under the ivy, something about its shape reminded me of the apartment building my mum and I had lived in when I was a kid. I remember reading a few years ago that they were going to tear that place down.

"Come on in," the old man said.

There was a small side-door at the edge of the foyer, nearly swallowed by the shadows in the corners of the room. The old man fished up a handful of keys from his pocket – house keys, car keys, locker keys – and chose a long black iron key, its teeth crooked and wrapped in dry rust. He forced it into the lock, then turned; the *jolt* of the lock bouncing off the foyer's vaulted domes. Beyond the door lay a winding staircase, spiralling down into the dark.

"Down here," the old man said.

He drew an old torch from his pocket and clicked it on, hand against the railing. I could tell his battery was nearly dead, so I offered my mobile phone for light. A single bar glared at me as I clicked the button, next to the dead Wi-Fi symbol at the corner of the screen.

"Do you know what you're looking for?" he asked me.

"Yeah," I said. "Yeah, I'm actually looking for a friend of mine – well, more than a friend, I guess, really. Her name's Crystal. Crystal Adams. Does that name mean anything to you?"

"Don't recognize it," the old man said, shaking his head. "But that doesn't mean she's not down here. I'm a long way from getting this place in any kind of order. Would you know her to see her again?"

"I think so," I said. Dark curly hair, green eyes, with a smile like summer sunlight and two piercings through her left eyebrow. Yeah. I'd know her.

"Right then," the old man said. "Stay close. It's easy to lose your way down here."

The light swept across a row of small niches in the wall, winding down the side of the stairwell. Inside each one was an item or two – outdated coins, phone chargers, and socks stained brown with dirt. I saw at once what he meant about the lack of order – there didn't seem to be any kind of pattern to the tangles of Christmas decorations, decks of cards, TV remotes, and crumpled sheaves of misplaced homework all lined haphazardly along the edges of the stairs. There was an old water bottle I'd left on the train once, and the penknife I hadn't seen since I'd used it to open a can of dog food in my granddad's garage. I took both from their niches for a closer look, then realized that the old man had gotten ahead of me. I pocketed the knife and moved on.

"When was the last time you saw this girl?" he asked, once I'd caught up.

"A few years ago, I guess. Back when we were still in school." I thought back to the day I'd first heard about what happened at the party, and about what it was she'd done there – then how I'd blasted out of the chemistry lab, classmates turning to watch as I barrelled down the school corridor, homing in on her like a guided missile. Then the argument – I'd kept my voice low, I thought, but by the end it felt like a sudden explosion and a pile of ash. She'd stormed away quickly, tears in her eyes, her friends Trish and Nejeen glaring at me before trailing in her wake.

I'd apologized the following day. We'd met for coffee after school that afternoon – and a long talk on the phone that evening. For the next few weeks we'd tried to work things out. I told her I needed to be able to trust her – that I was willing to keep trying if she was. She said she wasn't sorry – that she'd hardly said two words to Tommy Daniels that night, and it hurt her that I was quick to believe the worst. When she asked who had told me otherwise, I didn't answer.

For a while we tried to talk about other things – clashes with her co-workers at the restaurant, or the new guy my mum was dating, or the auditions we had coming up at the end of term. It almost felt normal – all the other things that mattered, all the things we used to talk about before I heard about the party. But even then, I think I knew I was losing her, somewhere in the long pauses and dead air.

By Christmas, we both knew it was over.

The old man reached the end of the stairway, and another oaken door. He put the key in the lock, and I followed him.

It was dark inside – unlike most of the crypts London opens to tourists, there were no electric lights along the walls. But the air was cooler inside than I expected, and smelled like stones wet with rainwater. More niches lined the walls, larger and deeper this time, some marked with placards, and many others blanked by the passing of time. They were filled with a sprawl of lost items – forgotten dentures, stolen jewellery, a rugby match, and piles of CDs long ago mislaid. A Jack Russell terrier was sniffing around a niche at the far end, and popped his head up to watch as we passed. I heard skittering in the shadows, and kept on.

The old man led me deeper into the crypt – to the end of the hall, and down another staircase to the level below. Some of it reminded me of the things I'd seen in my Uncle Henry's attic – there were 45s and eight-tracks, an Atari joystick, a few Oyster cards, and a cracked mug from Queen Elizabeth's coronation. We crept along the corridor (his steps were nearly silent in the bunny slippers), until we reached another stairway down.

"How deep does this place go?" I asked him.

The old man turned and peered at me. I squinted at the light of his dying torch. "Deep," he said. "Everything eventually makes its way down here." He glanced over at a couple of opportunities and a pile of hair.

"Right. Um, it really wasn't that long ago that I saw her – I really doubt that she'd be this far d—"

But the old man had moved on.

I trotted behind him, past worn mittens and bicycle tyres, and a bag of memories that had spilled out onto the floor. I found a summer day I'd spent playing computer games when I was nine, hiding under a *Green Arrow* comic I'd never given back. A few levels down I stopped to talk with Joey Chilvers, who wasn't sure how long he'd been down there, and was looking for the football we'd kicked into the creek behind his house. I hadn't talked to him in probably ten years.

"Why are you looking for her now?" Joey asked, once I told him what I was doing. "It's been a long time."

I thought carefully – thought of the last phone call we'd had, and the warnings I'd gotten from Trish and Nejeen. *Stay away from her*, they'd said. *Otherwise you'll just make things worse.* And I thought of Melissa – the girl with the hoop earrings and the spearmint gum, the girl who'd first told me about the party; about how she'd seen Tommy Daniels disappear into the loo, belt off, with Crystal's hand in his. I'd been scheduled to work that night. I'd never gone. Melissa thought I deserved to know.

She kissed me, that New Year's Eve. I still remember the taste of spearmint on her breath.

"I miss her," I told Joey.

Joey nodded.

I kept going.

The old man had vanished long ago, but I wasn't worried – it was just the one corridor, after all, and I'd probably still see the light of his torch once I reached the bottom of the next stairway. It wouldn't be too difficult to keep up.

But when I reached the level below, everything was dark.

"Hello?" I called out. "Hello!"

There was no answer.

I kept going, down one level, then another, past jobs and interests and dreams long forgotten, until I reached a small door at the end of the tunnel. It opened on a stairway, then down into a vast chamber that stretched far past the reach of my light. Still, from the top of the stairs, I could see the edges of the chamber's store – crumbling statues and jungle temples, and Alexandrian libraries next to sunken continents mouldering in ocean depths. I reached the bottom of the stairway, stepped into the maze, and marvelled. It would be a long time, I thought, before I ever came to the end.

"Crystal?"

My voice echoed her name back to me. The old man was nowhere to be seen.

I heard my own footsteps scratching on the pavement, *scratch, scratch*, like Velcro coming together and pulling apart. Once I kicked something hollow by accident, and looked down to see a golden chalice, rolling away into the dark.

I turned to make sure I could still see the exit. The battery on my mobile was getting low.

"Crystal?" I asked the darkness. It echoed the word back to me, but did not answer.

I wondered who else was down here. I hadn't thought about it much when I first arrived, but there could be lots of other people down here, people no one had seen in a very long time. It could go on for a lot longer than I'd been expecting. Maybe even forever. It's hard to keep things, after all. You squeeze, and most of the time they slip through your fingers.

I'm not sure how long I looked for her, wandering around corners or rooting through piles of debris. I don't know when I finally decided to turn around. But when I looked back for the stairway, it was gone.

I checked my phone. It had gone to low-power mode a while ago, and all the bars in the top corner of the screen were faded. I opened Maps, but the screen stayed blank. That made sense. I should've known there would be no maps down here.

I decided to turn back and look for the wall of the chamber. The stairway couldn't have *vanished*, I thought – I'd just gotten turned around, and as long as I made my way along the wall, I'd find it sooner or later. Things don't just disappear, I thought. Especially not down here.

I walked. It took a long time, but I walked – until the light broke along the corner of rough concrete. I reached out my hand to touch it, then followed the wall – sure that sooner or later I'd find the way out. All it would take was a long, dark walk.

And then I saw it.

Not the stairway, or anything like it. Instead I saw the nickname Crystal gave me, back when we'd first gotten together. We'd had a couple of bit parts in the school play together – *Peter Pan and Wendy* –and I walked her home most nights after rehearsal. The last few times we talked so long we missed her house. I'd asked her to come home with me for a coffee after final performance; I'd been a bit scared to ask, but when she'd said yes – God, it was cheesy, but I felt like I could fly.

I picked up the name and dusted it off. It was a little worn, but still whole. It had been a long time since I'd heard anyone use it.

It was the start of a trail – first the nickname, then her phone number, then the hoodie she'd nicked from my locker the following week. The TV series we'd watched together, and the rock music from the 80s we'd both loved. The long talks we'd had most nights that summer, about school, and work, and home, and everything that comes after, lying side by side on the football pitch five minutes from her house. We'd lie there in the grass, and our backs would soak as we tried to spot stars through the artificial glow of the London sky.

And then there were the things that *she'd* lost – like the job at the restaurant, the one she'd lost the last night of summer, when she'd heard about the car accident and left to look for me in the ER. She was still in uniform when she found me – found me bruised and sore, neck locked tight in a hospital brace, sprawled out on a gurney. The walk we'd shared a few days afterwards, back to that same football field, where we both lay down and she told me she loved me. It was the first time she'd said that to anyone, the last golden night of the summer. I could still hear the sound of it lingering along the trail.

There was more. The sleep I hadn't gotten the night after I found out about the party. And all the nights afterwards, too, lit by angry text messages and rasps into the phone. *I barely talked to Tommy Daniels that night*, she'd said, over and over again. *You can ask Trish and Tommy yourself if you like.*

And then, at last, the bottle of trust we'd shared together, the one we'd tried to hold onto in the months before our breakup. It lay in shards now, shattered and leaking on the smooth stone floor. I stepped around the glass carefully and wiped my finger in the puddle, pressing it to my tongue. It tasted like an old kiss. Bittersweet.

I moved on, picking my way further along the trail. I started to smell something new: a sickening, spearmint smell, floating over the role Melissa had asked me to turn down in the play the following year. She was proud I'd been cast as the lead – but between school, work, rehearsal, and a girlfriend, she was afraid I'd be stretched too thin. Especially if I wanted to go to Oxford with her after graduation.

I told her later I'd forgotten the application deadline. I wondered if that was down here somewhere too, lying around with all the other debris. But I never saw it.

Melissa's parents had agreed to pay for her first year, and threw her a dinner party in their Knightsbridge flat that summer to say goodbye. Melissa told her parents that night that she wasn't worried about leaving me behind; Oxford was close enough for me to stop by, of course, and once she came back at Christmas, it would be like we'd never been apart.

In early October I boarded a Friday afternoon train for a surprise visit, with a necklace I'd picked out as a birthday gift. When I knocked on the door of her rooms, a young man answered – he shook my hand, and Melissa introduced me as an old friend from school. She said that Brandon was taking her into London for a Saturday shopping trip, but I'd be welcome to join them for dinner that evening. I declined.

I got on the last train home to London, the necklace still heavy in my pocket. I could see it now – it was lying on the floor a little way off, glinting in the light of my dying mobile.

I walked over to it. Picked it up. I thought I'd sold it a few days later, but apparently whoever bought it hadn't thought it worth keeping either. I tossed it aside, towards an old shipwreck that loomed about a stone's throw away, coated in algae and shadow. A fragile *clink* sounded in the dark.

Then, silence. Long silence.

I waited.

It was quiet down there, in the crypt. Quiet as well as dark. It was so quiet you could hear your thoughts, roaring through your mind like a train through an Underground tunnel. I thought about Crystal, and wondered what she'd been doing down here, all this time. It's hard to know what to do when you're lost.

Maybe she wasn't lost, I thought. Maybe someone else had found her, or she'd found them, and they were together in the West End, maybe, rehearsing for a show. It had been a long time since I'd seen her, and these things happen. I'm sure I'm not the only one who's gone looking for lost things.

When you're a kid lost in Sainsbury's, you can go to the front desk and they'll page your mum over the PA. Then she'll rush to the front and find you, and throw her arms around you like she thought she'd never see you again. But there was no front desk down here.

Footsteps, like mine, *scritch-scratching* in the dark. I turned.

"Tootles?"

Her hand went down as I lowered my mobile. Dark curly hair, green eyes, and three piercings in her left eyebrow. I smiled at the nickname.

"Hey, Tiger Lily."

"Hey," she said. She smiled, like summer sunlight.

"What are you doing down here?" she asked. "You look like you're a bit lost."

"Yeah," I said, in a kind of fragile chuckle. "Yeah, I was."

"So was I."

I hesitated. "I'm sorry I didn't believe you," I said at last.

"That's alright, Tootles," she answered. And she slipped her hand into mine.

"My mobile's about to die," I told her. "And I'm not sure I'll be able to find the exit without it. Do you know the way out?"

Another smile, subtle but perfect. She reached into her pocket, and turned on the light of her mobile.

"No," she said. "But let's see if we can find it together."

The Time Keeper

Emily O'Malley Liu

It was the winter solstice of the year I turned twenty-one. The Time Keeper emerged from his tower, the bone-white of his mask shining in the light of the Cold Moon. The crowd beneath cheered, our arms laden with evergreen boughs and mistletoe and holly, which we would carry into our homes to decorate for the Yuletide festival.

For the first time, perhaps because I was no longer a child, the Keeper struck me as melancholy. Not his countenance, which was concealed, but his *stature*, somehow seemed sad. We were, after all, here for him only briefly, for the annual blessing, after which we would return to our own hearths and kitchens, busy with food preparation and chasing children and all the other occupations of normal life. The Time Keeper, meanwhile, kept time in his palace, beating his metronome to the pace of the planets as they moved against the stars, the moon and sun as they spun in the sky. Some said that he was disfigured; even that his disfigurement was self-inflected, an attempt to avoid looking like his father, which was Time itself.

Faces turned up expectantly, waiting for him to raise his arms. When he did not, the merry cheers sputtered, and upraised hands began to falter under the weight of their green treasures.

And then, he spoke.

"I have need," he said, in that voice that was neither clear nor memorable, but which vanished like smoke, "of an apprentice."

There followed a moment of pause, a wintery silence, and then the murmurs began. The Keeper had never made such a request before. Who could we send? There were voices that said to send the oldest and wisest – by which they meant the most expendable – but there were too many voices who valued their wisdom close at home. Someone said to send a hale child, of perhaps eleven or twelve, but their mothers objected that they were too young for such responsibility. No one dared to suggest sending a young woman, which left the young men, who were needed for their own ability to work in the fields and serve the village. The blacksmith could not be spared, nor the tavern man, nor the brewer, nor the horse doctor. The men who worked in the fields were resting from their summer labors, and in any case, many had young children who still needed tender care at home.

"I will go," I said.

I had no wife to object, no trade deemed essential to the village. The murmurs died; no voices rose in objection as I dumped my evergreen load onto a nearby child's sleigh.

I felt the Keeper's masked gaze upon my head as I pushed upon the gate with hands that I willed not to shake.

Then the Keeper raised his hands and blessed the crowd, a gesture which was met only with an astonished silence that ran behind me as I closed the heavy wooden door.

I still smelled of pine sap, a stench that only became more noxious as I stood in the dark and cold of the tower. I blinked into the blackness, willing my eyes to adjust, but there were no windows on this storey, and no internal source of light. The cold began to seep into my muscles, feeding the soreness that had begun to take root there, and I ached.

And then: a glow emerged from the end of a hallway.

He wore no mask, but his face was neither horrible nor disfigured. He looked like nothing other than a man, an ordinary man of middling years, with hair gathered into a long plait that hung down a back of intermediate height, and soft grey eyes that shone in the light of his torch. He looked at me with kind sadness.

"Come," he said.

He led me up a twisting staircase to an upper corridor and pushed open the door to an apartment that he said was mine. The rooms were far finer than anything that I, a woodcutter's son, was accustomed to, and briefly it occurred to me to be concerned as to what sort of assistance I was expected to provide. I turned anxiously, but the Time Keeper only bowed, and said in his smoke voice that food would be brought up, and that I ought to get some rest.

Outside, it began to snow, and I watched as the drifts floated past my window, which was wide enough to see the expanse of the Keeper's palace. I wondered if Time ever paused to visit here, or if it simply kept turning as it did in the village. A knock at the door sent adrenaline coursing through my arms, but when I opened it, the hall was empty save a tray of food on the floor.

* * *

The next morning, breakfast arrived in the same manner, this time with a note on a scrap of paper that read simply *the tower*, in a cramped, painful-looking hand. I finished the breakfast and downed the hot black coffee. In the light of day, fear had fled entirely and eagerness replaced it, for which I was grateful. I had not been known as a coward, but last night I had begun to fear I was one. But of what had I been frightened? A man with kind eyes, no bigger than myself? Supper delivered to my comfortable room?

The corridor was warm, though there was by now a thick blanket of snow on the ground outside. I had taken my coat with me, and I was warm enough that I began to sweat as I climbed the winding stairs. At the top was a room that could only belong to an astronomer-priest. Circular, and not large, it overflowed with golden instruments. Thick blue carpets on the walls and floors kept the chill at bay, despite the large windows, which looked out in all directions. Tables and highboys teetered under the weight of books and scrolls, scattered bits of paper and moleskins opened to pages littered with writing. A large golden instrument dominated the east window, teetering on spindly legs, the great tube of it pointed up towards the sky. A small desk stood opposite, curved to fit tightly against the round wall, at which sat the Keeper swathed in grey fur, though the room was warm.

By daylight, his greys were accentuated: though his face was smooth, the hair that hung down his back in a neat queue was an even shade of silver, and his skin was pale to the point of translucency. When I entered, he put down his book and turned to stare at me with eyes that looked like starlight in the middle of day. He was, I realized all at once, far from ordinary. "Did you sleep well?"

"I – yes, thank you." He was still studying me with those unfathomable eyes, and I felt a resurgence of nerves.

"I'm afraid there has not been a guest in the tower for some time. I was not sure what was needed to make it fully suitable for human presence." He paused. His voice was hoarse, as though he didn't use it often. Then he continued, with the lighter air of a man making a joke, "I don't think I fully qualify on that count, any longer."

So he was human then, or had been. "What about your other servants?"

"What other servants?"

"Aren't – there others?"

He shook his head once, just a tilt of the chin to one side. "None."

"Who cooked the food I ate last night?"

"I did," he said simply.

"Oh," I said. Then, belatedly: "Thank you."

"It is no trouble." He inclined his head again. "I'm grateful the village was able to spare you."

"I won't be much missed." I loved my village, but their silence still rang in my ears.

"No?" He spread his fingers across the volume on the desk. "Surely your family will miss you."

"Poets are a nicety, not a necessity." My father was a woodcutter, and my help, such as it was, had been superfluous. "There is no one who will materially hurt for my lack."

He gazed at me a few moments longer, then folded his hands in his lap. "Well. I have been in need of an auxiliary for some time."

"Of course. Where should I start?" I looked around the room. His was not the only desk; there were several buried beneath all the papers and books. "I could straighten up these – what are you doing here, exactly?"

"My research," he said vaguely. His eyes slid from one pile to the next without appearing to really see them. "I suppose you can read?"

"It's generally helpful in poetry writing."

He considered this. "But not necessary, I imagine. Very well, if you are so inclined, I would be very grateful if you could organize by subject – planets, stars and so on."

"Yes. Have you a blank journal?"

He didn't ask what it was for, but silently handed me a pen and codex that were near his hand. Then he opened his book and returned to it.

The room was overwhelming to say the least. The furniture was packed so tightly it would be hard to navigate through the room even if there hadn't been stacks of paper obstructing every route. I supposed I might as well begin at my feet. I settled myself cross-legged on the floor in front of the pile nearest me, pulled from the top, and read:

Saturn, Observations: 1100–1300

I looked up. "Have you been here two hundred years?"

He twisted round again in his seat, no hint of impatience at my question. "Much longer, I should think. But I no longer remember."

"Well, that certainly explains the chaos," I said cheerfully. I made a mark in the journal for Saturn and continued my work. Aside from the names of the major planets, I recognized little.

Luminosity Classes of Stars
Cosmic Background Radiation
Planets in Relativistic Orbits

The words meant nothing, but the sounds were as fine as any poetry in my head.

I'd only noticed that the light had begun to change when it became difficult to read: the sun had risen beyond the window over my shoulder, above the tower, and my little corner between the desks was in shadow. The Keeper looked at me. "It's noon," he said.

"Yes. You must always know what time it is," I said without thinking.

But he only grinned. He had taken off his furs at some point while he worked, and it was strange to see him essentially in shirtsleeves. "Usually. Though I've been known to be lost in my work as well. Come," he said, and I rose from my cramped position, feeling the tingling in my legs, almost painful as they came back to life.

We took the winding stairs down, then down and down again, past the corridor that held my own rooms and past the dark entrance hall where I had alighted yesterday. I fought back a yawn; yesterday seemed an age ago. At the base of the staircase we found ourselves in a kind of cellar, with a fire in a large hearth, which the Keeper stoked until it was roaring. He set a kettle over the flames and rolled up his sleeves, revealing forearms that shone like moonlight.

"What can I do?" I asked, uncomfortable in the silence. My parents always said that I was a poor fit for a poet, who people suppose must be a contemplative, solitary creature. I craved noise and conversation, wailing babies and the drunken laughter of the elderly. When I wrote, I wrote in taverns. The Keeper moved as silent as the moon.

He handed me a head of garlic and told me to mince. That much I could do. I flattened the little cloves and peeled their skins and got to work. The sound of my rolling knife was preferable to the silence. The entire tower was still, without so much as a mouse moving within the walls. I would've at least liked a cat, something to cause a bit of ruckus.

He was stirring something in a pot hung over the fire, and I thought he looked like a witch. He took the garlic and added it to the pot. "Smells good," I said. He gave me a look that suggested he had realized that I was the kind of person who cannot bear silence, and I thought perhaps he regretted his choice of apprentice.

He ladled a bowl for each of us and we ate. He ate as he moved, with the silent grace of the planets against the stars. I matched him, or tried to, timing my movements so that they made as little noise as possible. The only sound in the room was that of the crackling fire. The gentle click of spoons was as loud as thunder.

"Why have you not had an apprentice before now?" I asked. It seemed odd that a man as eternal as he might need a human apprentice at all. I could hardly become the next Keeper. The Keeper never changed.

He finished chewing the stew that was in his mouth. There was some meat in it, something rich and gamey. I wondered where it came from, if he frequented the village on the sly, unrecognized without his mask, or perhaps hired a boy to run errands. If so, I had never heard rumor of it. As far as we knew in the village, the Keeper was an entity unto himself.

"I have not had need of one," he said.

"And now you do?"

He waited, considering me. Then he raised his hands, and I saw that the fingertips shook. "I can no longer write as I once could."

I thought of the painful-looking hand that had appeared on the note with my breakfast. I sat back in my seat. "Of course," I said, relieved. A scribe. I could be a scribe. "Yes, that I can do."

When we had finished our stew, he took his bowl and mine and walked them over the to wash basin. "Go now and get some rest," he said, though it was only early afternoon. "The skies will be clear tonight."

* * *

He taught me his time keeping. I studied the phases of the moon, the way they pushed and pulled against the solar year, always in competition, never in alignment. We observed every night it was clear enough to do so, making use of both the naked eye and the golden telescope, which at first intimidated me but with which I eventually became acquainted. My neck ached from so much time spent either craned up at the sky or else down at my journal, taking notes, writing as fast as the Keeper could talk, recording his work, his life, its meaning.

I was happy most days, lonelier in others. I missed my family, and while the Keeper was kind, his presence remained distant, an untouchable figure despite our proximity. I learned to sleep through daylight, though my head pounded when I woke, and my stomach ached most of our working day, which of course was really the night. The Keeper made us tea seasoned with turmeric, but it barely cut through the fog.

My mind drifted away from me, and I caught myself unable some days to remember what day of the week it was, let alone where Venus stood in its convoluted orbit. Once, I asked him how he withstood the way time stretched up here in the tower, how he handled work that required such precision. He responded that the years slipped away like a sieve, each another data point in the sky, another point to observe, to measure and record.

"I've learned to let go of the years rather than the days," he said. "I know what stage the Moon will be in tomorrow, and the next day, and the next after that." His eyes flickered up towards the heavens. "I know where everything will be found. But where I will be a year hence…where I was years ago…" He shook his head at the stars, and I thought it remarkable that he did not shake his fist, that he could smile though his voice was so mournful.

I must have had an astonished look on my face, because he chuckled and said, "Don't worry, I shan't keep you that long. Next Yuletide, you will be home with your own family. But it helps to be reminded of the gravity of what a year is. To watch how a person changes in that time."

I thought of the year my sister had had a baby, how my niece had grown from a creature incapable of more than mewling to a vivacious creature of twelve months, toddling about and flirting with every adult she encountered.

So that was why I was here, enduring the time-altered schedule of the newly parented and the mad.

"I won't be very useful to you if I lose my mind," I said and suppressed a yawn behind my hand.

He smiled. "You will get used to it."

* * *

The nights moved, circular, from cold to cool to warm and back again, until the harvest had passed and the first snows had fallen.

And the Keeper and I – well. There is a certain intimacy that grows by matter of course between two people who share such close quarters, but this wasn't that. Our was not the sort of casual intimacy that makes for good housemates or family members, intimacy born of proximity and happenstance, though it might have been. It was a deeper thing, the sort of closeness derived only from gazing at the same cosmic bodies at the same time as another person. It was the closeness of lovers and contemplative friends, a closeness I had never shared with another human being, something I hadn't known I'd wanted until it had been offered, and I found myself falling into its warmth the way one falls into a soft bed at the end of a long day.

I never became truly accustomed to his schedule, but I learned to bear it, to live with it and around it, as human beings learn to bear all things. It helped when he began to insist that I close my eyes for an hour during our observations, at which I lay down on the rug and slept like one of the stones beneath my head.

It was nearly Yuletide, and we were sitting by the fire in the kitchen, both of us with a warm cup of wine, mulled with spices and oranges, in keeping with the season. I read to him, a little of my latest verse, in which I had attempted to capture what the season at home meant to me, the holly and the firs, the greenery on the walls and lights shining in the dark. My mother and father, dancing in front of the fire. My siblings, squabbling over the last bit of pudding. My niece, too young to remember the prior year, taking it all in again, as though for the very first time.

And me: observing it all, a part of it and yet set apart, the poet who watched from the corner. My throat closed unexpectedly, and I turned away mid-verse.

The Keeper looked at me with concern. His face, which had been so serene, as peaceful as I ever saw it, frowned. "What's wrong, dear one?"

"Tomorrow is the blessing of the boughs," I said.

"So it is."

"I'll go home," I said.

"You will," he said gently, and my throat closed, and I couldn't say any more. I longed to go to him, to put my head on his knee like a lover might. But for all our closeness, there remained a barrier.

For all our physical proximity, we never touched.

I told myself it was alright: the Keeper belonged in his tower, and I belonged with my people in the village. Even if I had found, for the first time, some sort of purpose here, even if my poetry was well-served by the movements of the spheres and the steady presence of the quiet grey man I had come to respect – admire – adore.

The next day, the Keeper donned his furs and his mask, and we stood out on the tower balcony in the wind and cold. No new snow had fallen overnight, and we could hear the crunch of the villagers' footsteps a mile away.

We had not spoken of it, but I knew without needing to be told that I would leave with the villagers when they came for the Blessing. I could feel the Keeper distancing himself, keeping himself apart from me. At arm's length. The mask felt like an extension of that distance, a last barrier between us that could not be broached.

At last, the villagers arrived, arms laden with feathery boughs and sharp holly, children dragging sleighs and singing, women red-nosed and rosy-cheeked, and men cheerful with good food and beer. When they saw us both standing above them, a great cheer arose for the Keeper and his apprentice.

Beside me, the Keeper tensed, reacting to the noise the way I did to silence. When the cheers reached their pinnacle, they began to die away, waiting for the Keeper's blessing. Silence fell like snow, its own blessing on the upturned faces, which waited and waited and waited.

The Keeper began to raise his hands.

And I grabbed his arm. He turned to me, and I sensed his confusion through the mask. "Come with me," I said.

"I cannot—"

"Not forever," I said. "Just for Yuletide."

When he held his breath, the stars paused, and waited.

"And then," I said, "we'll return." Though I thought that when we did, we should bring a cat.

He allowed himself to be drawn away from the balcony, leaving the crowd, still unblessed, in a confused rumble. I led us down the winding staircase, out the great hall, past the gates, and into the grounds. When they saw us, the crowd, which had been still muttering, let out an almighty silence.

We walked forward, into the crowd, which parted a little for us. A few people confusedly raised their greenery, then lowered their arms. Tradition had been broken. The Time Keeper was not in his tower; he walked among the people.

I kept tugging at his hand, until we were in the spot where my parents stood with my brothers and sister and their families. My niece slid down from her mother's arms and looked curiously up at my companion. The Keeper came down to one knee, so that he was at eye level with the child, and removed his mask. My niece regarded him quite seriously for a moment, before she turned to me and took my hand, and together, we all made our way back to the village, just as new snow began to fall.

The Wild Man of Uril

Mijmark

Othune had won the honour after the tough competition, which had begun at dawn. Driven by a fear of failing and disappointing everyone yet again, he'd persevered for hours. The oldest contender for the privilege; it was his last chance. As his reward for his triumph, the Hethamen then baptised him in the river as one of theirs, an acolyte. Just one rite remained to prove himself worthy enough to join these town elders and become one of them.

In his village called Gemmas, they would celebrate the Festival of Water tomorrow. Othune had to retrieve the offering from the sacred Spring of Uril before sunset. He'd been there before, during other solemn homilies. It would be an easy task to carry a river-clay urn by himself up to this local headwater of the town's river.

But still, his sometimes-dour patriarch remarked once alone from the crowds, while they walked together. "Finally, white clothing doesn't suit you, boy."

Hadn't he pushed his son enough? What more could Father want? The bleached tunic custom was how adolescents showed they were mature of age yet not of experience. From now on he'd badger his boy to marry.

After midday meal, Othune began his journey from the Houses of Man to the Houses of Wild. The passing of the day while he ventured deeper into this timeless place soon calmed him from his sullen mood. Here different rules governed whoever called nature home – all the forest denizens, both the ordinary and the extraordinary. Individuals changed, yet the people of Wild always stayed the same.

Under the live oaks and pines, the pungent scent of mugwort kindled forgotten memories as he brushed by them while listening to the inhabitants: noisy jays, the quail covey darting into the sagebrush and a descent of comical woodpeckers targeting a dead cedar already laden with holes.

By the time he reached the ridge where the steep dell sloped away then fell abruptly, his worries had abated. He listened for the water's rill as he scaled a slight trail along the abrupt downslope into the tangled grove of the valley. The harsh scrub encircling gnarled oak trunks had thickened, yet he managed to find the seldom-used path through the dense understory. This ancient coppice soon released the earthy scent of mushrooms as he trod moist humus. By following the trickling noises, he emerged through a stand of alder trees onto a flattened boulder, a water-worn, granite platform that jutted far into the spring – just as he remembered it.

He stepped out onto the holy site and saw both a deer drinking and a man drinking on the other side. Yet there was only one other living being here.

This man wore no clothing. His hair and skin had the fur and colour of a deer. His head had antlers, his nose was but a black slit of a button and his feet were hooves. This deer stood on two legs and had hands. Its forward-looking eyes and thick beard portrayed a calm yet weathered face. Crouched down, it sipped the surface of the stream running over a stone lip. Once finished, he raised his head and gave a blessing to the spring.

Those were the same ritual gestures that Othune used.

He moved closer. The deer-man looked up. They just gazed at each other. His whiteless eyes glistened, like an animal. However, their verdant green colour had black pupils, like a man. He seemed intense, feral, yet a shy sincerity also greeted the lad.

Then the wild-man looked down and easily disappeared behind the underbrush of mule-fat and willows downstream. Othune could hear no sound of him moving, so he sat, watching that very spot. He couldn't forget those viridian eyes. If he stayed still, perhaps he might convince the wild-man that he meant no harm.

In time he immersed his toes into the pristine stream. Here at the beginning of summer, birds merely murmured how hot it was that afternoon. However, by the trickling Spring of Uril, under the branches of tall bay and alder trees, cool water eddied over his feet.

When the shadows of afternoon stretched long, the mule-fat clumps began to permeate the air, a keen scent of sweet clarity always given off before dusk. At long last he put on his boots, performed the rite, filled the bright indigo urn, hoisted it and scrambled up the steep canyon.

At the ridge he yelled, "We dance the Festival of Water in Gemmas tomorrow. It's the village downstream." He then returned home in troubled haste. He knew what to expect.

* * *

It didn't surprise him when Father and two Hethamen rounded a familiar madrone tree. He thoroughly expected scorn, so he cast his eyes down. "I'm sorry. But I'm home before—"

"Quiet!" His father approached and snatched the deep-blue jar from him so forcefully he snapped the strap. "You made me feel *proud* this morning. Now you bring me *shame*!" Othune bit his lip and closed his eyes. Not only did the seizing hurt, but his remorse doubled. He almost hid his tears – almost.

Father presented the offering, "I deeply apologise. Our family will never dishonour traditions again. The sun hasn't yet set."

The younger Hetham had already taken the indigo vessel and sped away while the older matron remained. "The lad is young, still in white."

"Not that young, but he'll learn; he'll learn." In a sombre, curious tone she continued, "We did worry. What stayed you?"

Othune made the proper response and bow. "Thank you generous Hetham. The holy site was…of such beauty; time escaped me."

She considered him for a moment. "You know…this means someone else will pour the water tomorrow?"

"Yes, my Hetham." Othune wiped away extra tears while trying to hide this act.

"Do consider him worthy again."

His father's plea drew an impassioned regard. "His chances are forfeit. You remember very well how only one can be chosen." She curled both hands and hooked them together in the ritual gesture. "At peace."

"At peace." His father mimicked her and watched her depart. Othune kept silent. "You shamed yourself and me today. I hope you learn from this mistake."

He finally nodded. He'd escaped a beating, and his father was once again becoming someone he loved, not feared.

"Go home now. Tell your mother I'll be late. Keep this matter between us, until…" Father shook his head, cast his gaze down to his feet before he walked quickly away.

Othune didn't go home though, but wound his way to the outskirts of Gemmas, skirting trees, rounding a large wood pile, then a domed stone kiln and finally stopping at the shack where his mother's uncle lived alone. Great-Uncle was a man-loving-man, although now a widower.

Of all his family, he liked his great-uncle the best, a skilled craftsman of river-clay. Of all his teachers, his great-uncle remembered many tales and traditions other elders had forgotten or never learned. Of all people, his uncle told him of other distant and strange towns, of their different ways, and shared funny stories the serious Hethamen never mentioned. Out of everyone else, Othune shared secrets with him.

The lad revealed everything while his great-uncle prepared fragrant tea. Othune watched the amber liquid fill his cup before asking, "Did I see a wild-man? Or was he a spirit?"

"Well, this is a sacred time." His great-uncle's soft voice spoke slowly and clearly. "A spirit would not say anything. Did he speak?"

"Only to bless the water, like we do here." He looked up, enthused. "I told him we're dancing the festival tomorrow."

Those wizened brows lifted. "Maybe he'll come."

* * *

During the entire ceremony on the riverbank, Othune kept peering around for any sign or glimpse, to no avail.

The wild-man did come, but he'd forgotten how to walk among town-people. Instead, he hid under a porch and observed, until dogs came barking and snarling. Only the watchful eyes of Great-Uncle noticed the disturbance and glimpsed the retreat.

By the next month, the heat grew towards afternoon and buzzards moved high over crisp hills of yellow and drab green. Over and over and over again, that vivid stare haunted Othune. At long last, he'd summoned up the courage and slipped away from duties one lazy afternoon.

Uril Spring was merely drops and silty mud. On a rock next to the puddles, four green acorns tied together with yucca fibre draped over a serpentine stone. He recognised the offering and took out a gift, a polished, olive-wood flute, and set it on the same rock before speaking loudly, "I'll be making a salt journey to the ocean in a few days. I won't come back until the cold mornings return."

Months later, Othune managed to escape to Uril as soon as he had the chance. It hadn't rained yet, but the earth was releasing water held deep underground as a tiny trickle. Both the offering and the flute were gone.

He scampered up the canyon wall and soon returned, holding an obsidian chip. Then he lightly scratched atop a pale boulder, drawing the mark of the river-clay. "The Wine Ceremony is tomorrow. Please come." He hoped the man who'd lost his name would enjoy his father's bladder of fine vintage he left under the glyph.

The wild-man was watching, there on the opposite side, behind the alder stand, under the dry creek bank. He was always watching.

* * *

Othune's great-uncle urged him into his shack that evening. He cut some acorn-bread to offer him and warned, "This wild-man of Uril Spring, he left here long ago, before my time. He belonged to Redwood's house by marriage and carved serpentine rock.

"Jealousy from another exposed him as a man-loving-man, one who'd disgraced his wife with false vows. Grandmother Redwood and the Hethamen banished him. He became lost; he became Wild. You see, wild-men are as timeless as the forests they inhabit – part man, part spirit. They do things without meaning. You may be frightening him."

Othune remembered tales of how wild-men could return to live among the Houses of Man again. He also remembered that intense stare of verdant green. "Do hunters know where he lives?"

"The Houses of Wild – nowhere and everywhere."

He wouldn't trouble his great-uncle with more. His distress came instead from a harsher father, more and more displeased as time lagged on. Yet the youth felt no shame any more when Father criticised his more frequent visits with Great-Uncle to learn river-clay craft.

Those two men tolerated each other – one capriciously smiling and the other brooding in silence. Yet Mother always respected the oldest living member of her family, someone who'd chosen his status with the Hethamen's blessings.

* * *

Othune's attention to daily duties waned. How could he be frightening that lost soul? While helping his great-uncle work the clays after the first deep rain soaked the arid ground, he stole away and raced northward, enthused by the savoury smells of wet sagebrush saturating misty air.

Over the swollen pool, right beside his nearly washed-out icon was another recent glyph. Othune recognised the Serpentine Code and burst into a wide smile. "So! You are here!" He set down a cotton towel that held rolls of pickled grape leaf stuffed with boiled acorn-mash, dried fruits and honey-butter. He stayed, trying to see through the understory brush once more into those timorous eyes.

Weeks later his parents had business with another village and left him alone. He was quick to visit again. Uril Spring was running strongly. The heavier rains had washed away everything.

He offered a woven pouch filled with colourful yarns and strings. "They're better than yucca fibres. They'll begin singing Weaving Songs soon and we welcome all Houses of Wild to join us."

He stayed quiet, standing still after speaking for many minutes with unwavering patience. In time, he noticed movement through low branches and slowly shifted about to place himself better. He caught a glimpse of the deer-man's shoulder, one antler, and some of that kind face hiding behind wispy willows. Once again, one intense eye peered into his. Once again that verdant gaze seemed troubled, struggling between timorous concern and benign grace.

Soon the Wild-House denizen arose and pointed. Othune turned to where he who was once a man directed and saw the Serpentine Code drawn across flat rock. A crudely woven basket lay there, holding honeycomb, plump mushrooms and a handsomely polished serpentine stone. He'd never seen one so forest-green and jet-black. A slight reflection on its sheen beamed back his smiling face when he held it.

When he spun around, the lost one had disappeared. Why again?

The lad said meekly, "Thank you," and slowly made his way home.

* * *

On the first visit of New Year, the heavy rains of winter chilled him to the bone, despite his oilskin coat. The creek was roaring and foaming dirty yellow. With feet so numb from cold, it was difficult to find his footing as he descended slippery mud.

The grime hid his bruised, blackened eye. It covered the puffed up, purple corner of his mouth. He shouted over chattering teeth, over deafening torrents beating rocks against each other, "We're celebrating the World Blessing in Gemmas. No one comes here this year. I…I – have been too long in white. My parents…they'll be sending me to another village. I'm to marry." He shouted the news again, for he didn't know if the wild-man could even hear him.

Before he returned home, Othune disobeyed his father's command outright and snuck away to visit his great-uncle. He pitied the man who'd lost his name and wanted to save him; perhaps Great-Uncle knew how. However, the youth also feared being ridiculed or even shunned by everyone else if he attempted anything, or even voiced his concerns beyond the confines of his confidant's shack.

After revealing his troubles, he summoned up the courage. "What if I refuse my parents? What if I declare myself like you, a man-loving-man and never make those vows?"

"Are you?"

"I don't know. What do you think?"

After a long silence, his great-uncle replied, "I think you should ask the wild-man."

* * *

One week before the Moon Ceremony, the time for marriages, he'd made his decision, skipped supper with a bad excuse to his protesting parents, shut himself in his room and waited to escape that evening. He hid under his father's fur-lined cloak to disguise himself from any watchful eye of neighbours or Hethamen.

This time he took a different, longer way there to hide his trek. He hiked uphill and around the ridge running across the valley floor. He discovered a clearing once he entered the lower reaches to the dell of Uril Springs. Lying over one side, a hollowed-out digger pine had recently fallen over, propped up by a stony overhang. Underneath this lean-to lay a grassy bed and pillow, woven from the very yarn Othune had given the wild-man. Closeby were all the other gifts that he'd brought for him, every last one.

He removed his shirt and trews, spreading them out, and lay underneath his father's blanketing cloak upon this mat of straw. Still, the frosty chill pricked him like iced needles; his shivering increased. Maybe an hour passed until the nearly full moon rose high over the canopy…until he lightly fell asleep.

Othune woke in the colder half of the night, for a thawing breath fell on the nape of his neck. The wild-man was behind him. He had the faint smell of a washed animal. A calloused hand gently touching Othune's temple, then his cheeks, which had sprouted a soft beard all these months later. He kept patiently still, afraid to frighten this timid one. Othune could feel comforting heat from the deer-man's furry body once the wild-man nuzzled up to him, embraced him lightly and cradled him in welcomed warmth.

The lad was hesitant to speak, to think of anything except for that soft, furry body radiating comfort. The deer-man's sheltering frame breathed in deeply when his arms surrounded the youth. That snug embrace made Othune feel cherished and revered. His bliss and smile lasted until he fell asleep within those hirsute arms.

* * *

He woke well into the next morning, lying down with his clothes and cloak blanketing him. In plain view was his likeness, handsomely carved and polished out of serpentine, a paradigm of artistry.

On a flat stone beyond, however, the glyphs of ritual, marriage and honour sprawled across its face. Nothing else remained. The wild-man had carefully removed everything.

Othune felt empty, defeated. He had trouble speaking. "I – I'm to be wed in six days. You are welcome to come."

When he returned, he avoided his great-uncle's shack, for he knew Father was there or closeby. As expected, his mother busied herself just outside their home. When he approached, she buttonholed him.

"Where were you?" Her sharp, shrill voice carried. She was beyond concern of neighbours' opinions, and she wouldn't interfere later.

Last winter, Father's temper had risen when Othune voiced his anger. Today it would come from Othune's silence. He would remember the soft, furry warmth on his back instead of every lash from a thick belt.

* * *

After the ceremonies, he moved into the other village, into his bride's house, into the family's matriarchy as was the custom. These people had lost their river-clay artist to illness. They welcomed Othune's talent. He soon took to work with fury and drive.

From welcome to worry, public opinion eventually painted him with an ungrateful brush, of being indifferent to his betrothed, for he kept declining them of tradition and custom, of visiting friends as a new union of two. The longer they shared a life together, the more time he took to perfect his skill.

In time, a messenger from Gemmas told them that Great-Uncle was dying of the brain-fever, so the two journeyed to bid him farewell. They managed to arrive in time for the Ceremony of Passage, to be present when Great-Uncle took his last breath. That day, instead of taking comfort in company, of accepting his wife's sympathy and embraces, he sought silence and remembrance in his confidant's now-lifeless shack.

Othune exited hours later to overhear elderly women talking about himself, about his excursions to Uril Spring. It seemed his ranting great-uncle revealed everything and anything to everyone and anyone. No wonder his parents were wary earlier.

Once back at his new home, his new wife became more cautious. He figured his folks told her both credence and coincidence. In time their union soured. He honed his craft to an obsessive perfection.

He finished polishing a river-clay urn one day for the Festival of Water to come, giving it a glossy shine of deep blue. When he got home, he found his personal chest wide open. In the waste tip outside, he saw the gifts from the wild-man that he'd kept as precious reminders, now ruined and destroyed. He heard the pounding of metal on rock and once out of the house, he found her breaking that serpentine likeness of him with a hammer.

Without a word spoken, he turned and walked away, his back to her screaming rant. He walked away, his back to that house, his back to that town. He kept walking, carrying that urn along and marched for two days straight until he was once again at the sacred Spring of Uril.

He stepped out onto the flat rock that pushed into the pool, smiling and full of hope. It was just as he remembered. The scenery welcomed his nostalgia of that sacred day exactly one year ago. He called out, "I am no longer wed. I am no longer who I was."

Following the ritual he'd learned years ago, he filled the indigo urn, held it high and baptised himself with a steady trickle while chanting. "I sever myself from the House of Man. I belong to the House of Wild now. I choose to live here – with you."

He waited for hours, as if in a trance of benign patience, peering through wispy willow twigs, mule-fat clumps, russet branches and trunks of alders. He waited for the slightest movement or any other sign of his dear man.

When his endurance waned towards the aromas of evening, he crossed the rill. There among the willows and mule-fat he could smell decay to his left. He crept along and peered at the creek bank, under the overhang.

The lost man's body was already part earth. It lay crouched inside the twisted branches of young alders, tightly clasping many of those now-decomposing gifts.

No one ever goes to Uril Spring anymore. The Hethamen warn of the wild-man there.

Only a Summer Love

Trixie Nisbet

I had watched Peteris painting in the forest even before I had form enough for him to see me. I knew immediately that I wanted him as my summer love.

He was young, barely able to produce the straggle of bohemian beard that seemed to symbolize his freedom and disregard for convention. He lived for his art, working on paintings and sculpture according to his whim. His attention flitted. I saw in him a nature as transient as my own.

I drifted directly into his line of sight as he painted the great oak tree in the clearing. He looked through me, though I fancy he perceived an essence of me which he brushed onto the canvas in bold strokes of vivid green.

It was springtime. All around me, the Dzintari forest blossomed with new growth, and I felt in its regeneration the promise of my own revival. Velnius still constrained me in his vortex, but the equinox had passed, and I could feel myself becoming ever more corporeal. I reached out to Peteris as he painted. He felt me as a swirl of breeze. I teased at his hair and stroked the lean line of his cheek and jaw. Instinctively he knew I was there. His curious eyes scanned the clearing, but he could see only the change of season in the surrounding trees and sprouting greenery.

I followed him into the city. He has an untidy studio set into one of the narrow streets that branch from the cobbles of Riga's Town Hall Square. He deliberately made his way to stand at the square's centre. Instinct again. His canvas smock undulated to a draft that didn't stir the red-and-white flags which adorned the ornate buildings around him. He held his chin high; his eyes scanned again. I knew that he sought me in the wind.

It was a few days later that I was able to appear. Velnius could hold me no longer. Though he whirled the sky, I now had presence enough to seep from his control.

Peteris was sculpting. His slim hands were wet with clay which he kneaded and pulled, shaping a figure. Deftly, and with great concentration, he fashioned a woman. She was dancing, her arms a-flow with movement. He took his wooden tools to her face, smoothing her brow and drawing out her cheekbones and chin. He took great care with her eyes capturing an intelligence, and a headstrong sense of purpose. He was pleased with the result – as was I: the resemblance was uncanny.

I danced from the air, appearing before him in the clutter of his studio, a living, breathing version of his figurine. I was naked and could feel the warm spring air caress my skin. I revelled in the touch of the wooden floor under my feet.

Peteris showed no great surprise. I think he had been aware of me for some time and looked on me with awe and fascination. I wondered at his immediate acceptance of me. Did he see the desire and determination in my eyes? I reached out to his face and relished the unfamiliar sensation of physical contact. He, with the acceptance of youth, welcomed the embrace. We kissed, keen and needy. I felt the slide of his clay-slimed arms around me.

* * *

Peteris painted me and sculpted me. I used him as my summer love. He used me as his muse and his obsession. There was more nature in me, he said, than the whole of the Dzintari forest.

We walked often to the clearing with the oak tree. He sensed that I was more comfortable there than among the stone streets and spires of Riga. There he would paint me, blending my image with the vibrant colours of summer. It was as if he instinctively knew what I was. But still he peered at me over his easel and pierced me with his artist's gaze. "What are you?" he asked.

I basked in the slants of sunlight, like a plant savouring their warmth. "From mythology, you might call me a laumas," I said. "A woodland sprite. A spirit of summer." I sought his reaction.

He had guessed. And his concern betrayed itself in a wavering of his hand. My painted face warped on his canvas as if smeared into the background vegetation. "What happens," his voice was suddenly young and vulnerable, "at the summer's end?"

I smiled at him without humour, hinting my apology. This question, in many varieties, always arose at about this time. My spirit is fickle. Each year I select my companion, knowing our partnership to be temporary. After a winter spent in Velnius's sky all I crave is the sensation of a physical body. I always get what I want, but my selected partner often wants more. "Ours can be only a summer love," I told him. "My time in this realm is short. By the autumn equinox I must rejoin Velnius and the other sprites suspended in his care."

I saw Peteris react with horror at the mention of Velnius's name. There are legends of him, the one-eyed trickster, leading the host of the dead through the Baltic heavens. The truth, however, is less romantic. Velnius has command of the wind and, during the winter months, he acts as sentinel to the summer spirits, guarding their ethereal hibernation.

I sidled across the clearing and stroked the worry from Peteris's brow. "We must make the most of our limited time." I drew him into the shade of the oak tree and waved up into its verdant branches. "My mortal time is always measured by this tree. I am yours," I assured him, "until the last leaf falls." I lay on the blanket of lush ferns and grass. A whirl of warm breeze plucked a bobbled leaf from the tree above us; it spiralled like a sliver of jigsaw as I pulled Peteris down beside me.

* * *

A summer is merely a breath of time. But a breath was all that we were allowed. Peteris and I celebrated the midsummer festival, garlanded in fragrant wreaths of vegetation, and I had him make love to me beneath the Lingo moon of the year's shortest night. From then I felt the contraction of the days. I too felt squeezed and constrained by the lengthening night. Peteris and I spent less time in the forest. The oak tree was still covered in green leaves, but the growing number that littered the forest floor were like sand grains in an hourglass telling of the fleeting nature of our time together.

Peteris turned his hand to ceramics, creating miniature facades of the ornate churches and towers that spear the Riga skyline. He would enamel them in bold colours, often incorporating my silhouette into a doorway or window. A favoured subject was the lavish brick frontage of the Melngalvju Nems which sold well to visitors of the studio. Always, Peteris would stand at the very centre of Town Hall Square to fashion slices of clay into the shape of the building.

Here, he again felt the mystic wind that failed to stir the surrounding flags. He told me that he fancied the orientation of the buildings funnelled the breeze from any direction to this central point. My previous loves hadn't the sensibility to notice this phenomenon. Peteris was unique. He questioned me with a look, and I felt that he deserved to know the truth.

I indicated the white stone plinth that stood nearby. The armoured depiction of Roland, the city's protector, I explained, was not the only statue in the square. "There is a monument here," I told him, "to Velnius, god of the air and skies."

Peteris looked around, confused. Then he realised. “It’s right here,” he said holding out his hands. “Composed of wind.”

“A column of curdled air,” I confirmed. “Now that you know it is here, you will see it in the swirl of leaves in autumn, and the dance of snowflakes in winter.”

Peteris stepped free of the patch of wind as if it chilled him. “He’s watching you, isn’t he?” he said. “Waiting to take you back – take you away from me.”

“That is the cycle of my life,” I said. The words, for once, snagged in my throat like a sob. I reached out a hand to Peteris. I had thought to console him. But I found myself longing for his embrace. To my surprise, I was engulfed in sadness. Peteris folded me into his slim arms. With my face over his shoulder, he couldn’t see my tears. “I am a sprite of summer,” I whispered. “My time with you draws to a close.”

I felt the tenseness of his body. “I will not let him take you,” he said.

* * *

At the approach of the autumn equinox, I felt Velnius’s eye upon me. Day and night were becoming equal in length. Summer relinquished its heat and its glow of life. I felt the heavy fatigue of the trees as they dropped their leaves, and I sensed the coming of the snow that would chill the city and the surrounding countryside.

“I have never seen snow,” I told Peteris.

"This year, you will." He gestured from his studio door along the narrow street. "We will kick our way through the drifts. We will cross the square and defy Velnius to his face."

I admired his passion, but managed only a weak sigh. "That is not possible."

His artist's eyes miss nothing. He frowned. "Are you unwell?" he asked.

"I am like the trees," I said. "I become dormant in winter. That is why I ride the wind till springtime when I can blossom again."

"You look tired," he said, "and cold."

He led me to a chair by the fire, adding another dried log to the blaze. I had never been cared for like this. Usually, my summer love would accept from the beginning that we were compelled to part. I would appear, and I would vanish. There would be no drawn-out decline. I had chosen Peteris, as I had chosen so many others before him, simply for his youth and vitality. I hadn't realized that he would be so different.

"I will look after you." He placed a paint-speckled sheet around my shoulders.

I hadn't the strength to disagree with him, and was soon asleep.

After another week, I could no longer manage the walk into the forest. My legs were losing their strength and ached to their bones.

"How many forest sprites exist?" Peteris asked me.

I gazed up beyond the spires and clocktowers to where wisps of morning cloud scudded across the sky. "Most sprites are content to ride the wind with Velnius," I told him. "A few, like myself, follow the seasons of the forest to experience a more physical existence. But my vitality wanes." I managed a forced smile. "I am fortunate to know only the balm of summer, and not the harshness of winter." I slumped, and Peteris supported me on his arm. I had already survived beyond my usual summer span of life. "I don't think my physical body can endure much longer," I said.

Peteris looked suddenly so young and frightened. His eyes were pleading. "I can't lose you."

At the centre of the square, a whirlwind formed. Every particle of dust and grit was swept up from the cobbles to gather like a translucent column of smoke. The wind swirled the dirt into a shadowy figure. His outline was vague, but I knew that, with his single eye, Velnius stared down at me.

"It is time for you to return," sighed the wind.

Velnius was right. I could hardly stand. I longed to shudder myself free of this aching mortal body and drift into the lightness and freedom of the breeze. But I clung to Peteris – and I felt the strength of his resolve as he turned to defy the god of the skies.

"She stays with me!" he yelled. "There's nothing you can do to prevent that."

Velnius shimmered, specks of dust sparking in the slant of morning light. "You have contrived to prevent her return," snapped the wind. "But at what cost?"

I could support myself no longer, and slumped into Peteris's embrace. My life was drained. I was drying into a husk of my former self. Peteris could see the change in me. Perhaps, too, he saw my attempt to meld with the breeze, to be borne away under Velnius's winter care. But I remained human, bound to my physical body as if held here by the clasp of Peteris's arms. He was defiant of Velnius, but his eyes were clouded with uncertainty.

"What have you done?" I asked.

With a soft whisper of falling dust, the image of Velnius dispersed. It had planted a seed of suspicion in my mind and was no longer needed.

The skin of my hands itched and I felt them crisp like old bark as I stroked tenderly at Peteris's cheek. Our eyes connected. "What have you done?" I asked again.

* * *

Peteris took me to the forest and led me to the clearing. My progress was slow, painful and unsteady. At times Peteris practically carried me crunching over the uneven leaf-strewn ground. There, at the clearing's centre, stood the oak, national tree of Latvia, and the measure of my mortal summer life. Its skeletal branches zig-zagged into bare twigs. All the leaves had fallen – except one.

One leaf anchored me to my human existence. But it was no ordinary leaf. It was coated in clay. A ceramic leaf that was bound to its branch and enamelled a bright summer green in defiance of the season.

Peteris gripped my hand. "I won't let him take you," he said.

A wind plucked at his hair, then swirled, twisting the dry leaves from the ground in a rustling frenzied vortex. More substantial than the dust in the square, the manifestation of Velnius took shape towering above us, as tall as the denuded oak. His single eye stared down at me.

"To hold back nature," he thundered, "has dire consequences."

I felt the words reverberate around me. I knew he referred to my weakened body. Like the forest, I grew dry and brittle, fading like the glow of summer. Peteris still held me. Did he see me withering before his eyes?

"I don't care," he called back.

The wind whirled and screeched around him, buffeting him, scratching at him with the debris swept up from the forest floor. He shielded me with his arms and screwed up his eyes against the onslaught. "That leaf will never fall. You shall not take her back." He paused as if to stay the emotion that trembled in his voice. "I love her."

It was like a spell. A charm which blew apart the leaves of Velnius's whirling image.

For a moment, my pain vanished. Though supremely weary, I raised my head and felt more human than at any time of my summer existence. I pulled Peteris to me for a passionate kiss. He was my ultimate summer love. Never had someone fought for me like this.

Our mouths met – and my lips crumbled like dry paper. I drew back as he stroked at my face which flaked at his touch.

Somewhere in the wind, Velnius sighed.

Peteris held me at arm's length, confused and dismayed. "What have I done to you?"

The answer was obvious to both of us.

"My time is over," I said, sad and resigned.

Despite my desiccation, Peteris drew us together for a final embrace. I felt his careful kiss soft on my fragile lips.

He turned, intending to climb the oak. But, as he approached the trunk, Velnius swept him upwards in a gale of dead leaves. Peteris floated up to the branch where the ceramic-coated leaf still clung. He reached out and broke it free.

I felt the instant relief as Velnius returned Peteris to my side. He didn't need to speak. His eyes were swamped with sorrow and a trace of apology.

"Ours could only ever be a summer love," I said. I reached down to the ground and placed an acorn into Peteris's hand, closing his fingers gently around it. I allowed myself to relax thankfully into the air. My voice whispered from the breeze. "I need you, Peteris," I said. "Watch for me in the spring." My voice faded away. "I shall find you, my love, because you hold my heart."

A Midnight Hunger

Aggie Novak

That first midnight, when I visit your village to feast on nightmares, you're the only one who sees me.

You children think you're safe. You always do. The others wear river-smoothed stones with holes bored through the centres around their necks, and sleep with knives under their pillows. Babies rest in cradles with thick circles carved into the floor around them.

Such protections are often enough to drive away the nochnitsi, my much weaker sisters. Nochnitsi have no thoughts but of hunger, of pain, and of fear. It makes them easy to control. But I am Polunochnitsa, Lady Midnight, Night Hag, and Shadow Maiden, and I am not so easily deterred. Stones and blades of iron do nothing more than itch at my skin.

Even dreams that start sweet turn sour when I settle on a child's chest, their deeper instincts alerting them to my presence. I suck it all in – the horrors of their imaginings sustain me. But you – when I get to you – there is no fear.

That's not to say your dreams are sweet. Not at all. You dream of a child, your sister, laid out in the banya white-lipped and stiff-limbed. The healing steam had failed to heal her. There is sadness in you, yes, for you are not a monster – not yet – but there is curiosity too. About where little Sofiya's soul would go now, if it would be possible to go after her and bring her back.

No. I hiss the answer into your mind. *It is not, she is gone forever.*

I admit, while this is true, I say it to upset you, hoping that distress will season your dreams just how I like them. But you accept my pronouncement with a little sadness and no shock – you already held the truth in your heart.

Then you open your eyes.

I stiffen. It's not often that I am taken by surprise. I would have thought I'd be angry, but I find I am intrigued. I want to see what you will do.

From any other child – and most adults – I would expect screaming. Cries for help. To be shoved away while my victim flees from bed in a panic. Your parents sleep beside you, all three of you pressed close to the warmth of the stove. It would be so easy for you to rouse them.

But you reach out. Not in terror or in rage. And not for your parents.

Who are you? you ask. Your tiny fingers stroke my silky black hair.

To you I appear as another child, though a very strange one. My black hair falls straight to my ankles, a curtain of night. In contrast, my skin is moon white – or corpse pale. Unlike you, with your pink, round cheeks and gently curling hair, there is nothing soft about me. Sharp teeth poke into my lips, and nails like claws grip your bedding. I have the skeletal thinness of starvation, for I am always so very hungry.

I am Polunochnitsa. The more you stare at me with those wide, curious eyes, the more I want to know about you in turn. It's part of my power – or my weakness. We spirits bend our nature to those who believe in us, are shaped by the lore humans create about us. The less you fear me, the less terrifying I become.

Polunochnitsa. You say the word slowly, lingering on the syllables. You pat my hair again. *So pretty.*

What is your name? My name is but a title, and holds little power. But yours? Once I know it I will always be able to find you again.

Roza.

Wild and thorny. Pretty and sweet. It suits you.

Go back to sleep, Roza, I croon. With the power of your name behind them, my words act as a spell. Your eyelids sink shut, your breathing slows once more. *Sweet dreams.*

And they are. I gorge myself on them – the images of myself, crouched on your chest, your musings of our encounter. I linger in the midnight, relishing the taste, before finally letting you go, so that you can sleep yourself towards morning.

I will be here, at midnight, waiting. We will meet again.

You have always had the most delicious dreams.

* * *

Our second midnight comes later than I expect. It's my fault, of course. I got distracted – the night is long and full of terrors, and they all taste so good.

You are changed. Not a child anymore, but a young woman, on the cusp of marriage. I see your future in your dreams. A man called Pyotr Petrovich from a village a day's travelling away. You've met him once, and he's as boring as his name, both in appearance and demeanour. He works a farm, just like your father does. You will help him and raise his children, just like your mother. The next time you see him will be your wedding.

Once again, your dreams are neither fantasy nor nightmare – your lot in life met with a grim acceptance.

What if he is cruel, I taunt. *What if the children you must bear kill you with their birth*? *What if they are weak and sickly things*?

But these are thoughts you have already turned endlessly in your mind, worrying away the sharp sting of their edges.

They slide off you like droplets, and your dreams turn to other things. Slender fingers around yours. A tickle of breath at your ear. Soft skin and smooth cheeks. A hand at your thigh and a building ache between your legs.

I want to laugh in delight. It's not men you dream of.

I twist your gentle imaginings into something else.

Sharp teeth at your throat. Nails digging in. Hair pulled, skin pinched. Pain—

But you don't shrink away. The pain only sweetens your pleasure, and oh, the flavour is exquisite.

You open your eyes.

Hello, Polunochitsa. A rosy flush spreads from your chest to your cheeks and your breath comes fast. Under my palms, your heartbeat races. *I was starting to think I dreamt you up.* You twist a lock of my hair around one finger.

Roza.

At that, you smile. *You remembered.*

Of course. I never forget the taste of a delicious dream.

You push up onto your elbows, bringing our faces close. So close that the heat of your breath warms me. It tastes of honey.

Will you leave again? As fast as you did last time?

I press against the staccato rhythm of your heart. *I must. I exist only at midnight.*

Is that not awful, to be so trapped?

Trapped? I flash my pointed teeth. *You misunderstand. I live in all the midnights. Every one that ever was and will ever be. I couldn't be more free.*

Your soft brown eyes widen, pink lips part. Your free hand squeezes tight around my wrist. *Take me with you.*

I don't give you time to change your mind. In a blink, your bed is gone. The rumbling snores of your father and the gentle glow of the stove's fading coals vanish.

Around us, the night is bright.

The light of the moon, unhindered by clouds, reflects back off the white of snow and ice. A flat expanse stretches endlessly before us, shining wetly.

Where are we? You turn, taking in the half-buried rocks at our feet, the sparse, bare-branched trees at our backs. *What is this place?*

You haven't loosened your grip on me – just as well, for my presence protects you from the bitter chill of the winter wind.

Vodskaya Pyatina, your people call it. It is not so far from your home. I laugh. *Or perhaps farther than you could ever hope to go.* Human measurements mean little to one who travels from midnight to midnight. *This is one of my favourite midnights.*

It's beautiful. Your brown eyes glimmer, filled with the sight. You turn to me, and for a moment, I see myself reflected in your eyes. Young and lovely and as radiant as the moon. *Why is it your favourite?*

It is rare, here, to find a winter night so clear. Almost like daylight, from what I've seen in dreams.

I expect questions. What about the white nights, you might ask. Those nights when the sun never dips below the horizon, or when it stays close enough that true dark never falls before it's rising again. What about those midnights? Then look at me with pity when I reveal my slight omission – that all midnights *except* for those are mine, that the sun and I may never meet.

But you don't ask.

All you say is, *It's better.*

I twist in the circle of your grip, shift so our palms are flush and our fingers entwine. *And besides, who doesn't enjoy the feeling of walking on water? Come on.*

Wait, this is—?

The sea, I confirm.

Then there's no more need to pull you along, you're running right beside me, laughing wildly into the night.

We run until your bare feet – protected from frostbite by me – slip on a slick patch of ice. Clutching each other, we tumble to the frozen surface of the gulf. My legs between yours. Your hands at my forearms. My hair, long as it ever was, shrouding us from the world.

It's you who kisses me. Dreams are the only thing I ever took from a human without asking. Warm lips, wet tongues, clashing teeth. You kiss with the impatient, greedy hunger of someone who has wanted something for a long time and doesn't know when, or if, they'll ever get it again.

There's nothing gentle between us. Your grip is firm enough to leave marks, my bites sharp enough to break skin. Our kisses taste like blood.

I wouldn't have it any other way, for if you are hungry, then I am ravenous.

Afterwards, bodies bruised from each other and from the ice, I take you back to your bed and your midnight. Back beneath your blanket as if you'd never left.

Go to sleep, Roza. I breathe the words against your mouth. I'll see you soon.

And this time I won't forget.

* * *

There are many more midnights after that. Some last a minute, some an hour, some longer than we care to count. I take you to a thousand quiet midnights like the first. In deep forests, on empty plains, on the banks of rivers, and the peaks of mountains. All places we can be alone, with each other.

We talk, between kisses, and one night you say *I want to see you feed.* And so I show you how I feast on nightmares.

Must you get so close to them? you ask, after I climb from the bed of a young woman near your own age.

Yes. I relish the scent of your jealousy.

You tangle your fingers in my hair and pull our foreheads close. *Has there ever been another like me*?

I know what you mean – have I ever shared with another human, the way that I have with you? And of course I have. My life is infinite and boundless and your lives are so brief. Shooting stars across the night sky. One does grow bored, from time to time.

But each of you are so wonderfully different, and so I say. *No. There's never been anyone like you.*

Not all our midnights are quiet. I take you to Moskva, where men drink and stumble through the streets well past the midnight hour. To feasts and to celebrations. I take you further, too. Not just in space – to the paved streets and fruit trees of Cordoba and the towering pyramids of Giza – but in time. I take you to Delphi, and we go back, watching an abandoned city revert to life. We return to Moskva and watch as it fills with people, more people than you would ever have seen in your ordinary village life, and the buildings creep higher and higher. As the horses are replaced with shrieking metal contraptions that make you clutch at my side and tremble.

What is this? you ask.

The future.

We dance, bodies pressed tight, in a hot mass of writhing bodies. Lights flashing and music blaring. We stand in the open air, at the top of an impossibly tall building, the city spread below us in a sea of lights.

You take it in, like you do every sight I show you, with wide, curious eyes. *It's so loud.*

So we jump to another future, towering feats of concrete and metal, left as empty and silent as ruins. Thick dust coats objects neither of us have names for, and the few plants are brown and withered in dry soil.

Where did they all go?

I shrug. *They moved on.* I don't tell you that I do not know, that I feel just as out of place here as you. That I avoid distant futures, for I am far stronger where and when there are those who believe in me. That I worry if I push too far I'll find that the futures run out, just as the pasts do.

Every time I return you to your own midnight you yank me close and kiss me deep.

Promise you won't forget me, you whisper into the skin at my throat. *Promise you won't grow bored.* I'm your whole world, and you need to know you're mine. And you are, for now.

I promise. Growing bored of you would be like growing bored of a blink.

Of course, the spaces between some of my visits are longer than others. I must feed, and as much as I savour your dreams, they alone are not enough to sustain me. And in the spaces between our midnights, your world goes, your life continues.

You marry that Pyotr Petrovich and seem surprised when I don't care. As if I would worry about a human man replacing me in your dreams. The more time you spend with him, the more your hunger for me grows. We talk less, our mouths too busy with other things.

One visit, I notice the swell of your belly. For the first time, you taste of fear.

The next visit, an infant is cradled to your breast. Its dreams are tasteless, unformed things, but you, you still dream of me.

You were gone so long. You're hurt, I can tell.

I'm sorry. And I am. I forget how fast human lives move.

When I return you to your baby after a midnight that lasts weeks, the thing turns its face from you and screams. You coo and offer it your breast, but you've been gone too long, your scent now unfamiliar.

Just go, you hiss through gritted teeth, not even looking at me.

So I do.

When I return the next night you cling to me with desperate fervour.

I was worried you wouldn't come back. That you'd forget me again until I was old and unlovely.

I will never forget you, Roza. And I won't. My memory is as long as my life.

I love you. You say it like a command, like a prayer.

I trail my fingers over your lips. *And I, you*.

We have changed each other, in our time together. Each of us more like the other.

I am softer, less skeletal – no longer a woman starving. My skin, still pale, has taken on a pink hue, healthy and alive.

You, however, have grown wan, as if your midnights with me have stolen from your time in the sun. The hollows under your eyes are dark as love bites.

Any weight you gained in pregnancy is gone, your collar bones protruding sharply. Eaten up by the twin hungers of me and the babe. As if you don't have enough in you to feed us both.

Come with me, Roza? And I don't mean just for tonight. *You could live out your life at midnight. You need not worry I will forget you, if you stay with me always.*

You tilt your chin up, and my fingers glide down your throat. *You would spend your life with me, just the two of us?*

A part of me wants to remind you that our lives are not the same. That I exist long before and after you. Always have and always will. But that would be cruel, and though I give you pain alongside pleasure, I do not want to hurt you.

Yes. You know that my hunger for you does not fade.

What will happen? To me? To your body once it's run out of midnights.

They will find you dead, here in this midnight. No sign you ever left. *Is that what you want? To spend the rest of your life in the dark*?

You swallow hard under my touch. *If I say no, will you still come back to me? Will we still have our nights together*?

I look to your husband. To your child. Their dreams reek with hunger for you. Your body, your time, your love.

I am not jealous, no. I am immortal and unending and above petty squabbles over human affection. But I find I am annoyed.

I am insatiable, and there's only so much of you to give. And it's true that I do not want to hurt you.

I do not think, I say, *that I wish to share you. And I don't think that they* – I gesture to your family – *wish to either.* I pull back from you, but not too far. I still want you to follow.

The taste of your torment sweetens the air like honey, and a part of me yearns for the nightmares such a choice might bring.

All of your want is for me. Your desire and your longing. But for them you feel duty. Responsibility and obligation. The heavy pull of what is expected, of what you know you should do.

It thrills me that I don't know which force is the more powerful, which you will choose.

Eventually you step towards me, and take my hand in yours.

I want to spend it with you. All of it.

That's all the agreement I need. You blink and we're back in that first midnight. Hands tangled in hair, limbs twined together, teeth biting. So hungry for each other.

* * *

Our last midnight, well, it lasts a lifetime.

Rising Mountain, Made of Glass

Zach Shephard

The breezy platform atop the tower brought Kalanna eye to eye with the setting sun, whose warm kiss did little to calm her worried mind. Far below, the countryside suffered. The green hills had once rolled like bodily curves beneath gossamer bedsheets; the trees had swayed like fingertips brushing a smooth neckline. But now those same features retreated into themselves, cowering away from the dark void of the crater.

The black hole in the land's heart seemed bigger than yesterday. A mountain could rise from that crater. A mountain *had* risen from that crater, every other day for the last few weeks, before always shattering into a million glassy shards. Each time, the gap in the world spread wider. How long before it reached the city? How long before the seven towers of Breev sank into darkness?

The rim of broken glass around the crater's perimeter glinted in the waning daylight, a bright contrast to the nothingness within. Hypnotized by the spectacle, Kalanna didn't notice her visitor until the woman's voice sounded from behind.

"You really should rest," Ferryn said.

"It's too early for bed."

"I didn't mean tonight. You should rest tomorrow."

Kalanna turned. Ferryn's face, framed on one side by a long, loose curl of auburn hair, showed the same unamused concern it always had lately.

"The mountain's coming tomorrow," Kalanna said. "You know I can't miss it."

"It's going to kill you one of these days. Every time you step onto that glass slope, I have to wonder if you'll survive the crash at the end."

Kalanna turned back, squinting against the sun, surveying the ailing land. "Whatever's done this needs to be stopped. The solution's at the summit."

"Oh? So you've reached the top?"

It wasn't a real question. They both knew the answer.

"I get closer every time."

"Closer to not making it back, maybe." Ferryn stepped next to Kalanna, at the edge of the railless platform. The pair took in the sunset and breeze together, awash in the concentrated magic of the high airs. "The council voted to go forward with the festival, despite what's happening out there. You should come. There are plenty of fine gentlemen who'd love a dance under the floating lanterns with Breev's premier heroine." She leaned in close. "And they'd love it even more if she didn't always look so exhausted." Ferryn held up an oval pocket-mirror. Kalanna saw the fatigue in her ocean-blue eyes; she saw the frayed messes of her dirty-blonde braids, needing to be retied.

She eased Ferryn's mirror down. "I don't have the prep time required for gentleman suitors."

Ferryn wrapped her arms around Kalanna's shoulders. "That's what best friends are for." She grinned, kissing Kalanna on the cheek. "The festival's in two days. Think about it, at least."

Ferryn exited. Kalanna remained to watch the sunset, plotting tomorrow's climb.

* * *

She stopped at the rim of the crater, glass shards crunching beneath her boots. Kalanna stared into the black abyss. Anticipation tickled her stomach, like that time-frozen moment before a first kiss. This was it – another chance to fix things. She wondered how many more she'd get.

Sudden light replaced the crater's darkness, violent in its brightness. The land trembled. Kalanna squinted into the hot white glow, once again seeking a glimpse of the mountain's peak as it rose. She finally had to shut her eyes.

The rumbling stopped. The ground settled. Kalanna looked.

The glass mountain stood like a great jagged gem, no longer blinding-white, but instead filled with refracted beams of morning's light. Only its peak continued to blaze bright as a crystal sun, obscuring whatever may lay there.

Kalanna put her foot on a sparkling path surrounded by tall, knife-sharp rocks. "One more time," she told herself, and ran.

Over flat terrain, few could match Kalanna's speed. Climbing, however, was a matter of endurance – and like all things in life, she struggled with pacing. But how could she restrain herself? On every previous climb she'd failed to reach the mountain's peak before it disappeared; going slower wasn't the answer. She had to continue pushing through the pain until she was strong enough to reach the top.

Up the crystal trail, around a bend, over a clear rock that acted like a stair built frustratingly high. Her heart hammered away, but not in the way Ferryn would have liked. Kalanna didn't have time for suitors, nor the festivals where she might find them. The city's safety was more important than the love Ferryn so desperately wanted for her.

At the first switchback the trail rose sharply. Kalanna wouldn't be able to continue running much longer. Like always, she looked ahead for a goal marker: some standout feature along the trail, which she'd resolve to push past before slowing. She found what she needed off to the right, leaning against a tree-like formation of sunstruck crystal.

It was a flat shard of glass like a piece of broken mirror, showing Kalanna an image of herself. But as she got closer, she realized the face looking back wasn't huffing from the climb. This was no reflection – it was another version of her.

"Omro!" the Kalanna in the mirror screamed, desperation in her voice. The real Kalanna slowed. She stopped beside the mirror, chest heaving from the climb. She watched.

The shard shuddered as if jostled by quaking earth, rippling the image within. When the colors settled, Kalanna saw not herself, but a man, reaching for her through a narrow crevice within blackened rock. The dark cave he occupied trembled violently. Chips of glass rained down, bouncing off the lean muscles of his forearm. From between curtains of wild, golden-brown hair, the man looked right at Kalanna – the real Kalanna, there on the trail. Flecks of copper glinted within his concerned sienna eyes.

"Kalanna!" he yelled.

In the mirror, her hand reached toward his. Just before their fingers met, everything crumbled, sweeping the image away.

The shard beside the trail became a true mirror, reflecting the true Kalanna. She picked it up, gazing at herself.

Omro – not a name she knew. What had she just witnessed? And who was trying to save whom, reaching through the crevice for one another?

The mountain rumbled. Kalanna returned to the present. How long had she been staring into the shard? It had seemed only a moment, but the mountain's end was already upon her.

Kalanna resumed her sprint – not because she had any chance of reaching the top at that point, but because she needed to train her body. She needed to get stronger for next time.

Cracks in the glass raced her up the slope. Falling crystal chunks shattered against the ground. The trail split open beneath Kalanna's feet, too quickly for her to avoid. She tumbled down a transparent fissure, its walls alive with rainbow sheen.

The world went bright, exploding into a million pieces.

* * *

"Stop fidgeting." Ferryn brushed powder onto Kalanna's cheeks. "Men can tell if you've been fidgety."

Kalanna opened one eye, watching Ferryn work on her in the dressing table's mirror. "And that's something they don't like?"

"I don't know. I'm just trying to get you to sit still." Ferryn stepped back. She tilted her head, appraising her work through narrowed eyes. Her face broke into a grin. "Done! Some women have to fend men off with a stick – *you'll* need a battle axe. Might want to stop by the armory on your way to the festival."

Kalanna turned her head in the mirror, taking in her cider-gold complexion. All this primping didn't feel like her, but she couldn't deny Ferryn's skill: her friend had somehow turned an exhausted city-defender into something presentable.

"Okay," Ferryn said, putting her tools away. "No more climbing explosive mountains and waking up beside ominous craters until after you've found a man. I'm not doing this again. Go get 'em, gorgeous."

It was a perfect night for the festival. Stars sparkled in the cloudless sky, just as smiles sparkled in the bustling town square. A visitor would never have suspected what dangers the city of Breev had labored under lately. Everyone seemed happy to forget about it all for a night, dressed in their finest cloth and jewelry. They celebrated with music, dance, laughter. Lit paper lanterns rose into the sky, higher even than the scattered silhouettes of Breev's seven towers, to the altitudes where magic was strongest. At their apexes they flared into bright yellow spots like drips of molten metal, then faded into the night.

Kalanna sat on a lonely bench outside a darkened bakery, gazing at the animated sky, her legs crossed under a midnight-blue gown with pearly white trim. She idly swirled her wine glass, thinking.

"...but enough about me. I'd love to hear how such a beautiful flower got into the business of selfless heroics."

Kalanna drifted from her trance, noticing the well-dressed man standing before her. She'd forgotten he was there.

"Huh? Oh – heroics. Sure. My parents were members of the militia that fought off Rastiv the Colossus when I was a child. I suppose I'm just following in their footsteps."

The man smiled. His sideburns weren't quite even.

"I'm sure your parents are very proud of you."

"They're dead."

He flinched as if stung. He looked nervously aside. "I – well. Yes." The gentleman coughed into his fist. "I'm not quite old enough to recall Rastiv the Colossus, but I understand he was the greatest threat Breev ever encountered. Your parents did a good thing. Please thank them for their sacrifice."

"I'll pass that on next time I'm at the cemetery." Kalanna sipped her wine. The gentleman awkwardly raised his glass and smiled. He stepped away.

Ferryn, effortlessly beautiful in her silky tangerine dress, sat beside Kalanna on the bench.

"All right. That's the fourth man I watched walk away from you. It's like you're *trying* to repel them."

"Sorry. My mind's elsewhere."

"Obviously. Tell me about it?"

Kalanna recounted the story of the man in the shard.

Ferryn sniffed her wine. "What do you think it means?"

"I don't know. But there's more: when I woke beside the crater, the shard was in my hand."

"And?"

"And that's never happened before. I've never brought something I found on the mountain back with me. There's something significant about it, Fer. I need to find out what."

"How do you propose to do that?"

Kalanna looked at her.

"Right," Ferryn said. "More trips up the mountain. Not my favorite plan, but I also know I can't stop you. I'd love to see the shard before you go again, though."

Kalanna opened her handbag. She pulled out a piece of mirrored glass almost too big to hold in one hand, pointed like a sharpened raindrop.

"Shiny," Ferryn said.

"More than that. Watch."

Kalanna tilted the shard side to side, until it caught the light of the floating lanterns and stars just right. An image of Omro's face appeared in the glass, frozen in time.

"Wow – those eyes," Ferryn said. "Like whoever made him tossed in a dash of sparkly cinnamon. And you're carrying this beautiful man's image around with you?"

"I'm just trying to solve the mountain problem."

"Mm-hm."

"Shut up."

Ferryn finished her wine and stood. She smoothed out her dress with her free hand. "You know I don't like you throwing yourself at that mountain. But the man in the mirror makes it all a little more palatable."

Kalanna rolled her eyes, smiling despite herself. "Thanks for the talk, Fer. Now go get lucky."

Stepping away, Ferryn looked back over her shoulder. "Who needs luck?" she asked, and smiled mischievously. Into the crowd she flowed.

The people danced. The lanterns flared. In Kalanna's hand, the shard gave warmth.

* * *

It was hard to gauge things from the rim, but it seemed to Kalanna the crater had grown closer to Breev. The mountain was spreading wider every time.

She looked back to the city, standing proudly in the distance. Purple flags snapped atop Breev's seven towers, their color indicating the day of the week. Kalanna wondered how many more times those banners would change before the crater reached them.

The ground rumbled. The mountain rose. Kalanna wasted no time.

Onto the trail, up the rugged glass terrain. As always, she started with a sprint – but her routine changed after the first switchback.

Heart thundering and legs heavy, Kalanna reached the tree-like crystal where she'd found the shard. She didn't continue upward from there. Instead, she took a side-trail, mostly level, which she'd tried once on a previous climb.

Kalanna knew the trail would dead-end eventually, but its terminus had entered her mind last night, during the festival. Gazing into the shard for the remainder of the celebration, her attention had been focused mainly on the image of Omro – but at some point, his surroundings had caught her eye. She'd recognized the crevice Omro reached his arm through. It was a rare dark spot on that otherwise light-infused mountain. And it could be found at the end of her present path.

Kalanna slowed to a halt, huffing. To her right and straight ahead, the mountain dropped off into sharp, shimmering rocks below. To her left was a narrow crevice in the wall, starting at head height and widening as it rose. The surrounding glass was solid black.

Kalanna peered into the crevice. Darkness peered back. Things didn't look promising, but she had to try anyway.

Cupping her hands over her mouth, she yelled into the crevice: "Omro!"

Her voice echoed through, returning to her. It came alone.

Kalanna turned and stepped away, shading her eyes against the sun. The first faint tremor came. The mountain wouldn't last much longer. There was no sense in fighting it.

The trail she'd entered on broke away, tumbling down the crystal cliffside. The small shelf Kalanna occupied lost pieces of itself, its edge receding toward her. A crack ran under her boots, crosswise. She didn't bother moving.

"Kalanna!"

She spun. There in the crevice was a man, sleeve pushed up to his elbow by the shaking crevice he reached through. She recognized his hand, his forearm; his curtains of golden-brown hair, and the copper flecks in his sienna eyes.

The ground beneath Kalanna gave way. She jumped just as the glass fell.

Omro's hand clasped her forearm. She dangled against the wall, empty air below.

"Climb!" he said. "You have to climb!"

Kalanna pressed her feet against the glass, finding traction in the crumbling surface. She kicked. Omro pulled. Her free hand grabbed the edge of the crevice. She climbed until the point where the opening was wide enough to pass through. Into the dark cave she spilled. A pair of strong arms caught her, wrapping tightly. She and Omro fell to the ground together, Kalanna on top.

Feeling through the darkness, she took his face into both hands.

"Quick!" she said. "Tell me everything! We don't have much time!"

She felt his arms unwrap from her back, his hands gently taking hold of her wrists. "Kalanna," he said, "in here, we have all the time in the world." A finger curled under her chin, lifting her gaze to the crevice.

Beyond, glass fell like raindrops through the bright sky, accompanied by the occasional boulder. The cave itself trembled, but didn't seem to be falling apart. Kalanna looked back to the man she couldn't see.

"Hey," he said. "I'm Omro. Nice to finally meet you, Kalanna."

* * *

They sat with their backs to the dark wall, side by side. The crevice, previously a bright window to the outside world, had plunged into blackness. The mountain was finally quiet.

"So," Omro said, "you probably have a lot of questions."

More than Kalanna could count. But now that things had settled down, none of her recent concerns came to mind. Instead, she was focused on the mystery man to her side, his shoulder brushing hers in the dark.

"I suppose I'll start at the beginning," Omro said. "You know about Rastiv the Colossus, right?"

His voice was a smooth, baritone thing, coating the cave's walls like syrup.

"Kalanna?"

"Huh? Oh – yes. Rastiv." She sat up straighter. "I was too little to know what was going on when he came around, but I've heard the stories. They say he was banished deep underground, where magic doesn't touch."

"Right. Except it turns out magic *can* get that low, if you manage to bring it down there from the sky. Which is exactly what Breev's sorcerers did. They went to the top of the seven towers and funneled their powers into the central one. A master craftswoman up there cast the magic into a glass plate. Once the militia weakened Rastiv enough, the sorcerers used the plate to imprison him under the earth."

"I hadn't heard that part."

"It's something the council tries to keep quiet. They don't want any curious adventurers digging around, looking for a plate of pure magic."

A suspicion struck Kalanna. "Omro – what's your trade, exactly?"

"'Curious Adventurer'."

"You found the plate."

"I wasn't there to steal it – I just wanted a look. That's where I first saw you."

The mountain came to life once more, deafening in its rumbling. Kalanna instinctively grabbed onto the closest thing, which happened to be Omro's arm. He placed a calming hand over hers.

"It's okay – this'll only take a moment."

The crevice grew so bright Kalanna had to avert her eyes – just like she'd done whenever the mountain had sprung up from the ground. The world quaked.

All at once, the chaos ended.

"Let's go for a stroll," Omro said.

He gave Kalanna a boost through the crevice. The trail outside was restored, as if it had never crumbled in the first place.

Kalanna went to the cliff's edge. In the distance, she spotted the flags atop Breev's towers.

"No," she said. "That doesn't make any sense."

Omro came to her side. "I know."

"Orange flags. Not purple. You're telling me two days passed while we were in the cave?"

Omro rubbed the back of his neck. "I should probably finish the story."

"You absolutely should."

They sauntered down the trail, Omro leading. After so many sprints up the mountain, Kalanna appreciated the casual pace. It was also nice having someone to hike with.

"I found the plate lying on Rastiv's sarcophagus," Omro said. "Under my torchlight, I saw you in the glass – whoever you were. Then the patrol came.

"I'd snuck past the guards on the way in, but now one of them was wandering into the cavern. She fired her crossbow. I dodged. The plate didn't."

They reached what might have been a meadow on another mountain. Flexible glass strands covered the area like blades of grass, bending under Kalanna's boots. Flowers with pointed, starburst petals glinted prismatically in the sunlight.

"Are you telling me Rastiv is free?" Kalanna asked.

Omro spread his arms wide. "It's how we got all this."

"He's on the mountain?"

"No – Rastiv *is* the mountain."

The land shook with a brief growl. Glass flowers swayed.

"He's fused with the peak," Omro said. "He's the thing making the mountain rise over and over. It gets higher every time."

"Oh, gods. He's trying to reach stronger magic."

"He's still anchored to the mountain for now, but if he gets high enough..." Omro shook his head. He squinted up at the bright white light obscuring the mountain's peak. "This is all my fault. But I think I know how to fix it."

"How?"

"By reassembling the plate. It's what imprisoned Rastiv in the first place, right? So it's got to be what'll put him back in his cell. And I've already got one of the pieces." Omro opened a leather pouch at his hip and pulled out a glass shard. Kalanna produced her own.

"Damn! Look at that," Omro said. He reached toward her wrist. "May I?"

Kalanna nodded.

Omro lightly held her wrist, turning it until a familiar image showed in the shard. The scene at the crevice played out before them, each reaching for the other's hand.

"So that's how you knew to yell my name," he said.

Kalanna gestured at his shard. "What's yours show?"

Omro held it up. Before the image could materialize, something behind Kalanna roared.

"Get back!" Omro said, drawing the short sword from his hip and stepping around Kalanna. She peered past his blocking frame. Standing in the meadow was a beast of glass and light.

The lion, taller even than Omro, shook its head as if shooing a fly. The crystal chimes of its mane sent tinkling notes into the air. Sunbeams refracted through its body, throwing pieces of rainbow about the meadow. Its sharp-edged eyes, clear though they were, were filled with malice. The lion stepped forward on large glass paws.

Kalanna drew a dagger. She wished she'd brought a sword, but she always packed light for her climbs. She stepped around Omro to his side.

"Seen this thing before?" Kalanna asked.

"Yes – and I don't think we can kill it."

The mountain rumbled – not just a single tremor, but a steady thing, the likes of which Kalanna had felt many times before.

"We may not have to," she said. "We just need to stall."

The lion pounced.

Kalanna and Omro split to either side. The lion landed heavily, sending a crack through the weakening mountain. It faced Kalanna, fangs bared. She held her dagger ready.

Omro must have struck something on the lion's back end, because chips of glass sparkled through the air like a spray of fountain water. The lion roared. It spun, swiping. Omro flew across the field, sword fallen from his grip.

"Omro!"

The lion charged its fallen prey. Kalanna was right behind.

Glass boulders crashed down the nearest slope, tumbling across the meadow. One of them glanced off the lion's shoulder, forcing it aside and stalling its charge. That was the opportunity Kalanna needed.

She threw her dagger. The blade lodged into the lion's flank. It roared and turned toward Kalanna, but was too late in addressing her – she'd already reached Omro's sword.

She scooped up the weapon. A heavy crash sounded behind her. She glanced back to see a huge portion of the mountain had fallen away; the edge was approaching her heels.

Kalanna faced her stalking adversary. She took a half-step back. The lion padded forward, head low. It pounced.

Kalanna dodged to the side, swinging as she went. Her sword severed the glass lion's outstretched paw. The beast couldn't land in its usual nimble way, and instead rolled forward over one shoulder. It tumbled off the mountain.

Kalanna turned to Omro, laboring to his feet. Blood ran down his arm. He stood straight. They made eye contact.

The ground shattered beneath Kalanna, sucking her into the blinding brightness below.

* * *

At the threshold of Ferryn's front door, she shoved Kalanna with both hands.

"Two days! You were gone for two! *Days*!"

"Fer, I'm sorry—"

"I looked for you when the mountain came down. You're normally lying at the rim of the crater. But you *weren't there*, Kalanna. I thought you were dead."

Kalanna's gaze dropped. She knew exactly how Ferryn felt.

"Can I come in?"

There was a long silence. Kalanna looked up to see a stern face looking back.

"I cut up too much fruit. You're helping me eat it." Ferryn stepped aside. Kalanna entered. They made for the kitchen.

Over cantaloupe, honeydew and peaches, Kalanna told her story.

"And Omro wasn't by the crater when you woke up?" Ferryn asked.

Kalanna shook her head.

"Maybe he made it back to the cave. You said you waited there the last time the mountain fell, and you just sort of… stayed on the mountain."

"I don't know, Fer. The cave was so far away. Things were coming down fast."

Ferryn studied the piece of melon at the end of her fork. She shoved it into her mouth.

"I've got someone I can ask about this plate situation. Remember that magic scholar I dated last year?"

"The guy with the…?" Kalanna made a swirling gesture around the back of her head.

"That's the one. He might know how you're supposed to go about sticking the shards back together."

"Thanks. That'd be a big help."

"You know, you've got a full two days before the mountain rises again."

"So?"

"So," Ferryn said, planting her chin on both hands and grinning, "tell me more about this man."

* * *

Kalanna stood at the crater's rim. Ferryn was there for the send-off.

"You're sure your guy didn't have any more advice on the plate?" Kalanna asked.

Ferryn pulled out a scrap of paper. She read: "'Once they have all the pieces, they'll have to speak the right incantation. Or possibly make a gesture'." She stuffed the paper away. "I wrote it down because there was no way I was going to remember. He's an incredibly boring person. Nice jaw line, though."

"And he didn't know what the incantation or gesture might be?"

"He said he could dig into some books if we gave him more time. Any chance you could wait another few days?"

"Time passes differently up there. It's probably only been a few minutes since the lion swiped Omro. I need to get him these bandages."

"Then I guess this is what we've got. Good luck, gorgeous."

"Thanks, Fer."

They hugged. The mountain rose.

Kalanna ran.

* * *

He wasn't in the cave. He wasn't in the glass meadow. Kalanna's heart pounded from all the sprinting around. How long had she been searching? The mountain wouldn't last forever, and it seemed impossibly large just then. Desperation closed in like a roaring rockslide.

The ground vibrated under her feet.

No – not yet. She needed more time.

She rushed to the place where Omro had fallen, scouring. What clues was she expecting to find? The mountain rebuilt itself anew whenever it rose. There wouldn't be footprints, nor a trail of blood to follow. This wasn't the right approach. There had to be something else she could do. There had to—

"Kalanna!"

She whirled toward the voice. Across the meadow, at the base of a slope, was a cave: a black spot on the glass mountain, too small to enter without hunching. In its mouth knelt Omro, clutching his bloodied arm.

"Omro!" Kalanna ran over. Without thinking she wrapped him in a hug, nearly tackling him into the cave.

"Good to see you too," he said, and she could hear the smile in his voice. "Come inside. The mountain will be falling soon."

* * *

To a chorus of rolling thunder, Kalanna bandaged Omro's arm. Outside the tiny cave, glass fell like a heavy rainstorm.

Kalanna tightened the bandage. Omro hissed.

"Sorry," she said, touching his shoulder.

"Don't be. Thanks for doing this."

"Of course." Finished with her work, she looked for a place to sit instead of kneeling. Omro scooted over.

"We'll have to get a little cozy until this passes," he said, and opened his arm. Kalanna hesitated, stomach fluttering. Finally she lay against him, head on his chest. He was warm.

The rumbling intensified. The outside world went dark.

"So this cave is like the other?" Kalanna asked.

"Yeah. There are a few of these places on the mountain. I don't know how they work, but they don't shatter when everything else does. It's how I've been able to stay up here while I try to fix my mess. How was your trip home?"

Kalanna told him about Ferryn's scholarly friend, and what they'd need to do once the plate was reassembled.

"I'm no sorcerer," Omro said. "I don't have any incantations or magical gestures handy."

"Me neither. I guess we'll have to figure that out once we get the shards together. Hey – you never showed me what was in yours."

She felt Omro shift as he dug for something. The faintest silver light appeared in the dark, held within Omro's hand.

The image in the shard was a near reflection of the present moment: Omro and Kalanna, holding one another in a darkened cave, barely visible in the silvery glow. The Omro in the mirror said something; the Kalanna laughed.

"Look at that," Omro said, twisting the shard. "Guess you were destined to be my savior." He shrugged against her. "I don't make the rules."

Kalanna laughed. "So you always knew this was going to happen?"

"I wasn't certain what the image meant. Could have been just a dream. I'm glad it turned out real."

The cave mouth brightened. The world settled.

"That's our cue," Omro said.

Kalanna didn't want to go, but two days had just passed in Breev – the crater would be even closer now.

"Can I see your shard?" Omro asked as they exited the cave. Kalanna passed it over. He held the two fragments together, forming most of a plate. "Looks like there's just one piece left. And I know where it is." He squinted at the mountain's blinding peak.

"Up there? With Rastiv?"

He nodded. "I've spent a lot of time looking for these pieces. I got to the peak once; the light doesn't hurt once you're up there. Rastiv was guarding a shard."

"What'd you do?"

"Rastiv spotted me and sent his lion, so…I ran. I found a cave it couldn't fit into, and waited things out until the mountain fell. Haven't been to the peak since. And frankly, I'm not thrilled about going back. But I guess we've got no choice. Onward and upward, as they say."

The climb was arduous, but Omro always knew where to find caves for rest. Whenever they stopped, they held each other in the dark while the world rumbled away. Kalanna worried about the mountain's expansion. She worried about how close Rastiv was getting to the magic that would break him free.

Exiting one last cave, they gazed up a steep, slender path among the glassy rocks. Omro had been right – the light wasn't so intense anymore.

"This is it," he said. "No more breaks. You ready?"

Kalanna handed him one of the two daggers she'd brought. "Not sure how useful they'll be, but it's better than nothing. Lead the way, adventurer."

It was only a short distance up the trail. They passed between two huge crystal stones at the top and stepped onto the flat peak.

He was an extension of the mountain itself, its glass rocks transitioning into his waist and upper body: Rastiv the Colossus, who'd once threatened the city of Breev, until Kalanna's parents and other brave defenders had sacrificed their lives to stop him. Ten times a man's height, the huge, luminescent figure waved thick arms of chiseled glass overhead, as if stirring the very sky. Kalanna didn't have to be a sorceress to feel the intoxicating magic that high in the air.

Rastiv looked down from the energy he manipulated with his blade-sharp fingers. An evil grin bent the features of his transparent face.

"The one who freed me returns," he said, his voice shaking the world. "I suppose you expect thanks?"

"Not really," Omro said. "Especially not after what we're about to do."

Rastiv's grin became a sneer. "As a fool you've lived, and as a fool shall you die." The colossus reached into the whirlpool of nacreous light overhead and pulled out a sword, its blade transitioning from blue sky at the base to starry night at the tip. Rastiv swung the weapon down.

Kalanna tackled Omro aside, tumbling with him. The sky-blade of Rastiv cleaved into the ground where they'd stood, digging a furrow and throwing glass splinters everywhere. Kalanna and Omro covered against the sharp rain.

"There!" Omro said, pointing at Rastiv's base. "The shard!" Kalanna spotted the third piece of the plate, propped against the clear rocks from which the colossus grew. Reaching it would be a problem.

The sword lifted. They scrambled to their feet and ran for cover behind a crystal tree. Omro peeked around the trunk.

"Duck!" He cradled Kalanna's head and pulled her down with him. A loud crash sounded. More glass rained down. The tree's trunk fell to one side, hacked off just above their heads.

Kalanna spotted the leather pouch on Omro's belt. She snatched it, trading him her dagger.

"Think you can keep him distracted?"

"Kalanna—"

She grabbed his shirt front and pulled him into a kiss. It seemed longer than it surely was, but not long enough.

They separated. They looked at each other.

"We'll talk about this when it's all over," she said, and ran.

She circled the stationary colossus at a distance. His blue-black sword swung again and again. Every time, Kalanna hunched, leapt, or rolled aside. She never stopped moving.

From the corner of her eye, she saw something small spin through the air. She looked in time to see a dagger pierce the whirlpool above Rastiv's head. Pearly liquid bled onto the colossus.

"Insignificant insect! You'll not undo my work!"

Rastiv's focus changed. With furious strokes he attacked Omro, who dodged all about as the landscape shattered around him. He wouldn't be able to last forever; Kalanna had to take the opportunity.

She rushed to Rastiv's base. In his blind fury, the colossus didn't notice her until it was too late.

Mid-stride, Kalanna scooped up the final shard. She kept running.

"No!" Rastiv boomed. "I won't be imprisoned again!" He continued his attacks, sloppier now in his rage and desperation. He repeatedly missed Kalanna, but the damage he caused to the terrain threatened to topple the entire peak.

She ran behind the largest glass boulder, standing at thrice her height. Omro came rushing from the other side. He wrapped her in a hug, exhaling with relief.

"Don't scare me like that."

"I did it!" Kalanna said. "I got the shard!"

Rastiv's sword crashed down into the clear rock, cleaving a few feet through. The colossus growled, struggling to wrench his blade free.

"We don't have a lot of time," Omro said. "Let's get this done."

They pulled out the shards, kneeling to assemble the puzzle on the ground.

The pair looked at each other.

"Now what?" Kalanna asked.

Rastiv's blade ripped free. It came down on the boulder again, deepening the cut.

"I don't know!" Omro said. "We need an incantation. Or a gesture!"

The sword struck again. A chunk of the boulder's top half rolled away, crashing to the ground.

"I'm not a sorceress," Kalanna said. "And I don't know how to—"

"Wait – look!"

Omro pointed at the third shard: the newest one, whose vision they hadn't yet seen. It showed Kalanna and Omro, huddled behind a glass boulder, while a blade of sky and stars continuously slammed down. From the shard, Omro's voice:

Kalanna – I never told you what exactly I saw in the plate, when I found it on Rastiv's sarcophagus.

The real Kalanna looked at him. "Omro…?"

He smiled at the shard, as if understanding.

"Kalanna," he said. "I never told you what exactly I saw in the plate, when I found it on Rastiv's sarcophagus."

He stood, guiding Kalanna to her feet, the plate between them. The colossus's blade smashed into the boulder again, stopping just above Omro's head.

Omro took Kalanna's face into his hands. He kissed her.

Kalanna felt the magic of the high air whip around the peak, swirling into a tornado centered above them. Something warm rushed into her. Time slowed.

His lips were soft.

A loud humming sound arose from between their feet. They pulled apart, looking down. The pieces of the plate fused themselves together, white light erasing the cracks. It levitated into the air.

"No!" Rastiv yelled. "Not again! I won't go bac—"

Like so often before, the mountain exploded.

* * *

Like so often before, Kalanna woke on the ground outside the city. But this time there was no bed of broken glass beneath her. This time there was no gaping crater in the land. This time, she wasn't alone.

She and Omro sat up. The setting sun painted the landscape red and pink. The hills and trees, once withering in the presence of the dark pit, looked healthy again. They looked happy.

"It's gone," Kalanna said. "We did it."

Omro let out a long breath, gazing out at the colorful horizon. "I guess we did."

"So – are you going to tell me?"

"Tell you what?"

"What you first saw in the plate, on Rastiv's sarcophagus."

Omro smiled. The sunset didn't entirely hide his blush.

"No incantations," he said, "but I did see a gesture. The two of us, together. Kissing."

Kalanna punched his shoulder. "Why didn't you *tell* me that?"

Omro rubbed the assaulted muscle. "The adventuring life has its perks, sure, but it can get lonely. You go to a new place, explore its mysteries, make some coin and move on. You meet people along the way, but you know you'll probably never see them again. That's just how things go. It's how they've always been.

"But when I saw us in the plate, I saw a different life. Those people had something together. Whoever that woman was, she was special."

"That's sweet. But it still doesn't explain why you didn't tell me."

"What was I supposed to say? 'Hi, you don't know me, but I'm almost positive you're the woman of my dreams. A plate told me so'?"

"Okay. I can see how that would be a weird introduction."

Omro shrugged. "I'd never felt something like that before. I didn't want to screw it up."

Kalanna wrapped her arms around his shoulders. "If it helps any, you definitely did not screw up." She kissed him. "Come on," she said, rising.

"Where are we going?"

"We just saved the world. We deserve a fancy, relaxing dinner. And I know a great hostess who would *love* to meet you."

They walked back to Breev hand in hand, the sun setting at their backs.

A Hundred Lifetimes

Kathleen Stanley

The headache that erupts as I open my eyes is so tormentingly painful that the contents of my stomach immediately react to the pain. It is instinct alone that propels my body sideways, so the vomit hits the floor. I feel along the edge of my mattress and gain enough purchase to push my body into a sitting position. *Get it together, Iris*, I chastise myself. Did I even have wine last night? A sudden onslaught of images flash behind my eyes, hundreds, all of them versions of myself, assault my senses as I gain access to decades of lives I've lived before this one.

I can't remember if it's always like this, the pain so visceral it makes me sick. Maybe it's the velocity of the memories as they begin to unspool in my mind, the pure volume a tumbling snowstorm of colour and feeling. They blend into each other, refusing to settle, and like an eye in the storm I see his face, repeatedly, a life raft in the sickening sea of too many lifetimes to count. I hold onto the moss green of his eyes that ground me and pull me in like gravity hugging the earth. I let everything else pass by, and I take deep, calming breaths, feeling a longing settle deep within my body. It strums in my blood and a name begins to form on my tongue.

Evander.

As his name leaves my mouth, a fresh wave of memories threatens to overwhelm me. They tingle at my skin, raising goosebumps as I remember the lightest of touches, deep breathing in my hair, the fullness of lips on my mouth. It will take my mind time to sort and place each memory with the right lifetime. I can feel the line separating in my mind, who I am today and who I've been before, and all the times we've found each other. The headache recedes enough that I can get up and I immediately go to the window. The sun is only just beginning its ascent into the sky, and I breathe a sigh of relief. A full day to find him.

It won't be long before the household stirs. I have often taken to early morning rides and so slipping out at this hour won't raise suspicion. I dress in a comfortable pair of riding leggings and a flowing tunic, draping my heavier cloak over my shoulders. There is every chance I won't be returning here at all and sadness at leaving my current family stops me in my tracks. Should I leave them a note? What do I usually do here? A memory breaks to the surface…

* * *

The late afternoon sun is beating down on my back as I watch a broad and muscular frame tie a final pack to the side of his horse's saddle. He's moving quickly but efficiently, double checking the straps before moving to the second horse, my own. He sees me dithering, glancing back towards the small brown house that sits further up the meadow. Regret fills his face, as he gently takes my hand.

"You're worried about leaving them?" he asks.

"I'm worried about never seeing them again," I reply. "I love you, but I have loved this family too…" I trail off, eyes on the house, avoiding his eyes.

Evander runs a hand over his head, his hair shaved to the scalp in this life, a shock compared to the mess of golden brown curls that it usually is. He was a soldier this time and rode like hell to find me when he woke up five days ago, memory restored. I've only had an hour to adjust. The second our eyes connected I remembered him, remembered every lifetime we've done this. Still, he's had more time to adapt than me, as he always does.

He nods and gently he says, "Iris, my love, we have a plan for a reason."

I start at the name, but then remember my name isn't Emily. That's just the name I was given in this life. I shake my head; it's already late afternoon and we have to move if we are to outrun the King.

"I don't remember it," I admit quietly.

He pulls me to him, a hand gently brushing over my cheek. It's as if his hands need constant reassurance I'm here, in front of him, real.

"The first time you left a note, your father in that lifetime followed us. He found you and within half an hour the King caught up to us. It…did not end well for him. You are so loveable Iris, no family who raised you can just let you go. So we decided about twenty cycles ago that it was safer, and kinder, to just leave as quickly and quietly as possible…

* * *

I come out of the memory and the reality of it hits me like a slap. No note then. It makes more sense to treat this like any other morning ride anyway. Parts of the memory stick in my thoughts as I throw some supplies together. The irony of Evander's insistence that no family can just let me go rubs like a blister on my very soul. The curse family has left on us both has nothing to do with how loveable I am. I move through to the kitchen, finishing my pack and then to the stable, managing to avoid everyone. I have a horse saddled and ready to leave before the sun has fully crested the hill beyond the house. I keep my pace steady until I am well into the forest and out of sight. Once I am sure there could be no eyes watching, I ride as if I can outrun the hounds of fate that nip at my ankles.

* * *

The sun has well and truly risen above me as I make it into the forest and my mind is still trying to sort through my different lifetimes with Evander. I feel like something is different this time, and I can't quite wrap my mind around what it is. There is a connection I need to make, but it evades me, feeling like a loose ribbon flying in the breeze, refusing to lie still enough for me to tie everything together. Love, passion, desperation, anger, loss cycle on repeat as I see us find each other over and over again. By the end of each day that my memory returns the King always finds us, and we both die. I know I need to look closer at that part, to try and find a way to not let it happen again. My cowardice wins out though, not wanting to relive Evander's death, and not wanting to see the King. In every life we have ever lived he has been a tyrannical force, and he has ruled over this kingdom for close to 2000 years. I feel an itch at this thought, that there is something here that is relevant. I let my mind dive for another, safer memory instead…

* * *

…I stand at the edge of a secluded pool of water, hidden deep within the forest. The water is a shimmering kind of blue that made you feel like you were on the edge of the sky, and diving in would make you lose all sense of gravity. I have been desperately hoping for weeks that Henry would make a move greater than the shy kisses he had taken to stealing after our walks through the forest. Here at the water, he feels different. Less shy, more focused.

"Shall we go for a swim?" he says with a lazy wink, lifting his shirt over his head. His tumble of amber curls falls messily over his forehead, and I can't help but let my eyes wander over his impressive chest. His hands linger at the waist band of his pants, and I avert my gaze as he pulls them all the way down. Embarrassment makes my cheeks flush, even if he was stripping right in front of me.

"I'm going to get into the water, before you burn yourself with that blush," he laughs. I feel my skin burn brighter at his teasing. "Join me if you like, if you feel comfortable doing so," he adds as he pushes out towards the middle of the water, giving me space to decide.

The thing is, I do feel comfortable. Everything with him does. It's as if he knows a part of me I didn't even know existed. I feel I can trust him, and so I strip off and submerge in the water. The coolness of the pond is so luxuriously contrasting to the heat of the day I let out a small groan of satisfaction that has his head whip in my direction. The moss green in his eyes darkens and he slowly and deliberately swims closer.

"That kind of sound could bring a man to his knees, you know," he says, reaching out for my knees under the water and pulling me into him.

The whoosh of the movement has me reach out to grab his shoulders, and he moves me, so I straddle his body. He is careful enough to leave a small gap of space between us, letting me decide if I want to take this further.

"I think I would like to see what you can do on your knees," I murmur before I think better of it. My cheeks heat, but he looks at me so full of hunger and want, I feel my own desire flare through the very core of my being. I'm burning for a different reason now. I close the distance between us and feel the hard length of him against me.

"I think you'll find I know exactly how to please you, on my knees or not," he says as he captures my mouth in a devastating kiss. It feels like coming home, like a kiss shared a hundred times before and yet still burns with so much passion that I crush myself to him. He keeps one hand on my waist, whilst the other roams my body, gently teasing my nipples, then moving down and tracing my inner thigh.

"Tell me if you want me to stop," he breathes between kisses.

"Don't stop," I gasp out, breathless with want.

He strokes my core, gently inserting one finger, then two and using his thumb to massage my clit, and I feel something deep within me awaken. As the pleasure builds, a pressure begins to shape in my mind, and I beg him for more. He shifts upwards, removing his hand and then angles my body, sheathing himself deep inside me. He waits until I adjust and as he takes the first thrust, I feel undone, the sharp pleasure clenching my insides and the fullness making me want, no, need him to go faster.

"More," I moan. He increases the pace and uses his hand to brush on the nerves that are about to send me over the edge. Again, I feel pressure on my mind but the pleasure

and rightness of our lovemaking is so overwhelming I can't focus on it.

"Together, Iris," he groans. I barely register the name, overcome with so much feeling. The pleasure peaks and I come around him, and he follows, pulling me against him. I collapse against his chest, the pressure in my mind released and I realise he called me Iris. I look up into his eyes and a fog I didn't know was clouding my mind lifts. This isn't Henry, and I realise that I am in fact Iris.

"Evander," I cry, crushing my mouth to his.

"You're back," he smiles, as if finally, his life was back on its axis and all of it was because of me. "I love you."

"How long have you remembered?" I ask.

"I've remembered you for a year, but it took me weeks to find you. You didn't recognize me, so I've been trying to wake you up this whole time…"

* * *

I slam out of the memory, surprised to find myself still on my horse. Reliving being with Evander was almost as good as the real thing. The burning distraction of that memory could have easily unseated me, but I feel another part of our story slam into place. Evander had once again been the one to find me. He always found me and had to wake me up. I gasp; this time I had woken on my own. With my own name. Did this mean we might finally stand a chance at breaking this damned curse? The pressure in my mind nudges me sharply and I realised why the pain hit so hard this morning. It was trying to lead me to him. Embracing the strange feeling, the nudge takes over, urging me onwards, and I spur my horse forward, knowing where to ride.

* * *

It is late afternoon when I reach an open field and feel him. The beacon in my mind that had led me like a compass for most of the day must have been calling out to him too, and I see his pace quicken as I leave the last of the forest's trees. He leaps from his horse when we are close, and I slow enough to dismount, barely making it three feet before he has me in his arms. My face becomes wet with tears and he crushes me in his arms, so tight it is as if he is frightened I'll disappear if he dares to let go. Pressing his forehead to mine, breathing hard, we stand, staring deep into the depths of each other's eyes. A hundred lifetimes pass within them, bonding us and our love. He cups my face gently in his hands and our lips meet, the kiss sweet and binding, a promise of love that no number of lifetimes could lessen.

"You found me," he says, and I realise he too is crying.

"You know what this means then?" I ask.

He nods, the only confirmation I need that my ponderings were correct. We had broken the chain. A hundred lifetimes had passed, and this is the one chance we have to break the curse. I just haven't worked out how we are meant to do that yet.

"I know we've broken the pattern but what now? How do I defeat him?"

"Your magic, Iris. Please tell me you have it?"

His question loosens my grip on reality, and with a lurch I'm thrown almost 2000 years into the past…

* * *

…I'm lying on the cold stone floor with my hands and feet bound in strange golden ropes that sizzle when they meet my skin. I am groggy and confused, but see Evander tied to a chair across the room, bound and glaring at something behind me. As I try to move, his eyes shift to mine, and a pained look of love and fear crosses his features. Trepidation creeps under my skin and I turn to see my father standing over me. He has me placed in a marked circle on the floor, one that is interconnected with two others. He moves back with a sinister smile into the circle at the top, and I look to see my grandmother, the Queen, is similarly bound in the circle to my left. Rage crosses her face as she stares at her son, but I can see fear there too.

"This is a mistake, Orion," she says, "You cannot do this to your family."

"Oh, I assure you, Mother, I can," he replies. "Do you deny that you intend to pass me over and give the crown to her?" he spits, gesturing to me. The Queen blanches, but she doesn't deny it.

"I am entitled to name my heir apparent, and Iris is full of light magic. You have a darkness that has taken root, my son. I cannot risk these lands under your rule."

I know my father is a cruel man, but my grandmother is implying he is corrupted, and there is no coming back from that. I glance back at Evander who had gone paler than me at this revelation. My father opens a giant ancient text and speaks with quiet rage.

"Then you force my hand. I will not be denied what is rightfully mine. Tonight, a new reign will begin. My curse will wipe you both from existence, and I will rise from the ashes."

"You know the magic of the crown must be given freely..." the Queen begins but Orion cuts her off.

"Unless one is powerful enough to force it. And this spell will allow me to drain the very power from my daughter's soul. Her light will feed my crown. She will be reborn, and I will drain her, feeding the crown the power it needs. I will not just rule but rule forever. I WILL NOT BE DENIED!"

My father begins to chant, and a cold sweat breaks over my body in horror. As the spell starts to take hold, I notice Evander has worked his hands free. Hope flares in my chest as he unties his legs and dives for the circle I am in. My father glances up and raises a wall of fire around the circle. Evander is now trapped, doomed to the same fate as me.

"You should have run." I begin to cry as he cradles me in his arms, the bindings on me refusing to come loose.

"Never without you," he replies, dropping a kiss to my hair.

The Queen watches us, nodding to herself, coming to some silent decision. She edges as close to our circle as she can, gesturing us to do the same. She's quiet as she speaks to Evander.

"I have enough magic to alter his spell, to give you both a chance. I need your blood," she gestures to us both. "A drop will do, mix them together and smudge it into the centre point of all three circles."

The gold binding that I realise is blocking my magic has burnt a mark in my wrist bad enough that is has started to bleed. Evander gently takes some, mixing it with his own from a gash on his head, I'm guessing from when my father captured us. As quick as a flash, he smudges it across the middle point of all three circles, and my grandmother begins to chant.

"A hundred lives you will endure
Cursed to find each other forever more
Until reunited with the name she truly owns
Will she find a way back to the throne
For her love first awakened
Power returned, that once was taken…"

* * *

As I return from the memory, I feel it, the power that is simmering under my skin. It has been so long since I accessed it that I had forgotten what it felt like, but now I know for certain that this is our shot.

"Yes," I breathe, "I can feel it."

I lift my hand out beside us. A ribbon of light pours from it, a prism of colour like a rainbow floating throughout. Evander whoops and spins me around, the magic flaring around us, and he kisses me with unbridled joy. In the past, the King has always found us, as if my awakening was a beacon that allowed him to find and drain me before we had a chance to find a way around the curse, to access my magic. I suspect he is already closing in on us, especially now we are together. This time though, we have the advantage. I can finally stop running.

"Tell me, my love," I ask slyly, "how do you feel about laying a trap?"

* * *

We decide the meadow is as good a place as any to finish this. Evander's magic has also been restored, it coming to life with the appearance of mine. He will use it to defend against whatever the King attempts whilst I undo the damage my father has done to our lives.

We mark a circle out in the grass, lined with my magic, a beacon that should draw the King and bind him whilst I reverse the curse. One good thing that a century of lifetimes has given us is the power to figure out how to fix this when I did eventually get my magic back. Evander's tireless research until he found me has given us a counter spell, but we will only get one shot and must hope he's got this right. My nerves are palpable as Evander approaches me, rubbing his hand in soothing circles on my back. I want nothing more than to fall into his arms and lose myself in him, but night has already fallen, and we can't risk distraction now.

Wind tears through the meadow, and I know this is it. My magic is pressing against my skull, ready to restore the balance of my father's atrocities. It is like a living thing, and it's pissed that it has been used for thousands of years in corruption and deceit, ripped from where it belongs. Ripped from me. The King appears, right in the centre of the circle, like a moth to the flame, unable to resist the call my magic was emanating. His smirk fades when he sees us lying in wait for him, understanding darkening his gaze.

"So, after all this time, you think you can finally outwit me?" he sneers.

"I know I can," I say back. I raise my hands to lock a prism of magic around him, but he shoots his hands up too and a dark shadow escapes as I close the dome over his head.

The shadow forms into a monstrous wolf-like beast, and it snarls, leaping for me. Evander jumps into its path, his own magic forming a sword in his hand. The sword glows with light magic, and he swings it in a lazy arc, a grin at being reunited with it spreading over his face.

"I've got this, Iris," he calls to me, lunging towards the shadow beast, drawing it away from me and the circle my father is trapped in.

I turn back to the circle of magic, trusting in my love, and begin to chant the counter curse. Light flows from my hands, wrapping around the King, pulling at him, leeching the stolen magic from the very pores of his skin. I can't hear his screams through the magic dome, but I can see them on his face. I feel no pity, I want my life back, I want to be free of him. Free to love my people and the beautiful man who has endured so much just because he loves me. I push the magic as quickly as I can, and with a final triumphant swirl of rainbow light, the King is drained. He crumples to dust, as does his shadow beast, and Evander turns and runs back to where I stand.

Taking my hand, we look at each other with disbelief that this is finally over. No more lives resetting. The magic returns to my body, and in the centre of the dusty ashes that were once my father sits a crown. Evander reaches down and with a grin passes me what was meant to be mine thousands of years ago. Then the love of my life kneels before me, and says in a voice full of reverence, "Long live the Queen."

I lean down and capture his mouth with my own. The kiss burns with our victory, our love, and I can't resist whispering, "There are so many other things I would prefer you do if you're going to get on your knees…"

His laughter echoes through the night, and deep into my heart.

A Song of Smokeless Fire

Elise Stephens

Uncle,

I write these words because you refuse to listen when I sing them.

You think me too prying, too stubborn. You make choices for me as if I'm still a little girl, but I can no longer ignore the gnawing questions about another life from which you rescued me. I believe an event in our shared past is the root of our nomadic wanderings, you chasing after rumors like today's, of a strange death that befell a flutist and her friends while they sat in an open field. Their bodies were found burned, but no cause of fire found.

My memory holds clues to a home I barely remember, and it too is edged by flames. Why did you rescue me and from what? Today I've made myself a promise: I'll seek answers that I'm old enough to know. You cannot stop me.

Your niece, –Amal

* * *

When the swallows shifted their migration and flew patterns contrary to nature, when the lilies bloomed months before their time, and when the blood-feud rivals warmed overnight to friends, the jinni took notice of the music that had inspired this upheaval.

The singer, a young man named Hasan, was the eldest son of the Assad family, a well-established merchant bloodline. Hasan's music spanned the space between flesh and spirit, and once the jinni knew, he had to witness the gift firsthand. Such music as Hasan possessed could change the world, if properly nurtured.

When the jinni secretly entered the walled courtyard of the merchant's home, he found Hasan tending the jasmine vines. Still concealed behind the fountain, the jinni gathered his plans for helping this mortal ascend to greatness, then assumed human form. Hasan turned as the jinni approached and a coppery beam of sunset spilled through a window, turning his curls to fire.

"Welcome," Hasan said, slanting a glance from beneath dark lashes.

Between them stood a small table with two glass cups of tea. Hasan gestured to a chair with an embroidered cushion, folded himself onto the other, then told his guest,

"I don't fear angels, demons, or jinn, nor do I care which you are. I only ask: what do you seek, and do you come as foe or friend?"

The jinni's human-shaped heart lurched with imperfect rhythm. He saw centuries passing and wind eroding stone even as he stood fully in this one precious moment of eternity. He whispered, to keep the thunder of the jinn out of his voice. "I seek your songs."

Hasan arched an eyebrow. "To steal them?"

"To breathe them in."

"Very well. As to my second question…?"

"I wish only good for you."

Hasan grinned, showing a mischievous dimple. "Very well, jinni. You may stay." He rose again to tend his jasmine, limbs alive with mortal youth. As the jinni watched, he considered that Hasan would walk but a few years under the sun, then wither like the loveliest of flowers. All men did.

They talked late into the night, drained three pots of tea, and burned eight hours of lamp oil. Hasan shared scraps of verses from the song he was writing and the jinni sang a few lines with him, searching for the way to blend spirit voice with human.

When the jinni slipped away at last, he calmed his worries by telling himself that this was only natural: that a human who could alter the world's natural order with his songs would summon the love of a jinni.

* * *

Dear Uncle,

My first memory of home is also the memory of losing it. Fragrant flowers, I believe they're jasmine, the babble of a fountain, candlelight, and a glittering green jewel that I grip in my fist. You play a song that night and I understand the notes as words you speak to me. Resonant strings and a smooth wooden voice. I wonder, was that oud that you played the same one you carry now?

The music and the beauty break when a man screams for the song to stop. He drops his cup and wine splatters the tiled courtyard. Wind roars indoors and the hot, crackling air hurts my skin. Everything is on fire. The flowers blacken. The fountain turns to steam. The people scream as their hair ignites and their flesh chars. The smell is evil.

I weep, but the fire doesn't take me. I don't know why. You carried me away from it all.

Why did we live? Were we lucky, or spared? Guilty or innocent?

Is there blood upon my hands – our hands? – is there an unknown debt in my name that you're hiding from me? This is my history and my right to know.

–Amal Who Remembers

* * *

"What is your true form?" Hasan asked one night, his head in the jinni's lap while the jinni ran fingers through his lover's hair.

They sat in a high tower overlooking the city while a crescent moon smiled down on their secret happiness. Hasan's final notes were gently fading on the evening breeze. He'd been teaching the jinni to sing with him, their voices blending in a pleasure the jinni had never tasted in all three hundred and ninety-seven years of his life. Hasan was not the first human he'd loved, but he was the first he'd wanted to die beside.

"The closest thing you'd know to my form is fire," the jinni said. "But without smoke."

"Fire that wouldn't sting my eyes or burn my lungs? Sounds perfect."

The jinni cupped Hasan's cheek in his hand. "I'll show it to you someday."

Hasan sat up, dark eyes outshining the stars. "I've been writing a new song. For us."

"Is it ready? Can I—"

"Not finished yet. Soon."

When the jinni kissed Hasan, he wished with all his being that he were not a being of smokeless fire; that together they might age at a shared pace, that their music might mature the way time intended, or at least that their song might last beyond a few short stanzas.

That night, the jinni gave Hasan his ring of mastery.

His lover strung it on a gold chain with the vow, "Though I possess a jinni's ring, I am not your master. I will not use this to make wishes that bind you. Love must have the freedom to go or stay, and I shall never force your obedience."

* * *

Uncle,

I stepped into my past today. The ruins of the Assad house, once belonging to a merchant family, its courtyard charred. The fountain still stands, and some floor tiles retain their color. It is the place where my earliest memory turns to flames.

A friend of mine, a librarian, took me to this place after I described my recollection. My friend explained the tragedies that span more than a decade, and in each one a demon who descends upon a musical festivity and slays all present, consuming them in a fire that yields no smoke.

I connect these horrors to the night you carried me away from the fire that claimed the people of this house. The memory echoes with music, taunting me with shreds of meaning. What was this song? If anyone knows it, you do.

I can already imagine the chords you'll use to chide my uncouth curiosity: dissonant combinations to underline your annoyance. But can't you hear the building crescendo? Can't you see that I never fully forget a song, once I've heard it, and I will search

until I learn the musical prelude to the fire on that tragic night?
–Amal of the House of Assad

* * *

When the jinni alighted on the upper balcony of the merchant's house to meet Hasan beside the potted orange tree, the singer greeted him in a brocade vest and linen tunic, rather than his usual soft robe with its braided belt. Hasan no longer wore his ring around his neck, but on his little finger. An evil premonition rippled through the jinni, but he kept his smile warm as he drew near and said, "What's the special occasion?"

Hasan stiffened and pulled back. The jinni's heart became cold mist.

"We must stop seeing each other." Hasan's words were toneless and flat, stripped of all music. His eyes were dull stones at the bottom of a lightless pit.

The jinni saw an abyss gape between them, centuries-old, littered with bones of dead men and whistling with the screams of anguished spirits. He didn't reply.

"I've spoken to my father," Hasan went on. "He's made me see what is wise and prudent. You and I are from different worlds, and I must make choices to establish myself and provide for my family." Hasan straightened his shoulders, looking every inch a prince. "I'm engaged to be married."

The jinni tried to find his voice, unsure whether he wished to be a vapor or a thunderstorm. At last, he said, "I will share you, if I must."

"No, it must be a clean break. I'm to inherit my father's business, after all, and my focus must be directed to this end."

"Then you don't mean to sing?"

"For a living? No. A hobby, perhaps. But I must be practical."

There it was. The jinni heard the pain that Hasan was trying to hold back. It was a faint mewling, like a kitten as it drowned.

The jinni whispered, "At least let me visit you. If only to comfort you when your wife is absent, to listen to your songs when you sing them, to cherish you in the shadows if that's all that's left to us."

Hasan's eyes flashed once with longing and the jinni felt his hope, stoked by a hundred years of waiting, try to rise again, but then Hasan shook his head.

"No. Such conduct would not be proper. It's long since time I grew up." Hasan glanced down at his ring and, in the moment before Hasan broke his vow, the jinni's heart turned to ash.

Hasan said, "I wish to hereby banish you from my presence. You may not come near unless I explicitly summon you."

The jinni fled. He could do nothing else. He was a spirit bound by the power of his ring, and he had believed, like a foolish mortal, that he would not be betrayed. Nothing but the ring's mastery could have parted him from Hasan. He knew he would spend the remaining years of Hasan's mortal life waiting, praying, and begging to be summoned back into his beloved's presence.

* * *

Uncle,

You've taught me hundreds of songs, yet held back the One that means more than all the rest: the Song that woke my primary tongue, for I sang before I spoke, as you've told me many times. I knew musical harmonies before I understood grammar. This is that Song.

You saved me from the fire that took my home. In a way, I'm the sole heir of that fallen kingdom, a princess of sorts, and you were once our minstrel.

I've visited the archives in the capital. I've lied, disguised myself, and stolen into restricted sections; all things you didn't raise me to do. The archives told me the story of a merchant, Hasan al Assad, born with a legendary voice of honey and silk, who forsook his talent to follow in his father's business. How he was known to wear a large emerald ring on his finger and when his household perished in a mysterious fire, his daughter's body was never found.

This is what I suspect: that you played a song that night of the fire and it somehow summoned the fire-spirit that killed my family. I escaped death via my chance possession of this emerald ring, the one I still wear today because you've made me promise never to take it off.

If that's true, then I know why you chase these rumors of death. You loosed a cursed song onto the world, and have been serving penance ever since, trying to stop more people from learning and singing this same song. And yet, you have no voice with which to persuade them.

The first to die was my family, and the ring that protected me is a jinni's ring. The jinn are spirits of fire – is a jinni burning all these people because of that Song? Why does the Song enrage the jinni? Do you know?

–Amal of House Assad, Bearer of a Jinni's Ring

* * *

The jinni fled to the mountains, seeking places as cold, sharp, and barren as possible. For, though he could not die, he hoped to numb his mind with pain. All the while, his ears remained tuned to Hasan, hopelessly hoping. He was startled to attention when, only an hour after his exile, Hasan stood on his balcony and sang alone to the empty sky.

The jinni could not come, for he'd not been summoned, but he listened from afar. The music was their song, the one Hasan had mentioned but never sung for the jinni, a duet for two voices, raw and beautiful and incomplete.

The jinni's tears burned pocks into the mountain stone beneath him. He knew, without being told that, after this, his lover would never sing again, and the thought of Hasan silencing his divine gift was a pain that wounded the jinni more than his exile.

* * *

Uncle,

I love you. You taught me to parse the chords of human life, to absorb its intricate range of sadness, joy, and toil. You sheltered me from every threat you could imagine. Because of you, I hear birds sing and know when they hunt food for their young and when they worry about nest-building. I can parse the notes of an old man's whistle – the melancholy nostalgias from his contented thanksgivings. I speak music more fluently than anyone I know, and you have shut this part of me away from the world, for you will not let me sing anywhere but in a closed and shuttered room.

But while this demon-jinni still prowls our land, all who sing are endangered.

I must find the angry jinni and this Song. If the killings are to stop, if there's a cure for the jinni's rage, it lies within the Song itself.

–Amal of House Assad, Bearer of a Jinni Ring, Singer

* * *

No dreams, no music, only silence. In just the blink of an eye for jinn, Hasan would die, and the jinni's fragile hope of being summoned would be buried beside Hasan's corpse.

But then, decades later, the jinni was bewildered, for he heard the summoning song. It didn't issue from a human throat, but from an instrument, the notes sliding on the rich curves of an oud and it was undeniably Hasan's unfinished duet.

The jinni followed it like an arrow, unsure what he would do when he arrived. A hundred humiliations might await him, but so also might a tender reunion. And yet, it was clear, even before he reached the song's source, that the musician was not Hasan.

This intimate melody, sacred as a lover's body; this duet meant only for the jinni and his singer, was being played by another for cheap entertainment.

The jinni became a storm cloud, boiling with thunder, rage, thwarted joy, and descended on the scene, prepared to shred the music, note by note, that it might never again be played. With a touch of bitter poetry, the setting of the song's performance was the same tiled courtyard with jasmine vines in which the jinni had first met Hasan.

It was an elaborate feast, candlelight flashing on gold jewelry, rich tablecloths with shining threads, tender cuts of meat, and gleaming gem-like fruit. The guests were listening to the music of a slender minstrel.

Flames filled the jinni's mind. Tonight would be this minstrel's last performance and the last night for everyone. The jinni plummeted in a torrent of wrath, burning the life from each guest, one by one, swallowing all in a smokeless fire that flamed with indiscriminate passion.

He recognized the man he adored only after he'd slain him. Hasan had grown a belly and covered his handsome face behind a large beard. Even his voice was ruined, roughed by years of hookah. The jinni shouldn't have been able to kill Hasan under the ring's protection. But it wasn't on his hand.

After he'd finished with the guests, the jinni found a survivor: a small child sucking on the ring's emerald as though it were a sweet, its magic shielding her.

The jinni saved the minstrel's death for last. He paused on the verge of turning the man to cinders and ripped out the minstrel's voice instead. There were many fates worse than death, the jinni told himself, and a singer who could not sing seemed a fitting punishment.

* * *

Uncle,

Forgive me, for I've ransacked your papers and found the Song, transcribed in your child's scrawl. I can read the story in the melody and feel the broken edges of its unfinished harmonies.

You said you lost your voice when you were a young man, and I think I can piece together the rest: First, years before you lost your voice, when you were still a street beggar, you overheard the enchanting farewell song that my heartbroken father sang from his balcony. The melody was so haunting, you knew that it would bring you glory if you could one day attribute it to your name.

Years later, when my father was a rich merchant, and you were a young and budding minstrel, you were invited in to play at his house party. My mother liked the song you chose. She didn't know its nature or that my father had written it. My father recognized the notes once you'd begun performing it and tried too late to stop you – this is my memory of his shouting – and then the fire-jinni came for us all. The ring spared only me.

I lost my family. You lost your voice. The jinni is still angry. But I know the solution now. That incomplete song is pain, loss, and betrayal. It must be finished, and I must help that come to pass.

I was born for this.

–Amal of House Assad, Bearer of a Jinni's Ring, Singer and Music-Speaker

* * *

A transcendent talent such as Hasan's music was not so easily smothered, to the jinni's disappointment. Like a disease, the unfinished duet found its way into the world. It seemed someone had overheard it during the brief performance of the now-mute minstrel.

This eavesdropper had gone on to sing it at a dinner party. The jinni heard it and burned each and every dinner guest, but didn't think to burn down the house as well.

A few years later, a transcript of the duet was found by another with a musical ear who arranged it for two instruments and held a small concert in its honor. A musician needed only to hear the melody once to absorb it and, despite the jinni's efforts, he couldn't stamp out the song. Thus, the jinni's grief outlived his beloved, born over and over by the notes of their incomplete song. He'd managed to destroy one with his rage, but not the other.

Then there was the night the song clawed its way into a fresh wound of its most recent iteration. The singer was a young woman. Her choice of stage was poignant, for charred jasmine vines and a soot-streaked courtyard fountain were her only audience. The winds of an approaching storm screeched from above and warped her voice. No one else would overhear. She was not singing for human ears. None but a jinni whose life was woven through those notes could have heard her.

The jinni hovered before the woman in his form of smokeless fire, prepared to take her life, but curiosity slowed his vengeance. Her face, ringed in dark curls, put him in mind of another face. Her voice's honey smoothness was like another voice. The way she looked up through her dark lashes brought to mind a moonlit meeting in this same courtyard. Then he saw the emerald ring on her finger.

His ring of mastery. The child who he'd spared the day of Hasan's feast. He'd thought her just a child, worthy of sparing if only for her innocence. But now, in her voice and face, he saw Hasan. She was the singer's daughter, the incarnation of the life Hasan had chosen apart from him.

The woman sang Hasan's song like a native tongue and shaped each note to its truest color. Her voice shimmered with the sadness of loss, the ecstasy of pleasure, the mirror-shine of wonder, and she sang as one who understood the world first through song.

And then, more music, this time with an instrument's voice. The strings squeaked at first, like frightened throats. A man leaned against the scorched wall stones, storm winds tossing his silver hair as he cradled a battered oud in his arms.

Human age hid little from a jinni's eyes. This man was the minstrel who'd audaciously performed Hasan's song here in this same courtyard at Hasan's feast, accidentally summoning the jinni and murdering the guests, then lost his voice as punishment.

The jinni felt his heart sink. These two lives he'd spared that night had returned to torture him again with the same song. It seemed mercy had done no favors.

The jinni prepared again to kill them, or at least the minstrel, since he had no ring to protect himself, but the jinni was arrested by the woman's voice, as no music had done since Hasan had first sung to him.

His lover was dead, as was the fate of all mortals, but here, in the voice of his daughter, whose very existence was betrayal made flesh, he heard Hasan singing again.

Urgency filled the woman's song. With open vocal sounds, she pleaded, drenching the notes in compassion, grief, and beckoning kindness. She held out her palm, and in it lay the jinni's emerald ring, granting him self-mastery once more. She was surrendering the ring's protection, showing she did not fear him. Just as Hasan hadn't feared the jinni's power on the night they first met.

The jinni took the ring, then rumbled in his thunder-voice to see if the woman would cringe. The minstrel fumbled his chords, but regained composure and held his part. The woman began the song anew, eyes fastened to the jinni's face. She sang in true song. There was no deceit in this music. Somehow, she knew the jinni's love story and his sorrow. Had she learned it from the song itself?

Unlike the others, this woman wasn't stealing the unfinished duet and using its majesty to elevate herself; she was giving it back to the jinni, its proper co-owner.

My love, the jinni thought, your child is asking me to finish what we left undone.

The daughter with no family, the minstrel with no voice, the jinni with no hope.

This woman's song invited the jinni to enter its melody, to find his rightful place in the duet.

The jinni thought again of moonlight on fountain tiles; of jasmine blossoms and hot tea, of bitter laughter and joyful tears, of a mortal's music that could have changed the world and a spirit's thunder-voice that had barely begun to tune itself.

The jinni began to sing.

Song of Sedir

Gemma Sterling

Halver left to go a-viking five years ago and never returned. Each night for five years, Eira would stand on the shores of the fjords and wait to see the square sail of his longboat approaching through the strait. Each night she returned to her homestead with her stomach hardened, and her chest heavy.

She could still remember the feel of Halver's arms about her, their strength. His chest had been broad, a fine place to nestle her head on. She had spent hours lost looking into the blue pools of his eyes. When he left, it was as though he carved out a piece of her heart and took it with him.

For five summers, Eira tended to the homestead, cared for her son Leif, and waited. Always, she tried to show Leif strength, but, when the sad sickness was too much to bear, her friend Andora would come to her and hold her hand by the hearth. More than once, Andora mentioned the witch who could open a portal in time when she stood on her Sedir platform. It was said that she would only do so at a terrible cost.

Eira always blushed whenever Andora mentioned Sedir. It used the powers of the Vanir, the earth Gods, Gods of fertility and love. It was said some witches performed magic clothed only in their cloaks. It made Eira's cheek feel warm to imagine it. Besides, Eira had her son to think of. What terrible cost would the witch make her pay?

So for five years Eira worked as a man. She made her ox pull the plows. She met with men at market to barter, the only widow among them. She had learned to show strength, to stand tall and broad, and the men respected her for it. Still, inside, the missing piece of her heart remained, and she feared that deep down they knew she was heartbroken.

On the night of the summer solstice of the fifth year, finally, Eira could bear no more. Her son, Leif, had come home with a bloodied nose. The other boys had attacked him during their sword games, bloodied him, and told him that he would never be worthy to go a-viking because he had no father. He told her that he would prove them wrong, that he would sail the sea as his father had. Leif's words were like a dagger of ice in Eira's heart. He was still but a boy. He could not yet hold his own in battle. Should he set sail, she would never see him again. If only Halver had returned, he could make the boy stay, make him feel worthy by having a father. Eira's thoughts turned to Andora's words about the witch.

That night, Eira donned her cloak, barred the door, and left through the window so Leif would not notice that she had gone. The moon helped her pick her way through the trees of the old wood until she found the witch's hut deep in the forest's heart.

Smoke rose from the circle in the thatch. The witch was home.

Eira felt like a hand of ice closed on her heart when she first set eyes on the wild woman by the hearth. She wore the skin of a she-wolf as her cloak. Her hair hung in greasy clumps. Eira told her of her plight and told her how she wished to step through the portal of time to bring Halver back. She asked her what the terrible cost would be.

"The Wyrd is for the sisters to weave. When you tug at a thread, it unwinds their tapestry. Such is the power given to the All-Father. He was made to pay a cost for this knowledge. Like Odin, you must give an eye each time you pass through the portal."

Eira's heart clenched. If she came back once she had gone through, she would be blind. She would never see Halver's face, or her son's. She told herself she could not do it, that it would be madness. She turned to the doorway but paused on the first step.

Eira fooled herself. She knew that if it meant she could bring Halver back to her, she would give her spleen, her tongue, indeed her whole heart to save him.

She took a deep breath and nodded.

When the witch took her eye, she had never known such pain outside the birth of her child. The witch, mercifully, gave her a balm to ease her torment. Eira ripped a strip of cloth from her skirt to wrap around her head and cover the open socket.

When Eira looked out onto the flat world, another piece of her heart tore. She had given a part of herself that could never be returned. The thought of seeing Halver's face again, even without depth, eased the ache. The witch told her that she would have a day's time in the past, and should she want to return she must step through the portal that opened at day's end.

The witch led Eira to her Sedir platform, a dais of branches with runes carved in their bark – runes, the language of Odin. When the witch mounted the platform, she raised her arms to the starry sky, and to Eira's eye she took on the form of the skin she wore, a she-wolf, standing on its hind legs and howling at the full moon in the sky.

Her magic rent the air in front of Eira. The skin prickled on Eira's arm as she saw a shore through the rent, and Halver's longboat bobbing in the shallows of the fjord. She took a deep breath and stepped through the rent.

Suddenly, she found herself clad in the costume of a Viking, seated on one of the longboat's benches, her hands clasped on an oar, pulling it to the rhythm of the drum beating by the mast. A bare-chested man with twining braids of hair hit the drum, timing each beat to the strokes of the oar. Sprays of sea water drenched the deck as the longboat broke the tide.

Eira's eye searched hungrily for her love. A tingling rush of passion ran through her body when she saw Halver, tall and proud, standing on the prow, looking out on the sea. His golden hair shimmered in the light. His broad back rippled beneath his shirt. Every part of her yearned to release her oar, rush across the deck, and shower his face and neck with kisses. However, to Halver's mind, he had just left her on the shore. He would think her appearance here dark magic. She had aged five years. Would he think her a dark elf in disguise, here to do him evil? She decided she must wait until they set up camp, then would she reveal herself.

Halver's longboat sailed up a river and beached on a bank. A vast forest stretched before the stony shore of the river. They set up camp. Eira's helmet hid her long blond braid, and in her costume the others took her for a smallish man. She worked as hard as the others, helping pitch tents on the stones.

After the mead had been drunk and songs sung, the Vikings took their rest.

Eira stole from her tent into Halver's.

He stood half-naked at a basin, cleaning the dirt from his arms and chest, rivulets of water twining between the taut muscles of his stomach. When he saw that someone had sneaked into his tent, he jumped for his sword, resting on a stone by the hearth. He swung the blade towards Eira's heart. A wave of cold fear rolled down her back, yet she managed to pull down the hood of her cloak with her trembling hands, remove her helm, and let her blond braid fall over her shoulder.

Halver's sword clattered to the ground. His large blue eyes grew wide like moons.

"How…how did you come to be here?" he asked in hushed awe.

Eira walked to him slowly, staring into his eyes so intently that the world around her fell away.

"I have traveled through time. I have disobeyed the Wyrd of the Norns, all so that I can see your face but one more time."

He tenderly cupped her face.

"What has become of your eye?"

"I gave it as tribute to the witch to travel through time. I would have given my blood, my heart, my soul to look on you just once more."

She took his face in her hands, and drew him forward, kissing him deeply. His lips pressed back against hers. She felt the rush of heat she had when Halver lived, the long-forgotten sensation. He took her up in his powerful arms and carried her to his furs. Their love that night was the most powerful she had ever known. She lay back, exhausted, spent, her limbs robbed of their power. She fell asleep in his arms as she had in times past.

When the light of dawn broke through the tent, Eira awoke with a start. The witch had told her she had but a day's time in the past. She had only a few hours to save Halver.

She woke him with a kiss upon the lips, then took his head in her hands and fixed his gaze with hers.

"I have come back because some calamity befell you on your journey. You never returned. I beg you, bring the boat back to the fjords, return to me."

A troubled look passed over Halver's face. To go a-viking meant riches, fame. Whole kingdoms could be won. To retreat from a journey once you had set out upon it meant disgrace.

"I cannot think of such things," he said. "I cannot dishonor myself with retreat even should it mean death."

It was as though someone took Eira's heart and wrung it in their hands.

"I care not about wealth, nor fame, nor kingdoms. I would be happy living as wild people in the woods, should it mean that you stay with me."

A pained looked crossed Halver's face. She could tell that her words had worked their magic upon him, but would it be enough to make him return to her? Was his love more powerful than his sense of honor?

He opened his mouth to speak when the blast of a horn broke the silence of the woods. Eira's stomach dropped. Such was the horn of the Wildmen. Was this the attack in which Halver would be killed?

She tugged at his arm as he strode from the tent, trying to stay him. He threw the tent's flap back and stood tall in the light of dawn. Halver's men let out exclamations of surprise when they saw Eira. To their minds, she had appeared in the tent as though by magic.

A party of Wildmen stood by the edge of the woods. The breath caught in Eira's throat at the sight of their spears and shields. The largest of them broke from the others and strode across the rocky shore to Halver.

He stood a full head above Halver. The Wildman spoke in his language and his sage translated his words for the Vikings.

"If your champion can best our chieftain, we will give you tribute to be your vassals. Should he win, your lives are forfeit to us."

Eira's heart rent at his words. This is how Halver and his men met their fate. Halver could not defeat their chieftain.

She clasped his hand.

"Do not take his bargain. Yield. Return to your family."

Halver brought her hand to his lips and kissed it tenderly. He looked into her eye with the secret tenderness he only showed to her.

"Should I try to flee, they would slaughter my men. My honor could not bear it. I promise to you; I will defeat him. I will return to our homestead."

"No," Eira pleaded as Halver shook her hand free and strode to the Wildman.

"I accept," he crowed.

The Wildmen began to beat their spears on their shields, ululating wildly. Their champion drew his sword, as did Halver.

It was as though a dagger plunged into Eira's heart. Halver's and the Wildman's shields clashed. The thunder of each blow shook the earth beneath them.

Eira watched in horror as the Wildman brought his sword upon Halver's wooden shield. Halver's legs weakened beneath the blow. The iron on the rim of his shield shattered.

The boards broke. Halver fell to the ground, unable to will his legs to rise.

The Wildman drew back his sword and aimed its tip at Halver's heart.

Eira could not breathe. The tragedy she had given her eye to prevent was about to unfold. She dashed forward, flung herself in front of Halver and took the point of the sword into her own bosom.

Halver let out a scream of primal fury and drove his own sword into the Wildman's chest.

Then a pitched battle broke out between the Vikings and the Wildmen for the terms of the pact had been broken.

Eira felt her life blood drain from her body. Halver's rough hands smoothed her hair from her face. She saw tears brimming like diamonds in his eyes. With her last breath, she kissed him on the lips.

When Eira again opened her eye, she saw a golden haze in the sky rather than the sun. She lay in a vast empty field that stretched on in all directions until it met the golden sky. Elysium. Eira's chest fluttered as she rose to her feet and looked about. So was this the life after the mortal one? Her hands felt the spot on her bosom where the Wildman's sword had plunged. It was whole. She brought her hand to her missing eye and found the socket empty. Death could not break the terms of her bargain with the witch.

Galloping hooves in the far distance drew Eira's eye. She lifted her hand to her forehead to block the golden light.

She saw a black blob in the distance, growing larger and larger as it sped towards her. Soon, as the shape took form, Eira saw that it was a golden chariot drawn by two great cats, forest cats the size of lions.

Eira felt her mouth go slack. Amazement stopped the beating of her heart. She dropped to her knees. It was the chariot of Freya, the Goddess of love.

Eira dared not look up as the chariot drew alongside her. She bowed her head. The platinum light that emanated from the Goddess blinded her. It was as though the light of the sun had been turned directly onto her, yet the light did not burn but instead filled her with the warmth of love.

"Look on me, my child," Freya said, with a voice more heavenly than the music of a choir.

Eira forced her chin to turn upward.

The Goddess removed her helmet and her black hair cascaded over her shoulders. Her face was so beautiful that looking on it caused Eira's heart to ache.

"I have watched you since you crossed the door of time. A love such as yours is a precious thing, a flame that fate cannot snuff. When you sacrificed your life for the life of your love, you proved yourself worthy of the greatest of my gifts."

Freya dismounted from her chariot and walked upon the air to Eira. Freya ran her hand over Eira's face, and Eira's eye was whole again. Tears wetted Eira's cheeks. She kissed the Goddess's hand over and over.

Freya waved her Sedir staff, and a rent opened in the air. Through it, Eira saw the thatched roof of her homestead on the shores of the fjord.

"I return you to your family," Freya said.

Eira nodded.

She feared to step through the gate. She swallowed a lump in her throat. Had Halver died in the skirmish? Would there be no husband to greet her on the other side of the door?

Freya rested her hand on Eira's shoulder. The Vanir's touch calmed her. Even if Halver did not return, Eira had been given the greatest gift the Gods could offer, a day with her dead love.

Trembling, she stepped through the rent.

Eira stood again in the fields of her homestead, with the landscape of the fjords unfolding before her. She looked over her house, and in her heart, she still felt an ache for Halver. Seeing him had only made it worse. She sighed and strode back to her home, preparing to explain to Leif why she had left in the night. She heard chopping behind the house and realized that Leif must be making firewood for the hearth. She rounded the hut, and it was as though the earth shifted beneath her feet.

Halver chopped wood behind the house, bare-chested, his muscles straining from the effort. When he noticed her, he dropped the ax into the flesh of the stump and staggered to her. A rush of blood hit her head. She began to fall in a faint until Halver caught her in his arms.

She looked deeply into the blue pools of his eyes.

"That day, five years ago, I brought your body home and burned it on the sea. I buried my sword and vowed never to pick it up again. I made our son promise he would never go a-viking. He swore his oath to me."

Eira's head swam. He planted a kiss on her mouth and her body tingled all over.

"For five years I have waited, counting each day. The Goddess Freya appeared to me in a vision. She told me you would bring a new life with you."

He placed his hand on her stomach. In her heart, Eira knew life grew there, born from the love they shared that night in the Viking camp. Eira's heart brimmed with joy. She had been given the greatest gift imaginable by the Goddess of love, a child brought back from the grave. Tears streamed down her cheeks, and she kissed Halver's full lips, and held him so tightly that no sea, Wildman, or God could ever part them.

Not Yet, Little Witch

Celia Winter

Amandine throws the finger bones in the air; they twist like dandelion seeds on a breeze, spinning weightlessly for longer than they should.

"Where did you go, my love? When will I find you?"

Will always told her the best way to travel through time is to ask a question. Time knows when you need to go, so it's better to trust it and leave doubt in the present. Doubt is dangerous.

And Amandine has plenty of it – doubt that she could do this with only recollections of conversations with Will as training in temperie; doubt that painstakingly copying the necessary runes into these finger bones from the memory of Will's would be enough to make them work; doubt that he cared about her half as much as she cared about him.

Even if he doesn't love me, he would have come back. We weren't done yet.

He hasn't told me why he came yet.

The finger bones clatter on the smooth marble table in front of her and a portal opens, wind made solid.

It's frightening, Will told her once. *Trusting time to know what to do with you. But what choice do you have but to trust? If not time, then yourself?*

Amandine isn't sure she trusts herself, but she trusts Will.

So she takes a deep breath and steps through the portal.

* * *

Time reminds her of melted wax – an oddly dry form of wet. Her skin feels oily and dusty, her hair straightens and curls, her lungs strain because time is breathable but it still feels wrong.

But then again, nothing really has felt right since Will left. *He said he'd be back.*

Child, when a man says he'll be back and then he disappears, best let him go, the Mother Superior told her after three days of waiting. *He was never a man to begin with.*

But Amandine remembers the way Will looked at her, the soft crinkle of umber skin around eyes as wise as ancient poplars. There was always fondness there, and warmth, but was it a taste or the totality?

When are you, Will?

The question again, the determination she needs to overpower her doubt and get when she needs to go. She squeezes her eyes tight over tears she doesn't want to cry before stepping through the portal again.

* * *

Amandine arrives in the middle of a busy grey street, full of people wearing trim black and white clothing, which makes her voluminous lavender habit that splits over her wide blue skirt stick out like someone dropped a splatter of paint right in the middle of a mourning ritual.

Amandine ducks her head, pulling the hood of her habit closer around her face. Where is she? When is she? Now that she's out of time, doubt drenches her like a cloudburst. Everyone's shoes are so cleanly made, all their clothing practically identical like someone had finally figured out how to get string to obey the laws of magic and spelled them into a perfect match.

If this is the future, and she thinks it might be the future because everything feels too polished to be the past, then perhaps this is when Will came from.

"Can I help you?"

Amandine's breath locks in her lungs like they are still full of time wax.

"Will?"

Because it's Will. Will, with his beautiful long face that always reminded her of a forest at twilight. But the longer she drinks him in, the more her soaring heart notices little differences. Though she would hardly call her Will old, this Will is barely more than a boy; there are no delicate crinkles around his eyes, no silver coils breaking into the dark cloud of hair that puffs around his head, no sign of the scar at the corner of his lips he'd always refused to tell her how he'd gotten.

There's no recognition in his gaze; if anything he's puzzled. "Do I know you?" She hadn't expected that to hurt worse than knowing he cared about her, but not knowing how much.

"Not yet," she replies. If this is the Will she would know, had known, there would be a twinkle in his eyes, a *How'd you get here, Little Witch*, somewhere in the lines around his crooked smile.

Understanding flashes in his eyes – not of her bursting through memories he hadn't formed yet, but rather of the concept of her. What that single word *yet* means to a tempier.

He offers her his arm and she slides a shaking hand into the gap between his forearm and bicep. A jolt shoots through her like a tree struck by lightning on a clear day.

"Where to?" she asks breathlessly, peeking up at him.

He looks winded, unexpectedly dazed. Like he'd felt it too. "The library. We're least likely to be overheard there. And it sounds like you have something to tell me."

* * *

Will used to tell her about this library, about the breathless hours he'd spent researching time, a building architected like a cathedral because of just how many books it contained. *It needs the support of centuries of master masonry*, he told her, leaning back in his chair, hands behind his head so his elbows were flung out like wings. *You'd love it.*

How right he was.

She's never seen anything like this. Light ripples down the spines of books which swirl around columns like the ridges on seashells. Everything is neat and orderly, as clean as the lines on Will's jacket, which he takes off and hangs on the back of a chair in a little reading nook.

"What brings you to now?" he asks, rolling up the crisp white sleeves of his shirt so they sit just below his elbows.

"I'm looking for you." She pours the finger bones onto the little table between them.

She doesn't tell him of the sleepless nights she spent teaching him about wind reading, about how trees always know what's coming and if you know how to listen to the harmonies in their rustling leaves, you can know too. A time magic of its own.

She doesn't tell him of the rainy afternoon he arrived at the abbey, drenched from head to toe with mud covering his dark boots, begging to see her. *Why Amandine*? the Mother Superior asked with narrowed eyes because strange men begging to see acolytes could end very poorly.

I can't explain – not yet, he pleaded.

But he never explained. Another reason the Mother Superior told Amandine to forget him, and why she hasn't been able to.

She tells him he came to study with her, that she learned from him and he learned from her.

"You carved the finger bones yourself?" he asks sharply when she tells him how she came by them.

"Yes," she says as he leans forward, resting his elbows on his knees so that he could stare at them more closely.

"And I showed you how?"

She shifts uncomfortably. "Not quite. But I inferred it from things you told me. About how you move through time, how you get when you're going, how you know what to do."

"That was very dangerous," he says slowly. "What was I thinking, doing that? Finger bones like this should come from a master crafter. If you get one line wrong…" He pauses, tracing the runes with such delicate care. "But these are perfect."

They are, because she spent so many hours staring at them when trying not to stare at Will's graceful hands.

He looks at her intently, his gaze flicking from her eyes, to her nose, to her forehead, to her lips as though trying to find an answer. Then he leans back, closing his eyes. "Why do I even bother?"

Not once has she ever seen Will despair. But this seems to be despair.

"I've spent half my life studying time," he tells her. "Temperie is the hardest magic to master, and the hardest to achieve ranks in. You jumped a millennia and a half on your first try to find me. Do you know how hard that is? I should just give up."

"It's not like I haven't studied other magics," she points out. "And I learned from someone who was very good." A

Will who is older, who has more lines around his eyes and who smiles more easily. A Will who this Will would become. "I wouldn't have been able to do it without you. You can't give up."

He opens his eyes again, his lips twisted in embarrassment. "I suppose if I don't, then I might end up trapped in time anyway, but without you to come rescue me." He runs his fingers over the studs holding the leather to the chair's frame. "Forgive me a human moment. It gets to you, wondering if you're good enough."

"Oh yes," she agrees. "But doubt has no place in the mind when dealing with time."

His spine snaps straight, his eyes widening. "Where did you hear that?"

"From you?"

His lips pop open and his gaze goes distant as he looks at the books lining the walls. When he brings his attention back to her, it's as though he's trying to read her mind, read her secrets. "Did I teach you, or are you teaching me?" He runs a hand over his hair. "This is going to get recursive fast."

Recursion is one of the most dangerous things in time travel, Will told her as they sat in the cloister, watching a bee buzz around a newly flowered stalk of lavender. *It's too powerful to control. When you stop being able to identify a beginning or an end, when you meddle too much, you might die – or never exist at all.*

If Will knew that then, he'd know that now.

And the Will in the here and now is standing up. "When you took my arm, I felt something and I thought it was—" He cuts himself off, looks away as if suddenly shy, and Amandine's breath catches in her throat. "But what if it was just recursion? You're messing with both of our timelines. I need to think." He takes several steps out of the nook before pausing and turning. "Do you have a place to stay?"

"No," she admits.

"I'll find you somewhere to rest. Come with me."

* * *

The room Will finds for her is the empty bedroom of one of his classmates, who has gone for a week to celebrate a Holy Day. "She won't mind," he tells her, and it isn't like Amandine has a lot of options.

She opens the window and listens to the wind, but the trees don't have much to say. There aren't forests, just dots of them here and there in the university courtyards – enough for them to converse but not enough to sing. Would their language have changed? She'd never thought to ask Will that. He'd been so curious about the language of trees. She'd just assumed it was because it was new to him, but now she wondered if, in the millennia and a half between when she was born and he was, if that language had been lost.

Will finds her in the morning, three books tucked under his arm and a haggard, sleepless expression on his long face.

With the brusquest "Morning," imaginable, he leads her to one of the dining halls and opens each of his three books.

"You're from here," he says first, pointing to a chapter titled 'The Wind Witches of Gusthenère Abbey'.

"That's not how you spell it," she replies, which makes him crinkle his brow. Her heart stutters at that crinkle, at the beginning of folds that will fold so many times that soon they will just be a part of his face.

"Earlier? You jumped two millennia?"

"What do you mean earlier?"

"This is the modern spelling. The one that matches the current pronunciation." He runs a hand over his face. "Well then. This is—" He points to the second open book, whose chapter is titled 'Time Loss in Large Jumps'. "I think what's happened. I tried to jump too far, maybe even back to the present, and got stuck in time."

That strikes a nerve. "You'd never get stuck in time! You don't doubt like that."

"I doubted yesterday," Will points out. "The second the realization of how recursive this was hit me, I doubted a lot. Why wouldn't I doubt later on? Doubt is part of time travel. A very dangerous part."

Because you need to believe with every fiber of your being that you're going to get there, Will told her time and time again.

"And this," Will points to the last of the open chapters, titled 'Recursion Insanity', "is what we're risking by doing *anything* right now. I might go insane. And, to a lesser probability because there's just one you – so far – you might too." There's an intensity to Will's expression that doesn't quite hide the fear in his eyes.

"Then we won't let it happen," she says simply. "How do you prevent it?"

"How do you prevent it?" Will's eyes look close to bursting out of his head. "You can't. It's all in the mind. Most of what time is – the perception of time – is actually is in the mind. That's why it goes so fast and so slow both at once. You just have to be strong enough to face it and not go insane."

"Then we will," she replies. "I know you can. How else would you have come to me in the first place?"

"That's not how it works," he grumbles. "That's not remotely how it works. For all you know, the version of me you're trying to rescue will go insane at the sight of me now. Maybe this will be a tragedy, not a triumph."

"Doubt has no place in the heart of a tempier," she says. He'd told her that a hundred times. A thousand.

He looks down at his hands with their long, graceful fingers, then back at her. "You came to find me," he murmurs, his eyes unexpectedly soft. "Why did I come to find you?"

Amandine swallows, trying to force down the sudden lump in her throat. "You never said," she whispers, blinking furiously.

Understanding dawns in his eyes and Amandine wishes she hadn't said anything at all. Was that why Will never told her? Because so much could be said with so little sometimes?

Then, horribly, Will's gaze passes her and his expression goes slack. When Amandine turns, she sees a pair of men in black habits and square hats who are glowering at Will.

"I see the reports are true. You did bring someone back with you," says the first man, pushing a pair of round spectacles up his nose.

"I didn't. She came on her own."

But it's the wrong thing to say.

"Mr. Eze," the second man intones. "How would a Witch of Gusthenère Abbey come here of her own capacities?" Amandine doesn't even have time to flinch at the pronunciation being so wrong because Will is on his feet, squaring his shoulders as if doing so will hide the abject fear in his face.

"A violation!" the first bursts out, face purpling.

"Mr. Eze," the second continues, "if this is true, you realize what this means? This is much worse than a reprimand. This will have to go to the University Board itself."

"No!" Amandine jerks to her feet and both men startle back. One holds up his books like a shield. "No – you can't. It's not his fault."

"We mean you no harm, witch," the second squeaks. *Why would he be afraid of me?*

You speak of the trees as though they're friends. Will sounded so surprised when she explained to him.

Aren't they? she'd replied, confused.

She hadn't realized how much his silence had spoken until this moment.

"No harm will come to him," she growls in a voice so low it doesn't sound like her own, but that's what she wants. She wants them to think she's calling the trees. "You will not go to the board, you will not reprimand him. He did not do this." She grabs Will's hand and again, there's that jolt that neither of them seem to know if it is recursion or something else.

She digs her other hand into her pocket for her finger bones, and begins to whistle.

The two men back away in horror and she throws the bones into the air – *Take me to you* – and catches them.

* * *

Time melts like wax down the crevice between her nose and her cheek, through the gap between her teeth into her lungs. Everything is dry and wet at once, but Amandine clings to Will's hand, refusing to let him go. It feels different this time, but not because she isn't alone. It feels different because the wax is thicker. It's harder to breathe; time clogs her lungs.

"Where are you taking us?" he wheezes, trying desperately to find normal air again like he's gagging on a sea that's drowning him.

She tightens her hand; he tightens his back. "To him."

"But how—?" he begins before she coughs again. This feels wrong. Maybe it's just as risky for her as it is for him. "Recursion," Will grits out. "Come on."

He leads her through time, and all she can think with each step is that she's going to suffocate. But Will is with her. Not her Will. Will before he was her Will. Will who will become her Will. So she can't suffocate because he'll find her again, no matter how long it takes, or else she wouldn't be here at all.

His steps falter, but he keeps going, and she keeps going because he keeps going. With each step, her breath grows steadier, but after a few paces, he stops to cough. She rubs her fingers over his back, wondering if it will soothe him, wondering if he can feel her because she isn't entirely sure that she can feel him with all the waxen time between them. His gasps sound like the wind when trees are dying.

"You need to go back," she says as he heaves.

"No, we need to find him."

"It's killing you to be here." The words are true; there's still too much doubt in him. "Please, Will. Go back. Go back and live." She couldn't bear it if Will died here. She'd never be the same. She wouldn't exist the way she does now and she needs to. Needs to be this version of herself because of how empty she'd felt before Will showed up. "Please Will. Take my finger bones and go."

Will's eyes stream with tears. The whites around the poplar brown are bloodshot, tiny veins popping under pressure. "I can't leave you. You might die. You have no way to get out without the bones."

"I'm fine," she insists. Will is suffocating like a candle flame covered by a glass jar but she's not. The waxen feeling of time feels more like it had when Will – her Will – first showed it to her. "I'll be fine." She looks around. She recognizes this place. This looks like the willow bower, the one where she'd first taught Will the hum of branches, and he'd looked at her like she was the moon incarnate. "It's a recursion. That's why it's affecting you more than me. You're here already."

Somewhere. Somewhere she can't see but she could feel it like the thrum of a hummingbird's wings, like the trees singing that the wind was high and the day was beautiful. Will is here. "We've found you. Now go. Before it kills you."

"What if you can't get out and I've just left you here?"

She laughs. "If you do, I will. I'll stay here and keep you safe. And you'll keep me safe." He keeps coughing and wheezing, trying to speak but unable. Spittle flies from his lips and she presses her hand over his heart. "Go. Now! Please! I don't want you to die! You have so much to live for!"

Mid-cough, he throws the finger bones, catches them, then disappears.

The wind dies down. The wax begins to swirl again, and Amandine looks around.

Time weaves its branches like a willow tree and the wax ahead of her solidifies into someone else – another body. He drips back into existence, tall and square-shouldered, walking towards her, then breaking into a trot to get to her faster.

A moment later, Will lifts her into the air, into time, and swings her around with delight, whooping with joy that she's there, that she's found him. Her Will with his poplar eyes and the familiar crinkles in his brow. Will, with wide lips like dark, swollen cherries and that awestruck expression he always had when she just got something faster than he thought she would.

"I knew you'd come," he says, voice laced with wonder. "I doubted for just a moment – enough to get stuck – and then I knew it would be alright because you'd come."

"You doubted?" she asks dryly, because Will never doubted anything, except at the start.

He laughs. When he presses his forehead lightly to hers, she thinks it was supposed to be a quick gesture of affection, but then he lingers, presses harder, his fingers fumbling to twine between each of hers.

"I doubted when it would be the right time," he says. "I never saw myself. You didn't let me. I would have died if I had. So I didn't know when it would be right. When I would disappear. So of course, I did. Got trapped in my own doubt. But just for a second before you showed up."

"It's been months though!" Amandine protests. Months since she'd seen him, months since she'd heard his voice. Months that left her as exhausted as if she'd been fighting gale winds daily to find him.

"For you," he whispers. "And oh, my love, I'm so sorry. It was always going to pass longer for you than for me. But I had my own wait while I figured out how to find you again, if it helps."

Her breath catches in her throat. "My love?" she whispers. It's like the exact moment the lilac buds burst into aromatic florets that herald the incoming spring. Words they never said to one another for how could they – born of different times and different places? What does it matter if they can't stay together?

But who's to say they couldn't, really?

He presses his forehead to hers again. "You saved me twice – filled my boring life with a purpose I didn't know I was missing. I came to find you because when you sent me away, I couldn't let that be the end of it. I came because I love you, Amandine."

She pulls her forehead from his, but not away – no, never away. She surges up on the tips of her toes to kiss him, to pull his cherry lips to hers and taste them.

Time does not taste like wax.

Time tastes like spring.

When they break apart, they're breathless again, but not because of time. They're breathless the way the wind is after a storm. He lets go of one of her hands to fumble for his vest pocket and Amandine traces the backs of her fingers along his cheek.

Will draws out the finger bones and when she looks down, her eyes well with tears. It's the first time she's seen them since she'd made her own, the first time she notices not just the carvings she so painstakingly put into the bones, but the shape and size of them, so familiar not because they are Will's but because they are *hers*.

He locks eyes with her.

"Shall we, my love?" he murmurs.

Then he throws her finger bones into the air and her hand darts out to catch them. Hand in hand, they step through the portal that materializes and out of time.

The Prophecy

Maria Wolfe

Chrysanthe hurried through the busy market square. With every step, the lidded clay jars of pigments in her basket click-clacked. A warm breeze carried the salty scent of the Cretan Sea to the open-air stalls where vendors hawked their wares. Figs, olives, wine, they called out. As she passed old Pitaja selling his trinkets, he seized her arm and thrust a small terracotta bull at her. "It's blessed by the sea god, Poseidon, himself," the man cried. "Protection against the monster. Against Queen Pasiphaë's bastard."

Her tear-reddened eyes met his, and, with a gasp of recognition, Pitaja released her as if she were diseased. "It's her," he shrieked, clutching the figurine against his chest. "The sacrifice!"

A murmur spread through the crowd. News traveled quickly in the city of Knossos, faster than a white-hulled boat wind-blown across the Great Sea. In less than a day, everyone had learned her fate: an offering to Pasiphaë's son, the flesh-eating beast.

She skirted past the old man, bound for the Labyrinth, the Minotaur's lair. No guards accompanied her; none were needed. If she tried to flee, King Minos's soldiers would catch her. And no one on the island would dare offer her refuge. Even her father had refused to spirit her away on his trading vessel. "This is the will of the gods," he said before boarding the three-masted ship for his long voyage. "No one will face their wrath by challenging their decree."

But the gods hadn't condemned her – it was the queen, Pasiphaë.

A path cleared before her. Chrysanthe plowed ahead, toward the Labyrinth atop Fylaki Hill. A multitude of stares fell upon her, charged with a single question: what had she done for the gods to punish her so? The whispered speculations whirled around her: blasphemer, criminal, whore. Even the merchants she'd frequented for years joined in the hateful glares. She knew what they believed – to earn this sentence, her transgression must be abhorrent; only the Athenian tributes, fourteen per annum, had ever been delivered to the monster. Never a Cretan.

Until Chrysanthe.

If she'd committed an offense, the queen hadn't named it. Chrysanthe was a palace artist, unremarkable, one of many. Her paintings – never her – were noticed and admired.

And then a new project had brought her to the throne room: a fresco, her largest assignment. Kneeling on the paved floor, she'd stenciled the requested image onto the prepared wall: a single bull in motion, soaring, its front and rear legs in mid-air. Was that when the queen began to watch her? Chrysanthe focused solely on her painting, from applying wet lime plaster to layering the pigments with her brushes. Each day, she covered a section until the work was completed: a bull with brown hair spotted in white, against a blue background, framed by overlapping stones, motley in color.

"Your bull seems alive, as if it may spring off the wall." The queen had startled Chrysanthe as she gathered her stained brushes. "I have been observing you. How talented you are."

She'd blushed, stammering her thanks.

The queen had smiled, an expression that belied the evil of her next words: "Tomorrow morning, you will go to my son in the Labyrinth."

Chrysanthe had uttered a horrified cry: the queen was sending her to her death. Her brushes fell from her hand. Her legs weakened.

Queen Pasiphaë had guided her to a nearby stool. "No, my dear, do not be scared. Bring your paints. If you charm him with your art, he will not harm you."

"But he's a murderer." Half-man, half-bull – an abomination. He ate human flesh. Chrysanthe had hunched forward. "The storytellers say so."

"No, you will be safe. You do not believe me – you think me mad – but soon, you will understand." Queen Pasiphaë had stroked her back, her touch as gentle as a mother's. "When you meet my beloved boy, you will see."

As she crossed the market square, Chrysanthe murmured a final prayer to her mother: *Antheia, please, let me live.* But her past entreaties to the flower goddess had always gone unanswered. Why should she expect otherwise now? Her mother had abandoned her at birth, depositing her on Father's doorstep before decamping for Mount Olympus. A father who hadn't wanted her, either, not after his mortal heart had been broken by the callous deity.

When she arrived at the base of the hill, Chrysanthe lifted her head.

On the hilltop, the Labyrinth stood, massive and majestic. In the sunlight, its walls of selenite glowed as bright as a full moon on a cloudless night. Its red columns soared to dizzying heights. As always, her breath caught, from fear and from awe – despite its seductive beauty, its tortuous passages caged a monster.

She trudged up the steep stairway to the entrance, guarded by soldiers armed with bronze swords and spears, not to prevent admission but to secure their sole captive within. "Queen Pasiphaë sent me." Her hands trembled, and the jars in her basket clattered.

A soldier stepped forward. "Yes, the sacrifice." His face was cold, without compassion.

Chrysanthe cast a last look at a view she'd never again enjoy: Knossos spread before her. The palace atop Kephala Hill. Markets and villas. Fields of barley, olive groves, and vineyards. And, not far, the Port of Kaftor and the Cretan Sea. Beyond, her father's ship steered toward the horizon.

With a shuddering inhalation, she steeled herself to enter the Labyrinth.

The heavy wooden door was unbarred and opened, allowing her to advance inside unescorted. Chrysanthe flinched when it slammed shut behind her. Entombed within high walls of rough-hewn stone, sequestered from the sun, she shivered at the penetrating cold. Her every sense awakened, anticipating at any moment a furious roar, the pounding of feet, a nightmare emerging from the darkness.

Where was the Minotaur?

Her breathing was too loud. Could the beast hear her? Would he toy with her, or would her end be swift? Chrysanthe cowered near the door, its wooden surface scored and marked with old blood. Denuded bones were strewn along the packed dirt floor, most from small animals, but not all. Human-size bones, too, remnants of the tributes he'd slaughtered in years past. The unbearable stench recalled long-rancid meat. A wide corridor extended before her, lit by torches clever Daedalus had engineered never to extinguish. She dared not travel farther – this place was built to confuse, to lead its victims astray. But, for now, she was alone, unscathed.

She let her tears flow anew. How long must she wait?

Chrysanthe set her basket on the ground and crouched beside it, snatching glances down the corridor as she unpacked. The jars held the pigments she'd prepared the night before: red and yellow ochre, Egyptian blue, and more. When the Minotaur came to kill her, she'd be doing what she loved most: her art. On a palette, she wet the powders with linseed oil from a goat's bladder. Here, she had no wet lime plaster on which to apply her paints, just dry stone; she'd brought no brushes, preferring her hands. She faced the wall and, with her quaking finger dripping with color, drew.

One petal, then two and three. A stem, several leaves. The rough stone didn't abrade her skin, a consequence of her divine lineage. She added blues, greens, and whites. Her tears dried when, as always, Chrysanthe lost herself in her art.

A garden soon filled the blank space, from the ground to as high as she could stretch. Daffodils, gladioli, lilies. Then apple, fig, pomegranate trees. Under her bare fingertips, one by one, the elements of her picture came to life, her magic – a gift from her goddess mother – passing directly from her hands into her art. Chrysanthe hadn't realized how much she'd missed painting like this, unrestrained. Father had allowed her to create, but only with her brushes – the tool, with its boar bristles and wooden handle, impeded her power. Her talent reminded him of Antheia, and he was desperate to forget.

For now, she'd revel in her magic.

The noisome air became redolent with her blooms. Bees buzzed; butterflies flittered. A lazy breeze caressed her skin. Once she reached the end of the long corridor, Chrysanthe smiled at her work before shifting to the opposite wall to continue.

Where she saw the Minotaur, watching her from around the corner. She froze, her mouth gaping, a scream caught in her throat.

He was as the storytellers claimed: a dirty beast with the horned head of a snow-white bull, the powerful body of a man, bigger than any man she'd ever seen. His sole attire was a linen loincloth, tattered and soiled. A long tail flicked behind him, his only motion.

She expected him to attack. She thought she should run. He didn't, nor did she.

It was his eyes that stopped her. Dark and sad, so human. Beautiful, even.

Why *he* hesitated, Chrysanthe couldn't guess.

"Your name?" the Minotaur asked. His voice, deep and dark, thrilled through her.

That he, an animal, could speak astonished her. That he, a monster, would ask for her name… "Chrysanthe," she replied, shaky. Her mother had named her. "It means 'golden flower'."

He repeated it, made it sound lovely. "A golden flower has made me flowers," he said with wonder. The Minotaur inhaled, his wide nostrils flaring, evoking his sire, the magnificent white bull, a token from Lord Poseidon to King Minos. "Not since I was a child living in the palace have I smelled such sweetness."

The prison door swung open with a bang. She jumped, as did the beast. A soldier standing at the threshold motioned with his readied spear, his face betraying his shock that she still lived. Beyond him, the sky was made vivid by the setting sun – an entire day had elapsed. "Woman, come with me," he bellowed down the corridor.

Chrysanthe quickly gathered her jars. Only a royal command could have compelled the soldier to unbar the door. She wouldn't test his forbearance.

The Minotaur retreated farther into the Labyrinth, out of the soldier's sight. "You are not a tribute," he murmured. "Why are you here, Golden Flower?"

"The queen…" How could Chrysanthe explain what she didn't understand?

He braced his hands against the wall, his head lowered. Like all of Knossos, the Minotaur assumed the gods had sent her as an offering. "Go then, and never come back."

* * *

"Queen Pasiphaë has summoned you." The soldier led her through the twilight-empty streets to the palace. His repeated glances asked: who was she, that the gods had spared her?

Torches threw shadows over the frescoes decorating the walls of the queen's megaron, her private chambers. Among them, only the dolphins fashioned by Chrysanthe shone as if lit by a fire within, the sole trace of her animating magic, blunted by her brushes.

"Sit," the queen said from her alabaster throne, waving Chrysanthe to a wooden stool. Her long skirt and breast-baring blouse bore an intricate design in bold reds and yellows, fitting for the half-human daughter of the sun god, Helios.

"How did you know the Minotaur wouldn't attack me?" Crusted paint flaked from her restless hands onto her plain wool skirt. If it weren't for the prison dirt soiling its hem, Chrysanthe would have thought her sojourn in the Labyrinth a dream.

"I said you would not be harmed. That your art would enchant him. You simply did not believe me." The queen gazed down at her lap, obscuring eyes so like the beast's. "You met my son?"

Chrysanthe pictured the Minotaur as she'd first seen him: fearsome yet fearful, as if wary of her reaction. Almost… shy. "Yes, not long before the soldier came." She exhaled slowly. "He wasn't what I'd expected from the stories I heard as a child." For the smallest infractions, her elders had threatened to toss her in the Labyrinth as a meal for the bloodthirsty monster.

"Those stories are cruel, meant to punish me by hurting him. But you see him as he is, do you not?" Queen Pasiphaë stared toward some distant point, her expression dreamy. "When you painted the bull, I knew you would. It was how you made his eyes – he was more than a soulless animal." Her voice hardened. "My son is not an animal."

"You…love him?" The stories hadn't allowed for that possibility. How could they? His unnatural conception came not of passion but of a madness inflicted by a furious Poseidon upon the poor queen. Not for her own crime but as vengeance against King Minos for his deception: sacrificing not the snow-white bull but a lesser creature to the god. But now, Chrysanthe could imagine it well: the Minotaur could be loved.

Queen Pasiphaë nodded. "I never wanted to send him away from the palace, but the king insisted. An oracle told him it must be done: the gods willed it. My son was so young, just ten years old, when Minos jailed him in the Labyrinth. Before then, he was so gentle and kind." Her fingers worried her gold necklace. "Fifteen years, alone all this time. How he has suffered, racked with rage and despair."

Chrysanthe blinked back her tears. "Have you spoken with him?"

"No, Minos forbids it. And, after his expulsion from the palace, I suspect my son would not welcome me." The queen frowned. "Daedalus watches – I know not how – and reports how he fares."

"Was he observing today?" Chrysanthe hoped not. That encounter with the Minotaur…she didn't understand what it meant. Until she did, she was reluctant to share it.

The queen's lips curved into a small smile. "No, and he will not, not until my son is saved."

Chrysanthe gasped. "Saved? From the Labyrinth? Impossible." Its walls were impregnable, and its single entrance well-guarded. "Certainly, the king won't permit his escape."

With a sweep of her hand, the queen dismissed her concern: "Minos tarries in the east, at the palace in Zakros.

He will not return to Knossos until the tributes come." Yet only after scanning the shadowy recesses of the room did Pasiphaë speak again. "Though the king discredits it, there was more to the prophecy." Her voice lowered. "The oracle also foretold a young woman who will set my son free. You, I believe. For years, I have been searching for you, Chrysanthe."

"For me? But I'm an artist. What can—"

"How you will effect it, I cannot say." Queen Pasiphaë sighed. "But you will go to the Labyrinth. Every day until—"

Chrysanthe stiffened. "Until he kills me?" But, recalling his eyes, she wasn't sure he would.

The queen grasped her hand. "No, my dear. The prophecy was clear: that is not how this story ends."

* * *

As the sun rose, Chrysanthe again climbed to the top of Fylaki Hill. It was early, well before most quit their beds. She hoped to avoid the fearful gossip her reappearance would fuel, charges of sorcery or worse. Even the stoic soldiers guarding the door threw her suspicious glances.

"The queen ordered me here," she snapped. With an objective Chrysanthe certainly couldn't achieve: save the Minotaur. How to do it, she couldn't fathom. Whether he deserved saving, she wasn't sure.

Once inside the Labyrinth, her steps slowed. The corridor was deserted. But her presence reanimated her painted garden that, without her, had gone quiescent. The applied pigments vied with the torches to brighten the space. Floral scents wafted on the magical breeze. A winged insect flew by her ear. She toed aside the fig leaves falling onto the floor – underneath, the scattered bones were gone. The Minotaur – it had to be – had cleared them away.

Dropping her basket near the door, she crept along the corridor, pausing at the first turn in the maze. There, she strained to listen. Was he lurking around the corner? Chrysanthe jutted her head around the bend. The short corridor was empty – no Minotaur lay in wait. Here, the bones had also been removed. She dragged in a breath.

Where was he?

She advanced until the corridor branched. Recollecting the tales of wending, winding passages that would lead a wanderer astray, she halted.

The Minotaur would have to come to her. Whether she wanted him to, Chrysanthe wasn't yet certain. Yesterday's reprieve may have been temporary; today, he may kill and eat her. She backed away.

Chrysanthe retrieved her basket, setting it where her garden ended. Again, she mixed her pigments with linseed oil. With her palette in hand, she started to paint. Her fingertips smeared multiple shades of blue onto the wall, the source of a meandering stream. Its waters flowed, babbling and burbling. On it went, curving into the short corridor.

She added trees to its banks. Cedar, cypress, and bay laurel, their canopies an abundance of green. While she worked, she heard the Minotaur stirring. His rhythmic breathing. A cough. The sound of his body grazing a wall. Near, yet so far.

Where the short corridor bifurcated, she laid out a feast from her garden, perhaps to be kind, perhaps to entice him. "Thank you for removing the bones." Chrysanthe rushed back to retake her palette. Glancing over her shoulder, she noticed the fruit was gone.

Soon afterwards, the soldiers opened the door to the Labyrinth.

"I'll be back tomorrow," she called out to the Minotaur.

* * *

With each passing day, her steps to the Labyrinth became more eager. Before the door to the prison opened, Chrysanthe wondered if this would be the day the Minotaur would be waiting at the entrance. Apprehension became anticipation.

In her basket, she carried food she'd prepared for him: bread, roasted squid, a chickpea stew. Without revealing himself, he accepted it all.

Though she'd never dazzle like her goddess mother, Chrysanthe took greater care with her appearance. Her long, black hair, usually an unbound mess, she tamed into an elegant style, adorned with bronze bands. She chose her prettiest bodices and flounced skirts. A metal belt, she cinched around her waist.

As she painted, Chrysanthe spoke, her voice pitched for him to hear. She described Knossos, its people and places. With her fingers, amongst the trees and flowers of her painted garden, she sketched the villa where she lived with her father: its flat, tiled roof; the lower walls made of clay-mortared stone, the upper of unfired brick; the front windows glazed with thin sheets of alabaster. "It stands near a vineyard. During the growing season, breezes carry its sweet scent within." She added a bluebird that began to sing. "Upon waking, this is the song I hear."

Each day, her painted garden transported her deeper inside the prison.

Each night, she resented the guards who released her.

After a week, she glimpsed a horn, then a single eye, spying on her from behind a corner. "Do you have a name?" she asked. "Other than 'Minotaur'?"

The eye, then the horn, disappeared. "No. I am nothing but the Minotaur, the 'bull of Minos.' An abomination – the king told me so often. He loathes me." He snorted. "I remind him of his folly – that he tried to trick a god."

Chrysanthe approached the corner but came no closer. "And when you were a child? Your mother must have given you a name."

"If she did, I do not recall." His voice sounded quieter, as if he'd drifted away.

"Then tomorrow, I'll bring you one."

* * *

Chrysanthe decided on Asterius, for the stars that shared her dreams of him. She ran up the hill the following morning to tell him.

This time, he bided by the door. Up close, he appeared more magnificent than from afar. His linen loincloth, white with blue and gold trim, was clean. He'd washed the grime from his skin.

When she greeted him with his new name, he gifted her with a smile, at first hesitant, then widening to display his predator-sharp teeth.

Afterwards, day after day, Asterius sat nearby on a mattress of fallen leaves as she spread her vibrant colors onto the walls. With plump figs and sweet words, she coaxed him closer until he reclined by her feet.

To entertain him, she described the frescos she'd painted in the palace. "My leaping bull captivated the queen, I think. At least, once it was complete, she ordered me here. As an offering to you, I believed." At his low growl, she shook her head. "But after that first day, she told me about a prophecy." His ears pricked at her long pause. "It says I will save you."

"No, I cannot be saved." Asterius laughed, the sound harsh. "Daedalus devised the Labyrinth to be inescapable."

"Yes, even its walls thwart my magic." Her paintings of a hole and a door both remained stubbornly two-dimensional. The weapons she'd drawn, as well. "I don't know how to free you."

Asterius rolled onto his side, propping his head on his outstretched arm. "The prophecy is fantasy. Think of it no more."

So she told him stories of her life. "Though my father made me hide my magic, people recognized I was different. A demigod, thus a pariah. Now that the queen favors me, my tormentors have been silent, but their taunts haunt me." With her hands stained, she wiped her nose against her shoulder. He scooted closer. "If not for you, Asterius, I'd still be alone."

Asterius touched her ankle, trained his big hand up to her calf. There, he left it, his warmth a comfort. Despite his silence, Chrysanthe deciphered his meaning: he understood. He had endured far worse, not only here but also while living in the palace.

"I remember my first years in the palace as happy," Asterius surprised her by saying. Though they'd discussed art and poetry, he hadn't yet shared his own tales. "Mother made it so: she sang to me and taught me to play the lyre." His hand slid away. "My sole playmate and protector was my older brother, Androgeus. Minos's son. But after Aegeus, the Athenian king, had him murdered, Minos locked me in here. Soon after, the first tributes came." He picked at the leaves on the ground. "I miss my brother. My mother, too."

"And your sister?"

"Ariadne found me repulsive and screamed if I came near." Asterius shrugged. "Only when I played the lyre did the princess tolerate me at all."

"Horrible girl." Chrysanthe stooped to smooth the back of her hand along his powerful jaw. "When did you last play?"

Asterius nudged her, silently pleading for her caress. "Ages ago. Though I have destroyed my instrument countless times, Daedalus always replaces it. I have never seen him; I wonder how he knows."

Chrysanthe told him about the spying. When Asterius stood to inspect the walls, she explained, "Not now. Not since our first day together."

Deep in his throat, he growled. "Shall I play for you tomorrow?" In his question was his fear she wouldn't reappear.

But Chrysanthe did.

As she set out a feast of roasted goat and stewed okra, he played a song on his lyre. He grunted at his rare fumbles on the strings: "My fingers have forgotten what to do." When she handed him a cup of herb-flavored wine, he set aside the instrument to drink.

Chrysanthe picked up her palette. "I drew you on the wall of my bedchamber at home." She'd memorized him: his snowy head and well-muscled body with its sleek skin. Her magic, she'd hoped, would transform the image into a decoy to fool the guards. "You're so big the likeness required several nights to finish."

"Does it also come alive when you are near?" Asterius grinned when she peered down at him.

She giggled at his flirtation. "No. Only now am I beginning to understand my magic, but it doesn't work like that. It'll quicken elements of a landscape: plants, water, wind. Insects and creatures no bigger than my fist, as well.

But nothing more complex." Chrysanthe gestured at him. "No one like you."

* * *

Over the weeks, her garden expanded farther into the treacherous maze. With him guiding her, she wasn't afraid of becoming lost – she trusted him completely. "Soon," she told Asterius, "I'll enter the heart of the Labyrinth."

His great head shook. "No, there is not enough time before the Athenian tributes arrive." The seven girls and seven boys would be sacrificed to him, to be killed and eaten. "Once that happens, you will no longer abide me." Avoiding her eyes, he plucked the strings of his lyre. "I do not know why you do now. Why do you come? Because of the queen?"

"Not because of her." Chrysanthe had forgotten about the queen and her edict. That was more than a month ago, from another life. "At first, it was. But now, I choose to be here. With you." In this prison, she'd never felt so free: Asterius accepted her as she was.

"But look at me." Dropping his lyre, he grabbed his bull's head between his hands. "This is no curse; this is what I am. By birth and by deed, I am a monster."

Chrysanthe couldn't deny his monstrous acts: tearing the tributes apart, stripping the flesh from their bones. Bones that, until she came, had cluttered the ground. But she knew him now – how he hated the killing, the devouring of human flesh. He was gentle, a prince with an artist's soul. "No, I don't believe that. You haven't attacked me. Must you—"

"Yes, I must," he roared, slapping his hand against the ground. His shoulders quaked as he fought his anger. "Other than the vermin that find their way inside this prison, those Athenians have been my sole sustenance. Without them, I would have starved long ago." He hunched over his bent knees.

She joined him on the ground. "Then ignore the Athenians. Let them wander your maze unassailed." When he shifted away, she followed. "Every day, I'll paint; I'll bring you food. You won't need them."

Asterius blew out a snort. "As soon as he returns from Zakros, the king will stop you."

Chrysanthe grabbed his hand. "But the queen—"

"Is powerless." He drew her hand to his cheek. "You do not belong here." His words overflowed with bitterness. "You deserve more than a monster."

"Minos is the monster, not you." Chrysanthe stroked his white hair, so soft for such a fierce creature, and his dark eyes filled with tears. "I see only Asterius. I want only him." When the wetness spilled over, she kissed it all away.

* * *

As she made her way home through the market square, everyone was abuzz with the news – the Athenian ship carrying the tributes had just sailed into the bay, weeks early thanks to favorable winds. It can't be true, she thought. Chrysanthe dashed to the port, gaping at the two-masted ship in the clear blue waters. Her chest tightened. She feared an ending was near.

The soldiers grumbled when she begged to be readmitted to the Labyrinth that night. Chrysanthe sprinted through the corridors, shouting until Asterius appeared. "What has happened, Golden Flower?"

"The Athenians are here." In the morning, Minos would parade the tributes through the city before sending them to the Labyrinth. She sobbed. "What can I do?"

"Nothing. This is my life." Asterius stared at the decorated wall behind her until, finally, he smiled. "Except…please draw me a moon, perhaps some stars, to light our painted garden." His eyes met hers. "I remember them as beautiful. I would like to see them once again."

She tilted her head toward the ceiling. "It's too high."

"I will help you." Once her palette was ready, he lifted her onto his shoulder, steadying her with a hand on her hip as she applied color to the stone. His naked torso gleamed under her waxing moon. When she finished, they lay side by side on a bed of foliage and watched the painted sky as if it were real. To her, with Asterius beside her, this place was more real than the world outside.

He clasped her hand and kissed it, his breath warming her palm. "Now go home. Do not come back. Not tomorrow. Not ever."

"But I want to. I must – I have yet to free you." Chrysanthe rolled over to embrace him, her head on his shoulder, her hand on his heart. She told him of the life she'd imagined for them: "We'll find a remote area on the island, lush with vegetation and replete with game. I'll paint; you'll play your lyre. Together, we'll be happy."

"A wonderful dream." He nuzzled her hair. "But a dream is all it is. I would find no acceptance, no sanctuary outside the Labyrinth; Minos would pursue me until I am captured or killed."

Chrysanthe held him tighter. "Then we'll be happy here."

"I wish..." He sighed. "No, the joy you have brought me cannot last. Once the tributes come, blood will again stain these walls, and bones scatter the floors. You will see me as the beast I am." He stroked her back. "And that I could not bear."

* * *

The exuberant chirping of her painted birds woke Chrysanthe. From the ceiling, the moon glowed, and the stars shone. She was alone – while she'd slept, Asterius had withdrawn into the depths of the Labyrinth. Had she dreamed his whispered "I love you"?

The soldiers responded to her pounding on the door. Chrysanthe emerged to a sunrise, cruel in its beauty. Already, the day was hot and humid, with no breeze to cool it. She wandered the vacant streets. In the harbor, the Athenian ship bobbed on the waters, its two furled sails an unrelenting black.

A growing ruckus soon drew Chrysanthe to the market square. Onlookers jeered the tributes, dressed in simple white tunics, filing through the thronged space. Soldiers prodded the small group forward, toward the Labyrinth.

The tallest man in the group was named Theseus, people were saying, the son of the Athenian king. But what king would send his child to die at the hands of the beast?

She pushed closer to the royal stage. "Theseus intends to kill the Minotaur," Chrysanthe overheard Ariadne tell her female attendants. The dainty princess, draped in jewels, stood apart from her parents. Her features, though comely, favored her father, haughty and mean. "I pray to the gods he succeeds."

Kill Asterius? Chrysanthe scoffed at the idea. The Athenian prince might be muscular and strong. He certainly strutted as if he were a great hero. But without an iron-tipped spear or double-edged sword, he'd be no match for her beloved. Asterius would rip him apart.

Chrysanthe circled to the front of the stage where, from her gilded throne, Queen Pasiphaë surveyed the tributes. Though her expression remained serene, the queen's hands gripped the armrests. Unshed tears brightened her eyes. Was that sadness? Why? Soon, her son would be saved, as the gods had preordained. Chrysanthe would ensure it.

Once the tributes had mounted the stairway to the Labyrinth, the king and queen retired to the palace. Yet the princess lingered on the stage, her gaze trained on the retreating Theseus until he vanished over the hillcrest.

A horn blew from atop Fylaki Hill. Despite the relentless sun, Chrysanthe shivered at the sound – the tributes were inside the Labyrinth. Asterius's ordeal had begun.

The market square bustled on this Tribute Day. Musicians marked the occasion with ribald ballads of Pasiphaë and her bull-lover while costumed dancers pantomimed their coupling. Children with honey-streaked faces playacted as the Minotaur, threatening to eat passersby. Now that she knew Asterius, Chrysanthe cringed at the vulgar spectacle she'd once enjoyed – no wonder the queen had fled the stage.

Ignoring the revelers, Chrysanthe milled around the vendors' stalls, waiting for some sign the sacrifice was done. Would it take hours? A day or two? She wasn't eager for the tributes to die, only for Asterius's suffering to end. Despite his protests, once the carnage was complete, she'd return to the Labyrinth. He'd need her comfort, and she'd gladly give it.

Not even an hour later, a resounding hurrah started high on the hill, then traveled down to the market. Chrysanthe elbowed through the crowd to discover what had transpired.

A group descended the hill, chanting, "The Minotaur is dead." The tributes marched before Minos's soldiers, led by the brute, Theseus, his tunic stained with fresh blood.

From the masses in the market square, a new cheer arose: "Long live Theseus, the Minotaur slayer." The traitorous princess joined the celebration, throwing herself into the Athenian prince's arms to shower him with kisses.

Chrysanthe clapped her hands over her mouth to stifle her scream. No, Asterius wasn't dead – they must be mistaken.

The mob jostled her as she fought to ascend to the hilltop. Her lips repeated a prayer: *Please, let him live.*

When she reached the Labyrinth, the soldiers were gone, and its door was wide open. A body – *his* body – spanned the threshold, his beautiful bull's face, his human torso bathed in sunlight. "Asterius!" Chrysanthe raced to his side and dropped to her knees beside him.

Blood gushed from his ears and snout. His right arm was crooked, broken, the bone protruding. Red bruises marked his belly. The lacerations too numerous to count. He opened his eyes at her exploring touch. Despite the warmth of the day, his skin was unnaturally cold. "Told you not to come."

"You're hurt," she wailed. "I'll get the queen, the royal physician. He'll heal you."

"No, too late. Dying." Asterius tried to sit up but toppled down. "That Athenian beat me with his fists. Could have stopped it, but I let him win. Arrogant pup left…thought I was already dead." His mouth contorted with pain. "I dragged myself here…longed to see the sky, to feel the warmth of the sun. So lovely. I had forgotten."

Chrysanthe wanted to shake him – *Why, why, why?* – but instead gathered him in her arms. "I was supposed to save you. The oracle said so." With her skirt, she wiped the blood trickling toward his eyes. "I failed."

"No, my love." His hand, reaching for her, fell limp onto his chest. She pressed it to her cheek. "My mother understood the prophecy, as did I. Only death could deliver me from the Labyrinth; there was no other means of escape." He winced at his weak cough. "You saved me by giving me the courage to change my fate: to no longer be the murderous beast. Had I killed again, I'd no longer be your Asterius."

"But I needed you to win. To live. To stay with me. I didn't care how." Chrysanthe gulped down her sobs. "I love you. Why must you leave me now?"

Asterius shut his eyes. "Because of the sweet smell of flowers. The beauty of the sun and moon. And you." His breathing became labored. "Because of you, Golden Flower – my heart, my happiness – I remembered…"

Her tears dampened his snow-white hair. Under her hand, his heartbeat had slowed. Oh, gods. "Beloved…?" Her voice cracked.

"I remembered…who I am." Chrysanthe leaned close to hear his final words, so quiet: "Not the bull of Minos, but Asterius. Not a soulless animal, but a brother, a son…a man."

Biographies

Chase Anderson – *The Negative Serpentine*
(First Publication)
Chase is a weird, queer, digital storyteller who writes weird, queer stories full of magic and monsters. He dropped out of chemical engineering to pursue a journalism degree and escape calculus. But, as he's returned to school to study computer science and cybersecurity, he must face his old foe once again. He draws inspiration from biology, chemistry, novel attack vectors and whatever his neurochemicals are up to today. Find his writing and more at chasej.xyz.

Kim Claussen – *Shift*
(First Publication)
Kim Claussen (she/her) is a neurodivergent author, who writes mostly speculative fiction of different flavours, focusing on adventure and escapism. Her works explore themes of magic, self-worth, and found family dynamics. She has always had a particular love for timey-wimey stories of all kinds! When not writing, she can be found devouring other fiction in various mediums, playing D&D with friends and family, and chasing down her energetic golden retriever.

AnaMaria Curtis – *Stitching Time*
(First Publication)
AnaMaria Curtis is from the part of Illinois that is very much not Chicago, where she learned to be argumentative, competitive and nostalgic. She is the winner of the 2019 Dell Magazines Award and the LeVar Burton Reads Origins and Encounters Contest, and her work has been published in magazines including *Clarkesworld*, *Uncanny*

and *Strange Horizons*. You can get in touch or find more of her work at anamariacurtis.com or on Bluesky at @anamariacurtis.bsky.social.

Sarina Dorie – *Stupid Cupid*
(Originally Published in *Plasma Frequency*, 2016)
Sarina Dorie is the first-place winner of: Golden Rose RWA Award, Golden Claddagh RWA Award, Allasso Humor Award and Penn Cove Literary Award. She is the author of over 200 short stories published in markets like *Analog*, *Fantasy and Science Fiction Magazine*, *Daily Science Fiction*, *Orson Scott Card's Intergalactic Medicine Show* and *Abyss and Apex*. Sarina Dorie's steampunk series *The Memory Thief* and her cozy mystery series *Womby's School for Wayward Witches*, along with over 90 other novels, can be purchased on Amazon.

Kate Duarte – *When the Moon Cradled the Sun*
(First Publication)
Kate Duarte has a bachelor's degree in Anglo-American Studies, and her work has been published in *Reverent: An Anthology of Divinity*, curated by Quinton Li. She writes queer fantasy and horror, with a healthy dose of romance. When she's not writing, she's wandering through the nearest castle in her tiny village, or playing with the fiercest of dogs, Stitch. Kate is represented by Lauren Bieker at FinePrint Literary Management.

Corey D. Evans – *A Different Dance*
(First Publication)
Corey D. Evans is a groundskeeper living in the United States, but writing is one of his passions. He has edited theological works for Dispensational Publishing House and Trust House Publishers, and contributed short fiction to other anthologies by Flame Tree Publishing. More of Corey's work can also be found at his Substack: Corey's Story Stack. When not working or writing, Corey enjoys adventures with his wife and seven children.

Rebecca Ferrier – *The Hour-Glass Trap*
(First Publication)
Rebecca Ferrier writes poetry and prose with gothic leanings. Her historical fantasy debut novel *The Salt Bind* – a lyrical exploration

of feminism and the sea – was published in 2026. She is pursuing a Creative Writing PhD at Northumbria University, having been awarded a fully-funded studentship. She won the 2020 Bridge Award for an Emerging Writer and has benefited from Creative Scotland funding. She lives in Edinburgh, Scotland.

Janet Forbes – *The Wolf of Darkwater Loch*
(First Publication)
Janet Forbes is an author, game-writer and (accidentally) cofounder of World Anvil, the award-winning worldbuilding platform, writing software and RPG campaign-manager. An alumna of Mary Robinette Kowal's Short Story Cohort and the Milford UK Critique Circle, her fiction appears in *Kyanite Press*, Bona Books' *Wrath Month, Dream Theory Media, et al.* As a game writer, Janet has written for Kobold Press and Infinite Black, and was lead author on the official *Dark Crystal* RPG. Find more at janetforbes.com.

Amie Glazier – *A Fate Written in Fire and Blood*
(First Publication)
Amie Glazier works in content marketing by day, wrangles four kids by night, and dreams up the best meet-cutes and fantasy worlds after bedtime. After following her husband's military career around, Amie and her family now live near Seattle, Washington. When she's not writing about swoon-worthy moments or magical heroines, you can find Amie binge-reading by the fire, excelling at carpool karaoke and actually enjoying chemistry while home-brewing beer with her husband. Read more at amieglazier.com.

Somto Ihezue – *Paths, Littlings, and Holy Things*
(Originally Published in *Diabolical Plots*, 2025)
Somto Ihezue (He/Him) is a Nigerian writer, filmmaker and editor. He is an MFA fellow in Creative Writing at the University of Maryland. His works have appeared, and are forthcoming, in *Clarkesworld*, *The Magazine of Fantasy & Science Fiction*, *Uncanny*, *Strange Horizons*, *NIGHTMARE*, *Beneath Ceaseless Skies*, *Diabolical Plots*, *Podcastle*, *POETRY Magazine*, *Flash Fiction Online* and others. His work has been shortlisted for

the ALCS Tom Gallon Trust Award, the British Fantasy Award (Sydney J. Bounds Awards), the Nommo Awards, the Afritondo Short Story Prize, the Utopia Awards and others. He is the assistant editor of the *Publishing Taught Me* anthology (SFWA & National Endowment for the Arts sponsored), and co-editor of *Will This Be A Problem? The Anthology*. You can visit his website at somtoihezue.com.

E.E. King – *A Possession of Magpies*
(Originally Published in *Cosmic Roots & Eldritch Shores*, 2019)
E.E. King is an award-winning performer, writer, naturalist and painter. Ray Bradbury called her stories 'marvelously inventive, wildly funny and deeply thought provoking. I cannot recommend them highly enough.' Her books are *Dirk Quigby's Guide to the Afterlife*, *Another Happy Ending*, *The Truth of Fiction*, *Pandora's Card Game* and *Gods & Monsters*, which is on the 2025 Nebula Awards recommended reading list. Find her at www.elizabetheveking.com.

C.J. Larsen – *A Ballad for a Lady Love*
(First Publication)
C.J. Larsen lives in the Pacific Northwest with her family, a spicy cat, and two small dogs who aren't entirely convinced the cat was a good idea. She has had several short stories published in *Elegant Literature* magazine and is currently working on a historical fantasy novel. She hasn't yet quit her day job as a criminal appellate attorney. If C.J. isn't writing in her free time, she's probably climbing, baking pretzels or pickling something.

J.A. Legg – *The Crypt of Lost Things*
(First Publication)
J.A. Legg is originally from Oshawa, Ontario, and holds a degree in English and Creative Writing from the University of Windsor. He's been published in MTLS.ca, *On The Premises* and *Metaphorosis*, as well as anthologies like *From the Corner of Your Eye*, *Antares Vol. 1*, *Heart of a Man* and *Strange Religion*. In 2016 and 2024 he received Honourable and Silver Honourable Mention from L. Ron Hubbard's

Writers of the Future contest respectively, and won a novel excerpt contest at *Uncharted Magazine* in 2024 as well. He teaches at a private school in South Asia, where he has lived for several years. You can follow him on X at @TheJordanLegg.

Emily O'Malley Liu – *The Time Keeper*
(First Publication)
Emily O'Malley Liu grew up in Palm Beach County, Florida and has lived in the American Southwest, the Midwest, New England and Japan. Em now resides with her husband and three kids in the greater Washington, D.C. metro area, where she researches financial systems by day and devises magic systems by night. Her first novel, *Wine for Roses*, will be published by Shiraki Press in Spring 2026.

Mijmark – *The Wild Man of Uril*
(First Publication)
Mijmark is a writer and illustrator from Australia, an Australian/US dual citizen of Newcastle, NSW. Speculative fiction dominates his writing themes – for the possibilities of playing with an open canvas of creativity and hyperbole, for the figments of imagination that can and do develop into dalliance. He creates unique stories which have no equal, no counterpart, like an explorer of a new world. His published speculative-fiction writing includes, but is not limited to: coauthor of *Into Tordon* (Midnight Sun Press), 'Saving Face' in *Portraits* (anthology), 'Snoring Ugly' in *Of Beasts and Butterflies* and '2001, A Space Operetta' in *Rhapsody*.

Trixie Nisbet – *Only a Summer Love*
(First Publication)
Trixie Nisbet has had approaching 200 stories printed. She has written extensively for women's magazines, with some of her romances leaning towards fantasy. Using her husband's name, she also writes science fiction and has had, to date, seven audio scripts produced by Big Finish/BBC for their Doctor Who range. She has won several international writing competitions including the 2022 Kepler Award for a fantasy short story.

Aggie Novak – *A Midnight Hunger*
(First Publication)
Aggie lives with her wife in Australia, where she spends most of her time hiding from the sun and heat. She writes around working as a pharmacist and entertaining her dog. She loves all kinds of speculative fiction and often draws inspiration from Slavic folklore and mythology. When not writing she can be found drinking tea and reading everything in sight. Her published works can be found in Flash Fiction Online, *Aurealis*, *Hexagon* and several anthologies! For the full list see aggienovak.com.

Zach Shephard – *Rising Mountain, Made of Glass*
(First Publication)
Zach Shephard lives in Enumclaw, Washington, where he writes fantasy, science fiction and horror stories. During the summer he keeps active by repeatedly racing up a nearby mountain, always trying (and mostly failing) to beat his fastest time to the top. His fiction has appeared in *Fantasy & Science Fiction*, the Unidentified Funny Objects anthology series and several of Flame Tree Publishing's books – including *Lost Atlantis Short Stories*, which features another of his romantic fantasy adventures. For more of Zach's work, check out zachshephard.com.

Kathleen Stanley – *A Hundred Lifetimes*
(First Publication)
Kathleen Stanley lives in Adelaide, South Australia with her husband and children. She is currently in her final year of a PhD at Flinders University, where she studies small town Christmas romance fiction. She has several academic publications, including a creative writing piece titled 'Alden House', a contemporary romance recently included in *TEXT* journal. She loves to read and write all genres but holds a special place in her heart for romance.

Elise Stephens – *A Song of Smokeless Fire*
(Originally Published in *Troubadours and Space Princesses*, Hemelein Publications, 2024)
Elise Stephens (she/her) writes stories influenced by the themes of family, memory and finding hope after loss. She is a first-place winner

of *Writers of the Future* (2019) and a finalist for the Baen Fantasy Adventure Award (2021). Her fiction has appeared in *Analog*, *Galaxy's Edge*, *Escape Pod* and *FIYAH*, among others. Elise lives in a house with huge windows that help her absorb the vast quantities of light she requires to stay happy. Learn more at EliseStephens.com.

Gemma Sterling – *Song of Sedir*
(First Publication)
Gemma Sterling is a writer of SFF and Horror. As the grandchild of Norwegian immigrants, Gemma grew up hearing tales of Norse Gods and myths from her grandfather. Her fantasy writings draw on this tradition, informing her characters and worldbuilding. Her writing aims to transport readers to long-forgotten eras where magic was a part of everyday life. Gemma currently resides in Nova Scotia, Canada, with her husband, daughter and two cats.

Georgia Summers – *Foreword*
Georgia Summers is a half-British, half-Trinidadian writer, who spent most of her life living across the world, including Russia, Colombia and the US. When she's not doing bookish things, she's planning her next great adventure. She currently lives in London, but she dreams of one day living in a haunted château with a ghost that cleans. She is the author of *The City of Stardust* and *The Bookshop Below*.

Celia Winter – *Not Yet, Little Witch*
(First Publication)
Celia Winter is a Chicago-based award-winning knitter whose bachelor's degree in history only tangentially helps her in her career in Data & Analytics. Her speculative and romantic fiction has been published in *Plott Hound Magazine*, *Heartlines Spec*, *The Dark* and several anthologies. When not knitting, she can be found writing; when not writing, she can be found bothering her two fluffy cats.

Maria Wolfe – *The Prophecy*
(First Publication)
Maria Wolfe lives and writes in northeast Ohio, where she also practised as a surgical specialist. Her fiction has appeared in *The Examined Life*

Journal, *The Pink Hydra* and Flame Tree's *Weird Horror Short Stories* anthology. She has been an avid reader of Greek and Roman mythology since age eight, when her father gave her a copy of Edith Hamilton's *Mythology: Timeless Tales of Gods and Heroes*.

Illustrations

Key cover art: Xinyue Chen
Xinyue Chen is an illustrator and book artist based in New York, mostly working in traditional media. Since receiving their BFA from the Central Academy of Fine Arts in Beijing and their MFA from the School of Visual Arts in New York, they have provided editorial illustrations, book illustrations and designs for many renowned clients, including the *New York Times*, *Scientific American*, NBC News, NPR, Bloomberg and many more.

Illustration page 7: Flairiart
Flairiart's work has previously been featured in *Factor Four Magazine*, *Solarpunk Magazine* and *Promised Protagonists.* Flairiart is a Filipino digital artist, and her social media handle on Bluesky is @flairiart.

Illustration page 13: Louise O'Connell
Self-taught artist, sculptor and writer from Wakefield, UK, Louise loves to paint fantasy art, fan art and landscape art digitally, and also enjoys writing gothic and fairy-tale stories. Instagram: @lousfantasyart

Illustration page 404: Nemma Wollenfang
Nemma is a prize-winning speculative fiction writer first. Her stories have appeared in several venues, including books by Flame Tree. She can be found on Facebook and Amazon.

Illustration page 414: Vanina Velcheva
Vanina Velcheva is a freelance illustrator from Sofia, Bulgaria. She mainly does character art but has recently expanded into book illustration. Her work focuses on originality and storytelling. Find her at Instagram @nianski_ or DeviantArt @nianskii.

Romantic Fantasy

Flame Tree Romantic Fantasy is a captivating blend of our signature Gothic Fantasy collections with the passion and magic of Romantasy. This new series featuring stories selected from open submissions is an exciting addition to Flame Tree's Beyond & Within, Myths, Gods & Immortals, Gothic Fantasy, Classic Stories and Epic Tales Collections, all beautifully presented, perfect as a gift and offering a lifetime of reading pleasure.

FLAME TREE
MYTH, FOLKLORE & FICTION

A wide range of new and classic fiction, from myth to modern stories, with tales from the distant past to the far future, including short story anthologies, Folk & Fairy Tales, Collector's Editions, Collectable Classics, Gothic Fantasy collections and Epic Tales of mythology and folklore.

•

Available at all good bookstores, and online at flametreepublishing.com